By Ron Handberg

Savage Justice
Cry Vengeance
Malice Intended
Dead Silence

Published by HarperPaperbacks

DEAD SILENCE

RON HANDBERG

HarperPaperbacks
A Division of HarperCollinsPublishers

🔥 HarperPaperbacks
A Division of HarperCollins*Publishers*
10 East 53rd Street, New York, NY 10022–5299

This is a work of fiction. The characters, incidents, and
dialogues are products of the author's imagination and are not
to be construed as real. Any resemblance to actual events or
persons, living or dead, is entirely coincidental.

ISBN 0-06-101247-5

HarperCollins®, 🔥®, and HarperPaperbacks™ are
trademarks of HarperCollins Publishers Inc.

Cover photograph © 1999 by Index Stock.

First printing: March 1999

Printed in the United States of America

Visit HarperPaperbacks on the World Wide Web at
http://www.harpercollins.com

❖ 10 9 8 7 6 5 4 3 2 1

ACKNOWLEDGMENTS

I am again grateful to my wife, Carol, and to my family for their unflagging support and encouragement; to Nancy Mate, Carol Ellingson, Jack Caravela, Alan Cox, Cindy Johnson, Debbie Olson and Susie Moncur for their friendship, advice and criticism; to Garry Peterson, the Hennepin county medical examiner, and to Carol Watson, of Missing Children Minnesota, among many others, for their expertise and counsel; and finally, to my editor, Jessica Lichtenstein, for her continued guidance and enduring patience.

AUTHOR'S NOTE

This book is a work of fiction, although the premise of the novel is based on a real event that occurred in Minneapolis many years ago. While a few of the true facts from that event have been incorporated into this work, the bulk of it—including names, dates, places, and indeed, the story itself—is entirely the result of my imagination.

AUTHOR'S FOOTNOTE

On November 10th, 1951, the three young sons of Betty and Kenneth Klein disappeared while going to play at a park in north Minneapolis. Like the boys in *Dead Silence*, they disappeared without a trace—except for two of their caps found on the icy edge of the Mississippi River. And like the fictional Hathaways, the Kleins have never stopped believing that their boys—who would now be men in their fifties—did not drown and are still alive.

Somewhere.

If that is true, then there is a chance, however remote, that one or more of them, Kenneth, David, or Daniel, might read this book, and realize—despite the passage of nearly a half century—that their parents and siblings are still waiting for them to come home.

PROLOGUE

JULY 16, 1983

The last Matt saw of his mother, she was standing at the front screen door, hands on hips, watching them go. Shouting after them, as she always did, to keep off Mr. Albers' lawn, and to be home in an hour for dinner. There may have been more, but by then the distance had eaten her words.

As usual, Jed was out in front, looking over his shoulder, laughing at the slower pace of his two younger brothers. Matt could have run faster, but he hung back with Andrew, who was only four, trotting next to him, watching as his little legs churned, taking at least two steps for every one of his.

"Wait up!" Matt shouted, his words caught and flung back into his face by the hot summer wind. Jed, if he heard, paid no heed. He was flying down the path in the park, eyes to the ground now, arms pumping, tight to his sides, bound for the slide and swing set that lay ahead.

Jed was the natural athlete in the family. He could run faster and jump higher than any other eight-year-old in the neighborhood, even a couple of the ten-year-olds. Long-limbed for his age and as graceful as he was competitive, he excelled in every sport—playing them all fearlessly and ferociously.

Matt could see his little brother was tiring fast so he slowed his pace to a near walk. It was too hot to be running anyway. "It's okay, Andy," he said. "You know Jed always wants to be first."

Matt was the middle boy, six going on seven, slight of build and brainy. He could already read better than his older brother and was far above his first grade level in math. The teachers loved him and were pushing his parents to put him into the school's accelerated program.

He was also the family caretaker, the responsible one. Mature well beyond his years. "Six going on thirty," his mother loved to say.

Jed, sweating profusely from his run and the sun, was high atop the monkey bars when the other two finally arrived at the play area. "Slowpokes!" he shouted. "Where ya been?"

All three boys were clad in shorts, T-shirts, and sneakers—all hand-me-downs, except for Jed's. And each wore an identical baseball cap, courtesy of "Cap Day" at the Twins game their father had taken them to two weeks before.

The play area was only a small part of the sprawling Fairlawn Park, several lightly wooded acres of picnic tables, flower gardens, and bike and walking paths, bordering but high above the Mississippi River in northeast Minneapolis. On summer weekends it would be packed with people, but on weekday afternoons like this there would often be only a few kids from the neighborhood and maybe a mother or two pushing a carriage or stroller.

But today even they were missing—and Matt, the cautious one, found that strange . . . and unsettling. "I wonder where everybody is?" he said, looking around.

"Who cares?" Jed said from his high perch. "We've got the place to ourselves." And then, wiping away the sweat, "Jesus, it's hot!"

Little Andy looked up, then at Matt. "Jed's talking dirty again. I'm going to tell Mom."

"You do and I'll kick your ass," Jed shouted.

"Cut it out," Matt said. "Talk like that and you could go to hell, you know." With that, he climbed up several feet on the bars, standing just below Jed, shading his eyes as he surveyed the park. "I don't think Mom would like us here all by ourselves. It feels kind of weird. Maybe we should go home."

Jed laughed and crawled down. "Are you crazy? We've got an hour. Let's go look at the river."

"No way!" Matt cried. "Not again. You know we can't do that."

"Who's going to know? You see anybody? C'mon!" With that, he again took off at a run, heading for the bluff overlooking the river.

"Get back here, Jed," Matt shouted. "Dad will kill ya."

Jed was undeterred, not even looking back. Matt yelled again, but there was no sign of his slowing. What to do? He couldn't leave Andy alone, and he knew he could never catch Jed, let alone stop him.

"Make him stop," Andrew cried.

"Shut up, Andy!"

Finally, when it was clear that Jed wasn't slowing or coming back, Matt grabbed his little brother. "C'mon. We've got to go get him."

Andy, whimpering now, trailed behind as Matt walked slowly toward the river bluff, following the path his older brother had taken. He didn't dare think of what their folks would say if they ever found out. While it wasn't the first time they'd done it, they had been told over and over again to stay away from the river, to never venture beyond the play area. And they had promised, over and over again.

But Matt knew Jed wasn't much for promises, especially if he thought he could break one and get away with it.

By the time they reached the top of the bluff, Jed had disappeared. Matt grasped Andy's hand and looked over the edge, spotting his brother halfway down the grassy slope, sliding on his rear end, grabbing branches to slow his descent.

"Jed! What are you doing? Get back up here. Please!"

Jed's laugh floated up the embankment. "I'm going for a swim. Come on down."

Andy pulled at Matt's hand. "Make him come up," he cried, tightening his grip. But Matt was helpless to do anything except watch. Jed was now at the bottom, standing on a small strand of sand at the river's edge, looking up. "Are you chicken?" he yelled.

"Dad will give you a whippin'," Matt shouted back.

Jed had already begun to strip off his shorts and T-shirt. "Not if he doesn't find out. Not if you guys don't tell him. C'mon, scaredy cats."

Matt was again torn. His eyes roved the river, at first seeing nothing, then noticing a large boat, a cruiser, drifting downstream near the opposite shore. Someone on deck seemed to be looking in their direction. But it was too far away to be sure.

Would their folks ever know? Probably not, unless little Andy opened his mouth. And they could scare him out of doing that.

The boat seemed to be coming closer.

Jed was in the water, naked, splashing and laughing, daring them to join him.

The water did look wonderfully cool and inviting. And Matt knew Jed would be chiding him for days if he didn't come down. "Hold on to me, Andy," he ordered. "Around the arm. And don't let go!"

With that, they slipped over the edge and began their slide down the long slope.

1

Alex Collier didn't think too much about the story until he was walking back to the newsroom from the studio. After all, it had been only a small item in the newscast, plugged in between the weather and the sports. A fifteen-second reader included in the "Remember When" section of the newscast.

He wasn't sure why, but it kept tugging at his mind, and he paused in the hallway to shuffle through the news script, searching for the single piece of paper. He finally found it.

It was on this date fifteen years ago that three Minneapolis brothers disappeared without a trace. The Hathaway boys, aged four, six, and eight, were playing in a park near their home when they vanished, dominating the local news for weeks. Two of the boys' caps were found floating in the nearby Mississippi River, leading to speculation that all three had drowned. But none of their bodies was ever found . . . and their parents, Hazel and John Hathaway, still believe they are alive . . . the victims of a kidnapping.

As Alex leaned against the wall reading and then rereading the item, the newscast producer, Brett Jacobi, walked past. "Nice show, Alex," he said. "You and Maggie kept it moving right along."

Alex gave him a quick glance. "Thanks," he said, his eyes returning to the script.

"Was there a problem with the copy?" Jacobi asked.

"No, not at all. I was just looking at the story on those missing boys."

"The Hathaway kids?"

"Yeah. It's amazing. Three kids, brothers at that, falling off the face of the earth. It must have been a hell of a story back then."

Jacobi was watching him curiously. "I suppose so," he said, "but it was long before my time here."

Alex tucked the story back into the script and continued walking toward the newsroom, Jacobi by his side. "You know anything more about it?" he asked.

"Not a whole lot. We did a fairly long piece five years ago, on the tenth anniversary of their disappearance, but I wasn't involved and don't remember much about it. Should be easy to dig out of the files, though."

By the time they reached the newsroom, only a few people were still there. That's the way it usually was after the late news, everyone scattering quickly once the broadcast was over, some to the nearest bar, others toward home in time to see the bulk of Letterman or the *Tonight* show.

But Maggie Lawrence, Alex's co-anchor, still sat at her cubicle next to his, phone tucked between her shoulder and ear, looking perplexed—probably talking to some pissed-off viewer irritated by something he or she had just seen on the news. Alex refused to take such calls, having decided long ago that even his generous salary did not compel him to talk to the crazies who loved to vent their spleen or to proselytize the local anchor people about weird causes. Life was too short.

Maggie, however, was still young enough—and naïve enough, in Collier's mind—to feel responsible for answering every call.

The only other person within easy view was the overnight dispatcher, housed in a glass booth behind the raised assignment desk—monitoring the various police and fire radio frequencies and dispatching the station's news cruisers to cover whatever murder and mayhem happened to be plaguing the Twin Cities that particular night.

Alex filed the script in the wastebasket beneath his desk, except for the missing boys story—which he slid into his desk drawer. It might be worth following up on, although he rarely did any reporting these days. There simply wasn't enough time, with all of the other bullshit duties imposed on the news anchors—speeches, personal appearances, promotional tapings, meeting with the consultants, and hobnobbing with clients and sponsors. Alex hated those parts of his job, but he knew they came with the territory and paid the bills. Besides, he was getting too old to be out hustling stories. Leave that to the young reporters with the energy and ambition to tolerate the long hours and frustrations of being on the street, covering the news.

Sometimes—increasingly, these days, it seemed—Collier wondered if he still had the patience and the stamina to even keep doing what he was doing.

His thoughts were interrupted by Maggie slamming down her phone and hissing, "The same to you, lady!"

Alex laughed. "You'll never learn," he said lightly.

She glowered at him. "You know what was bugging her?"

"Surprise me."

"She doesn't like the way I'm doing my hair this week. Says it was much better last week . . . there was more curl to it. I asked her if it was really that important to her. She said that's the only reason she watches the news . . . to see what I'm wearing and how I do my hair. She says that Cynthia over at Channel Three must have a better hairdresser! Can you imagine?"

"I'd have to agree with her." He chuckled. "I liked that extra curl."

"Screw you, too," she scoffed as she began to straighten out the top of her desk.

Maggie Lawrence had come to the station three years before, a transplant from California, where she had worked as a weekend anchor at one of L.A.'s independent stations. As bright as she was beautiful, Maggie had quickly established herself as the preeminent woman anchor in the market—and a hell of a reporter, to boot. Only the year before, she and another reporter on the staff, Jessica Mitchell, had exposed and broken up a local child pornography ring—bringing down the state's attorney general in the process.

Alex had come to the station a couple of years before Maggie, also from California, and had his own scalp hanging from the station's mantel. That of a prominent judge who was about to become the chief justice of the state supreme court before Alex exposed him as a vicious pedophile who had been preying on children for years. That was the last piece of really solid reporting he had done, at least of a serious investigative nature. While he was not particularly proud of that fact, no other story had come along since to whet his appetite. And, to be honest, he hadn't gone out of his way looking for one. He'd been hired as an anchor, not a reporter, and he was content to leave it that way.

"Time to get out of here," Maggie said as she rose from her chair and stretched. "Have you seen Brett?"

Before he could answer, the phone on his desk rang, startling both of them. "I walked back from the studio with him," he said, ignoring the phone, "but I haven't seen him since."

The phone rang again, reverberating in the quiet of the almost deserted newsroom. Then again. Insistently.

"Aren't you going to get that?" Maggie demanded.

He shook his head. "No way. You know me. I'm off the clock."

On the fourth ring, and after an irritable glance at him, she reached over and picked up the receiver. "Mr. Collier's phone," she said with mock sweetness. "May I help you with something?"

Alex smiled. She *wouldn't* ever learn.

Maggie listened for a moment, then said, "Hi, Max. This is Maggie Lawrence. Sorry we've never met, but I've heard a lot about you. I guess we just missed each other by a few months."

Must be Max Douglas, Alex thought. A reporter who had left the station three and a half years before to go into the PR business. What the hell could he want at this time of night?

After another minute of conversation, Maggie said, "He's right here. I'm playing his secretary tonight."

Alex gave her a quizzical glance as she handed him the phone. "Hey, Max, what's up? You should be in bed by now."

Douglas wasted no time on small talk. "I was watching the news, Alex. Heard the short piece you read on the Hathaway kids."

Alex was surprised. "I was just talking to Brett

Jacobi about it," he said. "I'd never heard of them before tonight. You weren't around when they disappeared, were you?"

"No, no," Max said. "But I did an update on the story five years ago. On the tenth anniversary of their disappearance."

"So that was you. Brett said somebody had done a piece, but he didn't say who."

"No reason he should remember," Max replied, "but I think there's something weird about the whole thing. I thought so five years ago and still think so today. I'd kind of put it out of my mind until I heard the story tonight."

Maggie had started to walk away, but Alex waved her back. "Why's that?" he asked Douglas.

"It's too complicated to explain on the phone, Alex. It's late and I know you want to get out of there. But maybe we could have lunch and talk about it."

Alex hesitated. He was torn. Did he *really* want to know more? He had an uneasy feeling about it, but knew it would be difficult to turn Max down. While they had never been especially close, they'd worked together long enough for Alex to develop a real respect for him as a reporter. He also felt some guilt for not having spoken to Max since he'd left the station. "Sure. I guess so," he finally said, trying to hide his reluctance. "When and where?"

"How about tomorrow? Noon at the Rosewood Room."

Alex glanced at the calendar on his desk. He was free. "You've got it," he said. "I'll see you then."

Maggie had settled back into her chair, waiting impatiently. "What was that all about?" she asked.

"Remember that short piece in the show about the

missing kids . . . the ones who vanished fifteen years ago?"

She nodded. "Sure. Sounds terrible, doesn't it?"

"That's what the call was about," Alex said, quickly repeating what Max had said to him. "It was like he'd read my mind. I thought it sounded strange, too."

Maggie shook her head. "Just think of what those parents must have gone through. What they must still be going through. Losing three kids all at once . . . and never knowing what's happened to them. It must be a nightmare."

Before he could reply, she went on, "Just the thought of something happening to my Danny drives me crazy. But to have three of them . . ." Her voice trailed off.

Danny was Maggie's seven-year-old son, whom she had raised alone since shortly after his birth.

"I know," Alex said, staring off into the distance as the memories returned. "God, do I know."

Maggie watched him curiously, waiting.

"I haven't thought about this for a long time," he said, "but years ago, when I was growing up in Illinois, in a small town south of Springfield, one of my best friends, a kid named Tommy Akers, was kidnapped while he was doing his early-morning paper route. Just like that Des Moines paperboy, Johnny Gosch, only years earlier. They never did find Tommy or his body. Not to this day, as far as I know."

"Jesus," Maggie muttered. "How old were you?"

He stared past her, at the far wall of the newsroom. "Nine or ten, I guess. We lived just a couple of houses away. I used to walk the route with him once in a while, just for the fun of it. I remember thinking, back then, what if I had been with him *that* morning? Might he still be alive? Or might both of us be dead now? Buried in a field somewhere." He paused, the image of Tommy still fresh. "He was a scrawny little guy, red hair and freckles and a lisp so bad you could barely understand him. We were like brothers. I'll never forget him. Or what his parents went through. It was horrible. Day after day of wondering and worrying, fearing the worst, hoping for the best." He paused once more. "The town was never the same again, and we moved a couple of years later, in part—I think—because my folks were afraid it could happen again."

He put his feet up on the desk and leaned back in his chair. "Years later, when I was still with my wife, one of our kids, Christopher, got separated from us in a big shopping mall outside of San Diego. We panicked, let me tell you. The first thing that popped into my head was Tommy Akers, the thought of never seeing Chris again. It took us more than an hour to find him, even with all of their security guards helping to search."

Maggie leaned forward, listening intently. And with some surprise. Alex was a very private man who rarely revealed anything of himself or his past life.

"Turns out, he got scared when he couldn't find us and hid out in one of the dressing rooms at a department store, and no one spotted him until damn near closing time. I've never spent a worse hour in my life. He was frightened to death, of course, and so were we. All kinds of terrible things go through your mind. So in a small way I can picture what the Hathaways must have endured."

"I can't imagine," Maggie said, grimacing.

Besides Christopher, who was fourteen now, Alex also had a daughter, Jennifer, two years younger, both living with his ex-wife in Philadelphia. While he saw them only three or four times a year, they were never far from his thoughts. Perhaps foolishly, however, he seldom worried about them these days—knowing how adult they'd become and how cautious and vigilant their mother was. Still, a story like that of the Hathaway kids made him wonder. He promised himself to give his kids a call in the morning.

"You want to grab a quick drink with Brett and me?" Maggie asked as she stood up, preparing to leave.

Brett and Maggie were an item in the newsroom, an unlikely pairing of a producer and star anchor lady who lived together with her son. Newsroom scuttlebutt had the two of them announcing their engagement in the next month or so.

"Thanks, but I don't think so. I want to catch up on some things here."

"Okay. We'll be at Tinker's if you change your mind."

Tinker's was a small bar a couple of blocks away, tucked inside one of the high-rise office buildings. It was the staff's favorite hangout, the only place around that was halfway respectable yet did not cater to the Yuppie after-theater or concert crowd. And they still sold beer by the pitcher at reasonable prices.

Alex gave her a quick wave as she headed across the newsroom. Then, deciding not to wait, he turned to his computer and quickly punched up the station's archival database and entered the word "Hathaway," waiting as the machine hummed and searched.

The entry, when it appeared on the computer screen, displayed a transcript of the tenth anniversary story done by Max Douglas, plus the file number of the videotape copy of the report. Alex printed out the transcript, then headed for the newsroom library to retrieve the tape copy itself. He wanted to read along as he watched Douglas's report.

Quickly finding a vacant viewing room, he shoved the cassette into the playback machine. The first thing he saw was Douglas standing in front of what appeared to be a park play area, voicing the opening of the piece.

MAX: Ten years ago today, three young brothers ran out of their northeast Minneapolis home to play here in Fairlawn Park, a couple of blocks from their house, something they had done virtually every summer day or after school for years. Their mother, Hazel Hathaway, watched them go . . . but not without her usual warning to stay away from the river.

Next on the screen was a woman, looking frail and drawn, whom Alex guessed to be in her thirties, although she could have been ten years older. Her hair was tied tightly in a bun, her skin devoid of makeup. He knew—even before her name was superimposed over her picture—that this must be the boys' mother, Hazel Hathaway.

HAZEL HATHAWAY: They just waved and laughed at me. They were so used to hearing me shout that way, we used to joke about it. That's why I'm so sure they didn't drown. I don't care what the others say. The kids knew they'd get a whippin' if they went near the water.

MAX: The river was the Mississippi, which runs below a bluff at the edge of the park, only a few blocks from the Hathaway home. A high fence protects the bluff now, but it didn't ten years ago when four-year-old Andrew Hathaway, six-year-old Matt, and the oldest, Jed, who was eight, left the house and waved to their mother for the last time.

As Douglas named the boys, a picture of them appeared on the screen, arms around each other, mugging for the camera, hair slicked back, faces bright and shiny, dressed in what Alex guessed must have been their Sunday best. Three cute peas in a pod, he thought, as their mother continued.

HAZEL: It was a real hot day, I remember that. Hot even for July. The kids were wearing shorts and T-shirts and sneakers. And their baseball caps. They wouldn't go anywhere without those Twins caps.

MAX: It was about four o'clock in the afternoon when the brothers ran through this park, supposedly heading for the swing set, sandbox, and monkey bars just behind me here. It was their favorite place to play. They had promised their mother they would be back home in an hour, in time to get ready for dinner.

HAZEL: Jed had a watch. He got it for Christmas, and was real proud of it. When five o'clock came and they weren't home, I got a little irritated. Their dad would be getting home soon and he liked supper to be ready when he got there. When another half hour passed and they still weren't home, I stopped being angry and started getting worried.

MAX: Still another half hour passed. The boys' father got home and immediately began searching

for them. When that failed, they called the police.
The man who ran the department at the time was
Chief Tony Malay.

Although Alex had never met the retired police
chief, he knew of him by reputation as a tough, honest
cop. Square-jawed with ruddy cheeks, he stared directly
into the camera as he recalled that night ten years
before.

CHIEF MALAY: When we were first notified, we
thought it would be like most other lost-kid calls—
that they were just staying out late, or maybe were
playing at some other kids' house. But we sent
several squads to the area, just in case it was, you
know, something more serious.

MAX: More hours passed and the summer sun was
quickly setting, with still no sign of the boys. By
then, of course, the parents were frantic with
worry. The father, John Hathaway, will never forget
that night.

JOHN HATHAWAY: I can't tell you what I was thinking.
What would you think? Three boys gone, *whoosh*,
like the wind. Hazel was hysterical and I was damn
close to it. The cops kept telling us they'd turn up,
but by then it was dark. All of the neighbors were
out helping us search . . . I had no voice left from
shouting, but we kept looking, with flashlights,
spotlights, even candles, for God's sake.

As Alex watched the father, he couldn't help but feel
his enormous pain. And frustration. The anguish was

etched into every line of his face, the torment as evident now as it must have been to those who were by his side that night.

MAX: State patrol helicopters were in the air and police boats were patrolling the Mississippi, but the long hours of the night went by with no sighting of the brothers or clues as to what might have happened to them. Their friends were questioned, but no one remembered seeing the boys in the park . . . and the Hathaways said there was no chance they had run away, certainly not all three.

By morning's first light, one of the police boats patrolling downstream discovered two baseball caps, one floating in the middle of the river, the other hung up on a branch half-submerged in the water. There was no doubt they belonged to the Hathaway boys.

Alex watched as the police boat pulled to shore, the officer in the bow holding up the two soggy caps for the television cameras. The parents were not there at the time, but the caps were quickly brought to their home for the official identification.

HAZEL: Their names were written in the headbands, you know, with indelible ink. To keep them from getting mixed up. They were their caps, all right.

JOHN: What can I say? We were devastated. It was like all of the lights in our life went out. All at once. Our three boys, swallowed up by the river. How could it have happened? Did one fall in and the others try to help? But they knew they couldn't go near the river.

HAZEL: And they were such *nice* boys! They wouldn't have disobeyed us. They knew better.

MAX: But the police thought otherwise. It was a terribly hot day, like today, and kids, they said, will be kids. The water must have seemed very inviting, down there below the bluff. The search for the bodies continued for another two weeks, far downstream, even past the locks and dams, but no trace of any of the boys was ever found. Not even by now, ten years later.

JOHN: How do you explain that? Tell me! I could understand maybe one body not coming up, getting stuck on something down under the water. But three? You tell me what the chances of that are? No, they didn't drown. Somebody took them, I can tell you that.

MAX: To this day, the Hathaways have not retreated from that belief, despite the lack of even a shred of evidence of a kidnapping or other crime.

CHIEF MALAY: I have great sympathy for the family and for their loss, but we conducted a thorough investigation and found nothing that suggested anything but a tragic accident.

MAX: In the years since their three boys disappeared, the Hathaways have had two other children, both girls, one born only two years ago. That has helped ease some of the pain of their loss, but they say nothing will ever erase it. That is, unless the boys are found, someday, somehow.

This is Max Douglas reporting for *Channel Seven News*.

Alex put the transcript aside and stared at the now blank screen, his eyes unfocused, his mind still digesting what he had just seen and heard. Another five years had passed since Max had filed that report, and still— *still*—no trace of the brothers. Was the father right? That the river could not have consumed all three? It sounded right to Alex, but what the hell did he know about such things?

Sleep on it, he told himself. Think about it. Maybe you're getting excited about nothing. After all, what can you do that the cops and probably a dozen other reporters haven't already done? Or tried to do. It's an old story. History. Sad but true. Damn near everybody has long since forgotten about it.

Except for the Hathaway family.

Alex picked up his briefcase and headed for the door. He was the last one to leave.

2

While Minnesota may be best known for the raw, brittle cold of its winters, it can also produce more than a few hot, steamy days of summer. And this had been one of them, a July scorcher that left people panting, sweating, and thinking wistfully of those subzero days of January. As he left the building, Alex discovered that even the darkness had brought little relief from the day's suffocating heat and humidity.

It must have been a day and night like this fifteen years ago, he thought as he made his way slowly toward the parking ramp, shedding his sport coat as he walked. In this kind of heat, could those kids really have resisted the temptation of the cool river water—despite their parents' warnings? It would have been hard.

Even now, he could envision the three youngsters sliding down the slope of the bluff in daring disregard of their mother's familiar instructions, the younger boys following the older, slipping off their shorts, shirts, and sneakers and diving into the water, laughing and splashing, carefully planning to leave time to dry off before dashing home again.

Until . . . until what?

By the time Alex reached his car, his shirt was sticking to his body and he could feel the beads of sweat swimming on his forehead and running down the back of his neck. A cold beer and a cool shower awaited him at home, thank God, and then eight hours of blessed air-conditioned sleep.

Why was he so damned tired? It wasn't as though he'd been doing any heavy lifting. Like the guys who spent their days under the sun dancing with a jackhammer or laying sheets of blacktop. Maybe it was a midlife crisis. Or the humdrum routine of his job. Whatever, he could barely work up the energy to get behind the wheel of his Blazer and guide it up the almost deserted ramp.

Not too many weeks would pass before he turned fifty, a menacing date for almost anyone, but especially for someone like himself, competing in a business where youth was not only an asset, but, some would say, a necessity. He tried not to think of it often, but he couldn't ignore the recent research at the station— which showed his age becoming a negative factor for a growing group of younger viewers, the very audience that was the lifeblood of the station.

So far his boss, George Barclay, had made no big issue of it, although a couple of months before he had slyly suggested that Alex might want to darken his graying hair a bit. Not much, just along the temples. But even that, coming from Barclay, said a mouthful. He knew the news director must be feeling some pressure from above.

Few other cars were on the streets as Alex wound his way home, skirting the chain of lakes in south Minneapolis to the spacious house he had first rented, then bought, several years before. A two-story Tudor, it was only a couple of blocks from Lake Harriet in the midst of a quiet residential neighborhood of substantial and stately homes. While the house was far larger than he required, he loved the roominess, the space to wander, to stretch out. Besides, he had to have space for his kids when they came to visit for several weeks in the early summer, or for Thanksgiving or Christmas.

As it was, the only other full-time occupant of the house was Seuss II, a most ungracious cat whom Alex had adopted from the Humane Society the year before, a replacement for Seuss I, who had come with him from California but had died a most unpleasant death shortly after. But that was another story. The first Seuss owed his name to Alex's son Christopher, and to the fact that he was one of a litter born in an old hat in a California neighbor's closet. It was also Christopher who—on his most recent visit—had insisted that the new cat be tagged with the same name, despite the fact that he probably had never seen the inside of a hat.

Seuss was perched on the banister as Alex opened the front door, eyeing him irritably, telling him what he already knew—that he was late delivering his after-work meal. "Cool it, Seuss," he said as he picked the cat up and tucked him beneath one arm, carrying him through the cool, darkened house to the kitchen. Sure enough, once the lights were on, he found the cat's food bowl turned upside down in the center of the kitchen floor, a certain sign of his pique.

Seuss was a Siamese, with piercing blue eyes and a smooth, almost silky coat that ranged in color from light tan to the dark brown of his face and ears. Alex had no idea how old he was, except that he was no kitten. And wherever he had come from, he had learned to take care of himself—and to have no particular fondness for humans, including Alex. Except at mealtimes.

Alex quickly filled the cat's bowl, and then checked the answering machine on the kitchen counter. The light was blinking. "Hey, Alex," the woman's voice said. "If it's not too late, give me a call when you get home. Like before eleven, okay?"

He glanced at his watch. Almost midnight. She'd have to wait until tomorrow.

She was Pat Hodges, a local attorney and old college flame who had reappeared in his life when he came to Minnesota, and who had played a key role in his exposé of the pedophile judge. Their present relationship was complicated, however, by the fact that her husband, also a judge, had been involved in the scandal and had committed suicide in the midst of Alex's investigation. The trauma of that event, although now several years old, still lingered, as did her guilt, preventing a more firm, lasting bond between them. For her the pain was still too fresh, despite the years.

All Alex could do was wait. But aside from his kids, she remained the most important person in his life.

His kids. The Hathaway kids. Tommy Akers. He couldn't seem to get them out of his mind. He grabbed a Bud from the refrigerator, flicked out the kitchen light, and headed for the shower, Seuss trailing more content-edly behind.

Then to bed.

But sleep would come not easily. The recurring vision of three boys flailing helplessly in the river saw to that.

He was not the only one.

Across the city, in suburban Roseville, the lights still burned in the home of Hazel and John Hathaway. It was well beyond their normal bedtime, and hours after their two daughters had been tucked safely in for the night. The couple now sat huddled together on a couch in the family room, watching but not seeing the flickering images on the television screen across the room.

The muted sounds from the TV set, although unheard, seemed to make their own silence more bearable.

They had not needed the brief television news report hours earlier to remind them of what day this was. Indeed, not a day passed—not one in fifteen years—that their sons were not in their thoughts. But the ache was even more intense on these anniversaries, and the Hathaways had come to dread them, wishing they would simply disappear from the calendar.

But, of course, that didn't happen. They were left to deal with the day as best they could, filling the hours in any way that would make them pass more quickly. Hazel fussed even more than usual over the two girls, busying herself and them with whatever household chores and crafts would keep the memories at bay and their minds occupied. For his part, John left for work early and came home late, volunteering for overtime at the warehouse and then spending a couple of additional hours at Casey's, talking to no one, staring at the rows of bottles along the mirrored wall of the bar. Knowing that by now Jed and Matt would have been old enough to be sitting on stools next to him, swigging a beer, talking sports, and giving their old man shit.

Knowing, too, that it would never be like that with the two girls, as much as he loved them.

Andrea, who was seven, and Angela, who was eleven, knew their brothers only by the pictures scattered throughout the house, and by the stories their folks and other friends and relatives would tell them. Neither girl was yet old enough to fully comprehend the enormity of the family's loss, although Angie had begun to ask more and more questions about her brothers, and had come to understand the special significance and the unspoken silence of this particular day in July.

Andrea could only ponder why her mother and dad seemed so sad.

While the girls would join in their parents' daily prayers for the boys, they would sometimes wonder aloud—in their childlike way—if God was deaf or simply not paying attention. Otherwise, they asked, why hadn't their brothers come home by now?

The family had never held a memorial service. Or bought cemetery plots. Or erected any kind of marker in the boys' memory. Or sought to have them declared officially dead. Their friends and extended family thought this was odd, especially as the years passed with no sign of the children. But they knew better than to voice those thoughts more than once. To persist would make them unwelcome in the Hathaway home.

For the first several years, the family faithfully celebrated each boy's birthday, in absentia, but eventually they decided the practice was simply too painful to continue.

"We've got to get to bed, Hazel," John said, finally breaking the silence. "The girls will be up early."

His wife continued to gaze at the TV set. "We'll probably get more calls tomorrow, you know," she whispered.

"Maybe not," he said. "It's been too long."

In the past, whenever the story was resurrected by one of the television stations or newspapers, the family would be swamped by sympathetic calls from friends or, as often, by crank calls from strangers or psychics claiming to know something about the boys. More than one caller had claimed to have them, demanding huge sums to reveal their whereabouts, but nothing had ever come of them. And the number of calls had diminished with the passing of the years.

Earlier on, at the height of the harassment, John had urged that they get an unlisted number, but Hazel would have none of it. "What if the boys call?" she had argued. "They have to be able to reach us." In fact, when they'd moved from the old neighborhood to their new home in Roseville, she had persuaded the phone company to allow them to keep their same number. And now, with Caller ID, they could sort through the calls, bringing some relief from the weirdos, but not always from their well-meaning friends.

Frankly, they'd been surprised to see the report on the *Channel Seven News;* it had been a long time since they had been contacted by any of the media. Which, to Hazel, was a mixed blessing. While the lack of publicity had returned some normalcy to their lives, it had also meant that her missing boys had been all but forgotten by the media and the public. And she couldn't bear to think of that.

In the days and weeks after the boys disappeared, and after the police had abandoned their search, the Hathaways had pleaded for time on radio and TV and for space in the newspapers to seek leads and keep the story in the public eye. They never missed an opportunity to speak to their missing boys or to the unknown people they believed had taken them. For a time, with the help of friends and relatives, posters with pictures of the boys were distributed throughout the Twin Cities . . . taped to store windows, tacked on telephone poles or building walls, anywhere there was space and a willingness to display them.

That was all they could do. They couldn't afford to

hire a private investigator, not in those days, or now, for that matter. And in that era there were no national TV programs like *Unsolved Mysteries* to appeal to. Eventually, despite their efforts, and because there was no real evidence that their boys had not drowned, the media and the public tired of the campaign and the story faded from the headlines and the newscasts. Replaced by other mysteries. Other tragedies.

Except on the anniversaries.

John turned off the TV and made his way to the stairway. "C'mon, Hazel, you can't sit there all night."

She stood slowly, as though just awakening. "You go ahead," she said. "I'll check the doors and get the lights."

"It'll be okay," he said with a soft smile. "We got through another one."

She tried to return his smile, but it was not in her.

Andrea heard her father's footsteps on the stairs, heavy and slow, and then—through her half-closed eyes—saw the bedroom door open a crack and the hallway light spill in. Checking on them. Then the footsteps moved on. Moments later her mother was beside her bed, straightening the tangled sheet at her feet. Then the cool touch of her mother's lips to her forehead. Andrea continued to feign sleep as her mother moved across the room to Angie's bed, where she repeated the goodnight ritual.

Once she was gone, and the door closed, Andrea whispered, "Angie. You awake?"

There was a muffled, mumbled reply.

"Angie!"

She could hear her sister roll over. "What do you want?" Sleep filled her voice.

"Was this the day?"

Angela knew immediately what she was asking,

although it had not been spoken of during the day. "Yes," she replied softly.

"I knew it!"

"How did you know?"

"I don't know. I just knew. The way they looked, I guess. Like they were pretending everything was okay."

"Go back to sleep, Andrea."

Andrea lay back on the pillow, now speaking more to the ceiling than to her sister. "Will they ever be back? The boys?"

Angela sat up in her bed, straining to see her younger sister in the darkness. But she could only make out the dark shape of her head against the white pillow. "I don't know, Andrea. Mom and Dad think they will, but I don't think anyone else does. It's been too long."

"Do you miss them?"

"Jeez, Andrea, that's a dumb question. I never knew them. How can I miss them?"

"I do."

"They wouldn't be like their pictures anymore, Andrea. They were kids like us then. But that was a long time ago. They'd be big now. Men. Like Jerry next door. Going to college or something."

"I'd like to have brothers," Andrea persisted. "Even if they were big."

Angie lay back down. "Go back to sleep, Andrea."

"I dream about them, you know. Lotsa nights. They seem so real, playing with me. Tickling me. Laughing at me."

Angie didn't tell her that she had once had those same kinds of dreams. But they had stopped long ago. Disappeared. Just like that. Just like her brothers.

She hoped Andrea's would, too.

3

It took Alex a few moments to spot Max Douglas, sitting alone on the far side of the crowded restaurant, his head buried inside a menu. Alex quickly moved toward him, squeezing between the tables, ignoring the stares from strangers that a TV celebrity always encounters, returning the smiles and greetings of a few familiar faces.

It was one of the reasons he so rarely ventured out into public; he couldn't escape the discomfort of being stared or pointed at, or being asked for an autograph at moments meant to be private. Others with his prominence, he knew, basked in such attention, even sought it out, but not Alex. As a result, he tried to stay close to home or the station . . . or to public places he knew would be *so* crowded—like a baseball or football game—that he would likely escape notice.

He had made an exception today, as a favor to Douglas and because—despite himself—he couldn't escape thoughts of the Hathaway boys.

Max took his eyes off the menu in time to spot Alex's approach. "Long time no see," he said as Alex reached the table and shook hands.

"No kidding," Alex replied, sliding into his chair. "And I regret that."

"No more your fault than mine," Douglas said, smiling.

Alex had not seen Max since he'd left the station to join the PR department of a large local utility, but one glance told him Max had not changed much in that time, or even in the five years since he'd done the report on the Hathaway boys. He had managed to maintain the rugged good looks and imposing physique of the Penn State quarterback he had been a decade earlier, along with his quick and engaging smile.

He'd come to Minnesota as a fifth-round draft choice by the Vikings football team, but was cut a couple of years later and went to work for the station, starting as an intern but quickly earning a spot on the reporting staff.

To Alex, Douglas was everything the stereotypical ex-jock was not supposed to be: smart, curious, modest, and tireless. He became a hell of a writer and reporter, one of the best on the staff, in Alex's opinion. But marriage, a couple of kids, and a chance to make a lot more money in the corporate world had finally persuaded him to give up the long hours and the unpredictable life of a television reporter. "I can't deny I miss the place," he said now, "especially some of the people. But I'll tell you, life is a hell of a lot easier on the outside. No more middle-of-the-night calls to cover some fucking plane crash or crack raid."

Alex nodded understandingly, but said nothing— waiting to get to the point of the lunch. But Max was not through. "What about you?" he asked casually. "You ever think about hanging it up? Doing something else? You're not getting any younger."

Alex shouldn't have been surprised by the question, but he was. And it showed. He could feel his face flush.

"God, I don't know, Max. I haven't really thought about it," he lied. "Am I looking that old?"

Douglas knew immediately that he'd hit a tender spot. "Hell no," he sputtered. "I was just making conversation. But you have been in the business a long time. It gets to everybody eventually."

The awkward moment was saved by the waitress, who arrived to take their orders and to leave a glass of water for each. After she had left, and after a few more minutes of small talk about the station and the people there, Douglas said, "I'm glad you made the time to meet, Alex. It could be important."

Alex took a sip of his water. "It's not a problem. After you called, I dug out the tape of the piece you did on the kids. It's a pretty amazing story."

"And that didn't tell the half of it," Douglas said.

"What do you mean?"

"I think there's a lot more there, Alex, but Barclay wouldn't let me spend the time digging into it. He just wanted an anniversary piece. You know, to retell the story. I wish I could have done more, but I wasn't about to go to war over it. And I've regretted it ever since. Which is why I called you."

"I'm not sure I understand," Alex said.

"I know the kind of reporter you can be, once you get onto something. Exposing old Judge Steele proved that. And you'd have a lot more leverage with Barclay than I had. You're the goddamned star of the show."

"Don't be so sure of that," Alex said with a slight grimace. "Besides, I haven't done any real reporting in a long time. I'm not sure I've got the guts or the heart for it anymore."

"I don't believe that," Douglas said. "Not for a second."

The waitress arrived with their food, a club sandwich for Alex and steak and fries for Max. He clearly hadn't lost his football appetite.

Alex waited for the waitress to retreat, then asked, "So what do you think? That they really drowned?"

Douglas shrugged. "That's the point. I don't know. The cops certainly believed it at the time, and as far as I know, still do. Nothing has happened since to change their minds."

Alex said nothing, waiting as Max took another bite of his steak. "But there are too many unanswered questions," he said, still chewing. "Like, why haven't any of their bodies popped up? Not one in fifteen years."

"I've thought of that, too," Alex said. "It's weird, but I suppose stranger things have happened."

Max knew that was true. It was one of the fascinations of the news business, and—now that he was out of it—the part he missed the most. Witnessing and sometimes reporting on all of the inexplicable events that happen—almost daily—in this world. Bizarre coincidences, superhuman feats of courage, and unbelievable tales of survival. Miracle babies as small as the palm of your hand, families reunited after decades of separation, sometimes from across the world. The list went on and on.

"Despite Barclay's wishes," Douglas said, "I did poke around a little bit. Talked to the county medical examiner, for one thing. He said he'd never known of another case like it . . . where three bodies had stayed in the river for this long. One body, maybe, but not all three."

"Why is that?" Alex asked.

"From what he said, gas usually builds up inside the submerged body . . . and forces it to the surface within a matter of days, weeks at the most, depending on how warm or cold the water is. Sometimes a body will get hung up on something down under, but the odds against that happening to all three of the bodies are almost incalculable."

Alex ate as Douglas talked, finally pushing his plate away, his sandwich only half-eaten. "What about the cops? What did they say?"

Max shrugged again. "They claim they did a thorough investigation, but remember, this was fifteen years ago . . . they didn't have the kind of sophisticated tools and techniques they have today. When they found those caps in the water, I think they pretty much discarded any other possibilities. Chalked it up as accidental drownings. Despite what the parents were saying."

Alex leaned back in his chair. "You talked to the parents. How did they strike you? Crazy? Obsessed?"

Douglas seemed to bridle. "Not at all. Just decent, hardworking people. They were devastated, of course. Who wouldn't be? The mother, Hazel, had a nervous breakdown, I'm told, and had to be hospitalized for a while. But they've refused to let go of the possibility that their boys are still alive, even if no one else agrees." He went on to describe their refusal to memorialize their sons in any way. "I remember them asking me, 'How can we mourn at empty graves?'"

Not that unusual, Alex thought. In the aftermath of Korea and the Vietnam War, he knew of many families with sons or daughters missing in action who would wait years, sometimes decades, before finally acknowledging death—and then only when presented with long-lost but convincing evidence.

"Doing the story," Max continued, "I got pretty close to the mother. By the looks of her, a light breeze could blow her over, but she's now as strong as an oak. The real strength in the family."

Alex remembered the frail woman on the videotape, and Douglas was right, she hardly struck you as a tower of strength. "You said she was hospitalized?"

"For a couple of months, I guess. She doesn't want to talk about it now, but I'm told she was in pretty bad shape back then. Blamed herself for letting the kids go to the park alone. But then she bounced back . . . joined one of those support groups for parents of missing or dead children, spoke at schools, became active in the missing kids movement."

At that moment, the waitress returned, offering a tray of deserts. Alex declined but Max quickly selected a large slice of apple pie. A la mode.

"I remember getting some strange calls after the story aired," Douglas said. "Anonymous calls, a couple of them claiming to know where the kids were. The family got some, too."

"And?" The question hung in the air.

Douglas paused briefly before answering. "What could I do? I had no names or numbers. I chalked them up as cranks."

"Do you remember any in particular?"

Douglas thought for a moment. "Only one, really. A woman who seemed to know a lot about the case. More details, certainly, than I included in my report."

"Like what?"

"Like what the kids were wearing when they disappeared. Down to the color of their shorts."

Alex was taken aback. "Are you kidding me?"

"Afraid not. It was spooky."

"Maybe she got it out of the newspapers back then," Alex offered.

"And remembered it for ten years? Unlikely, I'd say."

"You have no idea who she was?"

"None. I do remember telling the cops about it, but there wasn't much they could do either. We had no name, no way to trace the call. And she never called back."

"What about the ex-police chief, Malay?" Alex asked. "Is he still around?"

"Sure," Max said. "He's retired, but still kicking. Spends the winters in Florida and the summers at a lake place in western Wisconsin. I ran into him at a Twins game a few weeks ago. Spent a few minutes chatting."

"Did you ever see the actual police records on the case?"

"No way. I told you, Barclay would never let me go that far. It was history as far as he was concerned."

By then most of the tables in the restaurant were empty and they were getting impatient glances from the waitress. Alex looked at his watch. "I've got to get going," he said.

"So what do you think?" Max asked. "Any chance of your doing what I should have done five years ago?"

Alex let out a deep sigh. "I don't know, Max. It's intriguing, I'll admit that. But the case is so goddamned old. I wouldn't even know where to begin."

"Consider this a beginning," Max replied. "I'd be willing to help in any way I could."

"I appreciate that, but you've got another job now. To say nothing of a wife and kids."

Max pushed back from the table. "Don't you see? That's part of it. Now that I have kids, I can better relate to the Hathaways and what the hell this has done to them."

Alex immediately thought of Tommy Akers' folks back in Illinois. Were they still alive? It had been forty years. The thought of them going to their graves without knowing what had happened to their son pained him. He wished now that he had somehow kept in touch with them over the years.

"Let me tell you something, Alex. I predict that if you pass on this, you'll have some of the same sleepless nights I did five years ago. It'll never quite leave your mind. These kids and their family need a white knight. A champion. I was hoping it could be you."

Alex got up. "I don't know, Max. I'll think about it. But even if I do decide to give it a try, there's no guarantee Barclay will be any more interested now than he was five years ago."

Max smiled. "You'll never know until you ask, will you?"

By the time Alex got to the station, it was shortly before three o'clock. Maggie Lawrence was already there; it was her week to arrive early to record the afternoon TV and radio promos for the early news.

"Hey, Alex," she said as he reached his cubicle. "We kept looking for you last night at the bar."

"Thanks, but I was beat by the time I got out of here. I went right home."

She was watching him closely. "You still look a little weary. Are you okay?"

There it was again. Was it that obvious? "Not weary, Maggie." He sighed. "Just old."

"Right," she laughed. "Ready to be put out to pasture."

She could laugh, he thought ruefully. But he had twenty years on her, and a hell of a lot of miles. Hard miles, at that. Years of moving from place to place, always seeking a better job and more money in a bigger market, never content for more than a couple of years in any one place.

And at what cost?

His family, for one thing. His wife, Jan, could simply not tolerate the transient life, trailing after him as he crisscrossed the country from one job to another. She wanted stability, a real home. Roots. He wanted success on the fast track. Finally, after their third move in five years, she had had enough, bidding him a bitter farewell and taking the children with her. He'd actually lived in Minnesota longer than any place in his adult life, but by now it was far too late. His family was long gone.

And what about friends? Until now, he'd never stayed anywhere long enough to form many, if any, lasting friendships. But hell, he tried to tell himself, making friends wasn't much in his nature anyway.

He slipped off his sport jacket and sank into his chair, quickly sorting through the mail on his desk. There wasn't much. Several news releases, a couple of speaking invitations, and assorted other junk that he quickly deposited in the wastebasket.

"Anything going on?" he asked Maggie.

She gave a big yawn. "Not really," she said. "A couple of drownings up north and a boating accident on Lake Minnetonka. Except for the hot-weather story, it's pretty bleak."

Par for the course in July. The dog days of summer. The bane of newsrooms everywhere. Everybody who could be making news was either on vacation or closeted in their air-conditioned offices, hiding from the heat. Even crime seemed to be taking a holiday. Too hot for robbing or killing, apparently. And it being early in the election year, there wasn't even the normal political bullshit to help fill the newscast. As a result, they spent a lot of time covering picnics and parades, or stories of people trying to cope with the heat.

"This time of year, you have to make chicken salad out of chicken shit," Barclay was fond of saying.

Alex had an appointment with Barclay in an hour—arranged the week before to discuss a new contract. His current three-year agreement with the station would expire at the end of the year and the news director had said he wanted to get an early start on negotiations.

Alex wondered if it might be more than that.

He had decidedly mixed feelings. Did he really want to stay for another three years, considering the way he'd been feeling? The boredom and the lethargy. And did the station really want him to stay—in light of the recent research? He had avoided giving it much serious thought until now, but he knew Barclay would be looking for some kind of indication when they met.

If he decided to leave, or if the station decided not to renew his contract, he would have to start looking for something else soon. Anchor jobs in a top-twenty market were not easy to find, especially for someone staring fifty in the face. The best chance probably would be in Florida or Arizona or somewhere else with a large senior citizen population. Elephant burial grounds for guys like himself.

He got up and walked across the newsroom and into the adjacent Green Room, closing and locking the door behind him. He stared into the makeup mirror, trying to view the reflected image objectively. Did he really look fifty? Maybe. Certainly older than when he had come to the station, but who wouldn't? His hairline had receded slightly and the hair itself was definitely more gray than brown now. That *was* a change. Maybe he should take Barclay's advice and try a little Grecian Formula.

Except for the razor-thin and barely visible scar along his left jawbone, his face was as smooth as ever.

Tanned from the summer sun, with no wrinkles save a few crow's feet that had settled on either side of his deeply set, dark brown eyes. From far too many nights of squinting under the bright studio lights. Older but not old, he finally decided. And still with enough sex appeal to draw a lingering glance from many of the women he encountered. But even those, he had to admit, were not as young as they once were.

A sharp knock on the door ended the self-examination. Maggie was waiting outside. "I thought I saw you head this way," she said, catching her breath. "You've got a phone call."

Alex was surprised. Maggie normally would have just taken a message. "Who is it?" he asked.

"A woman, Hazel Hathaway," she said. "She claims it's important."

Hazel Hathaway. How could that be? Max Douglas. He must have called her after their lunch. Son of a bitch!

He began to follow Maggie back to the newsroom. "Is this who I think it is?" she asked over her shoulder. "The boys' mother?"

He shrugged. "Must be. I'll explain later."

When he reached his desk, the voice on the other end of the line was weak . . . and distant. "Mr. Collier?" She could have been calling from Hong Kong.

"Yes."

"My name is Hazel Hathaway. Max Douglas suggested I call you."

Alex was right. "Yes?"

"He says you're interested in my boys' disappearance. Is that true?"

He hesitated. He didn't know what to say. It was too early to commit to anything.

"Mr. Collier? Are you there?"

"Yes, I'm sorry. You caught me off guard, Mrs. Hathaway. I didn't know Max planned to call you."

She ignored the apology. "Was he right? About the boys, I mean?"

He paused again. "I was intrigued by the story, yes. But the first I'd heard about it was on our news last night. It's too soon. I've made no decision—"

She cut him off. "Do you have children, Mr. Collier?"

"Yes, two. They live with their mother in—"

"Could you stand the thought of losing both of them?" Her voice had strengthened and now seemed on the verge of hysteria.

"Of course not, Mrs. Hathaway. But please—"

She was not to be deterred. "Have you read the book, *Deep End of the Ocean*?"

As it happened, he had. Several months before, he told her.

"Then you know what that mother . . . that family . . . endured after their little boy turned up missing. Kidnapped. Well, multiply that by three and you can begin to understand what life has been like for us for these fifteen years."

Alex took a deep breath, not bothering to remind her that the book was a work of fiction. "I know you and your husband have suffered a terrible loss, and you have my heartfelt sympathy. But it happened so long ago. I'm not sure there's anything I could—"

"Would you be willing to talk with us?" she asked, interrupting him again. "In person, I mean."

He looked helplessly at Maggie, who was listening to his side of the conversation. "I just don't know, Mrs. Hathaway," he said finally. "It may be premature. I'd like to do a little more checking first."

"I see," she said, deflated, the disappointment vivid in her voice.

Damn that Douglas, Alex thought. Putting me into a corner like this. "I'm not saying I won't," he said consolingly. "I just need more time."

He quickly scribbled down the family's address and phone number, and promised to get back to her as quickly as he could.

"I've heard that before," she said dejectedly. Then she hung up.

He stared at the phone. *Goddamn!* What am I getting myself into?

"What was that all about?" Maggie asked.

"She wants me to find her kids," he replied.

"What?"

He quickly described his lunch with Max Douglas and the additional information he had gained about the Hathaway story. "He said he had gotten close to the mother, but never said anything about calling her. Puts me in a hell of a box. Shit, I don't even know if I want to pursue this thing. And even if I decide to, I'm not sure I'm up to it."

Maggie leaned toward him. "What do you mean by that?"

"C'mon. You know what something like that will take. A hell of a lot of time and energy. I'm not sure I've got enough of either."

"Pah!" she said. "You're actually starting to sound old!"

He gave her a wan smile. "I'll see what Barclay has to say. He may not want to do anything anyway."

"Sounds like it could be a hell of a story to me," Maggie said. "And I'd be happy to help, if you need it."

Alex mumbled his thanks, and then, glancing at the

clock, opened his locked desk drawer to pull out a copy of his personal service contract with the station. He hadn't looked at it since signing it two and a half years before, but now, only a few minutes before his meeting with Barclay, he decided it was time to review it.

Once you plowed through all of the legal boilerplate, the agreement was fairly simple: a sliding salary scale that had brought him from two hundred and fifty thousand dollars a year to his current three hundred and fifty thousand. Not great for an anchor of his stature and experience in a TV market as large as the Twin Cities, but more than enough to keep him happy—and to keep those alimony and support payments flowing east.

There were also allowances for clothing, car, hair care, vacations, and assorted other perks. The result was that he had almost no expenses of his own except for food, shelter and nonstation entertainment. And, being the near recluse that he was, he certainly didn't spend much on entertainment.

In return, he became a virtual captive of the station, expected to do whatever was asked of him, including a pledge to work for no other station in the market for at least one year. The familiar noncompete clause.

Unlike many performers, Alex employed no agent. He liked to negotiate for himself, confident he could bargain as well as anyone and save the agent's ten or fifteen percent fee off the top. In the past, that had been no problem, especially dealing with someone like Barclay—as straight an arrow as you could find in the television news business.

He wondered if it would be any different this time.

4

Hazel Hathaway had been brooding ever since she'd hung up the phone, wandering the now empty house, straightening a rug here, a throw pillow there, flicking a dust rag at tabletops she had thoroughly dusted only hours before. The girls were playing at a neighbor's house, and her husband was still at work. But all of them would be home soon, expecting dinner.

She paused at a photo of the boys sitting atop the fireplace mantel, one of several scattered around the house. But this was her favorite, a snapshot they had had enlarged and framed after the boys disappeared. The three of them, wrestling on the front lawn, a tangle of small arms and legs, caught at a magic moment when they all happened to look up at the camera. Grinning, their hair a mess, their faces streaked with sweat and dirt.

Loving life. Fearing nothing more than a scolding for the grass stains on their pants.

Taking the picture down, she held it with both hands, blowing a speck of lint away, studying it closely, as she had virtually every day for these fifteen years. Mostly when she was alone like this, out of sight of her husband and daughters, hiding the pain that the girls, at least, could not fully understand. For many years, she couldn't look at it or any of the others without weeping, but eventually—she couldn't remember exactly when—the tears had largely stopped, leaving only a gnawing emptiness in their place.

Sometimes, to her surprise, she would break out laughing, a picture suddenly reminding her of what one of the boys had said or done. But that, too, happened less and less often now, as time took its toll on those recollections.

This particular photo had been taken only days before their fateful trip to the park, and represented the last preserved image of her three sons. Try as she might, she could not visualize what they might look like today. No way could she make them grow older in her mind, to thaw memories frozen in time.

As she returned the picture to its place on the mantel and turned toward the kitchen, she wondered if she had made a mistake in calling Alex Collier. While Max Douglas had urged her to do it, she had hesitated, reluctant to reopen old wounds. She knew her husband would disapprove; he had made no secret of his desire to get on with their lives, to finally put the horror of the past behind them and to concentrate on loving and raising their two little girls.

What's more, she didn't know this man, Collier, aside from what she had seen on the television screen night after night, and from what Douglas had said: that he was a good man, and an experienced reporter. But she could hardly take heart from their phone conversation. He had been polite, but to her, somewhat cold and distant. Max may have badly misjudged his interest in her boys.

Still, she was glad she had done it. Even if nothing

came of it, she had made the effort, however futile. That, she thought, was the least she could do.

Barclay was at his desk, shuffling through a stack of papers when Alex appeared at his office door and knocked lightly. Barclay glanced up, then at his watch. "Right on time, Alex. C'mon in and close the door."

Alex did as he was told, sinking into a chair across from his boss.

"So how goes it?" Barclay asked, pushing the stack of papers aside.

"Okay, I guess," he replied.

"The heat's a bitch, isn't it? I can't remember a hotter July."

Alex nodded as he studied the man, trying to gauge his mood. But Barclay was impossible to read, in part because his full beard and bushy, overgrown eyebrows helped to hide any expression that might prove meaningful. And his eyes, looking out at Alex over half-glasses, provided no clue either.

A few years back, when Alex first arrived at the station, Barclay was a hundred or more pounds overweight and growing by the day. A bear of a man who could barely squeeze into his shirts and suits, to say nothing of his chair. But a heart attack scare two years before had convinced him to listen to his doctor and begin a daily regimen of exercise and dieting, which so far had carved away some seventy pounds of fat and left him looking far healthier.

"So we're here to talk about a contract, right?" Barclay said.

"Among other things," he replied.

Barclay appeared puzzled. "What other things?"

Alex wanted to discuss the Hathaway case, but

didn't know if there would be the time or opportunity. "We can get to that later," he said.

He had considerable respect for Barclay. Not only was he a great news director, one of the few remaining in the country who believed more in content than cosmetics, but he had always supported Alex and treated him fairly. Once, during Alex's investigation of the pedophile judge, Barclay had actually put his own job on the line to get the story on the air. They both survived the crisis, and Alex had never forgotten Barclay's courage in the crunch.

Now, as he leaned back in his chair, Barclay asked, "So where do we begin, Alex?"

"That's up to you," he said. "You called the meeting."

"Then let's not waste time. How do you feel about another three years here?"

"I don't know, frankly," Alex replied, then turned the question around. "How about you?"

"I'd like to work out a deal, if possible," Barclay said, then paused. "But we may have to make some changes."

Alex froze. "What does that mean?"

"You've seen the research, Alex. What the demographics are telling us."

There it was. Out in the open. No beating around the bush with Barclay. While he was wise enough never to mention Alex's age directly, for fear of a lawsuit if nothing else, they both knew immediately what he was talking about. What Alex himself had been thinking only the day before.

"You know that some of the younger viewers are leaving us in the late news," he continued. "It's worrisome. We can't afford to have that happen."

"And you think they're leaving because of me?"

"In part, at least. That's what the research says."

"Since when have you become such a believer in research?" Alex asked, knowing Barclay's reputation for trusting more in his gut than in what the consultant's research told him. And that he'd been right more often than not. But he also knew the stakes were higher now: In the era of cable and direct broadcast satellite, there was far more competition for viewers, especially younger viewers, and for the advertising dollars they brought. Everyone was fighting to keep a piece of the pie.

There were also persistent rumors that the station might be on the sales block. As one of a diminishing number of major-market network affiliates still locally owned, its value had risen dramatically as the networks and chains built their broadcasting empires. If the rumors were true, it could explain the determination to keep the ratings and revenues healthy for any potential buyers.

"Since Mr. Hawke told me to be a believer," Barclay replied. "And in this case, I think he's right."

Nicholas Hawke was the station's general manager, widely considered within the station to be a prick of the first order. Especially by Barclay, who had had more than his share of battles with him. But he was Barclay's boss, he did run the place, and he was the man who would eventually decide Alex's fate.

"So what kind of changes are you talking about?" Alex finally asked.

Barclay didn't hesitate. "I'd like to move you to the early newscasts exclusively," he said. "As you know, the demographics are more favorable there."

You mean older, Alex thought. More of the fifty-plus audience. People just like me. *Shit!*

Of all the possibilities, this one had not occurred to him. He sat speechless for several minutes, trying but failing to disguise his disappointment. Barclay said nothing, waiting.

The late news not only was the most prestigious and important to the station, commanding the largest audience and fattest advertising rates, it also provided the greatest visibility and stature to the anchors. Now Barclay wanted to take that away from him. "I don't know, George," he finally managed. "I'm going to have to think about this. Cut it any way you want, it's still a demotion."

"I don't see it that way," Barclay said, "but I can understand how you might."

Alex started to rise, then sat back down. "What about the dollars?"

Barclay slid a sheet of paper across the desk. "It's all here in black and white. I don't think you'll be disappointed."

Alex folded the paper and stuffed it into his coat pocket without looking at it. "I'll let you know," he said, rising, eager to leave.

"Sooner rather than later, I hope," Barclay said. "We'll have to look for a new guy for the late news."

Standing at the door, Alex asked, "Any chance of changing your mind?"

"Not unless the research changes," Barclay replied. "And I don't see that happening. Trends like this don't often turn around."

Alex was already out the door when he heard Barclay shout after him. "What about the other things you mentioned?"

"They can wait," he answered, wanting to be gone.

"You did what?" John Hathaway asked incredulously. And more loudly than he had intended.

"I called Alex Collier," his wife replied calmly.

Hathaway was standing by the door of the kitchen. Home early from the warehouse, he was still clad in the coveralls and hard-toed boots that he wore to work every day. His wife was at the sink, scrubbing the last of the potatoes and carrots for dinner.

"The television guy? From Channel Seven?"

She nodded, her back to him.

"Why in the world would you do that?" he demanded, but more softly now.

She shrugged, but said nothing.

"Hazel. Turn around. Look at me!"

She did as ordered, but slowly. Her eyes were defiant. "I thought he might help find our boys. That's why."

"Jesus, Hazel," he muttered, slumping against the wall.

She quickly explained the call from Max Douglas and her subsequent conversation with Alex. "I don't think it's going to go anywhere, anyway," she said. "He seemed . . . I don't know . . . reluctant, I guess."

John stared at her, struck again by what the years of endless worry and waiting had done to her. She was but a whisper of the woman he had met and married nearly twenty-five years before. Thin but robust then, she was almost skeletal today, her waist fitting comfortably within his two broad hands, her wrist within one. She had seemed to shrivel in the first months after the boys disappeared, especially during her time in the hospital, and had never quite regained either the weight or the zest for life that had attracted him originally and made the early years of their marriage such a joy.

Not even the birth of their two daughters had brought more than a temporary respite from her malaise. Getting pregnant, he thought, had seemed more an act of desperation than love on her part, and as much as she adored her girls, he knew they could never completely fill the gaping hole in her heart.

John went to the refrigerator for a beer and then pulled a chair up to the kitchen table. Their daughters were upstairs, busily cleaning their room so they'd be allowed to watch TV after dinner. "What if this Collier does agree to do something?" he asked. "Are you sure you want that?"

She took a chair across from him. "I want my boys back," she said simply.

He shook his head, exasperated. "Of course you do. All of us do. But—"

"Nobody's looked at it for years," she said sharply. "You know that. Not seriously, anyway. I can't stand to just sit here, year after year, and do nothing. And Mr. Douglas said this Alex Collier seemed truly interested." She paused, wiping her hands on a towel in her lap. "Besides, what can it hurt?"

He didn't hesitate. "The girls, for one thing. Do you really want to put them through that? All the attention? Think of what they'd go through at school. And here in the neighborhood. They're doing so well now."

Hazel was not to be deterred. "They'd do a lot better with three older brothers back home. With a full family. Do you know how often I find Andrea standing and staring at their pictures? Almost every day now, sometimes several times a day. And this morning she told me she was having dreams about them."

John knew it would be hopeless to argue further. He simply didn't have his wife's resolve. While he would never openly admit it to her or to anyone else, he had finally admitted to himself years before that their sons probably would never be found alive. In all truth, he may even have acknowledged it subconsciously when the police first handed him the two waterlogged caps they had found in the river so long ago.

For the sake of their marriage, however, he had publicly and privately maintained the facade. To have done otherwise, he knew, without some compelling proof of their deaths, would so damage his relationship with Hazel that it would threaten the family that remained. And he would never allow that.

"So what do we do now?" he asked.

"Wait, I guess. See if he calls back."

"I hope it's not a mistake," he said, still hoping to discourage her.

She stared at him. Hard. "The only mistake would be to quit trying."

As Alex expected, Pat Hodge's car, a black BMW, was in the driveway when he returned home between the early and late news. He had talked to her earlier in the day, and—despite his protests—she had promised to drop by the house to fix a quick dinner for him and Seuss.

The heat was no less intense today than it had been the day before. He found Pat in the backyard, lounging next to the small swimming pool he'd had installed a year ago. Her swimsuit, a clinging one-piece teal and white striped affair, was still dripping as she sat on the pool's edge, holding what he guessed to be a gin and tonic. "Welcome home," she said with a grin. Then, holding up the glass, she added, "I hope you don't mind."

"Of course not," he replied, wishing he could join her but knowing it was impossible. He never drank between newscasts, learning long ago that one drink could quickly lead to another. The last thing he needed was a thick tongue and a fuzzy mind when he climbed behind that anchor desk.

"Dinner won't be ready for a while," she said. "Why don't you get into your suit and jump in? The water's wonderful."

Why not? He had a couple of hours before he had to be back to the station and the water did look wonderfully cool. "You talked me into it," he said, shedding his sport coat as he headed inside the house.

Seuss was sprawled on the kitchen table, dozing, enjoying the last warm rays of sun spilling in the window, leaving little doubt that he'd already been well fed. Alex was tempted to sweep him off the table, where the damn cat knew he didn't belong, but then decided against it. Who needed the grief?

Within minutes he was in his swimsuit and back outside, carrying an ice-cold can of Diet Coke. Pat was once again in the pool, treading water in the deep end as he settled into a lounge chair, sipping his Coke.

Her dark hair was shiny wet, glistening in the sun. Whatever makeup she may have worn had been washed away, leaving her skin pale and clear, her deep blue eyes as penetrating as ever. While only a couple of years younger than Alex, she seemed little different from the college sweetheart he had loved and left some thirty years before. And no less lovely.

"How was your day?" she asked as she paddled toward him.

"I've had better," he said.

She reached the edge of the pool and held on, looking up at him. "What do you mean? What happened?"

He took a sip of Coke, debating whether now was the time to reveal his conversation with Barclay. Might as well, he decided. He knew he couldn't keep it from her for long.

Disbelief was written across her face when he finished. "You've got to be kidding! He thinks you're too old?"

"Not in those words, but that's what it's all about."

"I can't believe it. You're the only TV guy in town with a speck of maturity. The rest of them are kids. Brainless, at that."

He smiled. "Whatever, that's the way things are."

She hoisted herself out of the water and sat on the edge of the pool. "It's not Barclay, is it? It's Hawke. He never has liked you. Not since . . ."

"No, it's the research," he said. "I've seen it. They're right. We're slowly losing the younger audience."

Pat reached for her drink. "So what are you going to do?"

He took a deep breath. "I don't know. But Barclay wants an answer soon. He's got to find someone else for the late news."

A slight shiver passed through her body, despite the heat. "Are you thinking of leaving?" she asked, a tremor in her voice as well.

"I should start looking, at least. See what else is out there for an aging anchorman."

She scoffed, but then said nothing for several minutes, staring off across the pool, away from him. Could she really lose him again? The last time was in college, at the University of Kansas, when he'd ended what she had believed would become a lifelong relationship by suddenly disappearing, leaving only a terse good-bye note—claiming he had to get away, to find himself.

He was out of her life so suddenly, so cruelly, that she never expected—never wanted—to see him again. And in the twenty or more years that followed, there was no contact, no communication between them. And no expectation of ever seeing each other again. Indeed, neither ever knew where the other was—until Alex came to the Twin Cities, a nomadic anchorman who had found a new place to pitch his tent.

Pat had settled there years before, a Harvard law school graduate who eventually married Nathaniel Hodges, another attorney who subsequently became a district court judge—a crony of the pedophile judge Alex exposed. In fact, it was Pat—in her job as a public defender—who had first suspected the scandal and who had convinced Alex to take on the investigation, never dreaming at the time that her own husband would be involved and would ultimately escape by taking his own life.

In the years since, they had taken up where they had left off in Kansas decades before, in love but never willing to move beyond that to marriage or even to living together. Not until Pat could fully shake the shadow of her husband's death and the unintended role both had played in it. And until she could put aside an unfounded, but deeply held fear that one day she would find Alex gone again, with only another note marking his departure.

Now, as she slipped back into the water and looked up, her arms were outstretched. "C'mon in, now. I don't want to think about it anymore."

He followed her into the cool water, actually feeling cold for a split second. Then she was in his arms, holding him tightly against the wall of the pool, her face buried in his neck.

They stayed that way until the sun disappeared behind the trees.

After dinner, as Alex changed into a fresh shirt for his return to the station, he casually asked Pat if she remembered the case of the missing Hathaway boys.

"Vaguely," she said after being reminded of some of the details. "That's when I was working in the PD's office. I'm sure I'd remember more if we ever had anything to do with it."

"There's no reason you would have," he said. "No one was ever charged with a crime. The cops chalked it up as a multiple drowning."

She got up to straighten his tie. "And you don't think it was?"

"Hell, I don't know," he said, repeating the gist of his conversations with Max Douglas and Hazel Hathaway. "The parents apparently still believe it was a kidnapping."

"Does that surprise you? That they'd be holding on to hope like that?"

"Probably not, but on the phone the mother sounded so pathetic . . . so desperate. I felt sorry for her."

"I understand," Pat said as she followed him out of the bedroom. "But it sounds like you've got other things to worry about right now. Like what you're going to do about your job. With your life."

"No kidding," he said, glancing at his watch. He was already late. "I've got to get going," he said. "Thanks for dinner . . . and for being here."

"No problem. I'll clean up the kitchen and be on my way. But Alex, please don't leave me out of this decision you're facing. It'll be important to me, too."

He gave her a quick hug. "Don't worry," he said. "I wouldn't do that to you again. Not ever."

5

The next morning, despite his reservations, Alex was downtown early. He had no trouble finding the history section of the public library, the place he'd been told he could locate old copies of the Minneapolis newspapers on microfilm. The woman behind the desk, an older lady with her gray hair tied in a ponytail, obviously recognized him and quickly put aside what she was doing. "We don't often get celebrities here," she said shyly. "What can I do for you?"

Without telling her why, he said he was looking for copies of the paper for the two or three weeks after July 16, 1983.

"Fifteen years ago, almost to the day," she mused. "I bet I know what you're looking for."

"Really?"

"The missing boys, right?"

He nodded, surprised.

"I saw the item on your news the other night," she said. "And I remember the story very well."

"Why is that?" he asked.

She leaned across the desk, keeping her voice low. "I lived in the same neighborhood. My kids, when they were younger, played in the same park. And my husband

and I helped in the search for the boys. Most everybody in the neighborhood did. I'll never forget that night."

Small world, Alex thought. Then, "Did you know the family?"

"Not really. We'd see them in the yard, working. And the kids playing. But we lived a couple of streets away, so we never really got to know them. And they moved a couple of years later. People said they just couldn't stand to live there anymore. Not after what happened."

"So what do *you* think happened?"

She drew herself up straight. "I don't think they drowned, if that's what you're asking."

"You don't?"

"Everybody thinks they went swimming and got caught in the current or something. Swept away. But, c'mon. Do you think they would have gone into that river with their clothes and sneakers on? Okay, maybe their clothes. But their shoes? No way."

She saw his puzzled expression. "Except for the two caps, not a stitch of their clothing was ever found. Not even their shoes. If they'd gone swimming, wouldn't they have left something on the shore? It never made any sense to me."

He smiled. "You should have been a detective, Mrs.—"

"Holcomb. Dorothy Holcomb. Besides that, as you must know, they never did find any of their bodies."

"I know," he replied. "That's what got me interested."

"Then I hope you stay interested," she said. "It's time somebody did."

Mrs. Holcomb returned with the rolls of microfilm a few minutes later, retrieved from the stacks in the base-

ment of the library. Alex had trouble stringing the roll
of film through the machine, but finally succeeded and
began searching for the news stories he knew must be
there. It didn't take long.

The first headline stared out at him:

THREE BROTHERS MISSING, FEARED DROWNED

And the next day:

CAPS FOUND, SEARCH FOR BOYS WIDENS

On the third day, hope was vanishing:

STILL NO SIGN OF MISSING BROTHERS

He learned little crucial new information from the old
stories, although he did get a better sense of the breadth
of the search, and details of what had proved to be several apparently erroneous sightings of the boys, one
from northern Minnesota, another from as far away as
Montana. He also learned that a tracking dog had been
able to follow the boys' scent across the park and down
the bluff to the edge of the river, and that the level of the
locks and dams downriver had been lowered in an
attempt to find the bodies. To no avail.

As the days passed, the stories of the search moved
from the front page to the inside of the paper, and finally,
after ten days or so, the story simply disappeared from
print. Already history.

He made copies of each of the microfilm stories and
tucked them into his briefcase. No doubt there would be
other stories in the months and years after, but he could
hardly plow through fifteen years of old microfilm. He

would have to dig into the *Star Tribune*'s own archives to find more. Clearly, however, there had been no significant new breaks in the case over the years.

He returned the roll of microfilm to the library counter and thanked Mrs. Holcomb for her help. "You gave me more information than the old newspapers," he said, "and I appreciate it."

"I was glad to help," she replied. "I think of those poor boys often. It could just as well have been my kids."

He handed her one of his business cards. "If you think of anything more, please give me a call. My home number is there, too."

She agreed, and then asked if he would mind giving her his autograph. "We always watch your news," she said. "My husband and I."

No doubt, he thought dolefully as he signed a small slip of paper. She had to be in her late fifties or early sixties. His prime audience.

Alex escaped the morning heat by using the cooler skyways to make his way from the library back to the station, navigating through a maze of downtown buildings. Despite himself, he felt a growing sense of excitement, stronger now than at any time since his investigation of the judge. He had all but forgotten how good it was to get his claws into what could possibly be a good story.

At the same time, he didn't want to kid himself. The two cases were quite different. He'd had some solid leads in pursuit of the judge, but here there was almost nothing but the convictions of the parents and the suspicions of people like the librarian. And the case was so damn old. Whatever trail might once have existed had long since disappeared. Just like the boys.

Still . . . if they didn't drown—and aside from their caps, there seemed to be precious little solid evidence that they had—what could have happened to them? Three kids just don't up and vanish. Could the parents be right—that they were kidnapped? If so, by whom and for what purpose? Apparently no ransom note was ever received, and from what little Alex knew of the Hathaways, they were in no position to pay a ransom if one had been demanded. But—if the boys were still alive somewhere, why hadn't at least one of them surfaced by now?

Leaving what possibilities? That they'd been killed? Then buried? By some madman? There certainly were enough cases of abducted children still unsolved in the country, including several in Minnesota that Alex could recall. But in each case, only one child was involved. In all of his years in the news business, he could not remember a multiple killing or kidnapping of siblings like this.

On the surface, it appeared to be an impossible task. But he could not forget the pain in the mother's voice. The helplessness. If nothing else, perhaps a thorough investigation—even if it proved fruitless—could put the parents' minds at ease. Let them put the whole thing behind them for good.

On the other hand, the worst thing he could do would be to raise their hopes, only to dash them by giving up too soon. Leaving the questions still unanswered.

What the hell? he thought. Whatever happens with the job, I know I'm going to be around for the next few months anyway. Why not spend them doing something useful? If I could only work up the energy.

The newsroom was unusually quiet when he arrived. Although it was still early, there was none of the normal bustle about the place, telling him immedi-

ately that it was another day of little or no news. By
now, he knew, the assignment editors had exhausted the
normal run of hot-weather stories: the drain on electric
power, the crowded beaches and swimming pools, the
poor souls who had to work in the heat, and the potential impact of the hot, dry spell on farmers' crops. The
list went on, as predictable as it was boring. And here it
was, only July. They still had August to go.

Maybe we'll get a nice little tornado to liven things
up, he thought.

As he settled in at his desk, he reread the articles he
had copied from the library archives and jotted down
some of the names mentioned or quoted in the old newspaper stories: two police officers, an attendant at a lock
and dam downriver, a woman who claimed to have seen
the boys in northern Minnesota, near the town of Virginia, the day after they disappeared. There were a few
others, but he had to wonder how many of them were
still around. Or still alive, for that matter.

He had searched the newsroom's own archives the
night before, but had found nothing on their own
reporting of the original story. It turned out the station
had moved into this building about that time, and many
records and tapes had been lost or misplaced in the moving process. What's more, the reporter who had done
the story was long gone, no one was quite sure where.

Alex still had to retrieve whatever the St. Paul
papers had reported back then, but he doubted there
would be much substantially new or different from
what he had found in the Minneapolis papers.

What else should he be doing? Talking to old neighbors, for one thing. Then he should find the retired
police chief, Malay, and track down whatever police
records might still exist. And there was the Hathaway

family itself. Best save them for last, he decided.

Maggie arrived an hour or so later, surprised to find Alex already there. "What brings you in so early?" she asked.

"I had some business downtown," he replied vaguely. And then, apologetically, "I should have called you. I could have saved you coming in early."

"No problem. Brett had to be here anyway. So I rode in with him."

Despite the fact that he had shared the anchor desk with Maggie for almost three years, he could not say that he knew her well. Like Alex, she was not particularly outgoing, largely keeping to herself, aloof but not unfriendly, forgoing much of the normal newsroom socializing in favor of a more secluded, private lifestyle.

Alex knew that she had raised her son, Danny, alone, but he knew nothing of the boy's father, or whether she had ever married, for that matter. Until she'd settled into a relationship with Brett the year before, she had seldom dated and rarely took part in any station activity.

She had been—and to some degree, still was—the mystery woman of the newsroom.

He respected her desire for privacy, never pressing her for more details of her past than she was comfortable providing, in part because he didn't want to intrude and in part because he wasn't eager to share more of his own history. While it was common knowledge in the newsroom that there had been an attempt to threaten and blackmail Maggie during her investigation of the child porn ring the year before, no one could say with certainty what it was in her past that had spawned such an attempt.

Which only heightened the mystery surrounding her.

What they did share, besides a mutual respect, were the details of their respective contracts. Each knew the salary and the various perks of the other, and while there were disparities because of the differences in their ages and experience, they found sharing information had worked to the advantage of both in their individual negotiations. It helped keep management honest.

In fact, there was an informal arrangement among all of the anchors in the market to share information about their own situations. Not that you could absolutely trust what you were told, or what you learned through third parties, but the information pool did provide a sense of where you stood among your peers, and whether you were getting screwed or not.

Understanding all of this, it came as no surprise to Alex when Maggie asked how his meeting with Barclay had gone. She knew his contract would be expiring soon.

"Not that great," he replied.

"What do you mean? Didn't he offer you a renewal?"

Alex debated his response. He knew Maggie had just gotten a three-year extension to *her* contract, a year early. Indeed, the same research that showed a decline in his popularity among the younger viewers revealed that her "favoritism" levels were soaring. She was now the hottest female property in town, and the main reason the station had been able to maintain its ratings leadership in the late news. And she was getting offers from stations in other, larger markets damn near every week. Even the networks were said to be interested in her.

"It isn't that," he finally said.

She moved her chair closer to him. "What, then?"

"You've seen the research. You know what the numbers say."

She scowled. "And you believe them?"

"What I believe doesn't matter. It's what Barclay and Hawke believe."

"So what did he say?"

What the hell? he thought. She'll know sooner or later anyway. So would everyone else. Keeping secrets in a newsroom was virtually impossible, and he didn't want her to hear it from someone else. "He wants me off the late news," he said softly. "He wants somebody younger in there."

Her mouth fell open. "You're kidding me?" she said, amazed.

"I wish I were."

"That's bullshit," she hissed. "Complete, utter bullshit."

He smiled sadly. Those weren't words that normally came from her mouth. "It happens, Maggie. The aging anchorman syndrome."

She ignored the comment. "So what are you going to do?"

He shifted in his chair. "I don't know. Think about it, I guess. I'm not especially eager to move on, but I may have to."

She was up and out of her chair, angrily looking in the direction of the news director's office. "Is there anything I can do?" she demanded. "I'll talk to Barclay myself!"

He was touched. She was clearly upset, more so than he'd thought she might be. A woman almost young enough to be his daughter rising to his defense. It only made him feel older. "Calm down, Maggie!" he said. "I can fight my own battles. I shouldn't have said anything."

"What do you mean? We're partners, right? I wouldn't have been so quick to sign that extension if I'd known something like this was in the works. Barclay should have told me."

Maggie found it hard to picture herself sitting next to anyone but Alex at the anchor desk. From the day she'd arrived as a relative novice, he had been her security blanket, her mentor, always encouraging, always forgiving of her mistakes, counseling, coaching, helping her to grow in confidence and ability. Quietly, without fanfare, without seeking or expecting any thanks.

True, they had never carried their close relationship beyond the newsroom, but that didn't make it any less special. And unlike most of the male anchors she had worked with in California, including some of his age, he had never made a pass at her or treated her as anything but another professional.

"Don't say anything to anyone, Maggie. Okay? Not even Brett. I've got to figure this out for myself."

She sat back in her chair and studied him. For a man who rarely revealed anything of himself, she could see that he was hurting. The pain was in his eyes and in the stoop of his shoulders. For someone who has known nothing but success and upward mobility in his career, she thought, this has to be a devastating blow. She wanted to reach out and touch him, to offer some word of comfort, but she knew the last thing he would want was sympathy.

"All right," she finally said. "But please don't leave me out of it. I have a stake in this, too."

It took him only a moment to realize that she was the second woman to tell him that in the past twenty-four hours.

Later that afternoon, Alex finally did what he'd been thinking about doing for days, what he should have done years ago. He picked up the phone and placed a call to the *Maxwell Press Gazette* in Maxwell, Illinois, his old hometown. He asked to speak to the editor, who turned out to be a young guy by the name of Earl Specter, whose family had run the weekly paper for three generations.

"I used to live in your town," Alex told him after introducing himself. "Many years ago, like forty or so."

"Okay," Specter said. "That was a little before my time."

No surprise, Alex thought, but then said, "I was best friends with a little kid named Tommy Akers. He was a—"

"A paperboy. I know the story," Specter said. "The old-timers around here still talk about it. Like it happened yesterday. Small town, you know."

"I understand," Alex said. *Old-timers?* "Did they ever find out what happened to him?"

"Nope. Never did find a body. Or who might have taken him."

"Are his parents still alive?"

"Oh no, they died eight, ten years ago. Within a few months of each other, actually. My folks knew them pretty well."

"Did they ever get over it, losing Tommy, I mean?"

"Not really. You know, they tried to put on a brave face and all, but you could tell that it still, you know, haunted them years later."

"Did they have other children?" Alex asked.

"Yes, a daughter. Madeline. But she left town to go to college and never came back. To live, I mean. I'm not sure where she's living these days."

Alex paused, absorbing what he had been told.

"Why the interest, if I might ask?"

"Just curious," Alex said, and then told Specter briefly about the Hathaway case. "To be honest, I hadn't really thought about Tommy for a long time. But this case brought it all back, and I guess I was feeling a little guilty for never checking up on him. Or talking to his folks. We were pretty close at the time."

"Well," Specter said, "there are still a few people down here who think he'll turn up alive someday. But I wouldn't bet the farm on it."

"I know what you mean," Alex said.

6

It took Alex two days, and several tries, before he finally was able to arrange an interview with the retired police chief, Tony Malay, and then only on a Saturday afternoon—and only if he'd travel to Malay's summer home near Webster, Wisconsin, about a hundred miles north and east of the Twin Cities.

Malay had given him careful directions, but Alex still had difficulty finding his place. The cabin was tucked away in a forest of white and red pine and scrub oak, along the shore of Lake Benjamin, a tiny body of water miles from the nearest highway and accessible only by what turned out to be little more than a logging trail. Alex was glad he had the high-riding Blazer to get him over the bumps and ruts.

Malay was in back of the cabin, splitting wood, when he pulled into the yard. The extraordinary heat wave had broken the day before, but Alex thought it was still too warm and humid for that kind of work. Malay, however, showed no ill-effects; he had hardly broken a sweat and the pile of split logs was almost as tall as he was. Which was saying something.

He paused briefly as Alex got out of the Blazer and walked toward him. But then the ax was slicing through the air again. And again. On target. Precise. A human machine. Alex waited, saying nothing, watching the wood fly, until Malay finally put the ax aside and straightened up. "You found your way, I see."

Alex held out his hand. "No problem," he lied.

"I've seen you on the news often enough," Malay replied, his handshake as firm as you'd expect from someone who spent his days destroying logs. "I feel like I know you already."

Malay had retired a couple of years before Alex arrived in Minnesota—after some thirty years on the police force, the last ten as chief. A cop's cop, Alex had been told. A rugged, no-nonsense guy who'd worked his way up through the ranks, disdaining city hall politics and the early rush toward political correctness. He had had little time for sensitivity training or coddling the bad guys. Somebody fucks up, you arrest him. If he gives you trouble, stomp on him. Forget his color or whether he'd had a deprived childhood.

Happily for him, this philosophy went out of style at about the same time he was ready to hand in his badge and head for the woods, eliminating the need for a more enlightened mayor and city council to seek his removal. But the cops on the beat still spoke of him with reverence, pointing derisively to the quadrupling of the Minneapolis murder rate in the years since he'd left.

Alex had been warned to be careful, that Malay had no more patience with reporters than he did with the gangbangers. A trait that had endeared him even more to the cops on the street, who themselves held most of the media in only slightly higher regard than pimps and panhandlers. Alex could only hope Malay had mellowed in retirement.

"I appreciate your taking the time to see me," he said, choosing his words carefully. "I know you must have better things to do." Like chopping down the goddamned forest, he thought.

"Time I got plenty of," Malay replied, "but you're right, I hate to waste it."

His voice was softer than you'd expect from a man of his size. He had to stand at least six-five and weigh a good two hundred and fifty pounds—still well muscled for a man of his age, but with a paunch beginning to slip over the belt of his jeans.

"You like to fish?" he asked as he led Alex toward the cabin.

"For bass, yeah," Alex said.

"You any good?"

"I've caught my share."

Truth was, fishing for bass was about his only avocation. It was one of the reasons he'd bought the house so close to the chain of lakes in Minneapolis, which he'd been told was home to lunker bass, along with healthy northern pike and even a few elusive muskies. He had spent many a summer evening between news shows casting from shore, or weekends fishing from a canoe, almost always successfully.

"Is that so?" Malay said. "What's your favorite bait?" Testing him.

"Depends. On the surface, I like the Devil's Horse. Or the Hula Popper, although it's kind of fallen out of favor. But it still works for me."

"You use plastic worms?"

"Sometimes, but I don't really have the patience for them. They're too slow. I'd rather use a spinner bait underwater."

Instead of leading him to the cabin, Malay detoured

around it, following a path to the lake. "Why don't we give it a try," he said. "I've got an extra rod and tackle in the boat."

Alex apparently had passed the test.

The path led to the top of a steep incline, with steps descending to a dock below. A fourteen-foot Lund boat, with what looked like a ten-horse Johnson motor, was tethered there. "We've got a problem," Alex said as they reached the dock. "I don't have a Wisconsin fishing license. And you're an ex-cop."

"Don't worry about it," Malay replied. "I haven't seen a game warden on this lake in twenty years. And we probably won't get anything anyway. It's a bad time of day and a bad time of year for bass. Too sunny and hot."

Alex knew he was right, but hadn't wanted to say anything.

Malay handed him a casting rod that was already rigged with a floating lure, a gold Rapala. "There are some lily pads on the other side of the lake," he said as he revved the motor. "We can try along the edge."

Crossing the small lake gave Alex a chance to study the man. His cheeks and nose were a ruddy red from either too much time in the sun or too many hours with a bottle. Alex guessed the former. Malay's hair, what was left of it, was sandy brown, ruffled now in the breeze from across the bow. His eyes were a deep blue and unblinking, even with the wind in his face.

Alex could see no other boats on the lake and no sign of another cabin along the heavily wooded shoreline. He wondered if Malay owned the whole thing, and if that was why he wasn't too worried about a game warden showing up.

Not until they were anchored off the pads and had

cast a half-dozen times did Malay finally acknowledge the purpose of Alex's mission. "So you want to know about the Hathaway boys."

"Like I said on the phone," Alex replied, "I'm only doing some preliminary work on it. I still don't know if there's a story there."

"It's history," Malay said. Where had Alex heard that before? "It's best left that way."

"Maybe so," Alex said as he watched his lure land only inches from one of the lily pads. He allowed it to rest for a moment, then gave it a small twitch. Then another. Nothing happened. "But from what I can gather, nobody's really looked at the case carefully since you did the original investigation. That's a long time."

"Because there's nothing to look at," Malay said, a slight irritation now evident in his voice. "We worked the case hard. Had our best people on it. But the kids drowned, plain and simple."

He went on to tell Alex much of what he already knew about the search for the boys. "Shit, we had fifty cops working day and night, even after we found the caps. Taking calls, following leads, cruising every street and alley in the goddamned city. And we weren't alone. Everybody was looking for those kids. But everything led back to the river."

Alex listened patiently, not wanting to ruffle more feathers, filing away the few new facts he was given. Then he posed the question the librarian had asked him: Why wasn't more of their clothing recovered?

"Valid point. The only thing we could figure is that one of the kids must have fallen in and the other two went in after him. Before they ever had time to take off their clothes to go swimming. If that's what they were planning to do."

"You really think a four-year-old would jump in to try and rescue one of his brothers?"

"Who knows?" Malay said. "Maybe it was the four-year-old who fell in."

That made sense, Alex decided, but it still didn't answer the crucial question. "And why do you think none of their bodies was ever recovered? Not one in fifteen years!"

Malay shrugged and threw his purple plastic worm deep into the pads, pulling it slowly, tantalizingly across the top of the lilies, waiting for a bass to lunge for it. Again, nothing. The fish were staying under cover, in the shade. "I've thought a lot about that," he said at last. "But the river does funny things. It doesn't always release its victims, you know."

Alex waited.

"We had a heavy snow melt and a wet spring that year . . . and even in July the river was still running fast. Their bodies could have been twenty miles downstream by the time we started dragging."

Alex made no effort to hide his skepticism.

"I know it seems strange today, fifteen years later," Malay went on. "But back then we had no way of knowing the bodies wouldn't pop up in a few weeks."

"And when they didn't?" He left the question hanging.

"By then we were on to other things. And nothing else had developed to make us change our minds."

"Did it ever occur to you that someone may have purposely thrown the boys' caps in the river to mislead you . . . to help persuade you that they actually drowned?"

Malay shook his head. "No, to be honest, I can't say that it did. And, I have to tell you, the idea seems a little far-fetched, even now."

"How about the parents' pleas? The calls they got? They still think their boys were kidnapped . . . or maybe killed."

Malay put his fishing rod down even as Alex continued to cast. "I bet we talked to those people twenty times in the first couple of years after the boys disappeared," he said heatedly. "They never could—or would—accept their loss. I can't say I blame 'em, but they never gave us anything more to go on. They were living on hope, not reality."

Alex picked up Malay's rod. "Mind if I try your worm?" he asked.

"Be my guest." Calming down.

He aimed for an open piece of water, maybe five feet by five, within the field of pads. A spot neither of them had reached before. The worm fell exactly in the center, sinking slowly. "Nice shot," Malay said with genuine admiration.

Not a second later Alex felt the strike. *Boom!* No nibbling. The line went taut and the rod bent, nearly doubling over. "Damn!" he shouted. "What a hit!"

The bass immediately began its run through the pads. The brake on the reel squealed as the line flew out. Alex held on for dear life, letting the fish run. He knew the bass—and his line—would soon be entangled in the stems of the lilies, testing both his strength and the strength of the fishing line.

Malay guessed what he was thinking. "Don't worry, that's a twenty-pound test line. He won't break it."

It was a genuine tug-of-war, as if there were an anchor at the end of the line. But slowly the fish tired and Alex began to reel him in, dragging half of the lilies along with him. It took twenty minutes, but the fish was finally by the side of the boat, enshrouded in the leaves of the lilies. Malay scooped him out with the net and held him up, stripping away the greenery. "That's gotta be six pounds of bass," he said admiringly. "I haven't gotten one this big out of this lake in five years."

Alex's heart was still pounding, his arms still feeling the strain. He took the fish, holding it up by the jaw, careful not to injure it. Feeling the weight. The bass eyed him malevolently. He didn't admit it, but it had been more than five years since he'd caught one of this size himself.

"Want to keep him and mount him?" Malay asked.

Alex was tempted, but said, "No way. I'll leave him here for you." With that, he gingerly placed the fish back into the water. And with one swish of his tail, the bass was gone—back to the cover of the lily pads. To fight another day.

Nothing more was said of the missing boys until after they'd left the lake and were sitting in Malay's cabin, each sipping a can of Pig's Eye beer. Catching the bass had seemed to wipe away whatever suspicion or animosity Malay may have felt at first. Alex was now a fishing buddy, not a reporter. Somebody who could put a worm in that open patch of water on his first cast. Remarkable.

If Malay had a wife, she was not around. And Alex decided it was not the time to probe. The cabin was small, two bedrooms, a bath, and a combination kitchen-living room overlooking the lake. A fireplace of hand-hewn stone dominated one wall, flanked by bookcases that stood from floor to ceiling—filled with a few pictures and row upon row of paperback books. Malay was not a hardcover kind of guy. At least a half-dozen fishing rods hung from a rack by the door leading to the deck, next to a mounted bass that had to go a couple of pounds more than the one Alex had just thrown back.

All in all, a comfortable place, he thought, modest but neatly kept.

"What about the calls you got?" he asked. "I read about one from northern Minnesota, claiming to have seen the kids."

Malay scoffed. "We had dozens of calls. Some of them were clearly cranks, but there were a few that could have been legitimate. On first glance, anyway. We checked them all out, as best we could."

"What does that mean?"

For the first time, Malay seemed less sure of himself. "Just what I said."

"But by then weren't you already convinced that they'd drowned?"

"Pretty much, but—like they say—we didn't want to leave any stones unturned."

"Looking back, do you think you did?" Alex asked, pressing him.

Malay crossed his arms and leaned back in his chair, hesitating. "I suppose if I had to do it over again, we, ah, we wouldn't have been quite so quick to jump to the conclusion we did."

They were sitting at the small kitchen table, covered with a red-and-white checkered oilcloth. A small bouquet of freshly picked wildflowers sat in the center, sticking out of an old jelly jar filled with water. It was hard to picture Malay, all six-foot-five of him, stooping over, picking flowers.

"What about the woman up north, the one the paper mentioned?"

"It's hard to remember," Malay said, leaning back in his chair. "But I think she's the one who claimed to have seen three boys, about the ages of the Hathaway kids, looking out the window of a van that was stopped at a filling station, somewhere on the Iron Range, if I recall. Said they looked scared, pushing their faces against the window. But she never got a license number and couldn't even describe the van very well."

"So you did talk to her," Alex said.

"One of our people did. By phone. I couldn't spare anybody to drive up there. It was too far and too flimsy."

"Max Douglas, one of our former reporters, said he talked to another woman five years ago who even knew what the boys were wearing when they disappeared. But she wouldn't give him her name."

"I don't remember that," Malay said. "But it's probably in the files."

Alex got up and wandered to the other side of the cabin, studying the pictures on the bookcase shelves. There was one of Malay, in full dress police uniform, standing in front of City Hall; another of him with a pretty, dark-haired woman half his size sitting on a picnic table in front of the cabin. There were no photos of any children.

"You have kids?" he asked, turning back.

Malay shook his head. "Afraid not. Married late. Too late for kids."

"And your wife?"

"Died three years ago. Breast cancer. Marie was her name. Wonderful lady."

He returned to the table, deciding with a glance at Malay's somber face to forget any more personal questions. Back to business. "Where do they keep the old records? The files of a case like this?"

"You *are* serious, aren't you?" Malay said.

"Maybe."

"They won't tell you anything I haven't told you."

"Maybe not, but I'd still like to take a look at them myself."

Malay could see that Alex wasn't easily deterred. "When I left, they were kept in the basement of City Hall. In a big old storage room. A real shitpile. The files are on computer now, I guess, but not cases as old as this one."

Alex took a chance. "Would you be willing to help me find them?"

Clearly surprised by the request, Malay asked, "Now, why would I want to do that?"

It was Alex's turn to hesitate. "I don't know," he finally said. "Maybe for the fun of it. Maybe because you might still have some doubts about what really happened to those boys." He paused. "Maybe because it must get boring sitting out here in the woods all by yourself, reading paperbacks and casting for bass."

Malay smiled for the first time. "You know, if you didn't fish, you could be a real pain in the ass."

"Well?"

"Let me think about it. I'll give you a call."

"Don't dillydally," Alex said. "I might not have that much time."

Driving home along Wisconsin 35, through small towns like Siren, Luck, and Milltown, Alex felt a small sense of satisfaction—not only from catching a hefty bass on a day when it should have been impossible, but also from the possibility that Malay might actually give him a hand. After all, he had actually *been there*, way back when, and despite his early defensiveness, Malay now seemed to concede that the original investigation may not have been as thorough as they had once claimed.

And he certainly knew the ins and outs of the police department, and could provide unusual access to the old records and files.

But Alex also had his doubts. What if Malay—now that he knew Alex was serious—were to react in the opposite way and actually try to hinder the investigation? To keep the department's old record clean, to prevent any potential embarrassment from arising out of the past?

Having met him, however, Alex thought that seemed unlikely. Although it had been a short visit, Malay had struck him as decent and well-meaning, despite his original suspicions. And far from the ogre others had made him out to be.

Stronger than anything, though, was his feeling that the ex-chief would love to get back in harness, if only for a little while. That's what he was counting on.

By the time he got home, the skies had begun to darken, not from the approach of nightfall but from the menacing clouds advancing from the west—erasing even a glimmer of the sun. The slight breeze of the afternoon had turned to a dead calm; the leaves on the maples, birch, and ash surrounding the house seemed suddenly to wilt, hanging lifeless. Even the grackles had stopped their squawking.

While he was driving from Wisconsin, the first streaks of lightning were so distant as to be barely visible, the sound of the thunder lost somewhere over the prairies. But the storm was coming on fast. Their weatherman had predicted it the night before, a low pressure system moving in from the Dakotas—bringing with it the chance of strong thunderstorms late in the day. And the car radio, too, had been alive with the warnings.

Now, as he stood by the Blazer, Alex watched and waited for the calm to end, for the winds to pick up, as he knew they would. The first sign was a slight rippling of the water of the swimming pool, then the leaves coming to life. Fluttering at first, then twisting and turning, before long clinging to the branches as the wind gusts sought to tear them free.

As a kid, he had grown to love thunderstorms, awed by their power and ferocity. By how quickly they would come and go. Huddled safely inside the house, he would listen to the wind and rain rattle the windows and tear at the shingles, to the crackle of the lightning and the booming of the thunder—so close, so deafening, as to be inside the house with him.

He had felt wonder but never fear, even when the thunderstorms spawned tornado warnings and his mother would hurry him to the basement, seeking shelter beneath the basement stairs. For him those were moments of excitement, not panic—prompting childhood dreams of a career as a meteorologist . . . of being able to trace and chase the storms himself. To be part of them. Those dreams, like a lot of others, had faded with time, but his fascination with the weather had not.

Over the years, while reporting on all sorts of natural disasters, hurricanes and tornadoes, floods and forest fires, he had never lost his strange attraction to old-fashioned thunderstorms. Perhaps because they were so indelibly linked to his childhood memories of home in Illinois, of the old house he grew up in. Of sitting, hugging his knees to his chest, while the storms huffed and puffed and tried to bring the old place down.

So he waited now, his face to the wind, for the first drops of rain. He wanted to taste them, to feel them touch his skin. To cleanse the air of the countless sticky days of heat and humidity. But when they did come, they came in a hurry, a curtain of rain, propelled by the wind, giving him scant time to savor them before scurrying into the house.

7

Despite her promise to Alex, Maggie was waiting by George Barclay's door when the news director arrived at the station on Monday morning. "What the hell are you doing here so early?" he asked, her expression telling him immediately that it wasn't simply a social call.

"We need to talk," she said bluntly.

Barclay unlocked the office door and she followed him in, taking a chair across from his desk, watching as he slipped off his suit coat and hung it over the back of his chair, then hoisted his briefcase onto the crowded credenza behind the desk.

The office was small, or perhaps only seemed that way because he was so large. It was tucked away in one corner of the newsroom, but with a view of the assignment desk and most of the reporters' cubicles. The door was almost always open, and little escaped his eyes. Piles of newspapers and videotapes cluttered the top of his desk, and were scattered on the floor around it. Although Barclay was not one to covet awards, several of the station's most treasured plaques were hanging on one wall, including a national Emmy, a Du Pont-Columbia award for investigative reporting, and a Peabody medallion for community service.

"Is there a problem?" he finally said, sitting down himself.

"I think so," she replied.

"What's that?" His frown told her a problem was the last thing he wanted to hear about the first thing on Monday morning.

Maggie straightened up. "Alex told me about your conversation last week," she said. Then, hastily, "I pushed him. He didn't volunteer."

Barclay slowly shook his head. He shouldn't be surprised. He knew there were few secrets between the two of them.

"Alex says you want him off the late news," she went on. "That you want someone younger. Is that true?"

"I didn't say *younger*," he shot back.

"But that's what you meant, isn't it?"

Barclay chose not to argue, turning in his chair to face the window and the street outside. He should have been prepared for this. Alex wasn't the only one getting old.

"Well?" Her voice was insistent.

He turned back. "I'll tell you what I told him. The research says we should make a change. The younger viewers are beginning to leave. They're telling us it's Alex; that he's of their parents' generation, not theirs." And then, "The situation would be even worse if you weren't sitting next to him."

Maggie could feel the flush rise in her cheeks. "If I weren't sitting *here*," she said, trying to control her anger, "I wouldn't believe what I'm hearing. Alex is one of the best anchors in the country and you know it. Head and shoulders above any of the pinheads on the competition. And he's not even fifty yet!"

Barclay knew what she was saying was true. He

didn't have to be convinced. Hell, he had hired the guy. And he'd seen scores of videotapes of male anchors from across the country, and few—if any—could hold a candle to Collier in looks, delivery, knowledge, or believability. Unfortunately, he no longer had the one thing the others possessed: youth.

"Look," he said, "I'm not going to argue with you—"

She cut him off. "It's Hawke, isn't it? He's the one pushing this, isn't he?"

She was right again, although Barclay would never admit it. In fact, he had made many of the same arguments to the general manager that she was making to him, but Hawke had been adamant: Get Collier off the late news. The advertisers wanted the eighteen to forty-nine, or twenty-five to fifty-four-year-old audience, the very viewers who had begun to slip away.

"It's my decision," he finally said, unwilling to shift responsibility. "Let's leave it at that."

But Maggie was not about to let it rest, angrily asking, "Why didn't you tell me about this when we negotiated my contract extension?"

The truth was, he didn't know it at the time, but he said, "Would it have made a difference?"

"You're damned right. I want to keep working with Alex."

"You will, if he decides to stay. Only on the early news."

"That won't cut it, George. I think I was misled."

He sat back, stunned. What the hell was she saying? That she might walk out on her contract? That would be disastrous. Hawke would go crazy. And Barclay would likely be out of a job. "You were not misled," he said heatedly. He didn't like to be threatened by anybody.

Especially by somebody like Maggie. "You know me better than that. I don't work that way."

Her eyes were locked on his, but she said nothing.

"We negotiated your contract in good faith," he went on, calmer now. "We didn't make the decision on Alex until after the latest research was in—which came *after* we made our deal with you."

She got out of her chair, ready to leave, but her eyes never left his. "The fact remains, you're trying to change the basic conditions of my employment—namely, eliminating the person I was hired to work with . . . the person I want to work with."

Barclay was out of his chair, too, moving quickly around the desk to block the door. "I want you to calm down, Maggie," he said, facing her. "Don't be thinking foolish thoughts. We've been through too much together. We'll work something out."

"I hope so," she said as she moved around him and out the door. "For everybody's sake."

After watching her march across the newsroom, Barclay returned to his desk, settling heavily into the chair behind it. Okay, he had expected Maggie to be upset by the decision; he should have talked to her first, before she heard it from Alex. But shit, he had never dreamed she would actually threaten to break her contract and leave. That was unthinkable. The station would sink like the Titanic, only faster. And there sure as hell wouldn't be room in the lifeboats for him.

What's more, he believed her.

Maggie was too bright, too strong a woman to be making an idle threat, one she obviously had thought through over the weekend. If she persisted, of course, the station could go to court and probably stop her. They did have a valid contract, and he knew—as she must—that it contained no guarantee—written or implied—that she would be working with the same co-anchor. But in the end, even if they won, they would lose. The publicity generated by a court fight would not only damage the station, but would ruin any possible future she would have there. The public wasn't stupid; they would realize she was working under duress.

And the newspaper gossip columnists would have a field day.

On the other hand, to simply let her leave was also unimaginable. She was their rising star, their future, sought after by damn near every major station in the country. She could have her pick of jobs, and knew it. That's why they had signed her to the damned contract extension.

Beyond all of that, Barclay liked the woman and had gained enormous respect for her, especially in light of what he had learned about her more distant past: that she had survived a tough childhood, abusive parents, and the perilous life of a teenage runaway on the mean streets of Los Angeles. What's more, at the age of sixteen—in a moment of desperation and hunger—she had appeared in one of the cheap pornographic films being turned out by the hundreds in L.A. in the early '80s. It was this part of her life that the blackmailers had tried—and failed—to exploit during her investigation of the child pornography ring the year before.

Yet, despite all of these obstacles, against all odds, she had managed to straighten out her life, to graduate with honors in journalism from UCLA, to fashion a career in television news, and to single-handedly raise a child abandoned by his father. What's more, she had proved to be a hell of a reporter.

In short, she was not someone to take lightly.

Barclay wondered if Alex had any inkling of what Maggie was doing. He doubted it. And he was certain Alex would never encourage it. In fact, he'd probably be outraged if he knew. He had too much pride to be part of something like that.

But that didn't solve the problem. And unless Barclay could come up with a solution, he knew he would have to take the matter to Nicholas Hawke. He dreaded that possibility, knowing Hawke would angrily blame him—even though Hawke himself had started it all by demanding Alex's demotion.

Maybe it's time to get out of the business, Barclay thought ruefully, not for the first time in recent years. It was getting too complicated. He remembered fondly the old days when a news director's job was simply that— directing the coverage of the day's news. Now he was hip-deep in budgets, set design, new technologies, advertising, promotion—and the care and feeding of the people who worked for him. On many days he was so busy with that kind of bullshit, he didn't even know what the news of the day was.

Give it some time, he told himself. Talk to Alex again. Talk to Maggie. There had to be a way out of this, short of suicide.

By early afternoon, when Alex arrived at the station, the newsroom was alive with rumors that *something* was going on. No one was absolutely sure what, or where the rumors had begun, but the speculation seemed to focus on him. Maybe someone had seen him leave Barclay's office, upset. Or perhaps a research document had been inadvertently left at a copier, or maybe someone in upper management had let some inside information slip over a beer, or . . . any one of a dozen other possibilities.

Secrets never remained secret very long in any news-room, even though—in this case—the precise details had yet to be ferreted out.

And it wouldn't stop there.

By the next day, reporters at the competing channels would also know that *something* was up at Channel Seven. And the stories would be even more inaccurate or exaggerated: That Alex had cancer. That he'd punched out Hawke. That he'd been caught screwing Maggie on the anchor desk after the late news. That's how quickly and haphazardly the grapevine grew.

Alex knew things were askew by the time he reached his desk; there was no escaping the furtive glances or the stilted greetings as he walked across the newsroom. And it didn't take him long to figure out what was happening. "That was quick," he said, more to himself than anyone else.

"What was that?" Maggie asked from the desk next door.

He looked at her with a knowing smile. "I see the word is already out."

"Not from me!" she blurted. "I haven't said anything to anyone."

"But the rumors are around, right?"

"Yeah," she admitted, "but they're way off the mark."

"Really?" He didn't want to know any more.

Maggie had been accosted by more than a half dozen people since she had come in, all of them want-ing to know what was going on with Alex. Or feeding her the latest scuttlebutt they had picked up. In each case, she feigned ignorance and urged restraint. To no avail. The rumor mill was grinding away.

Now, as he picked through the mail on his desk, she

said, "I took a couple of messages for you," handing him two slips of paper.

The first was from ex-chief Malay, calling from his Wisconsin cabin. The second was from John Hathaway. *Goddamn!* What the hell could he want? More pleas and pressure, Alex guessed.

He dialed Malay's number first. "Hey, Chief," he said when Malay answered. "Thanks again for the visit . . . and the fishing."

"I'm glad you came," Malay replied. "I enjoyed it, too."

There was a significant pause before the chief continued. "I've thought about what you said . . . about the kids."

"Good."

"That's all I've been thinking about since you left, actually."

"Okay." Alex tried to keep the impatience out of his voice.

"If you still want my help, I'd be willing to lend a hand."

Alex felt a surge of relief. "That's great, Chief. I know you won't—"

Malay cut him off. "I've got to tell you, though, that I still think it may be a wild goose chase. But if you're willing to make the effort, so am I."

"I still have to get my boss's okay," Alex said, "but I should know something for sure in the next day or so."

Malay said he planned to be in the Cities on Wednesday, two days away, and they agreed to meet that afternoon. "I'll try to locate whatever files there are by then," the chief told him. "Assuming you'll get the go-ahead."

Alex hesitated before punching in the next number.

What could he tell John Hathaway that he hadn't already told his wife? After all, he still hadn't decided to pursue the investigation. He still hadn't talked to Barclay. He still wasn't sure there was a story there. Too many questions remained unanswered.

Despite his reservations, he made the call. It took several minutes and two telephone transfers to finally reach him. And then it was difficult to hear, with what sounded like factory noise in the background.

"What can I do for you, Mr. Hathaway?" he asked, almost shouting.

"Let me get to another phone," Hathaway said, returning moments later on another line that was minus the din. "Sorry about that," he apologized. "It's hard to find a quiet spot around here."

"Where's here?" Alex asked.

"A heavy machinery warehouse. Atlas Industries. I've worked here for years."

Alex waited, saying nothing.

"I understand you spoke to my wife," Hathaway said.

"She called me, yes."

"She wants you to help find our boys."

"Yes. But I told her I wasn't sure I could. I'm still not sure."

"Just so you understand, Mr. Collier. I'm not calling to try and persuade you. Just the opposite, as a matter of fact."

Alex was taken aback. "What?"

"This has to be between you and me," Hathaway said, almost in a whisper. "My wife must never know I talked to you."

"I'm not sure I understand, Mr. Hathaway."

"Hazel is convinced the boys are still alive . . ."

"And you're not?" Alex asked, cutting in.

"It's been *fifteen* years, Mr. Collier. And no, in all honesty, I'm not."

Alex sat back in his chair, the phone pressed tightly to his ear. What was going on here? Max Douglas had said *both* parents were determined to find their sons.

"I don't want the whole thing brought up again," Hathaway continued. "It will be too painful. Too traumatic. Maybe not for my wife, but for our two young daughters. I'm afraid of the effect it will have on them. At school. With their friends. They'll be in the spotlight. It could haunt them needlessly for the rest of their lives."

"But what if the boys are still alive somewhere?" Alex demanded.

There was momentary silence at the other end of the line. "If they are alive, and I can't believe they are, they'd be like strangers to us, wouldn't they? They'd be adults by now, and God knows what they would have become after all of these years."

It was Alex's turn to be silent. Finally he asked, "Have you talked with your wife about all of this?"

"Some. But I can't push it. It would wreck whatever is left of our marriage. That's why this conversation must remain confidential."

"Are you telling me," Alex said, challenging him, "that if I do decide to pursue this, I won't have your cooperation?"

"No, not at all. Please understand. I just wanted you to know how I feel before you make that decision. That I don't share my wife's belief that it would be for the best."

Alex was confused, but decided nothing further could be gained now. "I appreciate the call, Mr. Hathaway, and it will remain between us. I'll let you know what I decide."

"Thanks for listening to me," Hathaway said.

Alex caught Barclay as he was about to leave the station after the early news. "Got time for a beer or a Coke?" he asked, with a nod toward the Hilton Hotel across the street.

Barclay glanced at his watch. "I guess so, but it'll have to be quick. I'm due at the Y for my workout in an hour and I've got to get home to change first."

"This shouldn't take long," Alex said. He knew Barclay lived in a downtown condominium only a couple of blocks away, and that the YMCA was not that far from the condo. There should be plenty of time.

"Okay," Barclay said, although he wasn't particularly eager to face Alex at the moment. He suspected that Alex and Maggie had spoken by now, and that Alex had probably also gotten wind of the far-fetched rumors sweeping the newsroom. He's probably pissed off, Barclay thought, although he appeared calm enough now. Wait and see, he told himself.

The lobby bar at the Hilton was filled with a noisy convention and after-work crowd, but they managed to find an empty table off to one side, away from the most boisterous of the drinkers. When the waitress finally appeared, each ordered a Diet Coke.

"So what's up?" Barclay asked, leaning forward, his voice low. "Have you made a decision?"

"About your offer? No, not yet. I'll need a few more days, at least."

Then what's this all about? Barclay wondered. "Have you talked to Maggie about it?"

"Yeah. Last week. She pressed me."

"Did you know that she came to see me?"

His shocked expression gave Barclay the answer. "Hell, no!" Alex said. "When? What did she say?"

"This morning," Barclay replied. "She was upset. Threatened to leave, in so many words. To walk out on her contract if we take you off the late news."

Alex took a deep breath and closed his eyes, picturing the confrontation. What was she thinking? She must have been bluffing. No, not Maggie. But why? She had everything to lose: a plum job with a great future and the stability she had so long been seeking for herself and her boy.

"Goddamn," he finally muttered. "She had no business doing that. I told her to stay out of it."

"It puts me in a hell of a spot, Alex. You can see that. Losing you would be tough enough, but losing both of you would be a disaster. For the station. For me. I can't let that happen. No matter what."

"I'll talk to her," Alex said quickly. "This isn't her battle. She'll back off, I promise you."

"I hope so," Barclay said as their Cokes arrived. "It could get real messy."

Alex downed half of the glass in one swallow. "Anyway, that's not why I wanted to talk to you."

Barclay checked his watch. He still had a half hour. "What then?"

"The Hathaway boys."

It took Barclay a moment, but then he asked, "What about them?"

Alex went back to the beginning, from the first night he had heard of the missing boys, through his meetings with Max Douglas and Tony Malay, to his library research and his phone conversations with the boys' parents. Barclay let him go on uninterrupted, listening intently but skeptically to the recitation. When he finally finished, he cocked his head and said, "So?"

"So I think there's a fair chance those boys didn't drown," Alex said. "That they may still be alive, somewhere. Or that they may be long dead and buried. Kidnapped or murdered. I'd like to try and find out what really happened. To put the whole thing to rest, if I could."

Barclay stared at him across the table for what seemed like several minutes. Finally he said, "You're serious, aren't you?"

"I think so. I'm trying to decide myself. That's why I'm talking to you now."

Barclay quickly raised many of the questions and cited many of the obstacles that Alex himself had been struggling with: the long, cold trail; the lack of any real evidence that the boys could still be alive; and the apparent conflicting interests of the parents, among others.

"I don't claim it will be easy," Alex said.

"I'd say it's impossible," Barclay argued. "I thought so five years ago when Douglas did his story. Too damn much time has passed."

Alex wondered if he should argue further. Maybe this was what he'd wanted to hear all along. To let Barclay take him off the hook. To escape what could be a long, tiring, and tortuous investigation with his conscience intact. He could simply tell himself and Hazel Hathaway that his boss had refused to allow him to pursue the story. Simple. No guilt. No regrets. John Hathaway, at least, would be happy.

But down deep, he knew he couldn't. He recalled Max Douglas's words: "It'll never quite leave your mind, believe me."

"Listen, George. Maybe you're right. Maybe it is impossible. But what if it did work out? What if we did—by some miracle—find those kids? It would be the biggest story of my life . . . probably of yours, too. Every one of the networks would be begging us for it. You'd have to build a goddamned warehouse to hold all of the awards."

"I don't give a damn about awards," Barclay snarled. "Or about the networks."

"Then think of the family, for God's sake. Living a nightmare all of these years. They need some kind of closure."

Barclay leaned back in his chair, clearly unconvinced.

"What do you have to lose?" Alex argued. "It's not like I'm an integral part of your reporting staff. As it is, I spend half my time fiddle-farting around, twiddling my thumbs, trying to look busy. And I've got at least another six months here, regardless of what I decide to do about the contract."

Was he trying to convince Barclay or himself?

Barclay pushed back his chair, preparing to leave. "I'll think about it overnight," he said, standing up. "Maybe we can make a deal."

"A deal? What do you mean, a deal?"

By then Barclay was halfway across the lobby, and the question hung in the air behind him.

It wasn't until after the late news that Alex had a chance to confront Maggie about her morning meeting with Barclay. He caught up with her in the hallway between the studio and the newsroom and guided her—despite her mild protests—into the Green Room, locking the door behind them.

"What the hell were you doing?" he asked, keeping his voice low. And calm. "I thought you agreed not to say anything."

They were standing virtually toe-to-toe, Alex a full half-foot taller than Maggie. "I'm sorry," she said, not backing off, "but the more I thought about it over the weekend, the madder I got. Barclay denies it, but I think they got me to sign that contract extension under false pretenses."

"I don't think Barclay would lie to you," he interjected. "He's always been straight with me."

"And with me," she said. "But this is ridiculous. Replacing you with someone younger. I don't want to work with anyone else."

He took her gently by the arm and sat her down next to him on the couch. "That's nice to hear, Maggie. I appreciate it. But you know the way this business works. Guys like me come and go all the time. I'm amazed I've been here as long as I have. It's a record."

She was defiant. "Whenever you've moved before, it's been on your terms, not theirs. This is different. Barclay's giving you an ultimatum, and I don't like it. Not after what you've done for the station. And for me."

He shook his head slowly. "You've got a contract, Maggie. You've also got a life here. A great future. Don't screw it up on my account. I'll do what I have to do. I'm a survivor, always have been. This has to be my decision."

She got up and walked across the room, facing the mirror, speaking to his reflection in the glass. "Whatever success I've had is largely because of you. Everybody knows that. I couldn't have done it without you sitting next to me."

"That's bullshit, Maggie. Don't sell yourself short."

She turned to face him directly. "What about Scotty Hansen? I've heard the stories. You went to bat for him, didn't you? Saved his job."

"That was different," he replied, although he could remember thinking then that he would someday find himself in the same situation as Scotty.

Hansen was the longtime sports anchor at the station, a former Gopher and Green Bay Packer football star, whom Hawke was ready to dump unceremoniously because their consultant said his age and old-fashioned ways on the air were hurting the ratings. Alex leaked the story to the newspapers, beginning what became a "Save Scotty" campaign in the local media that helped Hansen hold on to his job until he retired voluntarily a couple of years later.

"Why was it different?" she asked.

"Because I wasn't risking my own job. You are."

She returned to the couch. "Isn't that *my* decision?"

"Maybe so, but I promised Barclay I'd get you to back off your threats, Maggie. Don't make me a liar."

She heaved a deep sigh. "Okay," she said. "I'll drop the threats. But I won't stop trying to change his mind. I'll do everything I can . . . short of quitting . . . to keep you here, sitting next to me at that anchor desk. That's my promise to you."

8

Hazel Hathaway was in her nightgown, ready for bed, when she heard the telephone. Faintly, from the downstairs den. She glanced at the bedside clock: almost eleven. The two girls had long since been tucked in for the night and her husband was still in the bathroom, showering.

A second ring.

Who in the world? she wondered. She couldn't remember the last time they'd received a phone call at this time of night. Too late for solicitors. And well beyond the time any of their friends or family might call. Unless there was some emergency. Probably a wrong number, she thought, as she hurried to the stairway. Regretting again, as she often did, that they had never bothered to put an extension upstairs.

She flicked on a light in the den and reached the receiver after the fourth ring. Before picking it up, however, she checked the Caller ID and saw "OUT OF AREA." Which she knew meant long distance. Strange, she thought, debating whether to let it ring or to get John out of the shower. No time for that, she knew.

She picked up the receiver. "Hello," she said, her voice soft, tentative.

The first thing she heard were distant hisses and scratches, as though there was a bad connection. Then, clearly, "Mom, is that you?"

She thought her heart would stop. The room seemed to swirl about her. The air was sucked from her lungs; her legs went limp, and she fell into a chair next to the desk. She couldn't speak. She could barely breathe.

"Mom? Are you there? Mom! It's Matt."

She gasped for air, clutching her chest. Not believing . . . yet. "Is this some kind of joke?" she finally managed. "If it is, you're very cruel—"

"Mom, it's no joke. It's me, Matt. Please. I only have a minute."

The noise was back on the line. She wondered if he was talking on a cell phone. "Where are you?" she demanded, still unable to think straight. "Where are your brothers?"

"Jed and Andy? They're okay, but they're not with me now."

Was it *his* voice? How could she tell? It had been fifteen years. He was a child then. Yet he sounded like she thought Matt might sound. Or was that her imagination running wild? Get a grip. "Where are you?" she repeated. "Where have you been, for God's sake?"

"I can't tell you. I barely have time to talk."

She was regaining her composure. Her heartbeat had slowed, her breath was back. So were her doubts. Her suspicions. She had to be sure. "What's your father's name?" she demanded. Testing him.

"Dad? John, of course. How is he?"

"Your grandfather? My father?"

"Grandpa Gus?" he replied, without hesitation. "Is he still alive?"

"No, he died six years ago." But she was not through yet. "Jed's birthday? When is it?"

A slight pause. "Mom, I don't have time for this. Listen to me."

By then there was a shout from the top of the stairs. John was out of the shower. "Hazel? What's going on? Are you on the phone?"

She covered the mouthpiece and yelled back. "In a minute, John. Please."

"Mom, I have to hang up in a second. They're coming for me."

"Who's coming?"

"Never mind. Trust me. I want to come home, but I need money. Two hundred dollars. For the bus."

"What about your brothers?"

"We'll have to get them later. Send a money order to me care of General Delivery in Newark."

"New Jersey?" She had never been to New Jersey, never east of Wisconsin, actually. She knew only that it was close to New York. How could he be in New Jersey?

"Yes. And hurry, please. I've got to go."

The line went dead. "Matt? Matt!" The phone was heavy in her hand. She stared at it, willing it to ring again. To hear the voice again. But the only sound was her husband's footsteps on the stairs. "What's going on?" he said, coming into the den, a bath towel wrapped around his waist. Then, seeing the phone still in her grasp, "Who were you talking to, Hazel?"

"Matthew," she murmured.

"What did you say?"

Louder. "Someone who said he was Matt. Calling long distance."

John collapsed into a chair across from her. "Are you serious?"

She could see the doubt written across his face. "Yes. I spoke to him. He just hung up." She then repeated the entire conversation, as best she could remember it. "It sounded like he was afraid, John. In danger. Like he was taking a chance making the call."

"But he wants money, right?"

"Yes. Bus money, he said. To come home."

John got up and headed for the stairs. "Right. And next time he'll want four hundred or a thousand to buy a car to come home. It's a hoax, Hazel. Can't you see that?"

"You didn't hear him! He knew your name . . . even my dad's name. How could he know that?"

That gave him pause. "Maybe he lived in the neighborhood back then. A friend of the boys. Maybe he knows someone else in your family. There could be dozens of ways . . ."

"But he sounded so sure of himself . . ."

"What else did you ask him?"

"Jed's birthday."

"And?"

"He didn't have time to answer. He barely had time to talk."

"Convenient," John said sardonically as he paused by the door to the den.

"You just don't *want* to believe," she said angrily.

"I don't want to be taken in," he replied softly. "The first clue is when they ask for money, Hazel. You should know that by now."

With that, he left her there . . . still gripping the phone, not bothering to wipe away the tears.

As Alex thumbed through the *Star Tribune* the next morning over breakfast, he wasn't totally surprised to find that the television columnist had picked up the newsroom rumors of the preceding day. It was only a small item, tucked in at the bottom of the column, but it loomed large as life to him.

> Rumors are circulating at Channel Seven that veteran anchorman Alex Collier may be on his way out. Either voluntarily or with a slight nudge from above. Station officials deny it, but the newsroom buzz has Collier ending up elsewhere when his contract expires at the end of the year. Insiders say the beef is that the fiftyish Collier is losing his appeal to the twenty- and thirty-something viewers . . . who seem to like their anchormen as young as they are. Stay tuned.

He read the item three times, then pushed the newspaper aside. The columnist hadn't even bothered to contact him. Bastard. Somebody was obviously feeding information to the guy, but who? Not Barclay. Not Maggie. Maybe Hawke had let it slip to one of his cronies at another station. Alex knew they all but slept together.

Forget it, he told himself. Ignore it. But he knew that would be easier said than done.

When he walked into the station that afternoon, the receptionist pointed to a woman sitting in one corner of the lobby. "You have a visitor," she said. "She insisted on waiting. She's been here for a couple of hours. I didn't know if I should call security or not."

Alex immediately recognized the woman as Hazel Hathaway, with the same wan, drawn features he had seen in Max Douglas's report of five years before. "No, no," he said. "I know who she is. I'll talk to her."

As he walked across the lobby, the woman looked up from the knitting in her lap and rose to meet him.

"Please don't," he said, sliding into a chair next to her.

"I'm Hazel Hathaway," she said. "I'm sorry to——"

"I know who you are, Mrs. Hathaway. I recognized you from Max's story."

Obviously nervous, she clutched the knitting needles as if they might provide some support while she struggled to find her first words. Alex decided to help. "I'm sorry you've had to wait so long," he said. "If you'd only made an appointment . . ."

"I know, I'm sorry," she whispered. "But I didn't know if you'd see me, and it's important that we talk. I didn't know who else to go to."

"Relax, Mrs. Hathaway, please. There's no reason to be nervous."

He was surprised by how thin she was, a wisp of a willow, yet with the strength of an oak, according to Max. Her skin was pale, with no trace of makeup. But it was her eyes that caught Alex and held him: the deepest, most lustrous green he had ever encountered, as sparkling as the shiniest shooter he had ever played with as a kid. He found it hard to look away.

"Would you like a cup of coffee or something?" he asked.

"That would be nice, but I don't want to be more of a bother."

"No bother," he said. "We can talk there." He led her out of the lobby and down the hall to the station lunchroom, finding a table near a window. No one else was there. He got two cups of coffee from the vending machine and took a seat across from her. "The coffee's not great, but it's the best I can do."

"I'm sure it will be fine," she said, taking her first sip, unable to hide a grimace from either its heat or taste. The hand holding the cup began to shake slightly. Then, "Is it true what I read in the paper this morning?"

"About my leaving the station?"

"Yes."

"They're only rumors, Mrs. Hathaway. You can't believe everything you read."

"But are you? Leaving, I mean?"

"Maybe. But even if I do, it won't be for several months."

He expected still more questions, but when none was forthcoming, he asked, "Now, what can I do for you?"

She put the coffee aside and took a deep breath. "We got a call last night . . . long distance, I think."

"Yes?"

"The caller claimed to be one of our boys."

"*What?*"

"Matt, the middle boy."

Alex leaned forward. "Hold on, now. Start from the beginning. When did you get the call?"

"After your news. A little before eleven. I was getting ready for bed. Had no idea who would be calling at that hour. It almost never happens."

"Go on," he urged.

"It was a man's voice. His first words were, 'Mom, is that you?' I almost fainted, I'll tell you. 'This is Matt,' he said. The rest is kind of a blur. I wasn't thinking straight. At first, I thought it must be another crank call. We still get them, you know. Every now and then."

"Slow down, Mrs. Hathaway. How do you know this wasn't just another one of those?"

She looked down at her clasped hands. "I don't,

really. I mean, I have no real proof. But he knew John's name and my father's . . . his grandfather's . . . name. But, it was more the way he talked . . . I don't know, he just sounded like I imagine Matt would sound. Even the way he said 'Mom.' Maybe it's just my imagination."

"What else did he say?"

She repeated the rest of the conversation, as best she could recall it. "He said he wanted to come home, but had to have money for the bus."

"Aha!"

She frowned. "That's what my husband thinks. Another con game. But he said he needed only two hundred dollars. Said to send it to General Delivery in Newark. That didn't sound like a big rip-off to me."

"You must have asked him where he—they—have been all of these years?"

"Of course, but he said there was no time to explain. That he was taking a chance even calling. Told me to trust him. Then he hung up."

Alex leaned back in his chair, draining the last of his coffee. "He knew his brothers' names?"

"Yes. And there was no hesitation in saying them. I mean, it wasn't like he was trying to remember them."

"But your husband doesn't believe it?"

Her back seemed to stiffen. "I told you. He thinks it's a big hoax. But he didn't talk to this person. He didn't hear his voice."

"But you haven't heard it either," he said. "Not in fifteen years."

"I know," she replied, sadness now in her own voice.

They spent another twenty minutes talking before Alex said, "Come with me," leading her back down the same hallway, but now toward the newsroom, not the lobby.

Barclay was alone when Alex appeared at his office door with Mrs. Hathaway in tow. He quickly introduced her and asked if they could sit for a moment. Barclay agreed, but only after a quizzical glance at him.

With an encouraging nod to Mrs. Hathaway, Alex said, "Tell Mr. Barclay about the phone call, please. As briefly but as completely as you can."

She did as she was asked, with Alex filling in any details she left out. When she was finished, they both looked at Barclay expectantly, but his expression carried no hint of his thinking. "You've had these kind of calls before?" he finally asked.

"Never from anyone claiming to be one of the boys," she replied firmly. "From others who said they knew where they were, or who could help us find them, but never from one of the boys. That's why I came to see Mr. Collier."

Barclay asked a few more questions, then thanked her and told her they would discuss the matter and get back to her. But he urged her not to get her hopes too high. "I realize that you'd like to believe this call was for real, but as you know, chances are great that it's not. The fact that he asked for so little money now might only be the beginning of an effort to extort more from you and your husband later. The world is full of bad people."

"I don't have to be told that, Mr. Barclay," she snapped, hurriedly getting up to leave.

"I'm sorry," Barclay replied immediately, seeing her anger. "It was a careless comment."

As Alex led her back to the lobby, he asked her to call if she heard anything further from the man calling himself Matt.

"Do you think we should send him the two hundred dollars?" she asked, standing by the door.

He paused. "That's really up to you and your husband," he finally said. "You may be throwing your money away."

She let out a deep sigh. "I know," she whispered. "But what if it really was him?" Then she was out the door and away, not looking back.

When Alex returned to Barclay's office, he asked, "So what do you think?"

"I'm not sure I believe her," Barclay said.

He was taken aback. "What do you mean?"

"C'mon. Doesn't it strike you as strange that she gets this phone call at the same time that she's trying to convince you to look into the case? The first time she's heard from one of her boys just happening to come at this particular moment? What are the chances of that? And who's the first one she comes running to? Good old Alex."

He hadn't really considered that possibility. "You may be right," he said, "but did she look like a liar to you? You really think she was faking?" Before Barclay could reply, he added, "If she was, she's a hell of an actress."

Barclay shrugged. "I don't know. I'm not clairvoyant. I just think it's odd."

Alex pulled himself up and out of his chair. "Okay, you've got your doubts. So do I. But are you going to let me take a run at it?"

Barclay leaned forward, hands flat on the desktop. "How badly do you want to do it?"

"Pretty badly, I guess. Especially now, with the phone call. I think it could be a hell of a story."

"That's not enough, Alex."

He took a deep breath. "Look, George. I've been in this business almost thirty years. Except for sticking it to Judge Steele, what's it been? Thirty years of chasing stories that nobody really gives a rat's ass about. Or, better yet, sitting behind an anchor desk, smiling, looking pretty, and reading somebody else's copy. Yawning my life away."

"C'mon," Barclay said, "it's not been that bad . . ."

"You're right. And I'm not complaining. It's been fun. It's been easy. Good hours, good money. But for the first time in all those years, I may actually have a chance to make a difference in somebody's life. A real difference. To real people. Before some asshole like you sends me out to pasture for good."

There was a hint of a smile behind Barclay's beard.

"I want to find those kids, George. Dead or alive, I want to know what happened to them. It's that simple. Not just because it would be a great story, but because—for once in my life—I want to do something for somebody other than myself."

Barclay gave him a long, hard look. "Under normal circumstances, I'd say forget it. It's too chancy. But if you're so goddamned determined, then maybe we can make a deal."

Alex's antenna shot up.

Barclay had obviously given it some thought. "Here's what I propose. I say go ahead, and you agree to a one-year extension of your contract, with the dollar figures I gave you the other day. You agree to give up the late news without a public fuss as soon as we find a replacement, but no sooner than the first of the year. Then you stay on for at least another year doing the early news. If you're not happy then, you'll be free to go wherever and whenever you want."

Leave it to Barclay to come up with a quid pro quo, Alex thought, but it could be worse. "You'd give me the support I need to pursue the Hathaway story?"

"Within limits, sure."

"What kind of limits?"

"Depends on the progress you make," he said. "I'm not going to throw money down a rat hole. The more progress, the more support. But you've got to be straight with me. If it looks like a dead end, you'll get the hell out."

Alex considered what he had heard. "You'll put all of this in writing?"

"You can have it by tomorrow."

"What about the rumors in the newsroom? The crap in the newspaper? What will you tell the staff?"

Barclay thought for a moment more. "How's this? We'll announce that you've signed an extension to your contract, saying nothing about the move to the early news, and that you're going to be working on a special investigative assignment. That should quiet things down for a while."

"Let me think about it overnight," Alex said. "I'll get back to you tomorrow."

Pat was at the house, waiting, when Alex returned after the late news. He had talked to her by phone earlier in the evening, telling her briefly about his conversation with Barclay and about his visit from Hazel Hathaway. She had insisted on coming to the house to hear more about both.

He found her sitting in the darkened screen porch, a glass of ice tea by her side and Seuss curled up, dozing contentedly on her lap. For a moment, as he knelt next to her, he thought she might be asleep, too, but a whispered greeting and a quick kiss in the dark told him otherwise. She didn't want to disturb the damned cat.

"How do you rate?" he asked quietly, with a nod at

Seuss. The cat almost never climbed into *his* lap.

"He knows who loves him," she replied lightly, gently stroking the soft fur.

A light rain had begun to fall, which—along with a soft breeze—was bringing a cool breath of air to what had been a warm, humid evening. The only sounds in the porch were the purrs of the cat, the soft patter of the raindrops on the leaves and shingles, and the occasional chirp of a cricket looking for shelter.

Alex went back into the house to make himself a tall and icy gin and tonic, offering Pat one as well. But she declined, and for several minutes after he returned, they said little, enjoying the stillness of the night and the closeness of each other.

"Well?" she finally said. "Tell me."

He quickly repeated the essence of his conversation with Barclay, filling in some of the details he had not had time to relate on the phone.

"Sounds like extortion to me," she said, once he had finished. "He's using this story to keep you around and to keep you quiet when they take you off the late news."

"I understand that," he replied. "It's pretty transparent. He knows now how much I want to do the story. But give him credit. He could have told me to take a flying leap."

Pat shifted in her chair to face him more directly, trying but failing to read his expression in the shadows. No question, the prospect of having him here for at least another year was appealing to her; perhaps by then she would be able to shake off the ghosts of the past and make the kind of commitment she knew he was looking for. But, she wondered, if she hadn't been able to decide by now, would another year really help?

Still, she was surprised that he was even considering

the offer. To swallow his pride and accept the early news assignment for the sake of a story didn't fit the man she knew, despite his personal feelings about it. But perhaps it was more than that. Maybe he was way ahead of her. She took a flyer. "You think this story could save your job, don't you?"

She saw the sharp turn of his head, but before he could respond, she pressed on. "You think that if you find those kids, dead or alive, it'll be a big enough story to keep you on the late news. You'll be a hero. Probably win a Pulitzer——"

"Pulitzers are for newspaper people," he said, cutting in.

"Okay, a Peabody then. No way Barclay or Hawke would dare make a move with you after that. Am I right?"

He smiled. "I can't say the thought hasn't crossed my mind. But that's not the main motivation. I really would like to find out what happened to those boys. It sticks in my craw like a goddamned chicken bone. But hell, if the story works out and also happens to improve my stock at the station, all the better."

"And if it doesn't work out?"

"Then I spend a year in exile, doing just the early news. It'd take some of the wind out of my sails, but I'd survive. I'd still get a paycheck. And we'd have more time together. Every night, if we wanted. Maybe even be able to see a movie or a play during the week."

And then, as though he had read her earlier thoughts, he said, "It would also give us another year to try to figure things out. You know, between us. If we couldn't decide on something by then, it would probably be just as well for me to get out of town."

Pat didn't know what to say, whether to admit she

had been thinking the same thing. Better not, she decided. "So you're going to accept the deal?"

"I think so. I'll decide for sure in the morning."

Pat flicked on a small light as she got up to refill her glass of tea, bringing him another gin and tonic as well. She was wearing a pair of white shorts that contrasted with the deep tan of her legs, and a blue striped T-shirt that clung to her body, revealing the soft curves Alex had come to know so well. The years had treated her figure kindly, but he knew she had worked hard to keep the forty-something bulges and sags at bay. To him, she was as attractive now as she had been in college so many years before. Maybe more so.

"What are you thinking?" she asked, catching him watching her.

"That you're still gorgeous," he said.

"Right," she laughed. "What other lies do you want to tell me?"

"It's the truth," he said.

Seuss climbed back onto her lap, ignoring Alex. "So what about the Hathaway woman?" she asked. "She thinks she talked to one of her sons?"

He described the phone call and the subsequent meeting between Barclay and Mrs. Hathaway. "He thinks she could be lying. That the call may simply be a ruse to get me involved."

"What do you think?" Pat asked.

He shrugged. "She looked and sounded pretty sincere to me." He paused for a moment, thinking. "I guess I believe she got the call, but it's hard to believe it was really one of her sons. I suspect it may have been another crank."

"Is she going to send the money? The two hundred dollars?"

He shrugged again. "I told her that it was up to her and her husband. But if the old man has anything to say about it, I don't think they will."

"Then why don't you?"

"What? Send the money?"

"Sure. See what happens."

She was right. He should have thought of it himself. Where was his brain? Two hundred dollars was petty cash to the station. Or to him, for that matter. "We should put you on the payroll," he said. "I'll call Mrs. Hathaway in the morning."

Pat had agreed to stay the night, snuggling against him now as he lay awake, her breathing deep and even against his ear. The rain continued to fall outside the open bedroom windows, slowly and gently, with a slight, cool breeze stirring the curtains. Alex felt a chill, and cautiously reached down to pull the sheet up and over their naked bodies without awakening the woman next to him.

Their lovemaking had left him spent, but—unlike Pat—unable to sleep, his mind awash with a jumble of thoughts that he couldn't seem to sort out. Or through. Many of them dealing with her. Was he taking the easy way out by agreeing to stay for another year? Allowing Pat to again postpone the decision she eventually would have to make?

In the years since they had rediscovered each other, he had known no other woman. At least in any intimate way. Nor, as far as he knew, had she seen other men. He had made no secret of his wishes over those years, proposing more times than he could now remember, proposals that were always met by her pleas for more time.

But time was running out, regardless of the decision he might make about the job. Six months or eighteen months. He saw little difference. She would have to decide.

Try as he might, and despite hours of talking about it, he still couldn't fully understand her reluctance. He knew that she still felt great guilt over her husband's suicide, but he also knew their marriage had been falling apart long before his death. And long before Alex had appeared on the scene.

But that was years ago.

Pat would only say that she was still haunted by his death. Still having nightmares about it. That he would likely still be alive if she had not pressed Alex to launch his investigation. "I might as well have pushed him out that window," she would tell him, despite the fact that she had been nowhere near at the time. "That's what the nightmares are about . . . watching him fall, hearing his screams. Seeing him there on the ground. The blood. People looking up at me."

Alex had urged her to get therapy, to somehow put it all behind her. To move on with life. But it was only the year before that she had finally agreed to seek help, and while she said the nightmares were less frequent now, they had not yet ended. He had begun to wonder if they ever would.

He'd already spent too many years alone; he didn't want to live out his life that way. Without a wife, without many friends. Growing old with a goddamned cat . . . who didn't much like him in the first place. In a few years his kids would be adults, and he would probably see even less of them than he did now. Pretty depressing, he thought. But facing fifty can do that to you.

He felt Pat stir in his arms, the soft touch of her lips

against his cheek. "You still awake?" she whispered, sleepily.

"Yeah."

"Can't sleep?"

"No."

He could hear her giggle. "Didn't I tire you out?"

He smiled in the darkness. "It's not that."

"What then?"

"Just thinking."

"About us?"

"Yes."

She rolled on top of him, gently pressing her body against his. Feeling him stir. "Well, stop thinking," she said. "Things will work out."

Maybe so, but he was not so sure.

9

When Alex first spotted Tony Malay, sitting at a table in the bagel shop, he knew immediately that something was wrong. The retired police chief was slumped over in his chair, looking sour, with no hint of a smile or even a sign of recognition as Alex approached and took a chair across from him. By then he was staring stonily out the window.

Malay had insisted on meeting outside of the station, for fear of being recognized by someone in the newsroom and arousing unwanted curiosity. "It's too early for that," he had told Alex. "I don't want it known yet that I'm consorting with you news types."

Morrie's Bagels was only a few blocks from the station, a tiny place just off one of the downtown skyways, but seldom visited by anyone from the station. Especially at midafternoon, in the middle of the day's news crunch.

"Hey, Chief," Alex said when Malay finally turned to face him. "You're looking grim. Is there a problem?"

"They're gone," Malay said, his eyes returning to the window.

"What's gone?" Alex asked, puzzled.

The chief turned back, a tremor in his voice. "The files. The goddamned files."

Alex fell back in his chair. "You're serious. You can't find them?"

"I've searched every foot of that storage room. At least every foot of where those records ought to be. There's nothing. It's as though the case never existed."

Alex held up his hands. "Hold on, now. Let me get this straight."

"What's to get straight?" Malay asked, frustration and anger in his voice. "I spent three hours in the god-damned storage room. Searching. Just like I said I would. I knew exactly where the files should be, but they weren't there."

"Maybe somebody moved them," Alex said.

"Where?" Malay demanded.

He frowned. "How would I know? Somewhere else in the storage room, I suppose. Shit, it's been fifteen years."

"Dead files like that don't get moved. Not without a reason. Besides, I looked every other place I thought they could be. There's nothing."

A waitress, looking as though she'd already had a long day, arrived to take their orders. Each asked for a cup of coffee, black. No bagels. She didn't bother to hide her irritation.

Alex waited until she was back with the coffee and gone again before pressing on. "Who's in charge of the files?" he asked. "There must be some kind of checkout system."

Malay took a sip of his coffee. "Of course there's a checkout system, and yes, I checked it. I could find no entry relating to those files, either in the computer system or in the old log books we used before the computer came on-line. Unless I missed something, whoever took the files did it on the sly and then wiped out any trace of them."

"And who's responsible for the system?" Alex asked.

"Civilian clerks, not cops. There have been a number of them over the years."

Alex shook his head, confused. "Does this happen often? That you can't find files on old cases."

Not that often, Malay told him, at least not in his experience. "The county attorney's office used to give us shit if we misplaced or lost any files. You know, on some old case that suddenly got hot again. We had to make sure the system was tight."

"So if these files weren't misplaced," Alex said, "then . . . what? They were stolen? If so, by whom? And why?"

Malay glared at him. "If I knew that, I wouldn't be sitting here talking to you."

"So what do we do now?"

"I'll do some more checking. Talk to a few old hands around the department. And a couple of retired dogs like myself. Shake the tree. Maybe somebody will remember something. It's all I can think of to do."

As they left the place, Alex tried to cheer Malay up. "It's not the end of the world, Chief. Hopefully, you can locate the files . . . but if not, we'll figure something else out."

It was clear, however, that Malay felt a personal responsibility for the missing records, that their disappearance was somehow a black mark on him and the department he had led for so many years. "I'll bust my ass trying to find them," he promised, "or who might have taken them."

Determined words, Alex thought as they parted ways, but said with more bravado than he knew Malay actually felt.

When he got back to the newsroom, Alex found a

copy of a memo lying atop his desk, a memo he knew would be coming. It was from Barclay, addressed to the station staff:

I'm pleased to announce that Alex Collier has agreed to an extension of his contract with Channel Seven, which had been due to expire at the end of the year. In addition, Alex will be devoting much of his time in the next few weeks and months to a special investigative assignment, the subject of which must remain confidential for now. I know you will join me in congratulating Alex and wishing him the best of luck in his continuing association with this television station.

He read the memo twice. There it was . . . in black and white. No retreating now. He had officially signed the contract extension that morning, despite some lingering doubts. But what the hell? he'd told himself, it's only another year, and Barclay had assured him that the move from the late to the early news, when it happened, would be delicately handled. Besides, there was still the outside chance that they'd change their minds—if the Hathaway story came through. But he wasn't betting on it.

Maggie was the first to approach him, memo in hand, confusion written across her face. "What the hell is going on?" she whispered. "You actually signed an extension?"

"Just what the memo says," he replied with a slight smile.

She pulled her chair close to his desk. "Alex! C'mon. What's the deal?"

He knew he should tell her everything. She, more than anyone in the newsroom, deserved to know. But he quickly decided against it. He was not yet comfortable enough with what he had done to confide in anyone. Even Maggie. He needed more time to soothe his ego . . . to convince himself that he'd done the right thing. "I can't say anything, Maggie. Not beyond what the memo says."

She now appeared confused *and* hurt. "You're not going to tell me? *Me, Maggie?* What about the late news?"

"I'm sorry. I promised Barclay," he lied.

She pushed her chair back to her own desk, looking at him in a way she never had before. "After I tried to go to the mat for you? You're shutting me out? Thanks a ton."

Before he could respond, two reporters and a photographer came up to his desk to congratulate him. "Great news," one of the reporters, Tom Hardy, said. "You're the best in town. Glad that you're staying."

"Is this what the rumors were all about?" asked the photographer, Nick Avery.

Alex feigned ignorance. "What rumors are those?"

"You haven't heard them?"

He shrugged. "I guess not."

"That's just as well," Avery said. "Some of them were out in left field."

By the time Alex went to the studio for the early news, virtually everyone in the newsroom had stopped by to greet him and wish him well. Except Maggie. She wasn't talking to him.

The next morning, Alex was up far earlier than usual and in his car, driving across town to northeast Minneapolis, a city map spread out on the passenger seat. In all of his years in the Twin Cities, he had never been to this particular part of town before, and had to consult the map frequently. Even then, he missed several turns before finally finding Fairlawn Park.

Max Douglas was already there, in suit and tie, leaning against the fender of his car, chewing on a sugared doughnut and sipping from a cup of coffee when Alex pulled up behind him. "Sorry I'm late," he said, "I got lost two or three times."

"Not a problem," Max replied, taking the final bite of the doughnut. "I just got here myself."

Alex had called Douglas the night before, asking if they might meet at the park where the Hathaway boys had disappeared. He'd told him that Barclay had okayed his pursuit of the story, and that he wanted to get a first-hand feel of the area, to see for himself the path the brothers may have taken before they vanished. Max had readily agreed to serve as guide, but said it would have to be early so he could get to his job more or less on time.

"I can't tell you how glad I am that you're doing this," Max had told him.

"Don't get too excited about it," Alex had replied. "It's still a long shot."

It was just after seven, a gorgeous, sunny morning, cool and fresh from the recent rains, with no sign that the suffocating heat and humidity of the preceding week would return. It would be the kind of day that Minnesotans would dream of during the interminable months of winter.

"Where do you want to start?" Douglas asked.

"How about their house," Alex suggested.

"It's just down this block," Max said, pointing to the right. "The third house from the end . . . the white one with the blue shutters."

They began to walk in that direction, Alex studying

the house that Max had singled out. It was no different from any of the other homes on the block; small, story-and-a-half, well kept with small shrubs in front and a white picket fence in the back. Because of the early hour, there were no kids outside, no activity at all along the street.

The neighborhood was not unlike the one where Alex himself had grown up in Illinois, or those in most other towns in America, for that matter. Quiet and peaceful, from all outward appearances, not quite middle class but by no means poor. Starter homes, he guessed, populated mostly by young families hoping to build equity and move on to more affluent neighborhoods. Or by older, blue-collar families who never had been able to afford more.

"Probably hasn't changed that much in fifteen years," he said.

"Probably not," Max agreed. "Certainly not since I did the story here five years ago."

Alex wondered idly if the family who now lived in the Hathaway house knew of the tragedy that had befallen the previous owners. He suspected they must; a story like that would not die quickly, no matter what turnover there was in the neighborhood.

"What about the neighbors?" he asked.

"What do you mean?"

"Did the Hathaways get along with all of them?"

Max eyed him curiously, then shrugged. "Damned if I know," he said. "Why do you ask?"

"Just wondering."

Douglas clearly was not satisfied.

"According to the little research I've done," Alex said, "of the tens of thousands of kids abducted every year, almost all of them are taken by someone in the family or close to them. You know, friends, relatives, neighbors."

"The cops must have checked them all out," Douglas offered.

"I wonder."

By then they were heading back down the street toward the park. "From what we know," Max said, "on that day, the boys did what they did practically every other day of the year. Simply took off across the street and headed for the park. No one besides their mother can actually remember seeing them go, but there's no doubt that's what they did."

There was a bike and walking path that led from the street into the park, a crushed-gravel trail that wandered through the trees and bushes, the grass and foliage now a lush green from the rains, with picnic tables scattered here and there on either side of the path. Farther along, a large playing field had been carved out of the woods to the right, making room for two softball diamonds, one soccer field, and a basketball court.

"I'm not sure the playing fields were here fifteen years ago," Max said as they walked along. "Except for the paths and picnic tables, I think this was all pretty much undeveloped back then."

Alex judged they had walked about two blocks into the park when he saw the playground straight ahead, just behind the last softball diamond. From what he could tell, as they drew nearer, it looked about the same as he'd seen in Max's report: two decrepit swing sets, each with six swings, the cracked leather seats supported by heavy, rusted iron chains; a large sandbox largely grown over with weeds; a slide that sagged; and a climbing apparatus that rose some ten feet into the air. None of it, he thought, appeared to have been used recently.

Max seemed to read his mind. "It was probably in better shape fifteen years ago. The park board seems to spend more time and money on the parks in your neighborhood, around the lakes."

Alex squeezed into one of the swing seats, pushing himself slowly back and forth, grasping the iron chains, wondering if the Hathaway kids had once sat there. Maybe even on that July afternoon. Wondering, too, if Hazel and John Hathaway ever returned here, to try to reach out for their sons. He suspected they did. At least Hazel.

Max watched him. "They did find footprints. Around the swings and in the sandbox. It had rained the night before the kids disappeared. But because they never found any of their shoes, they couldn't be sure the footprints belonged to the Hathaway boys."

"All of them kids' footprints?"

"Yeah, I think so."

Alex got up and walked around the area, kneeling first by the sandbox, then climbing up a few rails of the monkey bars, looking out across the park. Hoping for what? Some vision, some message to find him through the years? Silly, he knew, yet he did feel closer to the boys now than he had before.

"The river's over there," Douglas said, pointing, interrupting his musings. Not that Alex could actually see the river from there, just an eight-foot-high chain-link fence, about fifty yards away. "The fence went up right after the boys disappeared," Max continued as they walked toward it. "Should have happened long before, I guess, but nobody thought about the danger until . . ." He didn't finish.

The fence and the poles supporting it were rusty, and sections of it were bent over, leaning toward the river—

as though they had been pushed down and climbed over many times during the years. "Doesn't look like it's kept the kids away," Alex said as he walked beside it.

By leaning over the fence, he could see the river below, perhaps two hundred feet or so down a sharp incline. The embankment was covered by long grass and bushes, with a few scraggly trees clinging to the slope. Even now, though, he could see the outline of a path down through the grass, apparently shaped by the rear ends of untold numbers of kids sliding down to the water.

The lessons of the past, he thought, were easily forgotten. Or ignored.

The river at this point was about a hundred yards wide, slow-moving and a muddy brown. Only by fastening his eyes on a floating log or other flotsam could Alex actually see the current move. But from what Tony Malay had said, it was much swifter fifteen years ago . . . after a heavy winter snow and wet spring.

"How deep do you think it is here?" he asked.

Max shook his head. "I don't know. Deep enough, I guess, but probably not as deep as it was back then. The silt builds up over the years."

They were about to walk away when Alex spotted them, all but hidden in the deep grass just on the other side of the fence: three tiny white crosses, no more than six inches high. "Look at this," he said, kneeling down.

Max knelt beside him. "I'll be damned," he muttered.

The crosses were unmarked, but stood straight and appeared freshly painted. "You've never seen them before?" Alex asked.

"No. If they were here five years ago, I didn't spot them. And nobody ever mentioned them to me. It would have made a nice picture to end my piece with."

"They must be for the boys," Alex said, reaching through the fence to touch them lightly, "and the family must have put them here."

"You'd think so," Max replied, "but they never told me about them."

So much for no memorials, Alex thought.

As they walked back to the car, Alex filled Max in on the recent developments, including the missing files . . . and the phone call Hazel Hathaway had received. "We sent the kid the two hundred bucks, like he asked, but by certified mail. So we ought to know if he ever picks it up."

"Did Malay check with Peter Osborne's widow about the files?" Max asked.

Alex stopped in his tracks. "I have no idea. Who's Peter Osborne?"

"The guy who headed the investigation fifteen years ago. A detective in the missing persons unit. Malay must have mentioned him."

Alex shook his head.

"I was told he knew more about the case than anyone. But he was dead by the time I did my story."

They resumed walking. "Dead of what? Old age?"

"Hit-and-run accident. On East Hennepin. Off duty, walking to his car from a bar late one night. Never did find the driver, if I remember correctly."

Alex let that sink in for a moment. "That's a little strange, isn't it?"

"Maybe so, but he was drunk at the time."

"Why do you think his widow might have the files?"

"A shot in the dark. I was told he was the kind of cop who took his work home. And that he'd maintained a special interest in this case."

Back at Douglas's car, as Max prepared to leave, Alex thought of one more question. "At lunch, you told me about a phone call from a woman who seemed to know a lot about the case . . . what the kids were wearing and so forth."

"Yeah. But I never got her name."

"I know," he said, "but did you get a sense of whether the call was from someone local . . . or long distance?"

Max thought for a moment. "Not really. If I had to guess, I'd say it was local, but shit, it was a long time ago. Why do you ask?"

"I don't know. Just an idea I'm knocking around."

Douglas waited expectantly, but when Alex offered nothing more, he put the car in gear. "If there's anything more I can do," Douglas said, "don't hesitate to ask."

Alex watched him drive away, but kept seeing those three small crosses in the grass.

10

When he arrived at the station that afternoon, Alex went directly to Barclay's office. Barclay was on the phone, laughing, but waved him in and pointed to a chair. Alex waited patiently, watching the pedestrian traffic on the street outside the window until Barclay finally cradled the phone, still laughing.

"That was an old friend of mine," he said. "A news director in Toledo."

"Must be a pretty funny guy," Alex ventured.

Barclay was still giggling. "The other night, this guy says, a house burns down in a suburb of Toledo. The family dog barks and wakes the family . . . saving the parents and three little kids. The dog becomes an instant hero. Two of the stations in town, his and the CBS station, get the story from start to finish, you know, the fire, the kids hugging the dog and all the rest. A real heart-tugger. But the ABC station misses it all . . . doesn't know anything about it until they see it on the competition's news."

Alex waited for the punch line.

"In an effort to catch up, the ABC guys dash out to the house, hoping to get pictures of the family and the hero dog. But in their rush to get there, to get the story, they made one little mistake. They ran over the god-damned dog."

Barclay doubled over, unable to contain himself. "Didn't kill it or even hurt it bad," he said. "But can't you see their late news promo? 'Hero dog hit by news cruiser. Exclusive story at ten.'"

Alex smiled, more at Barclay's reaction than at the story itself. But he had to admit, it would have been a funny scene.

Several more minutes passed before Barclay finally settled down. "So what's up?" he asked, wiping a final tear from his eye.

"I want to bring you up to date," Alex said, first reporting on Malay's missing files, then on that morning's visit to the park and his conversation with Max Douglas. Including the call Max received from the mystery woman five years before. "The problem with the Hathaway story, as we both know, is how old it is. Fifteen years wipes out virtually any tracks."

Barclay nodded, serious and alert now. "I warned you about that," he said.

"I know. So we have to figure out a way to jog people's memories . . . to get those who might know something to come forward. People who haven't been willing to do so up to now. Somebody like the lady who called Max."

"So?" Barclay let the word hang.

Alex had been thinking about this since he'd left Douglas at the park. He knew the chances of Barclay's support were slim, but he decided to try anyway. He could envision no quicker way to get a lead on an old story, and what the hell? It was better to try and be rejected than not to try at all. "Remember, George, when we made our deal, you said you'd give me the support I needed?"

"Within limits," Barclay replied cautiously. "What do you have in mind?"

Alex took a deep breath. "I think we should reopen the case on the air. Now, in the next week or so. Make a big splash. Offer a ten thousand dollar reward to anyone who can provide us with crucial information on what may have happened to the boys."

He'd expected an angry and immediate rejection from Barclay, but all he got was a steady stare. So he forged ahead. "Not only might that get us a lead we need, but think of the publicity for the station. The interest it would generate. We'd be the talk of the town. And shit, the most it could cost us would be ten grand, and not even that if we get no leads."

What seemed like minutes passed before Barclay finally spoke. "I don't agree," he said.

Alex pounced on him. "With what?"

"That ten thousand dollars would be enough. We should make it twenty-five."

"*What?*"

Barclay was smiling now. "You heard me. Twenty-five grand. I think it's a great idea. I'm not sure it will get you any leads, but you're right, it would be a terrific promotion for the station. And it'll give us something to talk about on the news besides the fucking weather."

Alex was astonished. At most he had expected a lukewarm response, a "let me think it over" reply. But this? An enthusiastic endorsement? Never in his wildest dreams.

"Of course," Barclay went on, "I'll have to run it past Hawke. It's his money. But knowing him, he'll jump on it. Anything to give the ratings a bump. He'll wish he'd thought of it."

They spent the next half hour discussing details:

Alex would prepare the report, using some of the same file footage Max had used, plus new interviews with the boys' parents, and perhaps with Malay and others familiar with the case.

"Don't expect miracles," Barclay warned. "Chances of this producing anything are slim. But who knows? Something could come of it. In the meantime, I'd keep searching for those files and anything else you can dig up."

Alex agreed, then said, "One other thing. Could I ask Maggie to give me a hand with this? She's already offered to help, and I'd like to get back in her good graces, if I can."

Barclay again took his time responding, but finally said, "It's okay with me, I guess. But I don't want it taking either one of you away from the anchor desk."

Alex assured him that it wouldn't, then left the office feeling better than he had in days.

It took some time, but he finally found Maggie in a videotape editing suite, just off the newsroom. She was sitting beside one of the editors as he put the finishing touches on a long puff piece she had produced on the opening of a children's museum in St. Paul.

The dog days of summer were still with them.

Alex stepped just inside the door. "Sorry to interrupt, but are you about done?"

Maggie turned in her chair, visibly surprised to find him there. "Another five minutes or so," she said. "Why?"

"We should talk."

The editor paused in his task, eyeing them curiously. "Want me to leave?"

"No, no," Alex said. "Keep going, please." Then to Maggie. "Meet you in the Green Room when you're finished?"

"I guess so," she said, not bothering to disguise her reluctance.

Five minutes later she joined him, closing the door behind her. Still looking less than eager to be there. "What's going on, Alex?"

"Sit down, please," he said. "I owe you an apology. And I'd like to get back on speaking terms."

She took a chair across from him, but said nothing, eyeing him intently, waiting for him to continue.

"You were right," he said. "You, of all people, should know what's going on." He paused. "I wasn't exactly proud of what I had finally decided to do, and guess I was a little ashamed to tell you."

"What do you mean?"

He quickly explained his deal with Barclay, leaving out nothing, watching as she slowly shook her head, clearly not quite believing what she was hearing. "I don't get it," she said when he was done. "Do you really care that much about this story?"

"It's more complicated than that, some of it personal, but yeah, I do care about the story, more and more every day, it seems." He went on to explain what he had already mentioned to Barclay: the chance to actually make a difference in someone's life. "Besides, I don't relish the idea of looking for another job right now. Maybe I'm afraid of what I'll find out there . . . that nobody really wants a middle-aged anchorman who's past his prime. At least in a market of any size. I don't want to end up in Keokuk doing the late news."

Maggie scoffed at that. "Somebody would scoop you up in a minute," she said. "And in a big market, too."

"A few years ago, maybe, but now, I'm not so sure. Everybody's looking for young studs these days. Guys without graying hair and wrinkles around the eyes."

"Did you even look?" she asked.

"Not really. Word would have gotten back and that would have created even more rumors around here. I didn't need that."

He didn't mention what Pat had guessed to be his other motive—that a successful pursuit of the Hathaway story could possibly force Barclay and Hawke to change their minds. Or to at least postpone their decision. Giving him more time to decide what to do with the rest of his life. He knew Maggie would probably figure that out for herself soon enough anyway.

"Nobody else knows anything about this, Maggie. Not yet. So please keep it to yourself for now. God knows it won't be long before everyone knows—once Barclay starts getting those audition tapes for the late news."

"I still can't believe it," she said morosely. "In six months I may be sitting next to some blow-dried jackass just out of journalism school who probably can't pronounce his own name."

"C'mon, Maggie, Barclay wouldn't do that—"

"But Hawke would," she shot back. "If the guy's young and attractive enough. If he thinks it will jump-start the ratings. You watch and see."

She got out of her chair to leave, but Alex called her back. "There's one more thing. Are you still willing to help me on this Hathaway story?"

She paused. "I guess so, if you think I can."

He quickly told her what Barclay had agreed to. "The reward could help, but we still have a lot of footwork to do. Grunt work. It may take some time."

Maggie hadn't forgotten the thrill of helping to break the child porn ring story the year before. But also the enormous amount of time and effort it took. "That's okay with me. With Brett at home to help out with Danny now, I should have the time."

"Good," he said. "I'll fill you in the first chance I get, but right now I've got to make a phone call."

Alex tried three or four places, including the Wisconsin cabin, before finally locating Tony Malay—still staying at a downtown motel. "I haven't given up trying to find those files," Malay said.

"Any luck?" Alex asked.

"Not so far, but I still have several folks to talk to."

"What about Peter Osborne?"

The line went silent for a moment. "I can't talk to him. He's dead."

"I know that now," Alex said. "Why didn't you mention him before?"

There was another long pause. "Never thought about it, I guess. Being that he's dead and gone."

Alex quickly repeated what Max Douglas had told him about Osborne and the possibility that his widow might have the files.

"That's a little far-fetched, I'd say," Malay replied. "Pete did lead the investigation at the time, and did maintain an interest in the case, but shit, he's been gone for seven or eight years now. I don't even know if his wife's still alive. And if she is, if she's still around."

"Can you find out?" Alex asked.

"Sure. But like I say, it seems a little screwy."

Alex then told him of the plans to reopen the case on the air, and to offer the large reward.

Malay was aghast. "*Twenty-five thousand dollars?* Do you know what you're doing? You're going to be up to your ass in alligators. Every nut, every fruitcake around is going to be on the phone or in your office. Claiming they know something. You'll go crazy by the end of the first day. Trust me, I've seen this kind of thing before."

"You're probably right," Alex said. "But I don't know how else to find people who might know what happened fifteen years ago. Especially with those files missing. We'll just have to separate the wheat from the chaff."

"You'll have chaff coming out of your ears," Malay exclaimed. "You'll be buried in the stuff."

"One other thing," Alex said. "I'd like to interview you for the story."

"You mean on camera?"

"Of course."

"What would you be asking me?" Malay wanted to know.

Alex was purposely vague. "Just your thoughts on the case. You know, from a historical point of view. What you thought at the time . . . what you think now."

It took Malay only a moment to decide. "Okay," he said, "but if you try to ambush me, make me or the department look stupid, I'll shit all over you and that camera of yours. Understand?"

"I understand," Alex said.

11

Nicholas Hawke was waiting outside the studio when Alex and Maggie emerged after the early news. Both did a double-take, for seldom was Hawke in this part of the building, and almost never did he take the time or trouble to speak to any of his employees, even the stars of the show. Not that anyone was complaining, mind you.

"You looking for us?" Alex asked, pausing in the hallway.

"For you, Alex, yes. I'll just need a minute."

He dismissed Maggie with a nod and an insipid smile and she moved on, but not without a sympathetic glance back at Alex.

Alex thought he could count on two hands the number of times he had actually spoken to Hawke, most of those occasions during his first couple of years at the station—in the midst of his investigation of the judge, who happened to be Hawke's good friend. Hawke had tried, unsuccessfully, to kill the story, and Alex was convinced he still bore him a grudge and had been waiting for the chance to put him in his place. The demotion to the early news might be it.

But Hawke was still the boss, the guy who signed the paychecks and would ultimately determine his future at the station, so Alex decided to try to be courteous. "What can I do for you?" he asked with mock civility.

If Hawke noticed the tone, he didn't show it. "I wanted to congratulate you on your contract extension," he replied. "But that's not all."

Short in stature, impeccably groomed and dressed, Hawke carried himself on the balls of his feet with his nose in the air, apparently hoping for added height, but instead giving him the look of a haughty dandy. Not a gray hair was out of place, not a speck of lint sullied his double-breasted blue suit. His shirt was perfectly starched, his tie properly dimpled, and he smelled of some exotic aftershave that made Alex want to gag.

He took Alex to one side of the hall and wrapped an arm around him, looking up. "George also told me about your story. About the reward."

Alex tried to move away. "Yes, he said he would."

"I want you to know that I think it's a terrific idea. Great promotion."

"It could cost you twenty-five grand," Alex offered.

"That's peanuts. You can't buy the kind of publicity this will get us."

Alex couldn't resist. "We're not really doing it for the publicity, you know. I mean, if we get some, fine, but what we really want is information about the missing kids."

"Oh, I know that. But what's the harm if we get some good press in the process? Can't hurt the ratings, you know. And that's what pays the anchor bills."

"Sure," Alex said, wanting to get away.

Hawke finally released him. "I'm going to light a fire under the promotion department. Get 'em moving on this. You know, if we push hard enough, we'll have this town seeing those little boys in their sleep. It'll be great."

With that, and a slap on the back, he was off—tiptoeing down the hall.

"What did the Little Napoleon want?" Maggie asked when Alex got back to the newsroom. When he told her, she laughed. "What a dork! He could care less about those kids."

"Doesn't matter to me," Alex replied. "As long as he's willing to put up the money. I just wish he'd keep his hands off me."

Now that Maggie had agreed to help, Alex asked her to search the *Star Tribune* and *Pioneer Press* archives for any additional stories on the Hathaway boys in the years after they disappeared. He was sure there must have been periodic updates, especially in the first few years. No story like that would be easily or quickly forgotten.

"Anything else?" she asked.

He thought for a moment. "Keep your eyes open for any stories about . . . I don't know, individuals or groups that strike you as weird. Maybe in the year or so before and after the boys vanished."

"What are you talking about?"

He sat on the edge of his desk, looking into space, thinking aloud. "Look, it's pretty clear that if those kids *didn't* drown . . . somebody had to take them. Or maybe kill them. They didn't run away. They were too young, and they never would have stayed away this long by themselves. Not all three.

"And if they were taken . . . or killed . . . who would have done such a thing? Either somebody who had no kids of their own and wanted some . . . or maybe a crazed killer . . . or some nutty group that needed unwilling young recruits."

Maggie was watching him closely. "You mean a cult of some kind?"

"Maybe. There were enough of them around in the early eighties, if you remember."

She gave him a sly smile. "Sorry. I was a teenager then."

He squelched a moan. "Spare me, please. But back then, it was pretty common for parents to hire deprogrammers to find their runaway kids, get 'em out of the cults, and get their heads back on straight. It happened all the time."

Maggie had been on the streets of L.A. in those days, hanging out with kids no self-respecting cult would want. Druggies, whores, thieves, and worse. But she was certainly aware of Jim Jones and the other notorious cult leaders of the day. And who could forget the Heaven's Gate suicides of just a couple of years ago?

"Doesn't that seem like a stretch?" she asked. "I mean, that some cult would swoop down and snatch these boys?"

"I don't know," he said, recalling for her the recent discovery of a Minnesota prison inmate, a pedophile, who was secretly developing a computerized database with the names, addresses, and hometowns of hundreds of boys in scores of cities and towns . . . gathered from local newspapers and magazines. No one was quite sure what he had planned to do with them, but the list was quickly destroyed.

"And did you happen to see that piece on the wires the other day . . . out of Ohio?"

She appeared puzzled. "I'm not sure. What are you talking about?"

"Seems like somebody has been cutting pictures of boys out of hundreds of books at several college libraries in Ohio. Not X-rated-type pictures. Just ordinary shots of young males, hundreds of them, sliced out of all kinds of books. Nobody can quite figure it out."

"What's your point?" she asked.

"That weird things happen, that's all. That there are a lot of strange people out there. There have even been reports of pedophile rings, perverts who steal kids and sell them around the world for sex. In short, anything could have happened to those boys."

Maggie appeared doubtful, but said she'd start the search as soon as possible.

Hazel Hathaway answered Alex's call on the first ring. And after a minute of small talk, he got to the point. "Mrs. Hathaway, we've decided to pursue the investigation."

"That's wonderful. I'm very pleased."

"My boss has approved the project, but I need to sit down with you and your husband to discuss our plans . . . and how you can help us."

"Anytime you'd like. I'll speak to John."

"Maybe this weekend," he said. "Like Saturday morning, if you're free."

"John's not home yet, but I'm sure that will be all right with him."

Judging from his phone conversation with her husband, Alex wasn't so sure.

"How about ten o'clock?" she said.

"Perfect," he replied. "If there's a problem, please call me."

"Of course. I can't tell you how thankful I am. It's the best news I've had in years."

He wanted to warn her not to get her hopes too high, but she had heard that kind of advice far too often. Instead, he simply asked for directions to their home in Roseville. "Saturday morning at ten," he said. "I'll see you then."

"God bless you," were the last words he heard.

He had no sooner hung up the phone than it rang. "Malay here," said the voice on the other end.

"Hey, Chief."

Malay didn't waste words. "I found Mrs. Osborne. She's remarried and lives in Edina. Name's Cornelius now. Her new husband's a lawyer, a widower who used to be a friend of Pete, her late husband."

The chief was telling Alex more than he wanted to know. "You've talked to her?"

"That's why I'm calling. Can you get away for an hour or so?"

Alex glanced at his watch. "Why?"

"She's invited us out to her house. I was cagey. Told her we'd like to talk to her in person, but didn't say why."

He checked his watch again. "I have to be back by nine . . . to get ready for the late news."

"Shouldn't be a problem. I'm at the motel, okay? I'll be in the lobby."

Could be a waste of time, Alex thought, but what the hell?

The Cornelius home was a two-story colonial, off-white with green awnings, set well back on a spacious lot with enough trees—maples, oaks, birch, and honey locusts— to all but hide the house itself. Two stone gateposts straddled the entrance to the driveway, but there was no gate between them. Just a small sign announcing that the property was protected by Gemini Security.

Edina was one of the old money suburbs of the Twin Cities, not far from his own house, and as Alex drove through it, he couldn't help but notice what a far cry this was from the Fairlawn Park neighborhood he had visited earlier. You could take three of those houses, he thought, and fit them into one of these lots, with room to spare.

"Mr. Cornelius must be doing all right," Alex said as he turned into the driveway. "To afford a place like this."

"He works for one of the bigger law firms in town," Malay replied, looking at the large and well-groomed lawn and finely trimmed shrubs. "And Lorna's sure as hell living a lot better now than she ever did on Pete's cop salary."

"Lorna? That's her first name?"

"Yup. A gorgeous gal in her day. But she must be in her sixties now."

Alex pulled his Blazer up behind a Lexus and a Lincoln Navigator parked outside a four-stall garage. "Remind me to ask you more about Osborne's death," he said as they got out. "A hit-and-run, right?"

"Right. He was drunk on his ass. The driver, too, probably."

Lorna Cornelius was waiting by the front door as they walked up. She might be in her sixties, Alex thought, but she was still a beautiful woman. Slender with silvery gray hair, high cheekbones, and radiant skin that showed few signs of aging. She wore a simple belted shirtdress, a pink print that accentuated her narrow waist.

"Tony!" she said, giving him a quick hug. "How nice to see you. It's been far too long."

"I know. I'm sorry. I wasn't even sure you were still around until I started checking."

"Not to worry. I know how busy things can get." Then she turned to Alex, extending her hand, holding his a moment too long. The hand was as soft as he imagined it would be. "And you're Alex Collier," she said. "I recognize you from the news, but," she laughed, eyeing him up and down, "you're even better-looking in person. Come in, please."

They stepped into a large entryway, most of the floor covered by a giant Oriental rug, and in the center, under a glimmering brass and crystal chandelier, a round mahogany pedestal table. "Excuse the look of the house," she said. "The cleaning lady is out sick and I just didn't have the energy to do much myself."

It looked fine to Alex. A spacious living room was to the right of the entry, dominated by a large marble fireplace at one end and a baby grand piano tucked into a nook behind a big bay window overlooking the front yard. To the left, where they were heading now, was a combination den and library with dark woodwork, a smaller, brick fireplace, two desks, a couch, and three side chairs, and two walls filled floor-to-ceiling with hundreds of books. Unlike Malay's cabin, there were no paperbacks here. Probably all first editions, Alex thought.

"I thought we'd be more comfortable here," Lorna said, offering them places on the couch. "Richard and I spend most of our time here. It's the only place I allow him to smoke his pipe."

Alex had caught the faint aroma. "Is your husband home?" he asked.

"No, he's in New York on business." And then, "He's gone a lot, actually."

Alex thought he detected a slight smile in his direction, but he couldn't be sure. Still standing, she asked, "Would you like some coffee? Or a drink? I have almost everything."

Malay shot a quick glance at Alex, who shook his

head. "No thanks," he said. "Alex has to get back to the station shortly."

She took a seat in one of the chairs opposite them. "Then what can I do for you? You were quite mysterious on the phone, Tony."

Alex explained their mission as briefly as he could, describing how he had first become interested in the Hathaway case and what had happened since. Lorna listened intently, nodding now and then as he went on.

"I remember it very well," she said. "It was really quite tragic."

"That's why we're here," he said. "I was told that your late husband continued to have an interest in the case long after it was officially closed."

"That's true," she replied. "He was almost . . . obsessed with it. We never had any children ourselves, you know, despite years of trying, and Pete seemed to almost adopt those missing boys. In absentia, if you know what I mean."

Malay leaned forward. "Pete never told me that," he said, clearly puzzled. "I mean, I knew he was interested, but never to the point of—"

"Pete kept it to himself," she said, cutting in. "But as the years went by he never really forgave himself for not finding the bodies. He was frustrated. He thought, you know, that he had somehow failed the family and the department. It was about that time that he started drinking more heavily."

"Are you saying he didn't believe the boys drowned?" Alex asked.

She leaned back, thinking. "Not in so many words, but I know he had his doubts. It was like his private passion, trying to figure out what really happened."

Alex could see by the clock on the fireplace mantel

that time was getting short. "The chief has searched high and low for the files on the case and hasn't been able to locate them. It was suggested that your husband may have taken them home . . . that after his death they never got returned. Is that possible?"

She settled back into the chair. "I suppose so. He brought a lot of things home from the office. Boxes of things. After he was killed, I didn't know what to do with most of them. And frankly, I kind of forgot about it, with everything else that had to be done . . . trying to settle our financial affairs and all. And then there was the burglary."

"The burglary?" Alex and Malay spoke, almost in unison.

"Yes. The day of Pete's funeral, somebody broke into the house, took some of my jewelry and a few hundred dollars out of the desk. I shouldn't have been surprised. That's pretty common, you know. Thieves study the obituaries and hit homes where the man of the house has died. Because Pete was a cop, I thought I'd be pretty safe, but it didn't turn out that way."

"Did they take any of the stuff he'd brought home?" Malay asked excitedly.

"I have no idea," she replied. "I didn't know what was there. But it did remind me to get rid of it all. So I called John Evans at the precinct, and he had somebody come and haul the boxes away. That's the last I saw of them."

Alex and Malay looked at each other. A coincidence? Osborne's death and the burglary?

"I'll get hold of Evans," Malay said as they stood, ready to leave, "and see if he made an inventory of what they took. That could help."

"I wish I could do more," Lorna said. "Pete was a

good cop. And a good husband, until the drinking got the best of him. I still miss him, but Richard has been great to me." And with another glance at Alex, "I just wish he didn't travel so much."

There was no mistaking the look this time.

"You deserve the best," Malay said. "I know it was hell for you toward the end."

She gave him another hug at the doorway. "Thanks, Tony." And to Alex, "If you need anything more, don't hesitate to call. And if you're out this way again, please stop by. We don't see many celebrities and I know Richard would love to meet you, if he's around."

Alex said he'd try, but knew already that it would never happen.

"So what do you think?" he asked once they were back in the Blazer and heading toward downtown.

"I think she was coming on to you," Malay said.

He laughed. "That's not what I meant, but you noticed it, too?"

"Hard to miss. Her hubby better stick a little closer to home."

The traffic was light on the Crosstown Highway and Interstate 35W, leading to the center of Minneapolis. Alex took it slow, trying to think as he drove. Could there really be a connection between the burglary and the missing files? The burglary and Osborne's death? Unlikely, but still strange. Perhaps Osborne never had the files in the first place.

Malay had been silent, too, probably thinking many of the same thoughts. Finally Alex broke the quiet. "You were going to tell me more about the hit-and-run."

"Not much more to tell," Malay replied. "Pete had spent most of the night in a cop bar, a place called Shorty's on East Hennepin. Which wasn't unusual for him in those days. Closed the place up that night. He was hit as he crossed the street to his car. Got thrown some fifty feet. He was dead when he hit the ground."

"And no one saw it?"

"Nobody we could find. Most of the other cops had already left the joint by then. From the debris on the street, we know the hit-run car was an '82 or '83 Chevy van, forest green in color, if I remember right. Because Pete was a cop, we turned the Cities inside out and upside down, but never did find the car or the driver."

"So it was chalked up as an accident?"

"If you mean, did we think it was intentional . . . that somebody set out to murder the guy . . . then, no. But there were no skid marks, no indication that the driver had tried to stop or avoid him. He may have been as drunk as Pete was. Who can know for sure?"

Alex chewed on that for a while. "You said he went to this same bar often?"

"Yeah, for the last year or so of his life. We tried to get him dried out, but he refused treatment."

"So somebody could have scoped it out . . . knew where he'd be. They could have been waiting for him."

"Sure. Anything's possible. But we had no evidence of that."

By the time they reached Malay's motel, Alex had thought of still another question. "When the boys disappeared, did you guys check out all of the neighbors?"

"What do you mean? As suspects or something?"

"I guess so, yeah."

"Probably not, but I don't really recall. That would be in the files, if we ever find them. But you've got to remember, there was no reason to believe it was a kidnapping at the time. Still isn't, as far as I'm concerned."

"Then why are you sitting here?" Alex asked.

Malay shrugged as he opened the car door. "To erase any doubt, I guess."

"That's all?"

Malay smiled. "And to keep your ass out of trouble, okay?"

12

When Alex arrived at the Hathaway house on Saturday morning, Maggie was with him, followed by two station photographers in a van loaded down with camera equipment. He asked the photographers to wait outside while he and Maggie went inside to prepare the Hathaways for the interviews he hoped would follow.

Maggie had asked to come along at the last minute, reasoning that she should meet the family whose sons were at the center of the story that was now partly hers. Alex had objected at first, fearing the two of them would overwhelm the couple, but finally agreed that Mrs. Hathaway might feel more comfortable with another woman present. He didn't know what *Mr.* Hathaway would be feeling.

The house sat on a tree-lined cul-de-sac, one of several attractive but very similar homes that must have been built by the same contractor a decade or more before. Although the siding of each home was of a different color, with a few distinctive design features, all of them were two-story structures with two-car garages, concrete driveways, curved sidewalks, and carefully groomed lawns. A snapshot of suburbia in the 1980s, already looking somewhat old-fashioned in the late '90s.

But definitely a step up from the Hathaway's old neigh-borhood near the park.

Two young girls in shorts and T-shirts were jumping rope on the driveway, watching curiously as Alex and Maggie walked up the sidewalk. "Hi," Alex said, paus-ing. "Do you live here?"

The girls held the ropes in check and nodded shyly.

"What are your names?" Maggie asked.

The older girl, whose hair was tied in a pigtail, looked at her sister and said, "I'm Angela. She's Andrea."

Alex walked over to them and shook each of their small hands. "I'm Alex and that's Maggie. Are your folks home?"

Both nodded again. "They're in the house. Are you from the television?"

"That's right," he said.

"Are you going to help find our brothers?" Andrea asked.

"We hope so."

"Good," Angela said. "We pray for them, you know. Every day."

"I bet you do." And then, "Would you mind if we took your pictures later? If your folks say it's okay?"

The two girls looked at each other and giggled. "You mean we'd be on TV?" Angela asked.

"Maybe so. If it's all right with your parents."

By then the front door had opened and Hazel Hath-away stood just outside it. "Hello, Mr. Collier. Thanks for coming. I see you've met the girls."

"Yes. They're quite the young ladies," he replied as he walked to the door and shook her outstretched hand. "And this is Maggie Lawrence. She's helping me with the story and wanted the chance to meet you and your husband."

"It's a pleasure," Mrs. Hathaway said, opening the door wider and leading them into the house. "As I've told Mr. Collier, we watch your news all of the time."

"Make it Alex, please," he said.

"And Maggie," Maggie added. "We're pretty informal people."

"Okay, but then I wish you'd call me Hazel."

Although Alex had warned her, Maggie was still surprised by how thin and tired the woman appeared. A loose-fitting white cotton blouse hung from her shoulders, and a knee-length floral print skirt dropped straight from her waist, as though she had no hips. At first glance, Maggie thought she could be anorexic.

"You girls stay outside, okay?" Hazel shouted to her daughters. "But don't leave the yard."

Alex and Maggie were led through a smallish living room with well-worn but comfortable-looking furniture and then into an adjoining dining room, where four places had been set at a square mahogany table. A coffee cake and coffeepot sat in the middle. "I thought we could sit here and talk," she said.

"That's fine," Alex replied, looking around, quickly noticing a framed eight-by-ten picture of three boys sitting on the buffet. He recognized it as the same photo Max Douglas had used in his report of five years before.

"John will be here in a moment. He's been working in the garage and had to get cleaned up."

Alex walked to the buffet and picked up the picture, studying it closely. Maggie joined him, peering over his shoulder.

"That's Jed, the oldest, on the left," Hazel said. "Matthew, the middle boy, is in the middle, and Andrew, the youngest, is on the right. That picture was taken just a few weeks before they disappeared. We'd planned to use it in our Christmas cards."

"Handsome boys," Maggie said. "My son, Danny, is just about Matt's age in the picture."

"They take after their father," she said, smiling, and Maggie noted that she still referred to the boys in the present tense.

They were already seated at the table, munching on the coffee cake and making small talk, when John Hathaway appeared, looking freshly scrubbed, with his hair slicked back. His expression was wary but not unfriendly, as he quickly shook hands and apologized for his tardiness. "I was fixing the lawn mower and lost track of the time. Got grease and oil all over me—and still can't get the damn thing to work."

A big man, who Alex thought had aged considerably since Max's report, his hair now mostly gray and his facial lines deeper. But there was a sturdiness about him, an aura of strength and competence that was in sharp contrast to his wife's apparent fragility. Yet Alex remembered Max telling him that it was she, not he, who was the real strength in the family.

John helped himself to a piece of the coffee cake, and then got right to it. "So you've decided to go ahead and bring the whole thing up again, huh?" he said, wasting no words.

"If we have your cooperation, yes," Alex replied, eyeing Hazel for her reaction. "But only then." He went on to explain their plans for the story and the offer of a twenty-five-thousand-dollar reward.

Hazel gasped at the amount. "You would actually give somebody that much money?"

Alex nodded. "If they can provide important information about the boys, yes. We think it may be the only way to get someone to come forward after all this time. But even that may not be enough. There's no guarantee of success."

"We also know we'll probably get a lot of false leads," Maggie added, "but we have to take that risk."

"I think it's wonderful," Hazel said. "We could never afford to offer a reward, not even a small one back then."

Alex leaned across the table. "You know this will bring considerable publicity. You'll be back in the spotlight again. Old wounds will be reopened. It may not be pleasant."

"Especially for our girls," John said, his voice tight. "I've told Hazel that they could get hurt in all of this."

Alex glanced from one to the other, their expressions clear evidence that this was not a new argument. "You'll have to decide that. We think it's important to include the girls in our story."

"We *have* decided," Hazel said, giving her husband a sharp look. "I don't want to go to my grave not knowing what happened to our boys. The girls will be okay, I'll see to that."

John got up and walked to the front window, spotting the station van parked outside. "Are we going to be overwhelmed by the other media?" he asked. "Flooded with calls? Cameras parked out on our front lawn, reporters snooping around?"

"I hope not," Alex replied. "In fact, I'd suggest that you talk to no one but us for a while, until we see what happens. Just refer any calls to Maggie or me, and we'll try to sort them out."

John walked back to the table and sat. He had one more question, directed at Alex. "Tell me again why you're doing this. Offering the big reward. To boost your ratings, or what?"

Alex smiled slightly. How often had they been accused of that? "Because, like you, we'd like to find out what really happened to your sons. And because, frankly, it's a good story . . . one that people out there, our viewers, can identify with. And maybe help with. If it also helps our ratings, so be it."

He went on to explain that they would like to do the on-camera interviews now . . . that the photographers were waiting outside, ready to set up the equipment.

"Then let's do it," Hazel said without hesitation. "Just tell us what to do."

They decided to conduct the interview on the Hathaway's back deck, where there was plenty of room for the camera gear and perfect light from the morning sun. It took about a half an hour for one of the photographers to prepare the equipment while the other taped Angela and Andrea with their parents and then by themselves at play—jumping rope and tossing a Frisbee back and forth in the backyard. Before long, several of the neighbors were leaning over the Hathaway's fence, watching with interest as preparations continued. All of them, Alex was told, were well aware of their missing boys.

"Are you going to be on TV?" a neighbor child yelled to the girls.

"Maybe so," Angela shouted back. "Cool, huh?"

John and Hazel sat together on one side of the deck table, facing one of the cameras, with Alex opposite them, facing the other camera—an arrangement that would allow the taped questions and answers to be intercut more smoothly in the editing process. It was agreed that Alex would do the interview alone, with Maggie off to one side, taking notes and keeping track of the time code on the tape.

His first questions were aimed more at making the

Hathaways comfortable with the cameras than with elic-
iting new information for his story. Questions dealing
with the disappearance of the boys and the subsequent
search for them—historical material that Alex was
already familiar with and which he would cover in his
eventual narration.

Then he got to the heart of things. "Mrs. Hathaway,
how have you and your husband been able to cope, to
keep your hopes alive over all of these years?"

Hazel glanced at her husband, then looked directly
into the camera. "It hasn't been easy," she said. "Most
people, even our closest friends and relatives, believe
the boys are dead. But in my heart, I know they're still
alive. Somewhere. Call it a mother's intuition, call it anything you want, but I know they're okay. I can *feel* it."

"Many people would call it false hope," Alex said. "A
pipe dream."

"We've quit caring what others think," she said tartly.
"They're *our* boys, *our* sons. No one else can know what
we're feeling. The emptiness. The heartache that never
goes away. Ever." She paused, composing herself. "It's
been fifteen years, but every time there's a knock at the
door, every time the phone rings, every time I see boys
about the age our sons would be today, I think it could be
one of them. I never stop hoping. Never stop believing."

They had agreed in advance not to discuss the recent
phone call from the person claiming to be Matt, but
Alex was interested in other leads they had received
over the years.

"In the first few years," Hazel said, "we had dozens
of calls. So did the police, I think. From all kinds of people. Some would say they knew where the boys were,
others claimed to actually have them. A few even
accused *us* of doing something horrible to them. Can

you imagine that? But we could tell most of them were cranks. None of them would ever give us their names, and most of them wanted money. Which, of course, we didn't have anyway."

"But there was never an actual ransom demand?" Alex asked.

"No, never. They were just trying to take advantage of us, I think . . . preying on us, looking for some easy money, I guess."

"And now?"

"We still get a few calls, especially when the case gets mentioned in the newspapers or on one of the radio or TV stations. It's maddening, sometimes, but we keep hoping the next one will be for real."

Alex turned to her husband. "How about you, Mr. Hathaway. What are your thoughts now?"

John Hathaway hesitated, his eyes welling. For the first time, he publicly expressed his doubts. "I'm afraid Hazel has more faith than I do. I would give anything to see the boys walk through the door, but do I think they will? Honestly? Probably not. It's been too long. Selfishly, I just keep thinking of how much I've missed. Watching them grow up, I mean. Playing ball with them, fishing, going to games, doing all of the things that dads and sons do together. Even if they are alive, nobody can bring back those years."

At Alex's urging, they went on to describe the boys as they were then: Jed the athlete, a risk-taker, rambunctious and fun-loving; Matt, a good student but too serious for someone so young, caring, a worrier who was as quiet as Jed was raucous; and Andrew, at four years old, just beginning to form his personality. "We all spoiled him," Mrs. Hathaway said, tears in her eyes, "but he was so little. He was the neighborhood sweetheart. Everybody loved him. He followed his brothers everywhere, mimicking them, always trying to keep up. They were his heroes."

"If they are still alive," Alex asked, "how would you expect them to be today?"

Hazel shook her head. "I just don't know," she said. "It depends, I suppose, on how they've been living all of these years. Where they've been, who they've been with. Have they been loved? Treated kindly? Or enslaved in some way? Brainwashed. There are just too many unknowns."

"We're not even sure we would recognize them," John added. "We could meet them on the street and never know it. We've tried to imagine what they would look like today, but just can't. Kids change so much, you know. They're men now . . . but all we can remember are the boys."

The interview went on for another twenty minutes, ending with Hazel's appeal for the public's help. "I know it's been many years," she said, reading from a paper in front of her, "but if anyone out there can remember anything about the disappearance of our boys on July sixteenth, 1983, we beg . . . we plead with you to call. Imagine for a moment that they were your sons . . . how badly you would want them back. This may be our last chance to find out what happened to them. We want our family together again, but we cannot do it without your help. Please."

For added emotional appeal, Alex had earlier asked to interview their daughters, but on that point, John Hathaway had stood firm. "I won't have it," he'd said angrily. "We probably shouldn't have let you take their pictures, let alone interview them. They never knew the boys . . . they could add nothing to your story."

Hazel didn't intervene this time, agreeing with her husband that an interview would serve no useful purpose and could prove harmful. "We've tried to be very protective of the girls, without suffocating them. I think you can understand that. The less said about them, the better."

It was also agreed that Alex would not publicly reveal the family's address or telephone number . . . that any calls resulting from the story would be handled at the television station.

"When do you think this will be on the air?" Hazel asked.

"I'm not sure," he said. "We still have some other work to do. But we'll get it on as quickly as possible. There will probably also be some newspaper publicity. So you should be prepared for that."

"We'll welcome it," she said. "Anything that might help find the boys."

As she walked to the car with them, her girls were beside her, holding her hands. Alex and Maggie said their good-byes and were ready to leave when Alex thought of a couple more questions. "Hazel, how well did you know your neighbors back in the old neighborhood?"

She gave him a puzzled look. "Not that well, really, except for the ones with kids like ours. Why do you ask?"

He ignored her question and asked another of his own. "Did you ever have trouble with any of them? Did any strike you as strange? Or overly friendly with your boys?"

She thought for a moment, then shook her head. "No, not that I can remember. But, like I say, we only knew those whose kids played with ours."

"So you don't think any of them could have been involved with this?"

She hesitated. "Gosh, maybe it's stupid, but I've never really thought about it. Not at the time, not since. I can't think of anyone."

Alex opened the car door for Maggie and waited until she slipped in. Then he turned back to Mrs. Hathaway. "One more thing. Have you or your husband been back to the park in recent years? Near the fence overlooking the river?"

"Not since we moved twelve years ago," she said. "I can't stand to go back there. It brings back too much pain."

He nodded and started to get into the car.

"Why would you want to know that?"

He thought of the freshly painted white crosses in the grass. If the Hathaways hadn't put them there, who had?

"No reason," he lied. "I was just wondering."

"Now that you've met them," Alex said to Maggie as they drove back to the station, "what do you think?"

"My heart goes out to them," Maggie said. "I damn near cried when she made that public appeal. I just can't fathom what they've been going through for all these years. It's horrible. But I do know one thing."

"What's that?"

"That I'm going to give Danny an extra hug or two when I get home."

He smiled. "I know what you mean."

Neither said anything more for several minutes, as Alex maneuvered the Blazer through the light Saturday traffic on the freeway. But then he asked, "What do you make of Mr. Hathaway?"

She didn't answer immediately, staring out the window, thinking. "He's hard to figure," she finally said. "But, in a way, I felt even sorrier for him than Hazel."

"Really? What do you mean?"

"Think about it. She still has her hope to hold on to, to keep her going. But not him. He's all but given up, it seems to me, leaving him with those two little girls to cling to. It's sad."

Alex agreed. "After talking to him a couple of times, I'm not even sure he really wants the boys back. I think he's afraid of what they may have become and of the disruption they'd cause to the family if they did show up. He seems content with the way things are."

"I'm not sure I'd go that far," she replied, "but he certainly doesn't have his wife's commitment."

As he pulled up in the ramp to drop Maggie off at her car, he asked, "So you're still sure you want to stick with me on this? It could be hopeless."

"I'm sure," she said, getting out. "More than ever now. I'll see you on Monday."

13

With Pat away at a Bar Association conference in Dallas, Alex spent the rest of the weekend around the house alone, catching up on bills that needed to be paid, reading the pile of magazines and newspapers that had stacked up, and giving the house—at least the part that he used—a good cleaning. While he certainly could afford to hire someone to clean for him, he actually took some pleasure in doing it himself. He wasn't sure why, but the work did require some physical exertion and did help pass the time.

Seuss would follow him around the house, watching intently as Alex went about his chores, supervising from perches on the furniture or the mantel of the fireplace, scurrying away and hiding only when Alex took out the vacuum cleaner. The noise terrified him, no matter how many times he heard it, a feline paranoia not helped by Alex chasing him across the room with the machine every chance he got.

On Sunday morning, he talked to his two kids in Philadelphia, spending almost an hour on the phone listening to them describe, in detail, their recent activities: Christopher playing Babe Ruth baseball and soccer, Jennifer attending Girl Scout camp and candy-striping at a nearby hospital.

"I got two hits on Friday night," Chris told him, "including a triple. I could have gotten all of the way home if I hadn't tripped coming around second."

"That's great," Alex said. "But how many strike-outs?"

There was a pause at the other end. "One," he finally said. "But the ump made a bad call on the last pitch."

"Sure," Alex said.

It had been more than a month since he'd seen them, since they had spent their allotted two summer weeks with him in Minnesota. He had taken both weeks off, spending the first week at a resort on Lake Mille Lacs, fishing and swimming, the second seeing some of the things the Twin Cities had to offer: A Twins game, a night at Orchestra Hall, and a day at the Minnesota Zoo. While the kids seemed to enjoy their time with him, it was also evident that they were eager to be back in Philadelphia with their own friends and their own activities. They were growing up fast without him, and Alex realized that he—not unlike John Hathaway—was missing out on much of the fun of watching his kids grow and mature.

"How's your mother?" he asked.

"She's fine," Chris said. "Do you want to talk to her?"

"No, that's okay. Just say hi to her for me."

"Okay."

Like Alex, Jan had not remarried after the divorce, although his kids had told him she was now seeing someone on a regular basis. "A nice enough guy," according to Chris, who came to see his ball games and helped him with his math. "And Mom seems to like him a lot." Alex had not pressed for more details, pleased on the one hand that she apparently had found someone, but on the other, silently simmering that another man might slowly be taking his place with the kids.

Jan had moved back to Philadelphia after the divorce to be closer to her parents, who lived in a Philly suburb, and to take a job at a large computer software company run by her brother. Despite an acrimonious divorce, they had managed to mend their relations in the years since—for the sake of the kids, if nothing else. They now spoke fairly frequently, and amicably, about any problems or issues that arose with the children.

But there was no discussion of their private lives.

Alex was sure the kids must have told her about Pat, since Pat spent a good share of her time with them when they were here, but Jan had never mentioned her . . . or the man she was now involved with. Nor had Alex ever asked.

"When does your baseball season end?" he asked his son.

"In a couple of weeks," Chris replied.

"That soon?"

"Yeah, why?"

"I thought I might try to get out to catch one of your games," Alex said. "But I don't think I can shake free by then."

"That's okay," Chris said quietly. "I didn't expect you to."

Before hanging up, they agreed that Alex would plan to be in Philadelphia for part of the Christmas holidays, and that they would talk again in a week . . . if not before. "If anything comes up, or is bothering you," he told his son, "you call me. And tell that to your sister, too. All right?"

"Okay. See you, Dad."

Later that day Alex got a call at home from Tony

Malay, sounding no more upbeat than he had at the bagel shop. "I talked to John Evans——"

"Who?" Alex asked.

"John Evans. Remember? The precinct cop who picked up the material from Lorna's house after the burglary."

"Right."

"Turns out, he did take an inventory of the stuff he retrieved. And after some pissing and moaning, he finally came up with the list. The Hathaway files were not there."

"Damn."

"My sentiments exactly," Malay said. "Another blind alley."

"So what do we do now?"

"I'll keep looking," Malay said, "and talking to people. Who knows? Maybe we'll get a break. We certainly could use one."

With the rest of the day facing him, and with nothing in particular to do, Alex decided to go back over all of the material he had collected on the Hathaway case, starting with the old newspaper stories he had found at the library. He spread them out on his desk, and began to reread them carefully, also checking the notes he had made the first time around.

He paused at the name of the woman in northern Minnesota who claimed to have seen three boys resembling the Hathaway kids the day after they disappeared. Probably the same woman, Alex thought, that Malay had recalled—the one who'd said she had seen the faces of the boys pressed against the windows of a van, looking scared.

The newspaper identified her as Alice Adams, living in Virginia, a town on the Iron Range, at the time. Would she still be around, or alive, fifteen years later? Alex decided to check. He called Information and was told there were four Adamses listed in the Virginia directory, but no Alice Adams. He asked for all four numbers and began to make the calls.

He hit pay dirt on the third call. "Alice Adams is my grandmother," the woman on the other end of the line said. "She lives with us. Who is this?"

Alex identified himself without saying why he was calling. "Is she around now, your grandmother?"

"Who is this again?"

"My name is Alex Collier. I work for a television station in the Twin Cities, Channel Seven."

"And why do you want to talk to her?" The woman's voice was full of suspicion.

"In connection with a story I'm doing. Could I speak to her, please?"

There was an obvious hesitation, then, "I'll get her."

He waited for several minutes, overhearing a spirited discussion in the background before a faltering voice finally said, "Hello."

He repeated his introduction, but then came right to the point. "Ms. Adams, I'm researching the story of the three little boys, the Hathaway brothers, who disappeared fifteen years ago."

"Yes?"

"You remember it?"

"Of course." Then, more sharply. "I might be an old woman, but I still have my memory, you know."

Alex chuckled to himself. "How old are you, if I may ask?"

"Seventy-six, thank you. And still sharp as a proverbial tack. Just ask my granddaughter."

"I'm sure you are," he said. Then, "At the time, the

newspaper said that you saw what you thought were the boys . . . in Virginia. Is that true?"

"Yes, it is. Plain as day. At the corner of Third and Chestnut, downtown."

"The police say that when they talked to you, you couldn't be absolutely sure it was the missing boys and that you weren't able to give them a very complete description of the van they were in."

"That's *not* true," she said, her voice stronger now. "At least, not all of it."

"It's not?"

"No. I saw pictures of those boys in our local paper. It was big news up here, too, you know. And I'm positive they were the same ones I saw in the van."

"You're positive?"

"Well, I'm more sure now than I was then."

"Why is that?" he pressed.

"I didn't know at the time that they had found two of the boys' caps in the river. I only heard about that later."

"So?"

"Only one of the boys I saw in the van was wearing a cap. The other two were bareheaded."

Alex sat back in his chair. She *did* have her memory. "What about the van itself? What do you remember about it?"

"It was dark green, that's about all. I never knew much about cars or vans. But it had big side windows. That's where I saw the boys, in the back. And it had whitewall tires, I do remember that."

"You didn't see the license plate?"

"No, and even if I had, I never would have remembered it. The only reason I remember what I do is because of the looks on those boys' faces. They were like . . . you know . . . the pictures you sometimes see of kids caught in a war someplace. Scared. Confused. Lost. I'll never for-get them."

He was ready to say good-bye, but before he could, she asked, "Why are you looking into this now?"

"Because we think it's possible the boys might still be alive. None of their bodies was ever found."

"I knew it!" she exclaimed. "I never could under-stand why they didn't listen to me back then. I *know* it was those boys I saw."

"Maybe so," he said, and then asked if he could call her back if something else came up.

"Of course," she said. "And I hope you find them. I've never stopped thinking about them. Not in all these years."

It wasn't until several hours later that Alex suddenly recalled what Tony Malay had told him: The vehicle that had struck and killed Peter Osborne was also . . . a dark green van.

On Monday morning Alex was at the station early, ensconced in a conference room, surrounded by a pile of telephone cross-directories from the early 1980s. He had found them tucked away in one of the station's storage rooms, collecting dust. The directories provided the names of residents who lived at specific addresses any-where in the Cities.

He was copying the names of everyone within a two-block area of the Hathaways' former house near Fair-lawn Park. The task was tedious and time-consuming, but he didn't know how else to get the information he thought he might need.

That's where Maggie found him, hunched over his laptop computer, entering the information. "What's this for?" she asked, looking over his shoulder.

"Probably nothing," he said, "but I want to find out which of the Hathaways' old neighbors have moved, and which are still there."

She responded with raised eyebrows.

"I'll compare this old list," he went on, "with a current list that we now have on the computer. It should tell me which families it would pay talking to, who might still remember something, and which . . ."

"Yes?"

"And which families moved after the boys disappeared. And how soon."

"Your neighbor theory, right?"

"Right. If those boys were taken," he said, "somebody must have known their habits. When and how often they went to the park. Who better to know that than one of the neighbors?"

She covered a yawn. "I'd say it's a stretch."

"Maybe so. But what the hell? Malay admits the cops probably didn't talk to any or many of them at the time."

When Maggie left, Alex bent back to his task, spending another hour collecting both old and current names. And another hour comparing the results. In the end, he was surprised to find that all but seven of the families who had lived near the Hathaways in 1983 were still there. If you could believe the cross-directories.

He highlighted the names of the closest neighbors for possible future interviews, as well as the seven who had moved in the intervening years. The next challenge would be to try to discover when those seven had left and where they'd gone.

As he was about to give it up for the day, he noticed that one of the names listed as still living in the neighborhood was Holcomb. It took him a moment, but then he remembered: Dorothy Holcomb, the librarian who had helped him find the microfilm of the old newspapers. He quickly placed a call to her at the library. "This is Alex Collier, Mrs. Holcomb. Remember me?"

"Of course. I've been wondering what happened to you."

He said, "I didn't realize at the time we spoke that you still lived in the Hathaways' old neighborhood. Is that true?"

"Yes. We've been in the same house for some twenty-five years now. Never could afford more, not with the kids' college expenses and all."

"Then maybe you can help me," he said, and quickly related the process he had just gone through. "Let me read the names of the seven families who have moved, to see if you recognize any of them."

He repeated the names slowly, along with their addresses. There was a lengthy pause at her end of the line. "I can only recall three," she finally said. "Whelan, Kennedy, and Clayborne. But we didn't know any of them that well. Why do you ask?"

"Just curious," he replied. Then, "Do you happen to remember when any of them left? In relation to the boys' disappearance?"

He thought he heard a slight gasp. "You think one of them might have been involved?"

"No, not necessarily. It's just part of my research. I'm trying to cover all of the bases."

"I know the Kennedys and Claybornes moved just a few years ago. After they retired. Went south, I think. To Florida, or maybe Texas. The Whelans left a long time before that, but I can't remember if it was close to the time the boys, you know . . ."

"Tell me about them."

"The Whelans?"

"Yes."

"There isn't much to tell. As I say, we didn't really know them that well. Went to the same church. A young couple, in their mid-thirties, I suppose. Larry and Emily, if I remember correctly. Didn't have any children. Kept pretty much to themselves."

As she spoke, Alex was checking the Whelans' old address. From what he could tell, they had lived four doors down from the Hathaways.

"How did they strike you?" he asked.

There was another pause. "As a little reclusive, I guess. But nice enough when they took the time to talk. I can't tell you much more."

"Do you know where they might be now?"

"I have no idea," she said. "Never did. And now that I think about it, they didn't even bother to say good-bye. They just picked up and left before their house was even sold, I think."

Alex once again repeated the four other names, in hopes that she might now recall one or more of them.

"I'm sorry, I can't. But I'll ask my husband. He may remember."

After he had thanked her and hung up, Alex quickly checked the current Twin Cities White Pages for a Larry or Emily Whelan. They were not listed. Nor were two of the other four names on his list.

Later that afternoon, Maggie reported that she had finished scouring the archives of both daily newspapers, going forward from the time of the boys' disappearance until now, and backward a couple of years before they vanished.

"And?" Alex asked.

She held up a fistful of clippings. "This is all there was," she said. "Besides what you'd found earlier."

He rifled through the pages.

"I can save you the trouble," she said. "There's nothing there, really. No smoking guns. The St. Paul paper gave the original story the same kind of coverage you found in the old issues of the *Star Tribune,* but since then, both papers have done nothing more than an occasional follow-up on the anniversaries. And there's been nothing at all in the last three or four years."

That was in sharp contrast, she told him, with the number of prominent stories both papers had done over the years on a couple of other unsolved cases of missing kids . . . kids who had clearly been abducted. "That says to me that everyone believes the Hathaway boys drowned. Publicly, at least, nobody except the parents seems to believe it was anything but a tragic accident."

As Alex continued to flip through the clippings, she went on, "The dead detective, Osborne, is quoted several times in the earlier stories, but even he never mentions the words 'abduction' or 'kidnapping.' If he had suspicions, he kept them out of the newspapers."

"Anything else?" he asked.

"I also saved the stuff the papers did on his hit-and-run death back in '89."

"Good. I hadn't thought of that."

"But they don't really tell us more than we already know."

"Why doesn't that surprise me?" Alex said, suddenly feeling a deep fatigue setting in. He leaned back and closed his eyes. More disappointments. More blind alleys. Would they ever catch a break? It had been a couple of weeks, but still there was nothing substantive to cling to. No police files. No real leads. If the offer of the reward doesn't open up some doors, he thought, he didn't know what they would do next. And he wondered again, for the umpteenth time, what the hell he had gotten himself into.

"Are you okay?" Maggie asked, eyeing him curiously.

"Yeah, just tired. And a little discouraged, I guess."

"Well, buck up," she said. "You knew it wasn't going to be easy."

He collected the clippings and stuck them into an envelope, to be read carefully later. But Maggie wasn't done. "Like you asked, I also looked for any stories of strange groups around the time the boys disappeared. You know, cults or whatever."

"Nothing there, either, I bet."

"Not much, but I did find one item that struck me as a little curious." She handed him yet another clipping. "This was in the paper about four months after the boys disappeared."

BCA ASKED TO PROBE MILITANT COMMUNE IN NORTHERN MINNESOTA

Associated Press

(VIRGINIA, MN) The state's Bureau of Criminal Apprehension has been asked by authorities in St. Louis County to investigate what they describe as a "secretive and militant" commune in a remote section of the county, some thirty miles northeast of Virginia.

Little is known about the group, reportedly called The Nation United, but neighbors complain they hear frequent gunfire in the area and suspect that war games are being staged within the group's thirty acres of heavily forested property.

The St. Louis County sheriff's officers have not been allowed into the compound, and say they have insufficient grounds to warrant a forced entry. Aerial surveillance, however, has located several buildings within the compound, and what is described as "a large number" of residents, including many children.

The BCA, the state's top law enforcement agency, has agreed to look into the matter, but declined specific comment on plans for its investigation. "It's not against the law for a group of people to choose to live together," one BCA official said. "The question is whether there are any illegal activities going on."

"It's probably nothing," Maggie said when he'd finished reading, "but what struck me was the Virginia connection. Where you said that woman saw the van. And the fact that somebody saw a lot of children there."

Alex read the article twice. "Did you find any kind of follow-up?"

"No, and that's also strange. If the BCA actually did an investigation, I couldn't find any word of it later in the papers."

"Probably turned out to be nothing," Alex replied, unable to shake his melancholy.

"Maybe so, but I've put in a call to the BCA to double-check. If there's anybody still around who might remember it."

14

Alex spent the rest of the week and into the next week-end working on several drafts of the Hathaway story, taking time out only to interview Tony Malay, Max Douglas, and the county medical examiner on camera and—with Maggie's help—to edit the earlier interview with Hazel and John Hathaway. He and a photographer also revisited Fairlawn Park, to shoot some of his on-camera "stand-ups" and a variety of other scenes, including a closing shot of the three tiny crosses in the grass by the fence.

Because of his concentration on these things, Maggie agreed to take up his search for the former Hathaway neighbors whose whereabouts were still unknown—with special emphasis on the Whelan couple. By week's end she had located two of the families, both of whom had moved within the past few years, but could find no trace of the Whelans, even using the computerized national telephone directories. "They either have an unlisted number or no phone," she told Alex. "At least, if you believe these national listings. Or maybe they're going by another name."

He suggested she try several other sources, like driver's licenses and death records. "It's probably a wild goose chase," he said, "but it would be nice to know what happened to them."

Alex had also hoped to travel to Virginia, three hours north of the Twin Cities, to interview the elderly Alice Adams on camera, but he simply could not find the time. He decided to paraphrase her strong conviction that she had seen the boys alive in the green van.

Despite their efforts to keep the investigation quiet, it wasn't long before the newsroom learned what they were up to, and several reporters—sensing a good story in the offing—volunteered to help in any way they could. Alex turned them down for the moment, but reserved the right to call upon them later.

"We have to get this story on the air as quickly as we can," he told Barclay. "The word's out around here, and sure as shit the other stations are going to know what we're doing soon, if they don't already."

Barclay agreed, and assigned two videotape editors to assist him and Maggie, full-time, in assembling the final story. Alex worked twelve to fourteen hours a day, spending the time between his anchoring duties either at the computer, writing, or in the tape-editing room. He barely had time to get home to sleep, and saw virtually nothing of Pat during this period, a situation she assured him she understood. In fact, she told him she hadn't seen him this enthused about his job in years.

He didn't even have to worry about Seuss; Pat had taken him home with her for the duration.

By the following Wednesday, ten days after he had begun writing and editing, the story was ready to air. But despite the risk of a leak, they had decided to postpone the actual broadcast until the following Monday— allowing enough time to promote the story without giving their competitors time to respond.

One of the promotions went like this:

Fifteen years ago last month, three little boys—brothers Jed, Matt, and Andrew Hathaway—disappeared from their northeast Minneapolis home and have not been seen since. At the time, it was believed they had drowned in the Mississippi River, although none of their bodies has ever been recovered. Did they really drown? Their parents still don't believe it, and Channel Seven has launched an investigation to discover the truth. Join Alex Collier Monday night at ten—as he probes this mystery and offers a substantial reward for your help in solving it. That's Monday night on the *Channel Seven News*.

Having completed his work, and with several days to wait for the broadcast, Alex caught up on his sleep, spent time with Pat and Seuss, and once again traveled to the Fairlawn Park neighborhood . . . this time without a camera. He waited until the weekend for that—in hopes of catching more of the old Hathaway neighbors at home.

From the list he had compiled earlier, he knew of several families who still lived close by, fifteen years later. He proceeded to go door to door, feeling not unlike an old encyclopedia salesman making his rounds. At each of the first three homes, he was quickly recognized and welcomed, but learned little new about the Hathaway case. All of the families, it turned out, had helped in the search for the boys, but beyond that, none of them could remember anything helpful except what they had read in the newspapers or seen on television at the time.

The fourth house on his list was the one that once belonged to the mystery couple, the Whelans. According to the directory, it was now owned by the Carlsons, Anita and William. It was Mrs. Carlson who answered the door and who—like the others—immediately recognized Alex. "It's really you, isn't it?" she exclaimed.

She was a portly lady who shouldn't have been wearing shorts and a halter, but was. "You look younger in person than you do on television," she said, intending it as a compliment.

Alex smiled and thanked her, as if he meant it.

He quickly learned that they had lived in the house for only five years and knew of the Hathaway boys only through neighborhood stories. Another family, the Scotts, had bought the home from the Whelans and had subsequently sold it to the Carlsons.

"Then you never knew the Whelans?" he asked.

"No, not at all," Mrs. Carlson replied.

"So you'd have no idea where they are now?"

"I'm afraid not."

"How about the Scotts? Have you stayed in touch with them?"

"No, we met them for the first and last time when we closed on the house. I think they were moving back east. Didn't like our winters."

Alex thought for a moment. "Okay, then. Do you happen to know when, exactly, the Scotts bought the home from the Whelans?"

"That I *can* tell you," she said. "We made a note of it when the deed was transferred. Wait just a minute."

She disappeared back into the house as he waited outside, reappearing a few minutes later. "The sale took place in October of 1983," she said, "but I remember the Scotts telling us that the house was empty when they bought it. The Whelans had moved out a few weeks before."

A few weeks, he thought. That would have been in August or September. Probably just a month or so after the boys vanished. Interesting.

There was no one home at the fifth house, but Alex left his business card in the mailbox with a scrawled note asking them to call at their earliest convenience.

He debated giving it up. The morning had turned hot and muggy. The sun had been blotted out by heavy, dark clouds that once again had moved in from the west, signaling that thunderstorms would not be far behind. In fact, faint streaks of lightning were already visible in the distance. He glanced at his list: four more homes to check. He'd have to hurry to beat the rain.

The sixth house belonged to somebody named Albers, down the street from the Hathaways, almost directly across from the park. Unlike most of the other homes on the block, this one was in a state of disrepair: blistered, peeling paint, cracked windows, a crumbling cement stoop, and unmowed grass that was more brown than green.

An older, unshaven man with sunken, reddened eyes answered the door, bare-chested and wearing what appeared to be a drooping pair of pajama bottoms. From the looks of him, he had just gotten out of bed, Alex thought.

"Yeah," he said through the screen door.

"Mr. Albers?"

"Yeah."

"Sorry to bother you," Alex said, introducing himself.

The man showed no sign of recognition. Not one of his fans, for sure. "You selling something?" he asked.

"No," Alex replied. "I'm looking for some information. About the—"

"I'm not interested," he said, starting to close the inside door.

"About the Hathaway boys," Alex said quickly.

The door opened again. "What about them?"

Even at a distance, Alex could detect the sour scent of liquor on the man's breath. And it was still well before noon. Alex glanced at the skies. "May I come in for a moment? It will only take a few minutes."

"We can talk here."

Alex quickly explained his mission. "We're looking for help. We have reason to believe the boys may not have drowned."

Albers stepped out onto the stoop, holding the pajama bottoms up with one hand. "Oh, yeah? What makes you think that?"

Alex ignored the question. "Were you around that day? The day they disappeared?"

"Sure. I saw them kids run to the park. All three of 'em."

"You did?"

"I just said I did. You hard of hearing or something?"

He shook his head and smiled. "No, my hearing's fine. Did you see anything . . . anyone else?"

"Not anyone, no."

The flashes of lightning were coming closer. So was the rumbling of thunder. The rain would not be far behind.

"What do you mean, not anyone?"

"I mean, I didn't see any people. I did see a car."

"A car? Where?"

"Over there," he said, pointing to where Alex's Blazer was parked, near the path leading into the park.

"Didn't belong to nobody around here, I know that. Never seen it before . . . or since."

"Did you tell the police about it?" Alex asked.

"They never asked."

"Then why didn't you go to them?"

"Because the cops and me don't get along. Never did. Never will. I wouldn't give 'em the fuckin' time of day."

"But you knew the boys were missing, right?"

"Sure, but it had nothin' to do with me. And I didn't even like the little turds. Wouldn't stay off my lawn."

What lawn? Alex thought. But then the clouds opened up, not with a light sprinkle, but with a gush. Albers quickly moved back inside the door, but made no effort to invite Alex in.

"What kind of car was it?" Alex asked, huddling against the house.

"Wasn't really a car," Albers said. "A van. Chevy, I think. A green one."

Then he disappeared inside, leaving Alex standing in the rain, but feeling not a drop.

15

Monday night finally arrived. Everything was ready. Everyone was in place. Alex and Maggie were at the anchor desk, impatiently waiting for the final countdown. Barclay was in the control room, making sure there would be no technical problems. Several newsroom employees were on the other side of the studio, manning a bank of telephones, along with a couple of newspaper reporters who had been assigned by their papers to monitor the broadcast and viewer reaction to it.

The floor director stood poised by the side of the studio camera, his right hand raised.

"Break a leg," Maggie whispered.

Five, four, three, two . . . the floor director's fingers counted down the seconds. Then his hand fell. The cue. They were on the air.

"Good evening, everyone. I'm Alex Collier."

"And I'm Maggie Lawrence. Thanks for joining us."

The opening two-shot quickly dissolved to a tight shot of Alex. "Tonight," he said, "we're going to depart from our normal routine and begin with a story that is really fifteen years old. The story of a family torn apart by the loss of three of their children, a family which has never given up the hope that the children may still be alive. And before we're finished, we're going to ask for your help in solving a mystery that has gone unsolved for far too long."

It had been years since Alex had felt this keyed up sitting in front of the cameras. He could hear a nervous tremor in his voice, could feel the beads of sweat creeping down the back of his neck. But who could blame him? Not since that unforgettable night when he brought down the pedophile judge was there as much at stake . . . as much of himself on the line. With the station's massive and provocative promotional buildup in the past week, he knew there would likely be a large audience out there, watching and listening expectantly. He didn't want to disappoint them . . . or the Hathaway family, whom he knew would be watching intently from their home.

He took a deep breath and went on. "It was only a few weeks ago, on this newscast, that we briefly noted that fifteen years had passed since Hazel and John Hathaway's three young sons disappeared . . . after going to play at Fairlawn Park, near their home in northeast Minneapolis. At that time, it was believed they had all drowned in the nearby Mississippi River, a theory that until now has gone largely unchallenged.

"Channel Seven has decided to launch a new investigation of the case because we believe—as the boys' parents do—that there is a chance, however remote, that their boys, who would be young men today, may still be alive."

The tape rolled, with Alex first covering much of the same ground that Max Douglas had covered five years before: showing how and where the boys had vanished, the old newspaper headlines, and scenes of the search that followed.

"What triggered our interest," he reported, "was the fact that none of their bodies was ever recovered, nor a single stitch of their clothing—except for the two baseball hats. The Hennepin County medical examiner, Dr. Peter Benning, admits that is highly unusual."

The tape cut to the medical examiner being interviewed by Alex.

DR. BENNING: Normally, a body will sink to the bottom and remain there until it bloats with gas, becomes buoyant, and floats to the surface. Usually in a matter of days. It would be virtually impossible, I believe, for all three of the boys' bodies to remain submerged for all of this time.

"The boys' mother, Hazel Hathaway," Alex went on, "has never accepted the idea that her sons are dead, and has somehow managed to keep her hopes alive for all of these years."

HAZEL HATHAWAY: In our hearts, we know they are still alive. Somewhere. Call it a mother's intuition, call it anything you want, but I know they're okay. I can *feel* it.

As the tape continued to roll, Alex described the doubts that other people still harbored, including the Virginia woman, Alice Adams, who was sure she had seen the boys in the green van, and the lead police investigator, Peter Osborne, who had died apparently not fully convinced that the boys had really drowned.

"The police chief at the time, Tony Malay, who is now retired, defends the original investigation of the boys' disappearance, but has agreed to join our investigation because of the possibility that the police may have rushed to judgment."

CHIEF MALAY: All we really had was the boys' hats and the fact that they had been playing near the river. But that seemed enough at the time. There was no evidence of foul play. No witnesses. No ransom demand. We had no choice but to chalk it up as a tragic accident. I'm still not sure that it wasn't.

Alex went on to report on some of the phone calls the police and the family had received immediately after the boys disappeared and in the years since. "A former Channel Seven reporter, Max Douglas, filed a story on the case five years ago and still remembers a curious call he got from an unidentified woman."

MAX DOUGLAS: She knew an awful lot about the case, considering it was ten years old at the time. Down to a description of the clothes the boys were wearing when they vanished. It was eerie. She also claimed to know that the boys were still alive, but she refused to tell me where they were or who she was. I have no proof, but I'd swear she was legitimate.

Alex concluded the tape portion of the report with scenes of the present-day Hathaway family, including more excerpts of the interview and shots of the two daughters with their parents and playing with each other. And with a picture of the brothers as they might look today, rendered by a forensic artist the station had hired to "age" an old photo of the boys. Finally there was Hazel Hathaway's plea to the public.

HAZEL HATHAWAY: This may be our last chance to find out what happened to our boys. We want our family together again, but we cannot do it without your help. Please.

The final shot on the tape was a close-up of the three small crosses, almost hidden in the grass by the fence. "Today, at the spot where the boys slid down the hill to the river," Alex said, "there are three small, freshly painted crosses—placed there by someone other than the family. We would like to know why . . . and by whom."

The camera was once again tight on him. "We do not know with certainty whether the Hathaway boys truly drowned . . . or were kidnapped, or perhaps killed. But we believe someone out there may know the answer. To discover the truth, we'll need your help. And we are prepared to pay for it. Channel Seven management has authorized a twenty-five-thousand-dollar reward to the person or persons who will come forward with concrete, relevant information that leads to the discovery of what actually happened to the Hathaway children fifteen years ago.

"If you are that person, we ask that you call us at 555-0112. We have news personnel standing by to screen your calls. Your name will be held in confidence, or you may remain anonymous and still be eligible for part or all of the reward. If you have information, please call. The lives of three boys and a family's peace of mind hang in the balance. Thank you."

Alex turned the rest of the newscast over to Maggie, and hurried to the bank of telephones on the other side of the studio. If he was expecting a flood of calls, he was disappointed. Only two of the four telephone lines were lighted, and it turned out that those callers—along with several others who followed—were more interested in getting information about the story than in providing it.

As he stood watching and waiting, George Barclay made his way from the control room to the studio. "Nice job, Alex. It was a good piece, and I thought you handled it well."

"Thanks, but so far it's not getting us any calls that are worth a damn."

"Don't get impatient. If somebody really does know something about this, they aren't going to rush to the phone. They're going to want to think about it for a while first."

"I hope you're right, but if this doesn't work, I don't know what we do next."

By then the two newspaper reporters had wandered over, one from the *Star Tribune*, the other from the *Pioneer Press*. Both had seen the story in advance, but both wanted to be at the station for the actual broadcast. And both carried clips of their newspapers' original stories on the case.

"Quite a yarn," said the *Star Trib* reporter, Barry Bruskin. "You get any calls?"

"None that count yet," Alex replied, with a glance at the telephone bank. "But it's still early."

"I've got to tell you," Bruskin went on, "my editor, who's a skeptical bastard to begin with, thinks this is just a big publicity stunt. To give the ratings a little boost."

"So what do *you* think?" Alex asked.

"Sounds like a hell of a story to me, but I must say your evidence of something other than a drowning seems a little skimpy."

"I don't deny that," Alex replied. "That's why we're

offering the reward, to try and jar somebody's memory . . . or maybe their conscience. We knew from the beginning that it was a long shot, but we think it's worth the effort . . . and the money. And, shit, you can tell your editor that we're not even in a sweeps period now."

The *Pioneer Press* reporter, George Emory, a tall, toothy fellow, had remained silent until then. "What about the parents?" he asked. "Will they talk to us?"

"I'm afraid not," Barclay said. "That's part of our deal with them. They talk to no one else for the time being. We'll give you a complete transcript of Alex's interview with them, but that's the best we can do."

"That's kind of shitty," Emory said.

Barclay shrugged. "Understand the family's point of view. While they're desperate to find their kids, they don't want to be overrun by reporters and camera crews. They want to keep some normalcy in their lives. And selfishly, of course, we would like to keep this story as exclusive as possible."

After another twenty minutes of discussion, the reporters prepared to leave to complete their own stories. Both had midnight deadlines.

"What kind of play do you think this will get?" Barclay asked.

"That's not up to us," Bruskin replied with a confirming glance at Emory. "People higher up on the food chain make those decisions. But I'll give it my best shot."

"That's all we can ask," Barclay said.

Maggie joined Alex and Barclay after the newscast, each relieving one of the other staff members on the phones. There were other callers, including several who chastised the station for trying to exploit the Hathaway family, but none who provided any new information.

After another hour, when the calls stopped, they all left, none of them bothering to hide their disappointment.

In contrast, the mood at the Hathaway home was as upbeat as it had been in years. Hazel, at least, could not have been more pleased with Alex's report. At long last, the story of her boys was once again in the public eye, and who knew what that exposure—and the reward— might bring? She couldn't remember feeling more hopeful, more confident. Her only regret was that it didn't happen years before.

Her husband was more subdued, but even he was surprised at the restraint Collier had shown in telling the story. His fears that the family would be exploited or the story sensationalized had proved groundless, although he still worried about the impact of the publicity on the lives of his daughters.

For their part, the girls thought the whole thing was too cool to be true. They'd been allowed to stay up well beyond their bedtimes to see the report, and despite their parents shushing, had squealed and laughed every time they saw their images on the screen.

When the report was over, and things had settled down, Andrea, the younger one, asked, "Will the boys come home now?"

"We hope so," Hazel said.

"If they do, will we be on TV again?"

Her mother smiled. "Probably so, yes."

"Awesome," she said.

The next morning, when Alex picked up the *Star Tribune* off his stoop and opened it up, some of the depression of the night before disappeared. There it was, above the fold on the front page of the metro section:

TV STATION OFFERS LARGE REWARD
FOR INFO ON MISSING BOYS

Beneath the headline was a three-column picture of the Hathaway boys as they appeared back in 1983, taken from the newspaper files.

Bruskin, the *Star Trib* reporter, was true to his word of the night before. His story was lengthy and complete, detailing the background of the case and the efforts by the station to reopen the investigation. It contained a number of quotes from the parents and others, including Tony Malay. It also quoted the current police chief, Sidney Bennet, who defended the department's original investigation and called Alex's story "a farce," and the offer of the reward, "nothing more than a ratings grab." To which Alex was quoted in response:

> The reward is not some kind of gimmick. It's the only way we could think of to reach out and get information in a case this old. We believe there are people out there who can help us, but who may need a financial enticement.

Since he did not have the *Pioneer Press* delivered to his home, Alex put in a quick call to Barclay at the station to see how it had treated the story. "Even better than the *Trib*," Barclay told him. "And they didn't quote the asshole police chief." He also said the Associated Press had picked up the story and was putting it on the national wire. "That should get us exposure around the country, if a bunch of other newspapers pick it up."

"That's great," Alex replied, "but only if it gets us the right call."

"One other thing," Barclay said. "The overnight ratings are in. We did a forty-three share last night. The best in six months. Hawke is dancing in the goddamned aisles."

"Good for him," Alex said. "Maybe he'll trip and fall on his face."

When Alex got to the station later that morning, he found two telephone messages that sounded promising, both from women. Neither had left a name or number, and both had insisted on talking to him personally and said they would call back later in the day. One claimed to be the woman Alex had mentioned in his report, the one who had talked to Max Douglas.

Surprisingly, there had not been the flood of crank calls they had expected in search of the reward. Instead, most of the calls had expressed sympathy for the Hathaway family and offered encouragement to Alex in his investigation. A couple had even volunteered to add their own money to the reward fund.

Sorting through his mail, he picked out a letter that apparently had been delivered to the station that morning. It bore no stamp or postmark. And no return address. He tore it open, and found a terse, handwritten message inside:

Forget the Investigation. Drop the Reward.
This will get you nothing but trouble.

Alex shoved the letter under the light of his desk lamp to get a better look. The writing had clearly been made by an ink pen, not a ballpoint, and had been fashioned with considerable care. Almost calligraphy. If it was a joke, or a ruse, someone had spent considerable time and trouble crafting it.

Should he take the warning seriously? Show it to Barclay? Nah. It must be a prank, he told himself. Somebody having fun. Maybe even someone in the newsroom playing a practical joke.

Still . . .

He quickly called the receptionist to ask if she remembered who had delivered the letter. "I have no idea," she said. "It was lying outside the front door when I arrived this morning. Someone must have left it there during the night."

That pretty much rules out anybody in the newsroom, he thought. But who then? He'd probably never know.

Putting the letter aside, he went through the rest of his mail. Not much there: the usual batch of news releases and press conference announcements, along with several personal cards and letters from viewers, most of them congratulating him on his contract extension, the news of which had finally made the newspapers several days before.

Remembering now that he hadn't talked to the Hathaways since the broadcast, he quickly punched in their number. Hazel answered on the third ring, but before he could say anything, she blurted out, "He picked up the letter!"

"What?"

"Matt. We just got the return receipt from the certified letter you sent to Newark. Can you believe it?"

Alex was as surprised as she was. What had it been? Two weeks? Something like that. "Hold on a second, Hazel. *Somebody* picked up the letter . . . probably the same person you talked to on the phone. But that doesn't necessarily mean it was Matt."

"I know, but . . ." He could hear the disappointment in her voice.

"Maybe it was, but someone else could have used a fake ID."

"You think so? How will we ever know?"

He was stuck. "I'm not sure. If it really was Matt, and if he's really using the money for bus fare, like he said, then we'll know soon enough. If it's a ruse, as I suspect it is, you'll probably hear from him again, asking for more money."

"What should I do then?" she asked plaintively.

"If he calls again?"

"Yes."

He thought for a moment. "If he asks for more money, tell him you'll need more proof that it really is him . . . that he and his brothers are still alive and well. Pictures or something. And be sure to call me right away."

"Okay," she said, almost in a whisper.

Alex then switched subjects, back to the original purpose of his call. "What did you think of the program last night?"

"I thought it was wonderful," she said, recovering. "We even allowed the girls to stay up and watch. They were thrilled to see themselves on TV."

"I bet. Have you had any calls?"

"Two radio stations called, and a couple of our friends. And two of our neighbors stopped by this morning for coffee. They'd seen the report, too."

"Did you talk to the radio stations?"

"No, I told them they'd have to speak to you."

"Good."

"How about you?" she asked. "Any calls?"

"A few, but nothing dramatic yet. I'm waiting on a couple of callbacks that could be important."

"I hope so," she said.

"One more thing," Alex said. "Did you and your husband ever know the Whelans? A couple who lived a few doors down from you before the boys disappeared."

"I remember them, but only vaguely," she said. "Did they have kids?"

"No, not as far as I know."

"I didn't think so," she said. "If they had, I'd probably remember them better."

He promised he would call again if there were any substantial new developments, and asked her to do the same. "Be patient," he told her. "This could take a while."

"If there's anything I've learned these fifteen years," she said, "it's patience."

16

Alex stayed close to the phone for hours, not wanting to miss the return calls. The first came at midafternoon. A woman's voice, so clear she could have been calling from the next desk. "Is this Alex Collier?"

"Yes, it is. Who's this?"

"Not now," she said.

He waited.

"You're looking for the woman who talked to Max Douglas, right? The one he talked about last night on the news?"

"Is that you?"

"Yes."

Alex wished now that he had Caller ID attached to his phone, but as it turned out, it wouldn't have made any difference. The woman seemed to read his mind. "In case you're checking," she said, "I'm calling from a pay phone."

"That's fine," he said. "What can you tell me?"

"You tell me. How do I get the reward?"

"Simple. By providing solid information that leads us to the Hathaway boys."

"I can remain anonymous?"

"If you choose, although it's more complicated that way. I'd rather deal with you in person."

"That's not possible," she said.

"Why not?"

"Because it could put me in danger, that's why. I'm taking a chance even calling you. You're not dealing with nice people here."

Alex's eyes immediately went to the warning letter on his desk. Maybe it wasn't a hoax, after all. "What do you mean?"

"Just what I said."

"You're telling me that you *know* the boys didn't drown, that they were taken?"

"That's right."

"By dangerous people?"

"Right again."

"How dangerous?"

"You don't want to find out."

"But you're telling me the boys are still alive?"

"As far as I know."

Alex could feel his chest tighten. He took a deep breath. "Where are they now?"

It took her a moment, but then she laughed. "C'mon, Mr. Collier. Get serious. You know better than to ask that."

He tried to assess the voice. Deep, husky. Even sexy. And confident. He could detect no hesitation, no fear. Sounding younger than she must actually be, if it was the same woman who had called Douglas five years before, who knew what the boys were wearing *fifteen* years before.

"Okay," he said. "Then where do we go from here?"

"You tell me," she replied.

"You know I can't hand out the money without some proof that you actually know where the boys are and who took them."

"And I won't tell you anything," she said; "without the money."

"Give me a minute," he said, trying to think. Then, "How about this? We could put the reward money in escrow . . . with someone, a lawyer or banker perhaps, whom we both can trust and who will preserve your anonymity. Then, if your information leads us to the boys, the funds will be released to you."

There was a long pause. "That sounds feasible," she finally said. "But what if I can only tell you who took them, and not where they are today?"

"That would be a start," he replied, "but not worth the entire reward."

"How much?"

"I'd have to think about it," Alex said.

"Let's both think about it," she replied. "I'll be back in touch."

With that, the line went dead.

The second woman called back an hour later, quickly admitting to Alex that she was the one who had put the white crosses by the fence in Fairlawn Park. "Did I do something wrong?" she asked, choking up. "I was shocked when I saw your report last night."

"No, no," he said. "We were just curious."

"My kids played with the Hathway boys. All the time, in that same park. I first put the crosses there shortly after they disappeared. It was my own personal memorial to them . . . you know, a remembrance. And I check on them every few months, to make sure they're still there. And to give them a coat of paint if they get faded, or dirty."

"That's very thoughtful," Alex said. "I'm sure the family appreciates it."

"I haven't told anyone, you know. Not in all of these

years. People might think it's silly. But I loved those little boys just like my own. And losing them was like losing my own."

She willingly gave Alex her name and address, but could provide no useful new information about what might have happened to the boys. "Like most people, we just assumed they had drowned."

"We think they may not have," Alex said.

"Well," she said, "if that's true, maybe my crosses and my prayers did some good."

"Maybe so," he said.

After she'd hung up, Alex placed a call to Barclay, arranging to meet with him, Maggie, and Malay after the early news. It would be the first time they'd all been together since the night Alex's story had aired, and there were several things to catch up on.

Once they were all in the conference room, Alex began with details of the conversation he'd had with the first woman, the one who claimed to know what happened to the boys. "If I had to bet, I'd bet she's for real," he said. "And if she is, it's the first solid evidence we have that the boys may still be alive."

Barclay was more skeptical, but said he'd reserve judgment until Alex heard from her again. If he did. "But remember," he said, "we're not going to be passing out any money until we're damn sure the information is genuine."

"Of course not," Alex said, "but look at this," showing them a copy of the warning letter he'd received. "I didn't think much about it at first, but now—after talking to that woman—I'm not so sure."

The letter was passed from one to the other. Maggie, who had received similar threats in her investigation of the porn ring the year before, urged caution. "I wouldn't ignore it, Alex," she said. "I'd be careful, if I were you. Use those eyes in the back of your head."

"I'll try," he said, "but I'm sure as hell not going into hiding."

He then reported on his weekend trip to the old Hathaway neighborhood, including what little new he had learned about the Whelan couple, and the recollections of the old man, Albers. "It's the third time somebody has talked about a green van. The woman in Virginia saw one, and Malay here says a similar van was involved in Peter Osborne's death several years later. It could be a coincidence, of course, but doesn't it strike you as a little strange?"

"Not me," Barclay said. "There must be thousands and thousands of green vans around. You're grasping at straws."

"Maybe so," Alex replied. "Still . . ."

Maggie and Malay said they had spent much of the afternoon at the Bureau of Criminal Apprehension, trying to track the results of the BCA investigation of the militant commune in northern Minnesota years before. "Nobody there could remember anything about it," Maggie said, "but after we showed them a copy of the AP article they agreed to dig into their files."

"Turns out," Malay said, picking up the story, "the investigation ended almost as soon as it began. By the time the BCA agent finally got to poking around up there, the group had pulled up stakes and moved on. Nobody is sure where. The property was abandoned and up for sale. End of complaints from neighbors. End of investigation. End of story."

"Shit," Alex muttered.

"Not quite the end," Maggie said. "When I got back here, I started surfing the Net and what do you know? I found that a group calling itself "The Nation United" has its own Web site. I don't know if it's the same bunch, but it could be, I suppose."

"What's on the Web site?" Alex asked.

"Lots of antigovernment, born-again Christian stuff. You know, the feds' war to take away our guns and our freedom. The UN's conspiracy to rule the world. Mixed in with a lot of Bible-thumping, religious stuff. When I get the chance, I'm going to keep surfing to see if I can find anybody who knows anything more about them."

Barclay got out of his chair, hitched up his pants, and asked, "Anything else? I've got to get to my workout."

"One more thing," Alex said. "Hazel Hathaway tells me somebody picked up the two hundred bucks we sent to Newark. She got a return receipt from the certified letter and was excited as hell."

Barclay scoffed. "If I were her, I wouldn't stand around waiting for the bus."

"I know," Alex said. "I tried to tell her the same thing."

Once Barclay had left, Alex, Maggie, and Malay stayed on in the conference room, saying nothing for several minutes, quietly digesting what they'd been discussing. Finally Alex said, "What should we be doing now?"

"Resting," Maggie said with a sigh and a smile.

He laughed. He knew what she meant. The last couple of weeks had been tough on all of them, but especially on Maggie, who still had a young boy at home to worry about. "I'm sorry," he said. "We'll try to ease up for a while."

"I don't mind," she replied. "But Brett is getting a little tired of all the extra baby-sitting."

"I don't blame him. I'll try to cut you some slack."

Malay got up and walked to the window overlooking the street. "I hate to say it, but I'm feeling like a third wheel," he said. "I'm not doing anything."

"What are you talking about?" Alex said. "You've already done a lot."

"Oh, yeah. Like what?"

"Keeping my ass out of trouble, among other things. Remember?"

"Right. Big deal."

"There *is* one more thing you could do," Alex said.

Malay sat back down. "What's that?"

Alex leaned into him. "Am I right that damn near every state must have an agency like our BCA, or state police force?"

"Probably," Malay said.

"Then . . . why don't you get on the phone to every state bordering the Mississippi River, between here and Louisiana?"

Malay looked confused. "Why?"

"To make sure we haven't missed something. To make sure that none of these boys . . . or parts of their skeletal remains . . . was ever found down river and never reported up here."

Malay was clearly skeptical. "You actually think a body, or even parts of a body, could make it that far? Through all of the locks and dams? Through the barge and boat traffic? I'd say it's impossible. I sure as hell have never heard of it happening."

"Look," Alex said, "assuming those kids were taken, we still don't know how they were taken. Maybe a boat picked them up . . . and took them a long way down the river before dumping one or more of them off. It could happen. I don't want to go through all of this only to discover that somebody along the river . . . five, six, or ten years ago . . . found a skull or some bones and failed to make the connection with the Hathaway kids. With DNA technology today, there's a chance we could make a positive ID."

"Okay," Malay finally said. "But it sounds a lot like busy work to me."

"Hey, you said you wanted something to do," Alex replied, grinning.

Before they broke up, they decided Maggie would keep working on The Nation United Web site and on the search for the Whelans, while Alex stayed close to the phone and also tried to contact the Hathaway neighbors he had missed the first time around.

"I can't think of anything else at the moment," he said. "Except to wait."

When Alex returned to the newsroom, he found Nicholas Hawke waiting by his cubicle, puffed up, a broad smile on his face, still wearing that repulsive cologne. Hawke clapped him on the shoulder. "First chance I've had to congratulate you on the Hathaway story," he said. "Damn fine piece of work."

Alex mumbled his thanks.

"George told you about the ratings, didn't he?"

"Yeah, he did. That's great."

"Great? They're unbelievable. Best in months."

Alex could only nod. He didn't know what else to say.

"And the press we got! We couldn't have asked for better coverage." Hawke rubbed his hands. "I've even gotten calls from friends around the country, who read the AP story. You are keeping it alive, aren't you? Milking it for all it's worth?"

Alex eyed him suspiciously, afraid to reveal any of the new developments. "There's not much new to report," he finally said. "But we do plan to do a quick update on the late news."

"A quick update? That's not good enough," Hawke said, frowning. "Shit, make something up, if you have to."

"*What?*" Alex was astonished.

"Hell, just take a little journalistic license. We've got to keep the momentum going."

"I don't make things up," Alex said quietly, but with heat. "Never have, never will. You couldn't pay me enough."

Hawke backed off a step, surprised by the anger in Alex's voice and in his eyes. Arrogant bastard, he thought. So high and mighty. Never did like him. Should have fired him years ago, when he had the chance. "Take it easy, Collier," he said, drawing himself up. "Get off your high horse. I was just talking about gilding the lily a little. Keeping the excitement going."

"I'll do what I can," Alex said, turning away, wanting to end the discussion.

"I hope so." Then, "You've got a lot riding on this."

When Alex turned back, Hawke was gone. *Journalistic license*. Fuck me! What was happening to the business? Maybe it was time to get out, after all. Hell, a week didn't go by that they weren't asked to plug some network program or movie on the newscast. Or to tailor the news to meet some desirable demographic target. *Make something up*. Shit!

Alex had not fully cooled off, hours later, when he met Pat for a late dinner downtown. She was waiting in the bar at Palamino, a fashionable bistro in the Hennepin Avenue theater district, just a few blocks from the station. Predictably, but to Alex's chagrin, he was quickly recognized by the maître d' and given the VIP treatment, immediately seated at a secluded table well away from the crush of the after-theater crowd that was now filling up the place.

It took Pat no more than a minute to detect his sour mood. "What's the matter?" she asked, reaching across the table to put her hand on his.

"Hawke," he said, quickly repeating the essence of their newsroom conversation. "Can you believe that? The prick. Asking me to make up something? 'Gild the lily,' he said."

She laughed. "C'mon, Alex. Does that surprise you? You know how he thinks."

"Trouble is, that's the way the whole business is starting to think," he said, putting a voice to his earlier thoughts. "Do whatever you have to do to get and hold the audience. Makes me wonder if I really want to keep doing this crap."

She watched him closely. And with amusement. It wasn't the first time she had heard this lament from him, but it did seem to come more often lately. And with more intensity. They had talked from time to time about what he might do if he ever left the news business, but there was never a clear answer. Like many news people, he viewed public relations with disdain, and couldn't picture himself in any kind of corporate setting. "Too stuffy," he had said. "And besides, what the hell do I know about business?" What he really wanted to do, he'd said laughingly, was to become a professional bass fisherman. But he knew there wasn't much money or future in that. In the end, the subject was always left unresolved.

"Did you tell Barclay?" she asked now.

"About Hawke?"

"Yes."

"Hell, no. He'd probably go punch the bastard out."

"So what did you end up reporting?"

"Basically, that we'd received a number of calls after the first broadcast, a couple of which had provided possible leads. But that we still needed more help . . . that the reward was still out there, waiting to be claimed. Actually made a bigger deal out of it than I had planned, thanks to Hawke putting the arm on me."

At that moment a large older woman with caked-on makeup appeared at their table, looming over them, then leaning down next to Alex, garlic on her breath and in his face. "Excuse me, but you're Alex Collier, aren't you?"

"That's right," he replied, pushing his chair back, glancing plaintively at Pat.

"I thought so," she said, pulling up an empty chair from an adjacent table and unabashedly settling into it. "I was just telling my friends," she said with a sideways glance across the room, "how wonderful it is that you're trying to find those poor lost boys. Just wonderful."

It was his worst nightmare. "I appreciate that, ma'am, but right now—"

"Their poor mother, what she must have endured . . ."

"She's a brave lady . . ."

"I have three sons of my own, you know. They're wonderful boys. One's a doctor, a heart surgeon, another is—"

"Ma'am, please," Alex said, and then, in his most conspiratorial voice, "I hate to interrupt, but you'll have to excuse me now, because I'm in the midst of a very important conversation with this woman. About that case, actually."

The lady gave Pat a sharp look. "Really? Well, I certainly didn't mean to intrude. I wouldn't want to do anything—"

"It's okay," he said. "No harm done."

The woman slowly rose from the chair, and after a quick squeeze of his hand and another appraising look at Pat, made her way back to her own table. Alex could see her whispering to her companions as they beamed at him.

"Jesus Christ," he muttered.

Pat smiled. She knew he would never get used to the attention. "Are all of your fans so cute?" she whispered. "Do you blame me for getting jealous sometimes?"

He glared at her, but after a deep breath, went on to tell her about the mystery woman's phone call and then showed her a copy of the threatening letter.

"My God," Pat said, studying the note. "This is a little scary."

He shrugged. "That's what Maggie says, too, but I don't know. Think about it. This case is fifteen years old. Even if the worst happened to those kids, would somebody still be around, worried enough to be making threats, after all this time? Not likely, it seems to me."

"Or to me," Pat said, sinking back in her chair, trying to choose her words carefully. "But to be frank, Alex, this whole thing strikes me as a little unlikely."

There it was. She'd said it. The first time she had dared express her own doubts, which she'd been harboring silently for weeks now. Ever since she'd seen him brush aside his own misgivings and throw himself headlong into the investigation. Truth was, the more he had told her about the case, the less she thought the odds were of his ever finding the truth. Or the boys.

Like a good lawyer, she had tried to weigh what little evidence there was, to sift through what was fact and what was mere theory or speculation. While she agreed the case was strange, that three little boys would simply up and disappear, it certainly wasn't beyond belief that they had simply drowned. In her years as a public defender, she had witnessed other cases just as strange, if not as tragic. And she knew better than most that suspecting a crime and proving it are two different things.

She had held her tongue, however, for fear of dimming his enthusiasm about the story. She hadn't seen him this energized in years. Let it ride, she had told herself, let it play itself out. He doesn't need another skeptic. But finally, she decided, the time had come to be honest.

If she had expected him to be surprised or shocked by her doubts, or her decision to voice them, she was disappointed. He simply smiled at her from across the table and said, "I was wondering when you'd speak up."

"You were?"

"Sure. You may be great lawyer, but you're not a great actress."

"Really? I thought I was being damn clever."

He laughed. He had sensed her skepticism from the very beginning, way back when. He had watched with some amusement as she had tried to maintain the facade, but it had long been clear to him—from a host of unconscious signals on her part—that she had serious reservations about the wisdom of his pursuit . . . and of the chances of eventual success.

"And you're not alone," he said now. "I can feel it in the newsroom, too. A growing sense that we may be on some kind of wild goose chase."

They were interrupted by a waiter arriving to take their orders. A young fellow who identified himself as Jeff, and whose deferential, almost fawning, table-side manner was clear recognition of Alex's status. After a moment more studying the menu, Pat decided on a chef's salad, Alex on the salmon special. And a bottle of California chardonnay to go along with it.

With the waiter gone, Pat picked up the conversation where they had left off. "So what are they saying in the newsroom?"

Alex thought for a moment. "It's not what they're saying. It's more subtle than that. The sly looks. Or the nonlooks. The whispered conversations. Chalk it up to paranoia, but I've been around newsrooms long enough to know what's going on. I suspect some of them may be getting shit from friends at the other stations, who see this as one big headline-grabbing promotion. A stunt."

"What about the woman? The one who called?"

"Hard to say. She sounded legitimate, but what can you tell over the telephone? And even if she is for real, it may not help us actually find the boys. She claims to know who took them, but indicated she may not know where they are now."

"So what are you going to do?"

He told her what he had suggested to the woman. "She's thinking about it, so all I can do is wait."

At that moment, Jeff the waiter arrived with their meals . . . and with a message. "You're wanted on the phone, Mr. Collier," he said with a nod toward the front of the restaurant. "I told the person that you're about to eat, but he said it was quite urgent."

Alex gave Pat a puzzled look. "Did you tell anyone we'd be here?" he asked.

She shook her head. "No, no one."

"Neither did I." He had left the station without saying anything to anyone about his plans, but perhaps someone had spotted him going into the restaurant. Still, it was strange.

"If you like, I can keep your dinner warm in the kitchen," the waiter offered.

"Thanks," Alex said, with another perplexed glance at Pat.

Halfway to the phone, he was momentarily tempted to turn back. If he didn't take after-hour calls at the station, why in hell should he here? But curiosity got the better of him, and he moved on to the phone. "Yes," he said.

"Is this Collier?" The voice sounded muffled, distant.

"Yes. Who's this?"

"Never mind. Didn't you get my note?"

Alex froze for a moment. Not in fear, but in surprise. It was the last thing he had expected to hear. "What note is that?" he asked calmly, when he'd recovered.

"I think you know," said the man. "Don't play fucking games with me."

The voice was gruffer now, closer. Alex looked around. No one was paying any attention to him, not even Pat, who was deep into her salad. Whoever it was must have followed him here, watched them be seated. He couldn't be that far away.

"What's your problem, buddy?" he asked, trying to sound unruffled.

"You're the one with the problem," the voice said. "Unless you forget about the Hathaway kids."

"You know something about them?"

"Keep your nose out of it, I'm telling you."

Alex laughed into the phone. "Fuck you and your hayseed relatives, too," he said.

"Okay, asshole. You've been warned. Twice. There won't be a third time."

Alex was about to tell his caller he was beginning to sound like a B-movie when the man suddenly hung up.

Alex quickly asked the maître d', standing nearby,

where the closest pay phone was. "Outside the restaurant and down the hall," she said, pointing. "But please, you're free to use this one again."

He thanked her, then hurried out of the restaurant and turned in the direction she had pointed. The pay phone was there, maybe a hundred feet away, but there was no sign of any man.

"What was that all about?" Pat asked once he was back at the table.

"Some little crisis at the station," he lied. "No big problem."

"I thought no one knew you were here," she said.

He shrugged. "I guess I was wrong."

He knew he should tell her the truth, but decided to delay it. Why spoil a nice dinner? But he couldn't wait for long. If this threat was for real, as he now suspected it might be, she would have to know. They spent too much time together for her to be left in the dark. And in possible danger.

For now, however, he was going to enjoy his warmed-over salmon and the rest of the wine.

It wasn't until he was filling their glasses that he noticed the slight tremor in his hand.

17

When the last of the wine was gone, and after they'd finished their coffee and were ready to leave, Alex decided he could wait no longer to tell Pat the truth about the phone call.

Her eyes widened in surprise. "You're serious, aren't you?" she said.

"It may be nothing," he said, "but the guy apparently followed me here . . . and may have seen us together."

He was especially concerned because she had driven her own car downtown to meet him and planned to drive home alone. "I'll walk you to your car and then follow you home," he said. "Make sure no one is following us."

"What about you?" she asked. "If he followed you tonight, he probably has before. And knows where you live."

"Maybe so. I'll just have to keep my eyes open."

"Stay with me," she suggested. "For tonight, anyway."

He was tempted, but quickly decided against it. For one thing, Seuss would go crazy, but more important, if the caller was hanging around his house, he didn't want to show any sign of fear or weakness. That could only make things worse.

"You're worried about the cat?" she said when he told her.

"I didn't put out any extra food for him," he said, "and you know how he gets. He'll tear the goddamned house apart."

But she knew it was more than that. Years before, the first Seuss, the cat he had brought with him from California, had been tormented and killed as a warning to him during his investigation of the judge. And despite his love-hate relationship with *this* cat, she knew he wasn't about to risk that happening again.

"Bring Seuss to my place in the morning," she said. "I've got a better security system than you do, and I'll see that he gets fed."

After a mild protest, he agreed—relieved to be free of at least that small worry.

They reached the parking ramp with no problem and without catching sight of anyone who looked the slightest bit suspicious. They had agreed that Pat would take a carefully planned, circuitous route home, involving a number of twists, turns, and stops. He would stay close behind, making certain no other cars were following.

They arrived at her town house in suburban Bloomington without incident, and Alex escorted her inside—carefully checking the garage and all of the rooms. It was possible, he told her, that the caller also knew who she was and where she lived. He urged her to keep a wary eye and take no chances.

"I'll be fine," she said. "It's you I'm worried about."

"Don't be," he replied. "Because I'm not."

Which was true. While certainly no macho man,

Alex had managed to stay in good physical shape over the years, working out fairly regularly and having learned enough karate years before to give him a level of comfort should the need to use it ever arise. So far it hadn't, and he didn't expect that it would.

"Maybe you should call Malay," she said.

"Tonight?"

"Is he still at the motel?"

"I don't know, but even if I did, I wouldn't bother him this late. Not for something like this."

"Maybe you should. I think he'd want to know."

Alex was standing by the door, ready to leave, when she added, "And forget what I said at dinner. About doubting that you might be on to something here. These aren't idle threats. Somebody's scared."

As Alex approached his house, he circled the block twice, checking for any parked cars that he didn't recognize or that appeared suspicious. Seeing none, and already feeling a little foolish, he drove through the alley behind his house and back again, pausing each time by the back of his garage. Stepping out of the car, looking and listening.

It was well past midnight and most of the neighboring homes were dark, with no sign of movement anywhere. No late-night strollers, no late-night parties. Not in this buttoned-up part of town.

He pulled around to the front of the house and into the driveway, hitting a switch on the visor that opened the garage door and triggered a yard light. Again he paused, letting the car idle as his eyes swept the backyard and pool area, as far as the light reached. Again, nothing stirred or seemed out of place.

Relaxing, he drove into the garage and lowered the

door behind him. Then, as a final precaution, he grabbed a flashlight from the workbench and quietly circled the house, checking the doors and windows and behind the shrubs and hedges. But as he turned the corner to the front yard, he was suddenly bathed in light himself. Momentarily blinded, he quickly turned away and ducked behind a corner of the house.

"Mr. Collier?" The voice was no more than twenty feet away. "Is that you, sir?"

"*Sir?*" Alex stepped around the corner. A white Minneapolis squad car was sitting by the curb, its spotlight now deflected, no longer directly in his eyes. A young cop was casually leaning on a fender.

"Yeah, it's me," he answered, leaving the shelter of the house and approaching the car. "What brings you around?"

"Dispatch got a call from Tony Malay. Said you might be having a problem."

Pat must have found him after all, he thought. He felt even more foolish now.

The cop was young, maybe in his late twenties. His partner was still in the car, hand on the spotlight, half-hidden in the shadows. "No problem," Alex said. "I've checked all around the house."

"Tony said you got a threat of some kind. That right?"

Alex was now standing next to him. "Yeah, but it must have been a hoax. I was just being a little cautious."

"Don't blame you," the cop said. "Have you been inside yet?"

"No, but I checked the doors and windows. Everything's locked up tight."

"Why don't I go in with you," he suggested. "Just to make sure."

Alex was too tired to argue, and led the way to the front door. As he expected, Seuss was waiting on the banister, but quickly scurried away and hid when he saw that someone was with Alex.

"Quite a watchdog," the cop said with a grin.

They walked through the house, turning on lights as they went, checking both upstairs and the basement. Finding nothing. "Sorry to be a bother," Alex said as the officer prepared to leave. "Tony shouldn't have called you."

"No sweat. That's what we're here for. Besides, things can get pretty dull this time of night."

Alex watched from the window as the officer got back into the squad car and drove off. It wasn't a minute later that the phone rang. Must be Malay or Pat, he thought.

It wasn't.

"Had to call the cops, huh? You chickenshit bastard."

Alex quickly doused the lamp by the phone and sank to the floor behind a chair, the phone pressed against his ear. The creep had to be close by, on a cell phone.

"Speak up, asshole," the caller said. "Or has your cat got your tongue?" Then he laughed.

Alex decided to remain quiet. Seuss had left his hiding place and was trying to paw his face, chattering at him. Hungry. Alex pushed him away.

"You dropped off that cunt, huh? A nice piece of ass, but a little on the old side, I'd say. Pat, right?"

Alex closed his eyes. So he did know.

"You don't want to talk, huh? Well, that's okay. I understand. Have a nice night . . . and sleep tight."

The line went dead. Alex waited a few moments,

then—feeling like a wimp—he crept to the front window and peered into the darkness. Again, he saw nothing. *Where the hell was he?* Maybe the guy had driven by the cop car and was long gone by now.

He stood and pulled the drapes, then went from window to window, shutting the blinds. He debated calling Pat, but decided she would probably be asleep by now . . . and was safe enough for the night.

He quickly fed Seuss . . . then headed for the bedroom, hoping sleep would come to him, as well.

Pat was still in her nightgown and robe when Alex showed up at her door before nine the next morning, lugging a cat carrier with Seuss bawling and clawing inside. "C'mon in," she said, giving him a quick hug before reaching down to free Seuss from his portable prison. "Poor thing."

With a sharp hiss, the cat leaped out of the cage and disappeared into one of the bedrooms.

"He's claustrophobic," Alex said, watching him go. "I have to chase him all over the house every time he sees that thing. And then he scratched the hell out of my hand getting him in."

Pat laughed. "He'll be fine," she said, "and you'll be fine, too," taking his wounded hand in hers and quickly examining it.

"Is the coffee on?" he asked.

"Of course, but have you had breakfast? I was just fixing some toast."

"Just some coffee, thanks."

While married, Pat and her late husband had lived in a large and lavish ranch-style home in Edina, but less than a year after his death she'd sold the house and moved into this smaller, but no less elegant town home in a newly developed section of West Bloomington. It was one step in her not entirely successful effort to shed the past and put the unhappy memories behind her.

She led the way into the kitchen, which was large and bright, all white and bathed in the morning sun, and proceeded to pour them each a cup of coffee. "So?" she asked when they were seated at the counter.

"So you found Malay last night," he said.

"I'm sorry, but I was worried. And he was still at the motel. I thought he could do something."

"He did. I found a squad car sitting outside my house."

"And?"

Alex went on to explain everything that had happened. "The guy had to be watching the house. And he knows your name. At least, your first name. Which might mean that he knows where you live, too."

In case he was wrong, Alex had been overly cautious again that morning, his eyes never leaving the rearview mirror for long.

If Pat felt fear, she didn't show it. "What else did he say?"

"About you? You really want to know?"

"Sure."

He grinned. "That you look like a nice piece of ass."

"*What?*" Somewhere between a squeal and a scream.

"That's true. And I had to agree with him, of course." She feigned throwing a punch. "You did not!"

"You're right. I didn't say anything. I just let him babble on. But he does sound like a mean bastard . . . and it seems clear now that he means business. This is no joke or hoax."

"So what are you going to do?" she asked.

"You mean, what are *we* going to do."

"Okay."

"We're going to be very vigilant, you and I. Watch our every move. Don't take chances. You've got a great security system here, but when you're away, try never to be alone. Stay out of parking ramps or anyplace else where there aren't other people around. Keep looking over your shoulder . . . and keep your car doors locked."

"I always do," she said.

"And it's probably best to stay away from my place."

"Really?"

"Unless you're with me. Okay?"

"All right."

With that, he took a final sip of his coffee and got up to leave.

"Are you sure you don't want something to eat?"

"Positive. I need to get to work in case that woman calls back."

She walked him to the door, holding his hand tightly. "Why don't you stay here tonight?" she said. "I'd feel better."

"You're sure?"

"I'm sure."

When he arrived at the station, Alex wasted no time finding Barclay and quickly reporting what had happened the night before. "There has to be something to it," he said. "Nobody would go to this kind of trouble to put a scare into me if he's not genuinely worried about what we're doing."

Barclay was at his desk, in his shirtsleeves, sweating. The station's air-conditioning had quit during the night. "Maybe so," he replied, "but let's forget that for a moment. Let's talk about how we're going to keep you safe."

Alex shrugged. "I'm not worried about it. Honestly. I'll keep my eyes open, but I can take of myself." He went on to explain the precautions that Pat was also taking. "I'll probably stay at her place for a couple of nights . . . or until her neighbors start gossiping."

Barclay was fanning himself with a legal pad. "Damn, it's hot! They said they'd have the air back on by now."

Alex hadn't even noticed the heat, but he wasn't going to argue the issue. "You should also know that Hawke is pushing me hard to keep this story front-and-center, no matter what."

Barclay put the makeshift fan aside. "What do you mean?"

Alex told him of the confrontation the night before.

"Jerk," Barclay said. "If he tries that again, tell him to come talk to me. But he does have a point, Alex: We shouldn't let the story fade away. We should work hard to keep it alive. Legitimately, I mean. No gilding the lily."

At that moment Barclay's assistant, Teresa Jensen, appeared at the office door. "Sorry to interrupt," she said, "but the desk says you have a call, Alex. They said you wanted to be told about any call."

"That's right, thanks." He hurried out of the office and back to his cubicle.

"This is Collier," he said once he got to the phone.

"I've thought about your offer." It was the same woman, the same husky, sexy voice.

"And?"

"There's a lawyer, Barney McSwain. He has an office on Lake Street, just off Hennepin. Catty-corner from Calhoun Square."

Alex was jotting the information down. "Okay."

"We know each other, and I trust him."

"But I don't know him," Alex said.

"Then you'll have to check him out. He's legitimate, I'm telling you."

"Okay," he said again.

"I've told him the essence of our deal. That I have information that you're willing to pay for. He's agreed to serve as a go-between. He'll hold the reward money until you're satisfied the information is genuine, then turn it over to me."

"What information, exactly?"

"Who took the boys and why."

"Not where they are today?"

"I told you, I don't know that."

Alex paused, thinking. "That would be worth ten thousand, if it's true."

"Fifteen," she said.

"Twelve-five, that's it."

"Deal. Talk to McSwain. He'll set it up."

Then she hung up.

Alex immediately reached for the phone book, flipping through the pages until he reached the listing for Barney McSwain, attorney. He quickly punched in the number.

"Law office." A female voice.

"Mr. McSwain, please," Alex said.

"I'm sorry, he's not here at the moment. May I take a message?"

"Please." He quickly gave her his name and number. "And tell him it's important."

"May I tell him what this concerns?"

"He'll know," Alex replied, becoming impatient.

"I'll give him the message," she said.

By the time Maggie showed up a couple of hours

later, he had gotten a call back from a friend at the county Bar Association, whom he had asked to check on McSwain's record and reputation. "He has a small practice," Alex was told. "Mainly family law, divorces, custody cases, that kind of thing. He's never been in any kind of trouble, from what I can learn."

McSwain himself, however, had not yet returned Alex's call.

Maggie, when told of the threatening phone calls to Alex, did not seem surprised. "When I saw that note, I figured it wasn't some kind of crank. Remember? I told you to be careful."

He remembered.

"So what are you going to do?" she asked.

He shrugged. "What can I do? Watch my step, I guess. Stay out of sight as much as possible. Keep my eyes open."

Maggie knew the feeling. She had gone into virtual seclusion the year before, when she herself had been the recipient of numerous threats. It had not been a pleasant experience. In fact, it had been downright harrowing.

Alex told her Barclay had already ordered beefed-up security at the station, adding another guard at each of the entrances—with orders to allow no one past without the proper credentials. He had also asked the staff, without telling them why, to stay alert for any strangers in the building.

"How about you?" he asked Maggie. "You've had no calls, have you?"

"No, nothing. But I suppose I could be a little more vigilant myself."

"Wouldn't hurt," he replied.

She went on to tell him that she still had had no success in learning the whereabouts of the Whelans, explaining that she had even used the on-line services, which find people through various private and public data sources. "There's not a trace of them anywhere. Nowhere. I've even called every other Whelan in the local phone books, you know, in hopes of finding some relative. But none of them seems to know anything about this particular couple. They must have changed their names, or moved to China," she said.

"That reminds me of something," he said, checking his Rolodex and punching in the library number of Dorothy Holcomb. She answered on the second ring. "Alex Collier again, Mrs. Holcomb. Sorry to be a bother."

"No bother," she said.

"Last time we talked, you said that you and the Whelan couple went to the same church. Am I right?"

"That's right," she replied without hesitation. "First Lutheran, on Edgewater Street. It's only a few blocks from our house."

He took down the information. "Do you still go there?"

"Why, yes. Not as often as we should, but . . ."

"Is the pastor the same one who was there fifteen years ago?"

"Yes," she replied. "He's been there for more years than we have. But he's about ready to retire. Pastor John Hankins is his name."

"Thanks so much. I appreciate it."

"You haven't found them yet? The Whelans?"

"Not yet, but I'm hoping the pastor may be able to help."

"I hope so, but you should know he's not as . . . uh . . . sharp as he once was."

After Alex got off the phone, Maggie glanced at the

note he had made. "I bet you'd like me to talk to the good pastor."

"Would you? Maybe you can jog his memory. If he still has one."

Shortly before the early news, Alex received two calls: The first was from the lawyer, McSwain, who agreed to meet the following morning at his office. The second was from the *Star Tribune* television columnist, a fellow named Jason Liggett, who was new on the job, and someone Alex had yet to meet.

"I'm trying to check out some rumors," Liggett said.

Alex had a sinking feeling. "You're actually checking them out this time?" he said caustically. "What a surprise."

Liggett ignored the jab. "My sources tell me they're taking you off the late news in a few months. Is that right?"

Alex took a deep breath. *Who the hell is talking?* "Really? And just who might your sources be?" he asked, playing for time.

"You know I can't tell you that. But I do trust them."

"That means you've got more than one?"

"C'mon, Mr. Collier. True or false?"

"You'd better talk to George Barclay."

"Then you're not denying it?"

"I'm not commenting on rumors. Period. Talk to Barclay."

As he hung up, he thought: George, forget the air-conditioning. You've just begun to sweat.

18

Barney McSwain's office was up two flights of well-worn stairs in an old brick building that housed a discount clothing store——Terwillingers——on the first floor street level. When Alex could find no elevator, he grudgingly took the stairs——surprised to discover he was breathing hard by the time he got to the third floor. Maybe, he decided, he wasn't in as good shape as he thought he was.

The interior of the building was more impressive than the run-down exterior. While old, it obviously had been recently remodeled. The hallway at the top of the steps was brightly lighted, the floor a polished marble, the walls covered by lustrous oak paneling. Alex passed by several other offices, including those of an accountant and a dentist, before finally reaching McSwain's at the end of the hall. A small sign in bronzed lettering next to the door said simply: BARNEY MCSWAIN, ATTORNEY AT LAW.

Alex didn't know whether to knock or walk right in, so he compromised by giving the door a quick rap, then opening it. He stepped into a tiny anteroom, containing a small desk and chair and two side chairs, none of them occupied. If there was a secretary, she was gone, and the desk was bare, except for a telephone. Maybe he uses a secretarial service, Alex thought, remembering the woman who had answered his call the day before.

Two paintings hung on opposite walls, one a Matisse print, he guessed, the other a Cezanne, maybe. He liked art, especially French Impressionists, but was no expert. Aside from the two prints, there was no other decor. The only other hint of habitation was the faint odor of cigar smoke.

He wasn't quite sure what to do. Another door apparently led to an interior office, but it was also closed . . . with no sign of light or movement behind it. Had McSwain forgotten the appointment? Hesitantly he walked to the door and again rapped lightly. "Anybody home?" he called out.

He heard what sounded like the scraping of chair legs on the floor, and a moment later the door opened. The man facing him had to be in his late sixties or early seventies, slight of build and bald except for a few strands of white hair combed back over his pate. Like the loose-fitting suit he wore, his sallow skin sagged—as though he had lost a lot of weight lately, maybe from an illness. He certainly didn't look healthy.

"Sorry," McSwain said, opening the door wider. "I must have dozed off in my chair. Forgot the time. Happens more and more often, it seems."

Alex introduced himself as he was ushered inside. "I appreciate your making the time," he said.

The old man's laugh was more of a gurgle. "Hell, you're the first person I've seen all morning. As you can see, I'm not exactly overrun with clients."

Alex settled into a chair across the desk from McSwain. This office, like the anteroom, was small and sparsely decorated. There was a sofa along one wall, with a large painting he couldn't identify hanging above it, and a head-high bookcase that ran the length of the other wall—filled from top to bottom with rows of law books. On the top of the credenza behind the desk were framed but faded photos of McSwain posing with three former presidents: Truman, Kennedy, and Carter. Not a Republican among them.

"Have you officed here long?" he asked, making conversation.

"Ten, twelve years, I guess," McSwain replied. "Ever since I left the Mullen-McCaron law firm downtown. Since they pushed me out, I should say. Thought I was too damn old." He paused, looking around him. "Business was pretty good here for a while, but it's dropped off year by year." Then he laughed again. "Coincides with my old clients dropping off, if you know what I mean."

Alex smiled. The old guy had a sense of humor, at least.

"You know why I'm here, I take it," he said.

"Yes, although I'm still a little puzzled by it all."

"It's fairly simple," Alex said. "Your client, whoever she is, says she has information that we need . . . that we're willing to pay for."

"She told me that much," McSwain interjected. "And I saw the story on your news."

"Okay. Then you know what we're after. But we won't know if her information is legitimate until we have time to check it out. We're prepared to give you a check for twelve thousand, five hundred dollars, made out to you, to hold in escrow for her until then. You'll have to work out your fee with her."

The old man was now sitting up straight in his chair. "And if you determine the information *isn't* legitimate?"

"Then you return the check to us," Alex replied.

McSwain picked up the stub of a cigar out of an ash-tray and began to chew on it, without lighting up.

"How long have you known this lady?" Alex asked.

"Long enough to trust her," McSwain said. "I wouldn't be doing this if I didn't."

"Long enough to know if she really does have what we're looking for?"

"No," McSwain said quickly. "I know nothing about the missing boys . . . or how she might have come to know about them. She's been quite secretive, even with me. She says she'll give me the information in a sealed envelope to deliver to you . . . and will expect to receive the check in the same manner."

Alex leaned forward. "Anything else you can tell me about her?"

"Not without violating the trust."

"The first time we spoke on the phone," Alex said, "she seemed frightened. Said we were dealing with dangerous people."

"She's told me the same thing," he replied. "Made me a little nervous, actually. But hell, I'm too old to worry about things like that."

"When do you expect her to deliver the information?"

McSwain shrugged. "In a couple of days, once I have the money."

Alex reached into his pocket and pulled out a check. "I'll need a receipt," he said.

At about the same time Alex was leaving McSwain's office, Maggie was arriving at the First Lutheran Church in northeast Minneapolis . . . a relatively small but beautifully constructed structure of stone and stained glass that—according to the faded cornerstone—dated back to the turn of the century.

She found the Reverend John Hankins in his office, just down the hall from the church narthex. He was alone, sitting at his cluttered desk, reading. Maggie couldn't see what. He was wearing a light blue short-sleeved shirt, a clerical collar ringing his neck. With his full head of pure white hair, pink cheeks, and—as she was about to see—warm and easy smile, he could have been anybody's favorite grandpa.

"Excuse me," she said from the doorway.

His head bobbed up. "Yes?" Then, recognizing her, "Oh yes, Ms. Lawrence, please come in."

He stood, smiling, to shake her hand.

"It's Maggie, if you don't mind," she said. "And thanks for seeing me."

"A pleasure meeting you in person," he replied. "As I told you on the phone, I've been a distant admirer of yours since you came to town."

At the outset, at least, she could detect no sign of the dementia that Mrs. Holcomb had hinted at. He probably has his good days and bad, she thought, but now, at least, he appeared fully alert; his eyes a bright blue and unblinking, his bearing steady and ramrod straight, and his voice deep and resonant, from years of preaching on the pulpit, she guessed.

They spent several minutes chatting, getting acquainted. He asked about her family and seemed surprised—but not shocked—to learn that she was unmarried with a young son. "His father left us when Danny was a baby, only a couple of months old," she told him, "and never came back. But we get along fine . . . and have made a new home for ourselves here."

When he didn't press the matter further, she quickly

moved the conversation on to other things. "You have a beautiful church," she said. "I peeked inside the sanctuary on my way in. It's gorgeous."

"Thank you. We take great pride in it, although it's harder and harder to maintain. The neighborhood has changed over the years, you know, with the white flight to the suburbs and all. Gotten a lot poorer. And our congregation has dwindled in size. We're barely able to make ends meet these days."

"Sorry to hear that," she replied, catching a flicker of sadness in his eyes.

"It's gotten to be too much for me, trying to keep it going at my age. It's time for someone younger, with new ideas and the energy to turn things around."

"I'd heard that you were thinking of retiring," she said.

"By the end of the year, I hope."

Earlier, in a phone call arranging the visit, Maggie had been deliberately vague about her mission, saying only that she was seeking information about two former parishioners, the Whelans. Hankins seemed eager to help but also reluctant, worried about a possible breach of confidence. However, she'd finally been able to convince him that anything he told her would itself be held in strict confidence and would never be made public.

But now, as they sat across from each other, he still seemed uncertain. "I do remember the Whelans," he said. "Very well, in fact. But I'm still not sure I understand what this is all about."

"Have you watched our news lately?" she asked.

He smiled. "When I manage to stay awake that late, yes."

"Then you might have seen Alex Collier's report on the missing boys. The Hathaway brothers?"

"I did, as a matter of fact. As you know, they lived in this neighborhood. And while I never knew the family, I remember the case vividly. Terrible tragedy."

Maggie took a deep breath. "The Whelans were neighbors of the Hathaways. They moved away soon after the boys vanished. Within a few weeks, actually. We'd like to talk to them, but they seem to have disappeared, too."

She went on to describe the efforts she had made to locate the couple. "We haven't been able to find anyone who knew them very well, or who knows where they may have gone."

The pastor sank back in his chair. "You think they may have had a part in the boys' disappearance?"

She shrugged. "Probably not, but we're trying to follow every possible lead. If nothing else, they may remember something about the case that no one else does. But we have to find them first."

"I can't help you there, I'm afraid. I have no idea where they are today."

"Then what can you tell me?" she asked. "It could be important."

"This is where it gets sticky," he said. "I'm not sure what I'm ethically free to reveal."

"It's been fifteen years, Pastor. What could it possibly hurt now?"

He rested his chin on his intertwined fingers. "I suppose you're right. Still . . ."

Maggie scooted her chair closer to the desk. "We've talked to another member of your congregation," she said, "a woman who was also a neighbor of the Whelans. She didn't know them well, but said they seemed a little reclusive."

"That was being charitable, I'd say."

"What do you mean?"

Hankin glanced at the door. "You're sure this will go no further?"

"Positive."

He got up and looked out into the hallway, then shut the door behind him before returning to his desk and asking, "Do you go to church, Maggie?"

The question came out of the blue and momentarily took her aback. "Uhhh, not as much as I should, I guess, but I have had my son baptized, and I do try to get him to Sunday school when I can. But I wouldn't say we're real regulars."

"Uh-huh."

"Why do you ask?"

"When you've been in this business as long as I have," he said, "you meet all kinds of folks. Most are just plain normal . . . nice, like you and your boy, I suspect. Maybe not as dedicated as we'd like, or as God-fearing, but good, decent people who are trying to live respectable lives and raise their kids right. I'm sure you've met people like that at your church."

Maggie nodded, not sure where this was leading, but reluctant to interrupt.

"On the other hand, as a preacher, you also meet people who are very troubled. For one reason or another. By their marriages, their jobs, their kids, or something in their past. Whatever. The Whalens were like that."

"Like what?" she asked.

"Troubled. They were really quite strange. Quite unlike any other younger couple I had met by then."

"Strange how?"

He held up his hand, urging patience. "Angry. About almost everything. Their marriage, their apparent infertility, the state of the world, everything, really."

"I take it you counseled them," Maggie said.

"Yes, over several months. They came to me looking for answers, I think, maybe easy answers, or in search of some kind of inner peace. But hard as I tried, I couldn't provide it to them, or else they weren't ready to listen. Then suddenly they were gone, without so much as a good-bye."

"You said they were angry. How angry?"

The pastor shook his head. "'Angry' may have been too strong a word. 'Disturbed' may be better. The woman, Mrs. Whelan, apparently came from a wealthy but broken family, with a dominating father. They were trying to make it on their own, but felt like victims, I think. That God, or society, or somebody, had not dealt them a fair hand. They talked about their dead-end jobs, their lack of friends, and how they desperately wanted kids, but couldn't have them."

She leaned forward. "Really?"

"Yes. I gave them referrals to all kinds of agencies I thought might help, but I'm not sure they ever went."

"Adoption agencies?"

"Yes, those, too."

"And you've never heard from them again?"

"No, never, but I've thought of them often, wondering what ever became of them. I felt it was my first real failure as a pastor, you know, and I've often pondered what I could have done differently. Or better."

Maggie had one last question. "This may strike you as strange, but were the Whelans the type of people who could have been drawn into some kind of a cult? Looking for those answers you were talking about?"

"Interesting thought," he said. And then, "Let's just say, I wouldn't be totally shocked to hear it."

*   *   *

When Alex returned to the station, he found a note on his desk from Barclay, asking to see him right away. Alex had a pretty good idea what he wanted, a suspicion confirmed when he found his boss alone in his office, looking peeved. "I take it you talked to Liggett from the *Star Tribune*," Barclay said.

"Yeah, last night. I told him to call you."

"He did. This morning."

"What did you tell him?"

Barclay got out of his chair and walked to the window, his back to Alex. "Forget that for a minute. I'd like to know how he found out."

"Damned if I know. I was going to ask you the same thing. I haven't said anything to anyone. Except for Pat, of course. And Maggie."

Barclay turned back to face him. "I haven't either, goddamn it!"

"Maybe it was our friend, Mr. Hawke," Alex said. "He's got loose lips, and I wouldn't put it past him."

Barclay shook his head. "I don't think so, not this time. He's got nothing to gain by it."

"Except to embarrass me. We're not exactly best buddies, you know."

Before Barclay could reply, Alex spotted a stack of videotapes on the corner of his desk. "Are those audition tapes?" he asked, pointing to the pile.

"A few of them, yeah," Barclay replied.

"Then maybe somebody in the mail room is talking," Alex suggested.

"I've thought about that, but they wouldn't know about the timetable."

Alex could only shrug. "So what did you tell him?"

Barclay settled into his chair. "I tried to fog it out.

Lied to him, as a matter of fact. Told him no decision had been made . . . that you had indicated you might want evenings off."

"Did he buy it?"

"Who knows? I asked him to hold off writing anything until we'd made a final decision, but I don't know if he will."

"Ten to one he won't," Alex said.

Maggie arrived back at the station a short while later, and quickly relayed to Alex what the good pastor had told her. "I'm not sure what it means, if anything," she said. "But at least we know now that our mystery couple was not exactly at peace with the world or themselves."

Alex was more skeptical. "I don't know, Maggie. There have to be lots of young couples like that. Troubled. Struggling. Half of them get divorced, for Christ's sake."

"But not all of them lived in the Hathaway's old neighborhood," she argued, "and not all of them are so troubled that they stick in a minister's mind for all of these years."

"Maybe you're right," he admitted. "But that doesn't bring us any closer to finding them, does it?"

The next morning Alex, still in his pajamas, picked the *Star Tribune* off his stoop and carried it inside the house, turning immediately to Jason Liggett's television column:

Although Channel Seven refuses to confirm it, sources tell us that Alex Collier will step down as co-anchor of the late news at the end of the year, but will remain on the two early-evening newscasts. Whether this move is voluntary or imposed remains a question, but it is known that news director George Barclay is reviewing audition tapes from would-be candidates for the late news slot.

For the record, Barclay says Collier has indicated he may want to curtail his schedule, but that no final decision has been made. As we've reported earlier, however, recent station research apparently has shown Collier losing his appeal among the younger viewers so prized by advertisers. Collier himself, who was recently given a contract extension by the station, had no comment on these latest reports.

But Liggett wasn't through yet, as Alex kept on reading.

Speaking of Collier and Channel Seven, competitors are said to be gleeful over the apparent failure of Collier's much-heralded "investigation" into the case of the missing Hathaway boys. Despite the heavy promotion and a big reward, the competitors claim Collier is no closer to solving the puzzle of what happened to the young brothers fifteen years ago. Even others in the Channel Seven newsroom are said to be skeptical . . . some say "embarrassed" . . . by the hoopla surrounding the investigation, and its apparent failure to yield results.

"You dirty bastard," was all Alex could think of to say.

19

Still angry, Alex had just shaved and showered, and was standing in the bedroom, debating what to wear for the day, when the phone rang. He walked to the bedside table and picked up the receiver.

"Is this Collier?"

For a split second, he thought it might be the stalker again. But no. The voice was familiar but different. "Yes, it is. Who's this?"

"Barney McSwain."

McSwain? He hadn't expected a call this quickly. "Hey, Barney. Good to hear from you."

There was a pause at the other end. "I don't think so," he finally said.

Alex sat on the side of the unmade bed, pushing aside Seuss, who was back home for a day or two and had been curled up comfortably in the rumpled sheets. "What do you mean?"

"I hate to tell you this, Collier, but . . ."

"What? Is she backing out?"

There was another pause. "Worse, I'm afraid. She's dead."

Alex felt his breath leave him. "You're not serious?" he finally managed.

"I wish I weren't."

Alex tried to collect himself, but the room seemed to whirl around him. "How? When?"

"Last night. Early this morning, actually. About two o'clock, the cops think."

"The cops?"

"Yeah. She was found hanging from the shower rod in her bathroom. Her son discovered the body when he stopped by her apartment this morning. He called the police, and then called me."

It took Alex a moment to absorb what he was hearing. "They think she committed suicide?" he asked.

"It's too early to tell, I guess. There was no sign of a struggle in the apartment, and the neighbors say they heard nothing strange during the night."

"Where are you now?"

"Still at the apartment. With her son."

"Have the cops left?"

"Yeah. And the medical examiner took the body for the autopsy."

"Could I meet you there?" Alex asked.

"I guess so, sure. Can't see the harm now. And I'll be here for a while."

"I'd like to talk to the son, too. If he's willing."

"I'll ask him," McSwain replied, and gave him an address on Penn Avenue, just beyond the Crosstown Highway.

It was not until Alex had hung up and hurriedly began to dress that he realized he did not even know the dead woman's name. But he could not forget her voice, or her possibly prophetic words: "I'm taking a chance even calling you. You're not dealing with nice people here."

Despite his rush to leave, Alex took time to make two quick calls: one to Phil Tinsley, a Minneapolis homicide detective he had come to know during his investigation of the judge, and the second to Tony Malay. Neither answered, so he left his cell phone number for both. He wanted somebody on the inside to get the results of the woman's autopsy as quickly as possible.

It took him no more than twenty minutes to get to the apartment building, a three-story brick structure that housed four apartments on each floor. Similar buildings, neither fancy nor run-down, lined both sides of Penn Avenue. Moderate-income housing, he guessed, probably occupied by people who wanted the convenience of living close to the freeway, the airport, and the giant Mall of America.

At first glance, there was no sign that anything untoward had happened there: no police cars, no crime scene tape, no gathering of the curious outside. In fact, the front door to the building had been left ajar, blocked open, perhaps by one of the cops or the medical examiner's people leaving with the body.

Alex walked in and went directly to Apartment 103, in the rear on the first floor. The hallway carpeting was well worn and smelled musty, made worse by stale cigarette smoke and the odor of cooked food. Fried bacon, he thought.

Barney McSwain answered his first knock. "C'mon in," he said, stepping aside as he opened the door. He seemed at a loss for anything else to say.

"Thanks," Alex said with a nod, his eyes quickly sweeping the living room, where he now stood. It was small, and furnished with a sofa, two overstuffed chairs, a rocker, an ottoman, and a large console TV set . . . more furniture than the room could really handle. It seemed to close in around him.

A small galley kitchen and eating area were off to the

right, a wall separating them from a hallway that he assumed led to the bath and bedrooms. There was no sign of the woman's son.

"You know," he told McSwain, "it's strange, but I don't even know her name."

"It's Stockworth," McSwain replied. "Marie Stockworth." Then, pointing to a photo atop the TV, he said, "That's her there in the picture."

Until now, the gold-framed eight-by-ten photo had escaped Alex's eye. He walked over to pick it up, then moved to a window for better light. The picture was carefully posed, no doubt in a photographer's studio, with the woman sitting properly erect next to a young man who must be her son. Alex guessed that she was about his own age or slightly older, dark-haired, with dark eyes, thin lips, and an angular face—which was pretty enough, but a bit too long and narrow to be strikingly attractive. A somber face, he thought, despite her obvious attempt at a half smile for the sake of the photographer.

He put the picture back in place and settled into one of the chairs while McSwain took the other. "Tell me about her," he said.

McSwain leaned back and clasped his hands behind his head. "Fifty-six years old, divorced, worked for Citizens Bank downtown. An assistant branch manager, I believe. Started out as a teller years ago and worked her way up until she bumped into the glass ceiling."

"How long has she been divorced?"

"Thirteen, fourteen years, I'd guess, but I'm not sure. I didn't know her back then. She came to me five or six years ago, to make out a will. I handled some other stuff for her, and we became friends. Not that close, mind you, but friends."

"Is her ex-husband still around?"

McSwain shrugged. "Damned if I know. She never talked about him."

"And the son? That's him in the picture?"

"Uh-huh. Her only child. Sean. In his late twenties, I'd say. Works construction around town. I'd only met him a couple of times myself, but his mother apparently told him that if anything ever happened to her to get in touch with me. That's why I got the call this morning."

Alex glanced over his shoulder. "Is he still here?"

"He's in the back bedroom. On the phone. Making arrangements. He's pretty shook up, as you can imagine. Finding her like that."

"How *did* he find her?" Alex asked.

"In her nightgown. Hanging by a cord from her robe, which was on the floor at her feet. They think she may have climbed up on the edge of the bathtub and just stepped off. She wasn't that tall, and her feet barely touched the floor."

Alex was doubtful. He knew from past stories he had done on suicides that most people used a gun or overdosed on pills or a combination of booze and pills. Or drove their car into a garage and let it run, dying from the carbon monoxide. Hanging, he knew, was not a quick or easy or painless method. People usually choked to death slowly.

"Was there any sign that someone had forced their way in?" he asked.

"No. No damage to the door, no indication the windows had been tampered with. No sign that anyone else was here."

Alex was still unconvinced, but decided to move on to the crucial question. "Did she give you the material . . . you know, before she . . . ?"

"No. I never heard from her. Not after I told her that you'd given me the check. Sorry."

"What are you talking about?" The voice came from behind Alex, and he quickly pivoted in his chair. Sean was standing just a few feet away, hands in the pockets of his jeans.

"The deal your mother made with Alex here," McSwain said.

Alex got up and extended his hand. "I'm terribly sorry about your mother."

Sean returned the handshake. "Thanks. Barney said you'd be coming by."

He stood the same height as Alex, which made him about six-one. But that's where the comparison ended. Broad-shouldered with a slim waist and biceps the size of Alex's calves, Sean more than filled the Marlboro T-shirt that clung to his upper body. Alex had no trouble picturing him on the working end of a jackhammer or hoisting a wheelbarrow full of cement.

His face was well tanned and his blond hair cut short. The only sign of his grief were red-streaked eyes and a nose that apparently would not stop running. He carried a handkerchief in one hand, pressing it to his nose between sniffles.

"Are you going to be okay?" Alex asked sympathetically.

"I suppose so. But it was a hell of a shock, let me tell you." With a glance at McSwain, he added, "Thank God Barney's around to help." He walked across the room and flopped onto the sofa. "Just so you know, until Barney told me, I didn't know anything about your deal with my mother."

"She didn't mention it?" Alex asked.

"No, but I haven't seen or talked to her for a week or

so. It was just by chance that I stopped by this morning."

Alex sat back down in the chair. "I hate to ask this, but did you have any hint that your mother was contemplating suicide?"

"Hell, no!" he said sharply. "If I had, I would have gotten her some help. She may not have been the happiest woman in the world, but trust me, she sure as hell wasn't suicidal."

"Unhappy about what?"

"Her job, mainly. They kept screwing her over at the bank. Promoting guys that she helped train."

"He's right," McSwain said, cutting in. "She came to me a couple of years ago about possibly filing a discrimination suit. But nothing ever came of it."

Alex got out of his chair and sat down next to Sean on the sofa. "As Barney told you, your mother was going to provide us with information about the disappearance of the Hathaway brothers fifteen years ago. That material may still be around the apartment somewhere . . . and if you happen to find it, we'd be willing to pay you the same thing we were going to pay your mother."

"I'll look," Sean said, "but I'd have no idea where to begin."

Alex edged closer. "Do you know how your mother might have come by that information?"

"No, unless . . ." He paused, thinking. "Unless it came from my aunt. I was only a kid back then, but I remember she and my uncle lived in the same neighborhood as those boys."

"Your aunt?"

"Yeah, Aunt Emily."

"Emily what?" Alex pressed.

"Whelan. Emily Whelan."

Alex was stunned. Paralyzed for a moment. He shot a quick glance at McSwain, then back to Sean. There was no hiding his shock, and the two men read it easily. "What's the matter?" Sean asked, puzzled. "Do you know her?"

"No, not personally," Alex replied, trying to recover. "But the name's familiar."

Sean leaned forward. "How is that?"

He took his time responding, trying to decide how much to reveal. "We've been trying to locate her, that's all," he said. "Her and her husband."

"Well, she's actually my aunt by marriage, I guess. My dad and her husband, Larry Whelan, are half-brothers. Same mother, different fathers. It's kind of confusing, I know, but I've always known her as Aunt Emily and him as Uncle Larry."

Alex decided to take a shot. "You don't happen to know where they are right now, do you?"

Before Sean could answer, McSwain held up his hand. "Hold on a second. If I'm reading you right, you think the Whelans may be the source of the information that Sean's mother was going to pass on to you. Am I right?"

Give the old boy credit, Alex thought. He catches on quick. "Maybe," he said. "I just don't know."

"Then I think we should set some ground rules," McSwain said. "If Sean here can tell you where these Whelans are, and if they prove to be a key to solving this puzzle of yours, then I think Sean deserves the money."

Alex thought for a moment. "I have no problem with that," he replied.

McSwain looked at Sean. "You understand what's going on here?"

He nodded. "I think so, but I don't know what difference it makes. I don't know where they are."

Alex felt a sharp twinge of disappointment. "You don't?"

"No, I haven't seen them for years . . . not since about the time my father took off."

"And when was that?"

"When I was a sophomore in high school. That would be the fall of '83."

Alex swallowed hard. About the same time the Whelans moved. "And where's your dad now?"

Sean took on a look of disgust. "I don't know and I don't care. He's a jerk. He left my mom and me hanging out to dry. Said he'd had it with both of us. That he wanted a new life. Told my mother to go ahead and get a divorce, that he wouldn't contest it. He said he'd send support money for me, but he never did. Not a god-damned dime."

"Is your father's last name also Whelan?" Alex asked.

"No, I told you. He had a different father. His name's Spangler. Marvin Spangler. My mother took back her maiden name after the divorce, but I've kept Spangler, even though I truly hate the bastard."

Sean went on to say that his father was a musician, a saxophonist who played with several local bands. "I never saw that much of him, even when he was living at home. He was always gone, playing some gig some-where. Sometimes for days, even weeks. My mother thought he was into drugs, maybe even dealing them, toward the end."

"Had your mother seen him . . . recently, I mean?"

"Not that she ever told me," Sean said. "And I think she would have."

Alex sat back, considering what he had learned. It

would take time to sort out, but there certainly was more than mere coincidence at work here. The relationships and timing were too close. Sean's mother must have learned whatever she knew about the Hathaways either from the Whelans or perhaps from her ex-husband. But how much did she know and why did she wait so long to come forward? Was she afraid? Now, of course, he'd never know, at least not from her.

Alex could see that both Sean and McSwain were getting restless. "I don't want to take any more of your time," he said. "I know you've got a lot to do. But tell me this: Were your father and his half-brother close?"

"Yeah, real. In fact, I think that's where he was a lot of the time when he wasn't home. Staying with Larry and Emily."

"Did your mother get along with them?"

"The Whelans?"

"Yes."

"Not really. She thought they were losers. Fucked-up people. I know she tried to keep me away from them."

"Do you have pictures of them?" Alex asked. "The Whelans and your father?"

"Not of the Whelans, although maybe my mother did. But I doubt it. I do have some pictures of my dad at home."

"Could I see them some time?" Alex asked.

"Sure. But they'll be pretty old."

As Alex got up to leave, they agreed to stay in touch . . . and Sean promised—once he had the time—to search the apartment for any information that his mother may have been ready to turn over to Alex.

"I'd appreciate that," Alex said. "It could be important. And again, I'm terribly sorry about your mother. I wish I'd had the chance to know her."

McSwain walked Alex out to his Blazer. "So what do you think?" the lawyer asked.

"I think we should wait for the results of the autopsy," Alex said. "But I'd bet a week's pay that she's not a suicide. Whether the medical examiner can prove it or not is another question."

McSwain studied him. "Tell me why you're so sure."

Alex stopped and opened the car door. "First of all, from what I heard in there, she wasn't the suicide type. Unhappy, maybe, but not suicidal. But more important, why would she kill herself when she's on the verge of making thousands of dollars? If not for herself, for her son. It doesn't make sense."

"You think it has something to do with the missing kids?"

Alex shrugged, but then quickly told him about the threats he had gotten. "If the same guy who's been bugging me somehow found out that Marie was ready to supply information, then . . . who knows? I can only tell you that he sounds capable of it."

"If she *was* killed," McSwain said, "that kid in there is going to go crazy. This has been tough enough on him as it is."

"I'll let you know as soon as I know," Alex said as he put the Blazer into gear and drove off.

He was on the interstate, halfway back to the station, when his cell phone buzzed. It was Tony Malay. "I got your message, Alex. What's up?"

He quickly explained the situation. "The ME hauled the body away a couple of hours ago. They're going to do an autopsy, but I don't know when."

"I know the people over there," Malay said. "I'll check."

"We'll need the results as soon as possible."

"Don't worry. It shouldn't be a problem."

"One more thing. I also put a call in to Phil Tinsley. You know him, right?"

"Sure. He's a good cop."

"If this thing turns into a homicide," Alex said, "I'd like to know someone inside the department. I've worked with Phil before, and I trust him."

"Okay, but I thought your boss doesn't like you working with the cops."

That was true. Barclay was of the old school who distrusted the cops as much as the cops distrusted the media. Especially working hand-in-glove with them. "What happens if we have to investigate *them*," Barclay liked to say, "and we're sleeping together? We're fucked, that's what. They've got their job to do, and we've got ours."

Barclay had made an exception in the case of Malay, because he was retired, and Alex told Malay now that he was sure he would do the same for Tinsley—since they'd worked with him in the past. And then, "By the way, Chief, how are you coming on the river search?"

"Slowly," Malay said. "I warned you. It's going to take some time. This is not a high priority for the people I'm talking to. They're checking their records, but they're not breaking their ass doing it."

"Okay, but . . ." At that moment, as Alex was about to ring off, there was a loud *crack!* and the world around him exploded in a shower of glass.

20

Momentarily blinded by the shock of it, Alex screamed. He dropped the phone and his hands came up to protect his face. The Blazer swerved sharply to the right, out of control. A horn blared from behind him, and he frantically grabbed for the steering wheel, yanking it to the left, feeling the right tires lift, then slam back down on the pavement, hard.

My God, what's happening? Stop this thing! Instinctively he hit the brakes and immediately felt the Blazer begin to fishtail. *Wrong!* he shouted at himself. Ease up. His foot came off the brake pedal and the car began to recover, steadying itself, slowing.

The side window next to him had exploded, covering him with shards of glass. It had been so sudden, so frightening that he felt nothing but panic. The window was mostly gone, the wind was in his face, hot and stinging, and the glass was everywhere . . . in his lap, on the seat, on the dash, embedded in his skin.

What was it? A rock? A bullet? Where had it come from?

Cars were passing him on either side, a few drivers casting curious glances his way. A couple tried to shout at him while pointing at their faces. Alex knew then that he must be bleeding. With a quick glance over his shoulder, he began to move into the right lane, heading for an oncoming exit ramp.

He had a moment to think. If it had been a rock, it likely would have come from the front, maybe from one of the freeway overpasses. Not from the side. He'd been stupid. He'd been so intent on the phone conversation with Malay that he had neglected to watch the rearview mirror or the cars around him. If it was a bullet, he had no idea who might have fired it.

Still shaken, he took the exit and pulled off onto a side street, parking the Blazer in the first spot he could find. He tilted the mirror and looked at his face: The left side was cut in several places and bloodied. He tried to blot the blood with his handkerchief and then got out of the car to carefully brush the glass off his clothes and the car seats.

It was only then that he spotted the phone on the floor where he'd dropped it. He picked it up. "Chief? Are you still there?"

"Yes, I'm still here," he yelled. "What the hell's going on? What happened?"

"I'm not sure," Alex replied, trying to keep his voice calm. "The driver's side window just exploded. Or imploded. Something. Scared the hell out of me."

"Are you okay?"

"A few cuts on my face, but otherwise, yeah. Damn near cracked up the Blazer, though."

"Where are you now?" Malay asked.

Alex looked around him. "Off the Lake Street exit, I think. Near Honeywell, you know. But I'm all right now. I'm going home to clean up, then head back to the station."

"I want to see your car," Malay said.

"Be my guest. It'll be in the ramp, first floor."

"You're sure you're okay?"

"Yeah. Still a little shook up, but fine."

Despite a shower and some powder makeup applied at home, Maggie was quick to notice the scabs on Alex's face when he got to the station a few hours later. "You didn't get those shaving," she said, standing close, softly touching the wounds.

"You're right," he said, and hurriedly explained what had happened on the freeway. "I'm still not sure what it was, but Malay's going to look at the car and try to figure it out."

"Jesus, Alex . . ."

"I know, it's a little scary. But it was partly my fault. I wasn't watching what the hell I was doing."

As they stood talking, Barclay walked up, took one look at Alex's face, and also demanded an explanation. Alex repeated the story, but before there were more questions, he quickly moved on to the bizarre events of the morning: the death of Marie Stockworth, including his doubts that it was a suicide, and the surprise disclosure of her relationship to the Whelans. "Her ex-husband may be involved, too, but nobody seems to know where he is either. At least, his son doesn't."

"Want me to do a quick computer check?" Maggie asked.

"That would be great," Alex said, jotting down the name of Marvin Spangler. "He was a musician who must be in his early to mid-fifties by now. And who may have been into drugs. That's about all I know."

Maggie started away, but Alex called her back. "You may as well check on Marie Stockworth, too," he said, giving her the woman's address and where she had worked.

When Maggie was gone, Barclay pulled up a chair next to Alex. "I know you're deep into this," he said, "but remember, it's my job to make sure nobody gets hurt around here. I'm serious. No story is worth that, understand?"

"I understand," Alex said. "I just let my guard down, that's all. It won't happen again."

Barclay shook his head. "Those sound like famous last words to me," he said.

"Look, George. We've finally got something to go on. We can't quit now because somebody's trying to throw a scare into me."

"If that woman was murdered," Barclay said, interrupting him, "then we're talking about more than a scare. We're talking about desperate people capable of doing desperate things."

"Let's get the facts first," Alex said, playing for time. "Maybe it *was* a suicide."

"Okay, but I'm going to ask Malay if he'd be willing to move in with you for a while . . . and to keep an eye on you at all times. I'll give him a desk and put him on the payroll as a consultant. We have so many of those already that nobody will give it a second thought."

"C'mon, George. That's really not necessary."

"Why don't you let me decide that," Barclay said.

Malay showed up at Alex's desk an hour or so later. "You're a lucky guy, you know that?"

"What do you mean?"

"You got shot at, my boy." He held up a tiny slug. "I dug this out of your dash, just below the glove compartment. A .22 slug."

Alex took the piece of metal and examined it. "How come I didn't see it?"

"Made only a tiny hole," Malay said. "Took me a half

hour to find it myself. Must have missed your head by only six inches or so, if that."

Alex could only stare at the slug. He'd been knifed once a long time ago, sliced across the lower jaw by someone aiming at his neck, but he'd never been shot at before, and sure as hell didn't like the idea.

"Do you remember a truck passing you on the left?" Malay asked.

"No, I was talking on the phone to you. I don't remember anything."

"From where I found the bullet, it must have had a downward trajectory, as though it was fired from above you. Like from the cab of a truck."

Alex could only shake his head. He could be dead. "Look, let's keep this to ourselves for now. Barclay's already freaking out because of the woman, and this could push him over the edge."

"Okay, but you'd better tell the cops or somebody," Malay said. "This is a goddamned drive-by shooting. It should be reported."

"Let me think about it. Phil Tinsley has agreed to meet us later today. Maybe I'll mention it to him."

Malay went on to report that the autopsy of Marie Stockworth was scheduled for later that afternoon, and that one of his old buddies in the ME's office had promised to call him with the results.

"Good," Alex said. "That should tell us a lot."

When Barclay got back to his office, his secretary told him Hawke wanted to see him. Like immediately. "And he didn't sound too happy, George," she said with a sympathetic glance.

What now? Barclay wondered as he slowly made his way to the second floor, which to him was enemy territory, where all of the sales and management suits hung out. Whatever it was, it probably wasn't going to be pleasant.

Hawke's spacious and richly decorated office was situated in one corner of the building, the nearly floor-to-ceiling windows overlooking a downtown park with a wading pool and bubbling fountains. His desk was more the size of a conference table, oblong and made of solid ebony, big enough to dwarf him as he sat behind it. Leaving him looking like some kid playing grown-up in his dad's office.

The door was open so Barclay walked right in. "You wanted to see me?"

Hawke looked up, a scowl on his face. "Is it true what I read in the papers?" he barked out before Barclay could take a seat.

"About what?" he asked, still standing.

"That we're making no progress on the Hathaway case . . . that our competitors are laughing at us?"

Barclay sank, uninvited, into a chair across from Hawke's massive desk, suddenly reminded of the time in third grade when he'd been berated and held after school by Mrs. McNulty for pantsing one of his buddies. "I don't know what the competitors are doing or saying," he said now. "And I don't really give a shit."

"Well, I do!" Hawke snapped. "Now, what about it?"

Barclay wondered how much longer he could put up with Hawke's childish tirades. He'd come close to quitting several times over the years, but had always reconsidered, recognizing that—despite Hawke's churlish personality—this was still a great television station, capable of doing great work. And one of only a few like it left in the country. Besides, he had grown to love the Twin Cities, and although he was not married and had no real ties here, he was reluctant to leave and start over again somewhere else.

But there would come a point, he thought, when he simply couldn't tolerate it anymore.

"The newspaper is wrong," he finally said. "We are making progress. There are new developments."

"Like what?" Hawke demanded.

Barclay debated telling him, but finally decided he should know everything. It took him about ten minutes, and when he was finished, Hawke asked, "You think this woman may have been murdered because of our investigation?"

"We don't know yet. It could have been a suicide."

"And how's Collier?"

"A little cut up and shook up," Barclay said. "But he'll be all right."

"You're sure?"

"Yeah. He's okay."

Hawke stood up and walked around the desk, leaning against it, not two feet from Barclay. "Speaking of Collier, how did *that* story leak? I'm already getting calls from his fans, for Christ's sake. Demanding to know why we're taking him off the late news."

Barclay had gotten many of the same kind of calls himself. And he knew the station switchboard was taking scores more every day. The unsolicited "Keep Alex" campaign seemed to be building momentum.

"He thinks you let it slip," Barclay replied, with some satisfaction.

"Like hell I did!"

"He thinks you may be trying to embarrass him."

"Bullshit! I don't like the guy, but I don't want another 'Save Scotty' campaign on my hands. I wanted this thing done quietly."

"Well, the cat's out of the bag now," Barclay said. "We're going to have to live with it."

Hawke leaned down, almost in his face. "Maybe so, but I want those leaks in the newsroom plugged!" he hissed. "Now! You understand me?"

"I'll do what I can," Barclay said, although he knew he had about as much chance of doing that as Hawke did of playing center for the Minnesota Timberwolves.

Hawke wasn't the only one upset.

Hazel and John Hathaway had both read Liggett's column in the newspaper, and Hazel, at least, couldn't believe what she saw: that Alex's investigation was going nowhere, and that people were actually laughing at the effort to find her boys.

For her husband, however, the column was confirmation of his earlier and continuing doubts. "I told you it was a waste of time," he said. "With or without the big reward. It's been too long."

Hazel remembered Alex telling her earlier not to believe everything she read, but there it was, in the newspaper. Would they print something that wasn't true? Adding to her confusion was the fact that Alex had not called her in days, not since she had spoken to him the day after his story aired. Wouldn't he have called to tell her of any promising leads? What's more, they had heard nothing further from or about the person who had called himself Matt, who had picked up the certified letter and the two hundred dollars in Newark.

He certainly hadn't shown up on any bus.

She found it difficult to hide her dejection, even from her husband. She could no longer work up the stamina to combat his pessimism. She simply stood by and listened without comment, fighting off the tears and a deepening melancholy of the kind that had once sent her to the hospital. Vowing to maintain her emotional balance for the sake of her daughters, if not herself, but knowing the last and best chance of finding her sons might, like them, be disappearing.

She was tempted to call Alex, to ask about the truth of the newspaper column. But she resisted, in part because she feared what she might hear. Give him time, she told herself. Pray. Keep the faith. But God, it was hard.

Phil Tinsley was still a uniformed cop on the streets during Tony Malay's final years as police chief, and while they didn't know each other well, Malay had been among the first to recognize Tinsley's abilities and potential for promotion. Now, years later, thanks to a push-start from Malay before he retired, Tinsley was a plainclothes lieutenant running the homicide unit . . . where Alex had come to know and respect him. For a time, Tinsley had been the significant other of Alex's former co-anchor, Barbara Miller, but their careers soon got in the way of the romance and they'd split up when Barbara went off to the network in New York.

While the two men had rarely seen or talked to each other since, Tinsley had agreed to meet Alex and Malay in the same bagel shop where Malay had first told Alex about the missing files. After several minutes of catching up on each other's lives, Alex asked if he knew about the death of Marie Stockworth.

"Not personally," Tinsley replied. "A couple of the other guys in the unit were out there. But I'm told it looks like a suicide, right?"

"I'm waiting to hear on the autopsy," Malay said. "But Alex here thinks it may not be."

"Why is that?" Tinsley asked.

"It's a long story," Alex said, and then launched into a brief recitation of what they had learned so far, going back to the original disappearance of the Hathaway brothers, but refraining from reporting the threats on his own life or the drive-by shooting. "It seems inconceivable that this woman would have chosen this moment to do herself in. She had too much to gain."

Tinsley had listened attentively to everything Alex told him. "So what would you like from me?" he finally asked.

"If it turns out she was murdered, and I know that's still a big if," Alex said, "but if she was, I'd like you to take on the case yourself."

Tinsley was obviously surprised by the request. "Jesus, Alex," he sputtered. "I don't know. I'm up to my ass in work already."

"I'm asking as a favor," Alex said. "I need to know, from the inside, how the investigation is going. From somebody I know and trust . . . and who trusts me."

When Tinsley continued to be hesitant, Malay said, "Tell him, Alex."

"What?"

"You know."

Tinsley appeared puzzled, his eyes moving from one to the other.

"I've gotten some threats myself," Alex admitted. "And this morning, somebody apparently took a shot at me on the freeway. The chief here dug the slug out of my dashboard."

"You're kidding? Is that how your face got cut up?"

"Yeah, from the smashed window. Whoever did it must have followed me from the woman's apartment."

"And you didn't report it?"

"I'm doing that now, to you. And I'd rather not see it all over the newspapers."

Tinsley could only shake his head. "You are a piece of work, Alex."

Malay gave Tinsley the recovered slug. "Maybe you can use this someday."

"So what do you say?" Alex asked. "About taking on the case?"

"Let's see what the ME has to say first. Then I'll let you know."

21

Alex had just stepped out of the studio after the early news when he heard himself being paged. He hurried to the newsroom and picked up the phone in his cubicle. It was Malay, calling from the medical examiner's office. "You were right," he said. "It was no suicide."

Alex felt a rush of . . . what? Excitement? Fear? Pity for the woman and her son? Probably all of the above, in no more than a second.

"I won't bore you with all of the technical stuff," Malay went on, "but the ME says she was dead before she ever got strung up from that shower rod. Someone strangled her, probably with their hands or the crook of their arm, from behind."

Alex shuddered at the image. "How do they know?"

"A couple of ways. First of all, there were deep bruises and contusions on her neck—worse, they say, than could have come from the hanging. And there was also damage to both the internal and external structure of the neck, including a fracture of her hyoid bone, at the base of the tongue, which they tell me usually occurs during a struggle, and rarely by hanging."

Alex was taking down notes as Malay spoke. "So the hanging was an attempt to cover it up?"

"I suppose so, but the ME says it was a pretty crude attempt. That they should have known it wouldn't fool anybody for very long."

"It apparently fooled the cops," Alex said, reminding himself to give Tinsley a call when he was finished with this.

"A couple other things," Malay said.

"Go ahead."

"The woman was not sexually assaulted. And there were no signs of any other physical injury. No scratches or bruises on any other part of her body. Or any indication that she put up much of a fight. No skin under her fingernails or anything like that."

"So what does that mean?" Alex asked.

"This is the old cop speaking, but I'd say that she was taken by surprise. Somebody got her from behind when she wasn't expecting it."

"You're saying it was someone she knew?"

"Must have been. You said there was no sign of a forced entry, right?"

"That's right."

"I'm going to wait around for a copy of the full report," Malay said. "I'll bring it over to your house tonight."

"Okay," Alex said. "Thanks." He had plenty of other things to keep his mind occupied in the meantime.

Maggie showed up a few minutes later, just as Alex was leaving a telephone message for Phil Tinsley. He quickly filled her in on the ME's findings, and asked if she'd mind trying to find Barclay to let him know. "Sure," she said, "if he's still around." Then, "Alex, do you really know what you're getting us into here? I mean, this is *murder* we're talking about."

"I know," he said. "That's why I want to get Tinsley involved. This is way over our heads."

With that, Maggie took off across the newsroom, muttering something he couldn't hear.

He next placed a call to Barney McSwain, finding him at his home near Lake Calhoun. "I've got bad news," Alex said. "We just got the medical examiner's report. Mrs. Stockworth was murdered, strangled by someone."

There was an audible gasp at the other end of the line. "My God. Then you were right."

"I'm afraid so. The hanging apparently was an effort to cover up the killing."

"What the hell am I going to tell Sean?"

"The truth, I guess. And the sooner the better, I suppose. He should hear it from you and not the cops."

"Okay, I'll try to find him. He may still be at the funeral home."

"Good luck," Alex said. "And please, keep in touch."

Maggie was back in a few minutes, reporting that Barclay was gone for the day. But she said she'd left a message at his condo.

"Good," he said, "but watch the shit fly when he gets the news."

"Why do you say that?"

"Because, like you, he thinks it's getting too dangerous. It's his job, he says, to keep us all alive and well."

"You should think about it, Alex. You're the one getting shot at."

He leaned back in his chair, hands behind his head. "What I can't figure out is why these people—whoever they are—are so goddamned frightened? Scared enough, apparently, to kill a woman and to take a potshot at me. What did they do to those kids to make them so desperate now? Fifteen years later? It doesn't jibe."

Maggie could offer no ready answer, but pulled out a couple of sheets of paper and passed them to him. "I ran those computer checks," she said. "There's nothing much on the woman. Just the kind of vital information you'd find on a driver's license. She has no criminal record that I could find, and from what little I could learn about her credit, it seems to check out okay."

"How about the ex-husband, Spangler?"

"Ah, yes. A horse of a different color. I could find no current address, and he has no valid Minnesota driver's license. But he does have a criminal record."

"Really?"

"Two drug-dealing busts. Both in Hennepin County. The first in 1984, the second two years later, in late '86. The first was for possession of marijuana. He got a fine, some community service, and a year's probation."

"The second?"

"More serious. Another marijuana charge, but this time with intent to sell. Because of his prior conviction and the amount in his possession, he spent two years plus in Stillwater prison. Out in '89. His probation ended in '92, and there's been no record of him since."

"So he was tootin' more than his saxophone," Alex said.

"It appears that way."

When Alex learned that Pat would be downtown to take a late deposition, he arranged to meet her for a quick dinner between the early and the late news, although he knew in advance that it wouldn't be a particularly pleasant meal. She was unaware of the day's developments and would have to be told sooner or later. He wasn't looking forward to it.

They met at a small restaurant in the IDS complex, but once there, he stalled, allowing her to do most of the talking over dinner, waiting to begin himself until they'd finished their cobb salads and had their coffee. And despite his efforts to soften the story, her eyes widened and her mouth fell open as he related what had happened on the freeway. It was only then that she noticed the small scabs on the side of his face.

"You could have been killed," she gasped. "My God, Alex."

"Could have, but wasn't," he replied. "You have to look on the bright side."

He went on to explain how inattentive he had been, the hard lesson he'd learned. "I won't be that careless again, believe me."

He told her the Blazer window had already been replaced and that Barclay had given him permission to park in the station's underground garage for the duration, however long that might be. He said Barclay had also persuaded Malay to move into the house with him, and that he was in the process of unpacking as they spoke. "He's still licensed to carry a gun," Alex said, "and knows how to use it. Which is some small comfort, I guess."

Pat had more questions, cross-examining him like the attorney she was. When she was done, he said, "But that's not the worst of it."

"What? There's more?"

"I'm afraid so," he said, detailing the death of Marie Stockworth and the information he had gotten from her son about the family's relationship with the Whelans. "There's obviously something there, but I don't know how we find out more until we locate either the ex-husband or the Whelans."

"Or one of the boys," Pat said.

"Yeah," he scoffed, "fat chance of that."

"So what are you going to do?"

He explained that he was hoping to get Phil Tinsley

involved and that Maggie was still trying to find the ex-husband.

"Maybe I can help," Pat said.

"What do you mean?"

"If this Spangler was busted in Hennepin County, maybe one of my old colleagues in the public defender's office represented him . . . and may know more about him."

"It's worth a try," he said, although he had little hope of success. It had been too long ago.

Before they got up to leave, Pat asked, "So what about us? In the face of all of this?"

Alex had already been thinking about that. "We should probably see less of one another for a while," he said. "Play it safe, until we get a handle on what's happening. I don't want to put you at risk. Any more than you already are."

She agreed it would probably be a good idea, but added, "Just don't forget about me, okay? And please be careful."

When Alex returned to the newsroom, he found an agitated Barclay waiting by his cubicle. He'd obviously gotten the word. Also waiting, a return message from Phil Tinsley. Alex asked Barclay to wait, then hit the PLAYBACK button on the answering machine. "I got the autopsy report on the woman and have talked to the guys who are on the case," Tinsley said. "They have no problem with me taking it over. I'll stop by tomorrow."

Neither Alex nor Barclay said anything for a moment, looking at each other, playing a game of stare-down. Barclay blinked first. "Well," he said, "what do you say now?"

Alex shrugged. "I'm just glad Phil has agreed to come on board."

"What do you mean, come on board? It's *his* investigation now. We're out of it."

Alex rose in protest. "Wait a minute, George. We can't give this up now. It's the first real break we've had, for Christ's sake."

"Don't play the hero with me, Alex. This is out of our league. We're reporters, not cops. And there *is* a difference."

Alex was not surprised by Barclay's reaction. He'd expected it, but hoped he could overcome it. "The murder investigation may be his," he said, settling back in his chair. "But the whole investigation of the Hathaway kids is still ours. You can't deny me that. Not after all of this."

Barclay was unconvinced. "Problem is, Alex, they're intertwined. You can't separate them. Whoever killed this lady apparently did it because of what she knew about the Hathaways. And it was probably the same person or people who took that shot at you. If you keep on poking around, they're going to try again. And I can't allow that."

"Isn't that my decision?" Alex argued. "I'm a big boy, George. And no dummy. I understand the risks. And if I'm willing to take them, who are you to stop me?"

"Your boss, that's who."

Alex was getting angry, but fought to retain his composure. "Does that give you the right to make personal decisions for me? If this were a journalistic argument, I'd say, okay, you're the boss. But it's not. This is like you telling me not to climb mountains or skydive or something else that you think may be too dangerous."

Barclay was on his feet. "Wrong! Those things have nothing to do with your job. If you want to risk getting killed by jumping out of an airplane, that's your fucking business. But if you want to risk getting killed pursuing a story for this television station, than it *is* my business."

At that moment Maggie walked up and quickly realized she had interrupted a scrap. "What in the world is going on?" she asked, looking first at Alex, then at Barclay.

"A slight disagreement," Alex said, somewhat sheepishly.

"Not so slight," Barclay said, still angry.

"Well, you might want to hold it down," she said, "since the whole newsroom is watching and listening with interest."

Both looked around, but then Alex continued, more quietly, "Look, George, you've already got Malay watching me like a hawk. If you want, I'll sign a waiver or something, relieving you and the station of any responsibility in case the worst were to happen to me. But don't deny me this story. If the cops take over the investigation and finally get to the bottom of it, we'll read about it in the goddamned newspaper. Don't let that happen. You've never turned your back on a good story before."

Barclay could only shake his head. "I'm not worried about the legal liability. I'm worried about you."

"And I appreciate that. But don't cut off my legs to save my life. Please."

Barclay started to walk away. "I'll give it some more thought," he said. Then he stopped, staring back at him. "You know, I hate to admit it, but I'm starting to agree with Hawke. You are an arrogant, obstinate prick."

But he was smiling as he turned away.

That night, for the late news, Alex wrote a short item

on Marie Stockworth's death, treating it as routinely as he would any other homicide.

> The Hennepin County medical examiner has con-
> firmed that a Richfield woman, fifty-six-year-old
> Marie Stockworth, was murdered in her Penn
> Avenue apartment early this morning. The woman
> was found hanged in her bathroom, and while it
> was originally believed that she had committed
> suicide, police are now treating her death as a
> homicide. So far no suspects are in custody.

When he arrived home later that night, Alex found both the front and back yards bathed in light and new dead-bolt locks installed on the doors. He had no key for the new locks, but Malay was waiting inside and quickly let him in. "What the hell have you been up to?" Alex asked, looking around him.

"What you should have done weeks or months ago," Malay answered as he moved to shut the door behind him. "Providing a little security."

Malay said he had ordered the new and brighter yard lights installed that afternoon, along with the new locks. "And someone's coming out tomorrow to update your security system," he said. "It's years out of date."

Alex was amused but slightly irritated. "Shouldn't you have talked to me first?"

"Why? You can afford it. And if I'm here to help pro-tect you, I'd like to have the house secure. I'll sleep bet-ter. And so will you."

Alex chuckled, but wondered what the neighbors would think. The house was going to look like an armed camp.

"I also want you to keep all of the curtains closed,"

Malay said, "and the lights down. And I don't want you stepping outside, to go to the store or even to pick up the paper off the goddamned stoop, without me next to you. Or better yet, let me do it."

"Let's not go crazy," Alex said, wandering through the darkened house. "I don't want to feel like a prisoner."

Malay trailed after him. "Look, if these people had the balls to take a shot at you on the freeway, in broad daylight, they're not going to hesitate trying to pick you off in here. I'd rather not see that happen."

Alex went to the kitchen to fix himself a light gin and tonic, but Malay declined the offer to join him. "I'll take a beer now and then," he said, "but I haven't touched the hard stuff in years. I got to liking it too much."

Alex wanted to take the drink to the screen porch, but Malay advised against it. "Best to keep solid walls between you and them," he said.

It was then, in the light of the kitchen, that Alex first noticed the holstered pistol on Malay's belt. He had never owned a gun himself, and had not fired one since he'd left the Army almost three decades before, and then only a rifle. "What is that?" he asked, pointing.

"A nine-millimeter Smith & Wesson automatic," Malay replied, taking it out of the holster and holding it up. "I've had it ever since I left the department."

"Have you ever used it on anyone?" Alex asked, leaning against the kitchen counter.

"No, not this one," Malay replied as he reholstered the pistol, leaving Alex to wonder about his previous guns. He decided not to press the chief.

Malay had left the full ME's report on the kitchen table, but as Alex studied it now, he could decipher nothing new, beyond what Malay had told him on the phone. Marie Stockworth was dead, murdered. That was the bottom line . . . and none of the report's fancy medical verbiage could change that fact.

"I'm off to bed," Malay said. "I can't take these late hours like you young guys."

Right, Alex thought. Young compared to you. "So you found a place to sleep?"

"Yeah. The downstairs bedroom, if that's okay. I'm all unpacked."

"Fine," Alex said. Then, as Malay began to walk away, "You don't sleep with that thing, do you?"

"What?"

"The gun."

"Sure. It's under my pillow."

"I hope you don't walk in your sleep," Alex said.

Once he was gone, Alex added more ice to his drink and—feeling defiant—slipped out onto the screen porch to finish it.

22

Malay was up long before Alex the next morning, and had already finished the newspaper and half a pot of coffee by the time Alex groggily made his way down-stairs. "Are you always up this early?" he asked as he poured himself a cup of the coffee.

Malay laughed. "Hell, yes. I thought we might go cast for some bass at Lake Harriet."

"No thanks," Alex replied, slumping into one of the kitchen chairs, sipping at his coffee. His eyes were barely open.

"You've already had two phone calls," Malay said.

"I have?" Alex had not heard the phone ring. He must have been sleeping hard, maybe from that night-cap.

"Yeah. Phil Tinsley for one. He's going to be over here in an hour or so."

"Really? Then I'd better get my ass in gear."

"The second was from the dead woman's son, Sean. Barney McSwain gave him your number. He'd like to meet with you as soon as possible. I told him you'd get back to him."

Alex glanced at the kitchen clock. Not yet nine o'clock and the workday had already begun. A couple of months ago, before this all began, he *could* have been fishing at Lake Harriet. Now he barely had time to drink his goddamned coffee. "I'd better get dressed," he said, draining the cup.

True to his word, Phil Tinsley showed up at the front door less than an hour later. By then Alex had shaved, showered, and dressed . . . and was waiting. He'd also tried a return call to Sean, but got no answer at the number he had left.

As they sat around the dining room table, Tinsley brought out a copy of the report filed the day before by the homicide detectives who had been at Marie Stockworth's apartment. "There's not much here that you don't already know," he said as he flipped through the pages. "I'm afraid our guys didn't do too thorough a job out there. They were pretty much convinced it was a suicide from the get-go." He paused. "I chewed a little ass, and they're back there today, trying to lift some prints and talking again to all of the neighbors in the building."

Alex and Malay took turns skimming the report: no sign of forced entry, no evidence of a struggle, no indication that anything had been taken. The apartment was neat and tidy when the cops arrived, and a quick canvass of the neighbors had found no one who had heard or seen anything suspicious during the night. The report also indicated that the detectives had confirmed that the son, Sean, had been with his live-in girlfriend all night.

"So where do you go from here?" Alex asked.

"That's why I'm here so bright and early," Tinsley said. He pulled out a small tape recorder and put it on the table. "If you're right, that this woman was killed because of your investigation, I want you to tell me everything . . . from the beginning. You told me some stuff yesterday, but I want to follow your every step. Don't leave anything out, no matter how unimportant you think it might be."

"That's a tall order," Alex said, "but I'll try." He then went back to the first night he heard of the Hathaway boys . . . and worked forward, trying to recall everything he had done and everyone he had spoken to. It took him the better part of an hour, with Malay filling in any details he might have missed and Tinsley interrupting now and then with questions.

When he was finished, Tinsley said, "That's a hell of a job, Alex. I wish you'd called me sooner."

"I didn't think anyone would end up dead, for God's sake. And besides, your chief told the newspaper our investigation was a farce and nothing more than a ratings grab."

"Doesn't surprise me," Tinsley said, with a sideways glance at Malay. "He's a jerk."

As he prepared to leave, Alex said, "You'll keep in touch, won't you? I mean, if you get a break or happen to locate the ex-husband or the Whelans?"

"Sure, if you'll do the same. But I don't want you getting in our way. Or getting yourself hurt, okay?"

"No problem," Alex said. "As you can see, I've got myself a bodyguard now. He won't let me take a piss without him."

When Alex finally reached Sean Spangler, they agreed to meet an hour later at a Perkins restaurant near the Southdale shopping center. Sean was already there when Alex and Malay arrived, hunkered down in a back booth, a cup of coffee and an uneaten piece of pie in front of him. Alex quickly introduced Malay, and then both slid into the booth.

Alex was immediately struck by the change in the young man's appearance. He looked as if he had not slept in the twenty-four hours since Alex had seen him last. He was unshaven, his hair was disheveled, and there were small, bluish bags beneath both eyes, as though someone had just worked him over. And his nose was still running. Even his body, so impressive the day before, seemed to have lost its strength and power.

"Pardon me for saying this," Alex said, "but you look like hell. Have you gotten any sleep?"

"Not really," Sean replied. "I was up most of the night, after Barney called."

"I'm terribly sorry things turned out this way," Alex said. "Especially since we may have played some role in it."

A waitress brought a pot of coffee to the table and asked if they'd like anything else. All of them declined. Sean still hadn't touched his pie. "That's what I wanted to talk to you about," he said. "Barney says you think she was murdered because of the information she was trying to get to you."

"That's a theory," Alex said. "But nobody knows for sure yet."

Sean slumped back in the booth. "I tried to get back into the apartment this morning, to look around like you asked, but the cops were there again and told me I'd have to wait a few hours. Until they were finished." His eyes welled. "It's unbelievable. My own mother, murdered. I can't get it out of my mind, what she must have gone through. The pain. She never hurt anyone in her life."

No one said anything for a moment, as Sean tried to wipe away the tears.

"Have you heard from your father?" Alex asked finally.

"Of course not. But he probably doesn't know. And even if he did, I doubt that he'd call." He went on to say that the funeral would be held in two days, once the medical examiner released his mother's body.

Malay leaned forward. "Sean," he asked, "do you know anyone, besides yourself, who had a key to your mother's apartment, or who she might have let in that late at night?"

Sean took a tentative bite of the pie. "No, but that may not mean much. I didn't know many of her friends. Or if she was dating anybody. We weren't that close lately, to tell the truth. We'd kind of lost touch. She didn't like the woman I'm living with, and made no secret of it. It pissed me off. That's why I stopped by yesterday, to see if I could begin to patch things up."

Before Alex could ask another question, his cell phone buzzed. "Hey, Phil," he said. "What have you got?" He pressed the phone against his ear. "Okay," he said after a minute. "Anything else? All right, I'll talk to you."

Malay was watching him expectantly, eyebrows raised.

"That was a homicide detective we're working with," Alex explained to Sean. "He says they've finished at your mother's apartment."

"Good. Did they find anything?" he asked.

"Yeah, that's what he called about. They found a scrapbook hidden away in one of her closets." He paused. "Filled with old newspaper stories about the Hathway boys. Pictures, too. Including some snapshots of the boys he thinks were taken with a long-lens camera. Snapshots that never appeared in any newspaper."

"Jesus," Sean muttered. "I never knew anything about it."

"I believe that," Alex said. "Your mother had kept the secret a long time."

"Is there anything I can do?" he asked.

Alex thought a moment. "You can see if the cops missed anything at the apartment. Anything to do with your father, or with the Whelans. Addresses, phone numbers. Friends. Check her computer, if she has one. Aside from that, no. Just take care of yourself. Get some sleep. And try to get through all of this somehow."

When he walked into the newsroom that afternoon, Alex knew something was awry. And it didn't take him long to figure it out. All he needed was the sight of Hawke and Barclay escorting a tall, good-looking young guy with blond, carefully combed hair, across the newsroom.

A potential successor, he knew immediately. Brought in for a tour and interview. Scandinavian, by the looks of him, Alex thought. Fair skin to go along with the blond hair. Like the sun had never touched him. He'd go over big in pearly-white Minnesota.

Alex could feel the sympathetic eyes of the newsroom on him as he slipped out of his sport coat and into his chair. He ignored all of them except Maggie, who slid her chair close to his. "That takes some nerve, doesn't it?" she whispered. "Parading him around the newsroom like some kind of prince."

"Well, he looks young enough," he said.

"Hawke is fawning all over him," she said.

"Better him than me," replied Alex with a smile.

Actually, he felt some empathy for the guy. He had been in the same position often enough himself in his well-traveled days as vagabond anchorman. Being sized up like a prized steer, trying to appear casual yet states-manlike. Enduring the hostile stares of the newsroom grunts, who didn't know him but knew he'd soon be making five or ten times the money they did, replacing some old duffer who had probably been a godfather to half of their kids.

Trouble was, he was now the old duffer. The shoe was on the other foot.

"What's his name?"

"Chuckie."

"Be serious," Alex said.

"All right. *Charles*. Not Chuck, not Charlie. Not Chas. *Charles,* like the prince. Charles Johnson, I think."

"Have they offered him the job?" he asked.

"I don't know. I don't think so," she said. "But they want me to do an audition with him in an hour or so. To see how the 'chemistry' works between us. Makes me want to puke."

Alex laughed. "There, there, young lady. He could be our salvation."

"Screw that. I think I'll put my hand on his thigh in the middle of the audition. And squeeze. See how he reacts!"

"He'll probably take the job at no pay," Alex said with a smirk.

He knew there was no chance that he would be introduced to the guy. At least not until *Charles* had been officially offered the job. It would appear unseemly, although Alex could think of no one better than himself to judge the fellow's potential as an anchor. Maybe Barclay would show him the audition tape.

Meantime, he had other things to tend to.

Hazel Hathaway was watching her two girls playing in the backyard when the phone rang. Watching and marveling at how they'd both shot up in the past year. Especially Angela, who would be twelve in the fall. No longer a little girl, she'd become a young lady, almost overnight it seemed to Hazel, tall and slim and unusually graceful at what was usually an awkward age. And uncommonly patient with her little sister.

The phone rang again.

Hazel left the window and hurried to the den, picking up the receiver after its third ring.

"Mrs. Hathaway?"

"Yes?" She glanced at the Caller ID, which read PAY PHONE and the number 555-2036.

"Do you love your daughters?"

"*What?* Who is this?"

"Would you want to see them disappear like your sons?"

Hazel collapsed into a chair, her hand to her heart. She could feel it pumping, could feel her face flush. Hang up! she told herself. Now. Quickly. But the receiver stayed in her hand, as if attached. "How dare you!" she shouted.

"That's a nice pink outfit the little one is wearing," the voice said calmly. "Andrea, right? And aren't those little titties I see popping out on the big one? Angie. The one wearing the jean shorts and the T-shirt?"

Hazel's hand went to her mouth, holding back a scream. He was describing exactly what the girls were wearing. Now, in the backyard. She dropped the phone and ran to the window. "Get inside, girls! Right now. Hurry. No arguments."

The girls looked at her, puzzled. But they didn't hesitate. They rarely heard her scream like that.

As they ran for the house, Hazel tried to spot any strange cars or people loitering around. She saw nothing. But he had to be . . . had to have been . . . nearby.

"What's wrong, Mom?" Angie asked once they were inside, breathing hard.

"Yeah, Mom?" Andrea echoed.

"Never mind," Hazel said. "Just stay inside. And away from the window."

She returned to the phone and picked it up, not knowing if he was still there. "You leave us alone, you bastard!" she screamed. "Leave us alone."

"Be happy to," he said. "But there's a catch."

She said nothing as she tried to memorize the voice, knowing that she had never heard it before.

"You tell Alex Collier to end his investigation. Now. Today. Or your little girls will be history. Just like the boys."

Then the line went dead.

Still panicky, still shaking, Hazel couldn't decide whom to call first: Alex or her husband. She settled on Alex, in part because she was deathly afraid of what John would say. And knowing he'd be right. That in her determination to find the boys, she was endangering what remained of their family.

She tried to calm herself as she waited for Alex to answer. Please, she prayed, be there. He was.

Working to keep the quaver out of her voice, she hurriedly explained what had happened, repeating every word of the conversation as clearly as her roiled mind would allow.

"It was from a pay phone?" Alex asked.

"Yes, but I don't remember the number."

"Are the girls all right?"

"Yes, they're fine. They're with me now."

Both daughters were sitting at her feet, chins resting on their pulled-up knees, listening intently to what was being said.

"Have you talked to John?"

"No, not yet. I called you first."

"Okay. Call him. See if he can come home early. I'll be at your house in an hour."

"He's going to be very angry," she said.

"I know. I'll do my best to calm him down," Alex said. "And I'll bring you up to date on what's been happening."

"Good. From what the paper said, I thought nothing was."

When Alex arrived at the Hathaways, Malay was with him—as he was wherever Alex went now. John Hathaway met them at the door, blocking it, and before Alex could introduce Malay or say anything, he spat out, "Are you satisfied now?"

Alex was not surprised; he knew this would be the reception. "Cool down, John. Let's go inside and talk about it."

But Hathaway didn't move. "I told you it could hurt the girls. But you wouldn't listen, would you?"

Then, from behind her husband, hidden by his body, Hazel spoke out. "John, let them in. This isn't helping."

He glanced over his shoulder. "I told you I'd handle this," he said.

"Not this way. Move. Let them in, John."

He slowly, reluctantly stepped aside, and when he did, Alex saw immediately that there must have been a hell of an argument. Hazel's eyes were red-rimmed, her face pale, washed out. And she looked even thinner than before, if that was possible.

As they stepped across the threshold, Alex introduced Malay. "You may remember him. He was the police chief when your boys disappeared. He's retired now, but has been helping me in the investigation."

Hathaway refused to shake Malay's hand. "Damn

right I remember him," he said. "You didn't do squat for us back then, did you?"

If Malay was offended, he didn't show it. "We did the best we could to find your sons, Mr. Hathaway. Maybe we gave up too soon, but at the time, we thought we had done everything possible."

"Leave it alone, John," Hazel said. "And welcome to our home, Mr. Malay." She led them through the house to the back deck. "The girls are upstairs. I thought we could talk out here."

Before they sat down, Alex said, "I hope you know how badly I feel about what's happened. I would no more knowingly put your daughters in danger than you would. And we'd like to help protect them."

"You've done enough already," Hathaway shot back.

"John." There was a warning in his wife's voice. "Let's sit, please."

They all took a place at the patio table. A pitcher of lemonade and glasses were already there. "Do you have any relatives who live outside the Twin Cities?" Alex asked.

"In northern Minnesota, yes. A brother and sister-in-law. Near Bemidji."

"Would they be willing to take the girls in for a while? With all expenses paid by us."

Hazel looked at her husband. "I don't know. We could ask. They live on a lake and the girls love it up there."

Hathaway cut in. "Why don't you just give up the investigation?" he demanded. "Like the caller said. It would be simpler. And safer."

"Too late for that, I'm afraid," Alex said. "Let me bring you up to date."

For the next half hour, he detailed everything that

had happened since they had last spoken, including the death of Marie Stockworth and the attempt on his own life. They allowed him to go on uninterrupted, but he could see the spreading disbelief in their faces.

When he was finished, Hazel asked, "You think this woman was killed because of this?"

"That's the way it looks," Alex replied. He then brought out copies of the snapshots that the homicide detectives had found in Marie's scrapbook . . . copies that he had picked up from Phil Tinsley on his way to the Hathaways. "Can you guess when and where these pictures were taken?"

Hazel and John huddled over the photos, moving from one to the next, then holding them up to the sun. There were ten pictures in all, some of which Alex assumed had been taken on different days—since the boys were wearing different clothes in a few of the shots.

"My God," Hazel whispered.

"Most of them were taken in the park, I think," John said. "Even the ones where you can't see the playground equipment."

"And two from our old front yard," Hazel added. "That's a rose bush at the corner of the house, behind them. I recognize it."

When they finally put down the pictures, Hathaway asked, "So what does this mean?"

"Someone obviously had your kids under surveillance," Malay said. "Shooting them from a distance. Maybe for some time."

Alex picked up the pictures again, sorting through them. "Were the clothes in any of these photos the same ones the boys were wearing the day they disappeared?"

"No," Hazel said immediately. "I looked for that. What's more, they're not wearing their baseball caps. So the pictures must have been taken before John took them to that Twins game. Because afterwards, they wouldn't go anywhere without those caps."

"And when was that?" Alex asked. "Two weeks or so before . . ."

"About that, yes," Hathaway said.

By now Hathaway had mellowed, but the thrust of his chin was a sure sign that he was still on edge and could be easily aroused again. Alex wanted to be careful. "Like it or not, John, there's no turning back the clock," he said. "The police are now handling the murder investigation, and we'll certainly alert them to the threats against your daughters. But I think we should take it upon ourselves to make sure they're kept safe."

"You want us to send them up north?" Hazel said.

"There, or someplace else out of town. We can move them secretly. While I don't think anything would actually happen to them here, I know you'd feel better. And so would I."

After a glance at her husband, Hazel said, "I'll call my brother right away and let you know."

"Good. Are you in agreement, John?" Alex asked.

"I guess so. It's too late to do much else, isn't it? I just wish we had never gotten ourselves into this in the first place. But nobody would listen to me."

"Maybe you won't feel that way," Alex said, "if all of this eventually leads us to your boys."

"Right," he said as got up and began to walk away. "And if you believe that . . ."

By then he was back inside the house.

23

Deputy Sheriff Jim Gibbons had been sitting on his ass most of the day, assigned to the office because the sheriff was on vacation and the deputy who usually sat there was at the hospital getting his hemorrhoids fixed. No wonder his butt itched, Gibbons thought, stuck in a chair like this every day.

So far there hadn't been one goddamned call worth getting excited about. A couple of dogs on the loose, a kid seen pissing in the park, and a fender-bender in the northern part of the county. That was it. He had three other deputies in patrol cars cruising around without a damned thing to do. Probably sitting somewhere, he thought, reading *Penthouse* and jacking off.

McLaren County, Missouri, was not exactly a hotbed of criminal activity. Mostly rural, it bordered about thirty miles of the Mississippi River across from Illinois, with no town of more than seven thousand population. Trinity, the county seat, was the largest—with sixty-eight hundred people. And Gibbons knew most of them, having lived there all thirty-two years of his life.

The only good thing about being assigned inside was that it was so damned hot outside. In the upper nineties, according to the thermometer on the bank, and humid as hell. The air conditioner in the office was running nonstop, and it still wasn't all that cool.

Out of boredom, Deputy Gibbons had read practically every piece of paper in the office, including some that he probably shouldn't have seen. Tough shit. He'd also looked over every FBI "Wanted" poster, but decided that no criminal in his right mind would stay long in McLaren County. Too boring.

It wasn't until he'd reached the bottom of the stack of paper on the desk that he noticed a memo to the sheriff from one of the honchos at the state police headquarters in Jefferson City. It was a form letter, apparently sent to every sheriff of every county that bordered the river, and Gibbons read it with interest.

> *We have been asked by the former chief of police in Minneapolis to search our records for any John Doe whose body or remains may have been pulled from the Mississippi River anytime in the past fifteen years. The remains would be those of a boy or boys who disappeared and were believed drowned in the river in July of 1983. A television station in Minnesota, with the assistance of the former chief, has reopened the investigation of the three boys' disappearance, prompted in part by the fact that none of the bodies has ever been recovered. If you can be of any assistance, please advise me.*

> *John Stone,*
> *Supervisor,*
> *State Police Records Bureau*

Gibbons sat back in his chair. Could it be?
The August morning six years ago was still fresh in

his mind. Who could forget it? First of all, it was even hotter than today, a goddamned oven at ten in the morning. Not a whiff of a breeze, not a fart's worth, and the river looked like it was standing still.

Gibbons was the first to arrive and the kid was still there, still clinging to his fishing pole, the lure at the end of the line ghoulishly hooked to the eye socket of a skull. The boy was shivering, Gibbons remembered that. Shivering on a hundred-degree day. Traumatized. And mute.

When he finally was able to speak, he told Gibbons he had been casting a deep-diving Rapala along the edge of the river bank, hoping to get a bass or maybe a sucker to smoke. He thought he had hooked a small log, but when he reeled in, he pulled up the skull.

Gibbons wondered now if the kid had ever gone fishing again.

Before the authorities were done, they had dragged that section of the river over and over again, and had sent divers down, in hopes of finding more of the skeletal remains. But the river proved too murky for the divers, and too filled with junk for the drag lines.

A pathologist determined that the skull was male, probably a young Caucasian male, but he would not go beyond that. And since there were no missing young males in McLaren or surrounding counties, or across the river in Illinois, the skull was filed away as a John Doe. As far as Gibbons knew, it was probably still sitting in a drawer or box somewhere, collecting dust.

Gibbons had never heard of the missing boys in Minnesota, but then again, they had disappeared before his time in the department. And Minnesota was a hell of a long way away, too far probably for a skull to be carried by the river's currents. But still . . .

He read the memo once more, then turned to the phone. What the hell? He had nothing better to do.

Malay was sitting at a makeshift desk in the newsroom, not far from Alex's, when he got the call. He didn't recognize the guy's name right away, but the Missouri twang was familiar. John Stone of the Missouri State Police.

"You've got something for me?" Malay asked after the requisite small talk.

Stone told him about the phone call from the deputy in McLaren County. "It's probably nothing, but I thought you'd want to know."

"For sure," Malay replied.

"But I have to tell you, I doubt that it's what you're looking for. Can't see how any body part could travel this far down the river."

"I know," Malay replied. "But the guy I'm working with thinks the kids may have been carried off in a boat. And that one or more of them may have gotten dumped further south."

"Okay, if you say so."

"Where's the skull now?"

"Still in McLaren County, as far as I know. Tucked away somewhere."

"What condition is it in?"

"Not great, I'm told. It was in the river a long time. But I guess there's still a few teeth left."

"How do I go about getting it?"

"The skull?"

"Yeah."

"There'd probably be a lot of red tape," Stone said. "But assuming I can find it, why don't I just send it to you? On the QT. It's doing us no good down here."

"Great."

"But I'd have to get it back."

"No problem."

Malay gave him the address, then hurried away in search of Alex.

Across town, at the Hennepin County courthouse, Pat Hodges was visiting with the chief public defender, a man by the name of Howard Stewart. Years before, the two had worked together in the department, but when Pat had left to enter private practice, he had stayed on . . . and had been named to the top job the year before. While they had remained friends, she had not seen or talked to him for several months.

Now, after catching up on each other's lives, Pat came to the point of her visit. "I'd like you to check your records," she said, "to see if anybody here ever defended a guy by the name of Marvin Spangler back in the mid-eighties. He was convicted in a couple of drug deals."

"What's this about, Pat?" he asked.

"I'm asking as a favor to Alex," she told him. "This Spangler is involved in some way in an investigation the station is doing."

"The missing kids thing?"

"Right."

"I've seen it on the news," he said. And with that, he turned to his computer and punched in Spangler's name. Pat watched from across the desk as the data scrolled across the screen. "You're in luck," he said finally. "Rawlings had him as a client back in '86. Entered a plea on a marijuana possession with intent-to-sell charge. According to this, that's the last time we've been involved with him."

Ted Rawlings had come to the public defender's

office shortly before Pat had left. She knew him, but not well. "Is he around?" she asked.

"Should be, unless he's in court. Let me check."

Moments later, Rawlings appeared in the office, tall, square-shouldered, with a dimpled chin and a mop of brown hair. "Hey, Pat," he said. "It's been a long time."

They shook hands and she quickly explained why she was there.

"Spangler?" he said. "No. Offhand, I don't remember the name."

"Take a look," Stewart said, pointing to the computer screen.

Rawlings leaned across the desk, reading the data. He shook his head. "I don't know, Pat. A couple thousand guys have come through here since then."

"Think hard, please," Pat said as she settled back in her chair. "We're trying to find out where he may be now. It could be important."

"Let me check my own files," he said. "Sometimes I make a note to myself that never finds its way into the computer. It'll only take a few minutes."

He was back in fifteen minutes. "This is all I could find," he said, handing Pat a small piece of paper. "This lawyer apparently called me in '89, asking for information on Spangler's case, but I have no memory of the call."

The name scrawled on the paper was that of Barney McSwain.

When Malay found Alex, he was headed for the station garage. "Where are you going?" he asked.

"To the Hathaways."

"Without me?"

Alex laughed. "You were on the phone, and Hazel is

about ready to leave with the girls. I thought I could make it without you."

"Forget that," he said. "Where you go, I go."

As hoped, Hazel had arranged for their daughters to spend a couple of weeks, maybe longer, with her brother's family on Lake Pleasant near Bemidji, in the heart of the state's resort country. She was going to drive them and stay for a few days herself, and Alex had insisted on making sure they got out of town safely, without being followed.

As they pulled out of the station garage, Malay quickly told him of the call from the Missouri state police. If he'd expected Alex to be excited about the discovery of the skull, he was disappointed. "It's certainly worth checking out," he said, "but I'd say the chances are pretty slim that it's one of our boys. Missouri is a hell of a long way away."

"You're the one who suggested the goddamned search," Malay said grumpily.

"I know, I know," Alex replied. "And I'm glad you found something, but I'm not about to jump to any conclusions."

"You're just hoping it's not one of them," Malay said.

"That too," Alex admitted. "I'd hate to see it."

Neither spoke again for the next few minutes, but as they neared the Hathaway house, Malay said, "We should try to get whatever medical and dental records they have on the boys. X rays or whatever. Before the mother leaves."

"Why?"

"Because the ME is going to need something to compare the skull to when it arrives."

"How in the hell am I going to ask her for those? What will I say?"

"That's your problem," Malay said. "You're the journalist. But the skull will do us no good without those records."

Hazel and her daughters were packed and waiting inside when they arrived at the house. It was a several-hour trip to Bemidji, and the girls, especially, were eager to get going.

Alex and Malay helped load their luggage into the car, alertly watching for any unusual activity in the neighborhood. There seemed to be none. "Is John going to join you up there?" Alex asked.

"When he can get a few days off from work," she replied. "Maybe this weekend."

Alex outlined the plan: She should take Highway 10 north and pull into a rest stop about thirty miles outside the Cities. Alex and Malay would be following closely, making sure no one was shadowing either of their cars. "We'll leave you at the rest stop," he said. "By then, we'll know that you're going to be okay."

Hazel agreed and got the girls into the car, and was about to pull away when Alex finally worked up the courage. "By the way," he said, "do you happen to have your boys' medical and dental records here at the house?"

Not unexpectedly, she was startled by the question. "Of course, but why in the world would you want them now?"

Alex hesitated. He could think of no easy way out of this. "I don't want to upset you," he said, leaning into the car window. "But at my request, the chief here has been talking to law enforcement people up and down the Mississippi River . . ."

"*What?*" Looking at Malay. "Why would he do that?"

"To make sure we weren't missing anything," Alex

replied, hoping she would not push him further.

She whispered, "Like one of their bodies, you mean?"

There was no escaping it. "To be frank, yes. I thought we had to do it, to eliminate any chance that one or more of them may actually have drowned."

She opened the door and got out of the car, out of the girls' earshot. "And?" she asked simply.

Malay stepped up. "The authorities in Missouri discovered a skull in the river six years ago. It was never identified. All they know . . . all we know . . . is that it was that of a young male."

"Sweet Jesus," she whispered. Her knees seemed to weaken, and she grabbed the handle of the car door for support.

"We have no reason to believe that it is one of your sons," he continued reassuringly, "but we need the records to be positive."

She closed her eyes and put her hand to her head, breathing deeply.

"Are you okay, Mom?" one of the girls asked from inside the car.

"Yes, Andrea, I'm fine." Then to Alex, "We've kept the records all of these years in case . . . well, you know, in case the boys are found. We'd have to be able to prove that they were really ours."

"I understand," Alex said. "If you'd get them for me, I'll return them as soon as possible."

"Okay," she said, turning back toward the house. "But please don't tell John about this. Not until you know for sure."

Once they'd seen the Hathaways safely on their way, with no problems, and were halfway back to the station, Alex's cell phone buzzed. "Hey, Pat," he said. "What's up?" He listened for a few moments, but then said, "That can't be right. McSwain told me he didn't know Spangler. At least, that's what I think he said." He listened for several minutes more. "But nobody over there knows where Spangler is now, right?" A pause. "Okay, thanks. I'll talk to you later."

Malay was watching him curiously.

"This gets stranger and stranger," he said after filling Malay in. "Why would McSwain lie to me, if that's what he did?"

"Maybe he was just trying to find Spangler to get back-support payments for his ex-wife," Malay suggested. "Or some other kind of settlement, maybe for the kid."

"Could be," Alex said. "But why wouldn't he have told me so?"

"Maybe you should ask him," Malay said.

24

He would have his chance the next day, at the funeral for Marie Stockworth. The services were held in the morning at the Rivkin Mortuary in Richfield, only a few blocks from the apartment where the woman had lived . . . and died. Besides Alex and Malay, no more than twenty people were there, including several from the bank where she had worked, a few from her apartment building, and some of Sean's friends.

And Barney McSwain.

Alex suspected that more friends would have been there had Marie died a natural death. But murder, especially an unsolved murder, tends to make people uncomfortable and shy away. Too spooky.

Before he entered the chapel, Alex glanced at the guest register, but found no other familiar names. Certainly not those of Marvin Spangler or the Whelans. To attract minimum attention, he and Malay took seats toward the rear of the chapel, alongside a man they would later learn was a detective from Tinsley's homicide unit.

The casket in front was metallic gray with chrome handles, the cover closed with a wreath of red roses on top and surrounded by several other floral arrangements.

Sean was already sitting in the first row, head bowed, with a woman who Alex figured must be his girlfriend on one side of him, Barney McSwain on the other.

The small, printed program told Alex what he already knew from Sean: Marie had been an only child whose parents had passed away years before. And aside from her son, she was survived by no living relatives, save for an elderly aunt who lived in California and was too ill to travel to the funeral.

The service was brief and strangely sterile. Since Marie had attended no church, her son had had to hire a minister the mortuary kept on call, a man who until then had no knowledge of Marie Stockworth or the life she had led, and whose homily was so generic it could have been about anyone sitting in the chapel. The hymns, too, were uninspiring and sung by a mortuary employee standing somewhere out of view. Or perhaps they were on tape. It was hard to tell.

As Alex sat there, he couldn't help but think of what his own funeral would be like. Not much different than this, he decided sadly. Of course, his kids would be there, and probably his ex-wife. Pat, too. And a contingent from the station, if he was still working there. But beyond that? A few friends, but no more than he could count on two hands. And the curious, the gawkers eager to see how a celebrity anchorman would be ushered into the hereafter.

And where would he be buried? Here, he guessed, since there was no other place he could really call home. Pretty depressing, he thought, no matter how you cut it. Another reminder, if he needed it, to start making a life for himself when all of this was over.

Because McSwain was one of the pallbearers, Alex had no chance to speak to him until after the funeral and the burial at the Oak Hill cemetery in Richfield. Like the service at the mortuary, the graveside ceremony was short and simple, attended by even fewer people than had been at the chapel.

Once it was over, Alex again expressed his condolences to Sean and then pulled McSwain aside. "I thought you told me you didn't know Marvin Spangler," he said.

McSwain looked at him, puzzled but wary. "What are you talking about?"

"At the apartment, when I asked about the ex-husband . . ."

"I told you I didn't know where he was, and that Marie never talked about him."

"But did you know him?" Alex asked, pressing him.

McSwain started to walk away. "I don't like being interrogated," he said.

Alex followed him. "We've been told that you did know him. Is that true, Barney?"

But McSwain kept right on walking, without looking back, until he reached the mortuary limousine that would take him and Sean back to the funeral home.

Once Alex was back at the station, Barclay stopped by his cubicle to ask for an update. He gave it to him, as briefly and concisely as he could.

"You've still got a long way to go, don't you?" Barclay said.

Alex admitted he did.

"What do you hear from Tinsley?"

"Nothing, but one of his cops was at the funeral, checking things out. And Malay is trying to get hold of him now."

Barclay pulled up a chair next to his. "What do you do if this skull does belong to one of the kids?"

"I don't know," he admitted, "but if it is one of the kid's, it doesn't necessarily mean that he and the others drowned. Someone could have killed him and thrown him into the goddamned river."

"You don't give up easily, do you?" Barclay said with a shake of the head.

"It's not that. Something has to explain these threats and the killing."

Unwilling to argue further, Barclay got up and started to walk away. But Alex called after him, "How did the golden boy do?"

Barclay stopped and turned back. "You mean *Charles*?"

"Yeah, the tall Norwegian."

"Hawke and the consultants think he's great. Loved him and Maggie together. Two young blonds at the anchor desk. What more can you ask?"

"And you?"

"He's a pip-squeak. Doesn't know the first fucking thing about news. And doesn't care to learn. But he's as smooth as a baby's behind."

"Are you going to hire him?"

Barclay suddenly got very serious. "I'll tell you what I told Hawke. If this kid comes, I go. And that's the way it could play out."

Alex fell back in his chair. "You're kidding?"

"No way. When the day comes that somebody else does the hiring around here, I'm gone."

Maggie came by a few minutes later, with her own version of the audition with Charles Johnson. "You can't believe it, Alex. There wasn't one hair out of place. Not one. And he has the most brilliant white teeth and smile you've ever seen. He seemed to leap out of the damned studio monitor."

Alex smiled. "Barclay said Hawke and the consultants loved him . . . and the two of you together."

"Yeah, well, they must not have spent much time talking to him. He's vacant, Alex. I mean, there's nothing up there. I asked him what kind of stories he'd been covering, and he said not that many. That he got into the business to be an anchor, and didn't plan to be out on the street all that much.

"He's a kid, Alex. A simpleminded kid with stars in his eyes who happens to be blessed with incredible good looks and a flawless delivery. I mean, he doesn't miss a word. He even pronounced Koochiching County on the first try. I felt like a rank amateur sitting next to him."

Alex told her what Barclay had told him. "Good for George," she said. "But I wouldn't put it past Hawke to call his bluff. He's in love with this kid."

"I don't think Barclay was bluffing," Alex said. "He seemed dead serious."

"Then may the Lord help us all," she replied.

To their surprise, Pat was waiting at the house when Alex and Malay returned after the late news. She had provided no advance notice, but assured them now that she had not been followed. "I did all of those things they do in the movies," she said. "I took several quick turns, double-backed, and kept my eye on the rearview mirror. Actually, I felt kind of foolish. Like a bad Double-O Seven."

"And you saw no one?" Malay asked.

"Nobody, I'm sure. It was like I was alone on the road, doing funny things," she said.

"This guy can't be everywhere," Alex said. "We've got to relax."

"Yeah, but when you least expect him," Malay replied, "best watch out."

They settled in around the kitchen table. "Any trouble getting into this fortress?" Alex asked her.

"No, the new key and the security code worked fine," she said. "But those new yard lights can be a little intimidating."

"Just like Stalag Seventeen," Alex said. "Minus the barbed wire."

In the time she had been there, Pat had baked a blueberry pie, which was just out of the oven. "I was getting lonely," she said as she placed a slice of the pie in front of each of them, along with a cup of decaf coffee. "It's like I haven't seen you in weeks."

The pie was a welcome sight to Alex, who had eaten dinner on the run at the station. Half a Subway sandwich, to be exact, shared, of course, with Malay.

"I know. I'm sorry," Alex said. "There just hasn't been time."

"So tell me."

Between bites of pie and sips of coffee, Alex related the latest, including his impressions of Marie Stockworth's funeral. "It was sad, you know. Somebody lives fifty-six years on this earth, and that's what they end up with. Fifteen or twenty people who took the trouble to say good-bye, some of whom didn't even know her."

"Some people don't even get that many," she said.

"I know."

So what's the deal with this McSwain?" she asked.

"I wish I knew," he replied. "He brushed me off when I tried to talk to him."

"What do you know about him?"

"Not that much," he said, repeating what his friend at the Bar Association had told him earlier, and what McSwain himself had revealed at their first meeting.

"What law firm was he with?" she asked.

Alex pulled his notebook out of his briefcase and flipped through the pages. "Mullen-McCaron. It's downtown, I guess."

"I know where it is. It's a big firm."

"He said they kicked him out ten or twelve years ago because of his age."

Pat smiled. "And you believed him?"

"I had no reason not to then. Why?"

"Because it's rare for a big law firm to 'kick out' a senior partner, unless he isn't producing or has gotten into some kind of trouble. Usually they just let them retire quietly or make them of counsel to the firm."

Alex mulled that over. "So what do you suggest?"

"I know a few people over there," she said. "Especially one woman who's part of that group of women lawyers I meet with. I've told you about them."

He nodded. "You think she'll tell you anything?"

"I don't know. She's been there a long time. Maybe I can get something out of her."

Malay had been sitting quietly, listening, but when he finished his pie and coffee, he got up and stretched. "I think I'll leave you kids alone," he said. "It's night-night time for me."

"You're really going to leave me alone?" Alex asked.

Malay ignored him. "Thanks for the pie, Pat. It was delicious."

"Goodnight, Tony," she said. "We'll see you in the morning."

He cocked an eyebrow and grinned. "We?" And then, "Have fun, but don't rattle the rafters."

*   *   *

When Alex walked out of the bathroom and into the dimness of the bedroom, he found Pat lying on the bed, in the sheerest of teddies. "I travel light," she said with a small smile.

"I can see," he replied, sitting on the edge of the bed next to her, lightly touching the fabric. "But even this seems a little heavy."

Coyly she said, "I'm not sure I can get it off by myself."

"Then let me help."

She sat up as he gently, gingerly pulled the whisper of silk over her head. Her dark hair fell over her bare shoulders, to the swell of her breasts. His hand ran through her hair, then lightly brushed her skin, still slightly moist from her shower.

"You always did have a wonderful touch," she whispered. "Even way back when."

He smiled, but said nothing. She was being kind. He remembered with embarrassment his first awkward attempts to make love to her, back in Kansas, a lifetime ago.

Slipping off his shorts, he lay next to her, continuing to caress her with his touch . . . then with his lips. Moving over her body, inhaling her freshness, hearing her breath come more quickly. And then his own, as she reached for him and slowly, exquisitely brought him to life.

Her tongue was in his ear, then between his lips and in his mouth, circling, caressing in its own erotic way. There was no sense of urgency, only a slow, deliberate exploration of their bodies and their senses. Even now, making new discoveries, finding new pleasure points. He could hear her low moans, mixed with his own.

"Come to me," she said finally, as her legs spread and he moved above her. "But we have to be careful," she whispered, smiling up at him in the darkness, "and remember the rafters."

He chuckled. "I don't care if we knock him out of bed."

When he was within her, it was all motion, all feeling. His face was buried in the warmth of her neck, the sensations building, ever building, until the final explosive eruption. And then the aftershocks, rippling, tingling, one after the other until there was only a serene stillness.

Later, as they still lay intertwined, Pat stroked his cheek softly, and said, "That was wonderful, you know."

"It always is . . . for me, anyway," he murmured, eyes closed, sleepiness already creeping into his voice.

She propped herself up on one elbow, looking down at him. "Do you still think we should make this more permanent?" she asked.

His eyes snapped open. "What?"

"I asked—"

"I heard you," he said. "But what are you saying?"

Her head fell back onto the pillow. "Since somebody took that shot at you," she said, "I've had to think even harder about what my life would be without you." Then, after a moment, "It's impossible to imagine."

He said nothing, but turned his head slightly to study her.

"I don't know how you've put up with me for as long as you have . . . with all of my ghosts and goblins," she said, staring at the ceiling. "You have amazing patience."

"Because I happen to be in love with you," he said. "That's not complicated."

Rolling over, she put her arm across his chest, the length of her body tight against his. "So do your old offers still stand?" she asked, a whisper in his ear.

He didn't hesitate. "Of course. If you're sure you're ready."

"I'm sure," she said. "As sure as I will ever be."

25

They decided to make no formal announcement until Alex had finished the investigation and both of their lives had settled down. Besides, he had yet to buy a ring, and wanted to be able to tell his kids about the engagement in person. Maybe, he thought, his ex-wife would have made a similar decision by then, taking some of the onus off him.

Knowing his kids, they'd probably demand a double wedding.

As it was, he was already feeling guilty because he had not spoken to the children more than three or four times in the past several weeks. He had blamed his workload, without going into any of the details, but they had seemed less troubled than he was. While they welcomed his calls, they did not appear to notice how infrequent they'd become.

Another reminder that they increasingly had their own lives, quite independent of his.

Back at the station, there was a worrisome lull. He had not heard from Tinsley on the Stockworth murder; the Missouri skull had not yet arrived; and they seemed to be no closer to finding Marvin Spangler or the Whelans. Even the threats against Alex had ceased, perhaps because he was constantly shadowed by Tony Malay.

Or perhaps because the investigation appeared to have come to a halt.

Alex had spoken a couple of times with Hazel Hathaway, who said her daughters were doing just fine up north, and wouldn't mind staying even longer than planned. But he had heard nothing more from Sean Spangler or Barney McSwain since the Stockworth funeral.

Meantime, two more candidates for Alex's late news anchor position had shown up, and were given the same kind of tour and audition that the first guy got. One appeared to be Hispanic, the other a black guy who looked enough like Denzel Washington to be his son. But Barclay reported that Charles was still Hawke's choice, and that he and the consultants had been increasing the pressure on him to hire the guy. "Fuck 'em," Barclay said. "They're going to have to fire me before they hire him."

Alex could only sit back and watch. And he was actually beginning to enjoy it all.

The first ripple in the calm came a couple of days later from Pat, who said she had finally been able to speak to her lawyer friend, Joanne Fraser, at the Mullen-McCaron law office, McSwain's old firm. "She's been on vacation all week," Pat reported. "But we finally got together for a few drinks last night."

"And?" Alex said.

"First off, she was very reluctant to say anything. Said it could cost her her job. But she's also a little bitter about the place. Made partner seven or eight years ago, but still isn't making the money the 'good old boys' are. She claims she bills just as many or more hours and brings in as much new business as they do, but still gets the short end of the stick."

Alex waited patiently.

"It took about three vodka martinis before she finally started to open up. She says McSwain was there one day and gone the next. Without an explanation, without a good-bye. But whatever got him fired, it wasn't old age. Several of the senior partners were older than him at the time, and are *still* there."

"What then?"

"She's not sure, and says nobody is, except for the firm's executive committee that cut him loose. And they've never talked about it, even after a few martinis themselves."

"She must have her suspicions," Alex said.

"Oh, sure. Rumors abound. The most prevalent is that he got caught with his hand in the firm's till. Overbilling and embezzling clients' money. Like that business with Clinton's buddies down in Arkansas. Only here, they kept it hushed up. Simply fired his ass. Never did get as far as the lawyer's board."

Alex pondered what he had heard. "But how could that tie him to this Spangler character?"

Pat sat back in her chair. "Who knows? Maybe it doesn't. Or maybe Marie told him about the whole Hathaway business years ago, and he decided to try blackmailing this Spangler. If he needed money badly enough to steal from his firm, he sure as hell wouldn't blink at a little blackmail."

Possible, Alex thought, but not likely. Still, it was better than anything he could come up with. What *was* clear was that McSwain had lied to him, both about how he had left the firm—but who could blame him for that?—and about knowing Marvin Spangler. What other lies were there?

"That's good work, Pat. Maybe it will all make sense at some point."

"My friend has promised to poke around a little more, discreetly, of course, and will get back to me if she can come up with anything else."

Out of boredom and frustration, Alex put a call into Phil Tinsley at his homicide office. "Haven't heard anything from you," he said. "What's happening?"

"Sorry, I should have called," Tinsley said. "But I don't have much to report. We found no strange prints in the Stockworth apartment; in fact, the place appeared to have been wiped clean. And a recanvass of the building got us nowhere. Nobody seems to have heard or seen anything unusual that night. We're talking to some of her friends and fellow employees at the bank, but again, we're drawing a blank."

"What about Spangler and the Whelans?"

"Nothing. We're having no better luck finding them than you are."

"Shit," Alex muttered.

"Keep your cool, Alex. We'll catch a break. We almost always do. But it may take some time."

Right, Alex thought. But how much time? "Okay," he finally said, "but please keep in touch."

"Trust me. You'll be the first to know, if we find anything."

That evening after the early news, Alex got together with Maggie and Malay. "We're at a goddamned standstill," he complained. "What the hell are we missing?"

Both responded with an embarrassed shrug of the shoulders.

Alex reviewed the notes he had made in the past weeks. "What about that Nation United Web page?" he asked Maggie. "You were going to check it out."

"I can't make any connections on the Internet," she said. "And when I call the number they list on their Web page, I get a message machine. I've left a phony name with my home number, but so far, nobody has returned the call."

"Is it worth a trip up to Virginia?" he asked. "To see if anybody remembers anything about them?"

"Alex, they pulled out of that enclave fifteen years ago," she replied. "Who would still be around now?"

"Maybe the people who bought the property from them," he replied.

"You're reaching," she said. "Let me keep working the Internet."

Alex continued to flip through the pages of notes. "You know, one guy we never talked to was the fellow who was manning the lock and dam the day the boys disappeared. He was quoted in the newspapers at the time, when they lowered the river level searching for the bodies."

"What could he tell us?" Malay asked. "Assuming we could find him."

"I don't know," Alex admitted. "And I don't want to beat a dead horse. But if those boys were picked up by the river, it was more than likely by somebody in a boat, right?"

"Maybe not," Malay said. "Don't forget the green van that was sitting by the park . . . and the green van that the old lady in Virginia saw with the three boys in it."

"But they could have been transferred from a boat to the van, couldn't they?"

"I suppose so," Malay said. "But if they were, none of their skulls would have wound up in Missouri."

"True," Alex said. "But what the hell? Maybe the boat went through the lock and dam before the boys were even discovered missing. Then transferred to the van. There are several hours unaccounted for there."

Malay could see the handwriting on the wall. "What's the guy's name?" he said resignedly. "The one who was working the lock and dam?"

Alex checked his notes. "Elmer Jonkowski, according to the newspaper. They didn't give an address."

"Can't be too many guys around with that name," Malay said. "I'll give it a try."

26

With the weekend facing them, Alex asked Pat if she'd like to take a little trip with him. "Where to?" she asked.

"North. To Virginia, or at least around there. It should be a nice drive."

Despite Maggie's reservations, he had decided to visit what had been the old Nation United wooded compound. In part out of curiosity, in part because he had nothing better to do at the moment. What's more, it would be a chance to get away with Pat by himself—since Malay had to attend the funeral of an old police buddy and had agreed that Alex could, on this one occasion at least, go somewhere without him.

But he had insisted that they leave before dawn on Saturday, and take the necessary evasive actions to make sure they weren't being followed.

The BCA had given Maggie the exact location of the site, and she had laid it out on a map for Alex to follow. Actually, it was closer to the towns of Tower and Soudan than it was to the city of Virginia, a thirty-acre tract beyond the border of the Superior National Forest. She didn't know who presently owned the place, but speculated that someone might be there on the weekend.

Watching the sun rise, they traveled north on Interstate 35 as far as the town of Cloquet, then along State Highways 33 and 53 to Virginia. It was a beautiful, cool morning, with little traffic, and the hours passed quickly. As they drove, Alex briefed Pat on what they were looking for, but like Maggie, she voiced her doubts that they would find anything after all these years.

"You're probably right," he told her. "But it can't hurt, and I got tired of sitting on my butt, waiting for something to happen."

From Virginia, they headed northeast, through the lower portion of the national forest, toward Lake Vermilion. They passed small farms carved out of the woods, tiny country churches, and what looked like small logging operations, with huge piles of timber—aspen and pine, mostly—stacked nearby, ready to be hauled to the pulp or paper factories.

Alex had been told the property he was searching for would be bordered along the road by a head-high barbed wire fence, with a spike-tipped steel gate at the entrance. The new owners apparently had not changed the security features of the place since the former residents abandoned it years before.

It took about twenty minutes of driving the back-country roads, carefully following Maggie's map, before they finally came upon the entrance and slowed to a stop. The gate was open, and beyond it, a narrow gravel road that led into acres of towering pine and poplar.

"What do you think?" Alex asked as the engine idled.

"You didn't come all this way to sit out here, did you?" Pat replied.

He put the Blazer into gear. "I guess not."

As he drove slowly into the woods, the sun all but disappeared. The canopy of trees left them in deep shadows, a virtual tunnel, silent but for the crunching of the tires on the gravel and the sounds of birds chirping and flitting among the branches above and on all sides of them.

"It's beautiful, but kind of creepy," Pat said, staring out the open window.

So far there was no sign of human habitation, although the road had obviously been used before . . . and often. It was smooth and well maintained, clear of weeds and fallen branches or other woodsy debris. Occasionally they would see what appeared to be trails branching off from the road through the trees, but it was impossible to know if they had been made by deer or humans.

After a quarter mile or so, they saw their first building, off to the right, a garage-type structure, only larger, with half-log siding and only two small windows. Like a bunkhouse of some kind. Then, a hundred yards or so farther on, two more buildings just like it, all of them half-hidden, built into the woods. Alex slowed to a near stop by each of them, looking for some sign of life, but finding none. Not even a stray dog. "I wonder where the hell everybody is?"

He got his answer around the next bend in the road, as the forest opened up into a large clearing. In the middle of it stood a lodge-like building, two stories high with wings that spread from either side of the main structure. To the right of it, a four-stall garage, and to the left, another of the bunkhouses.

A small stream was now visible behind the lodge, maybe twenty feet wide and slow moving. They had not caught sight of it before.

Two cars were parked in front of the lodge, a Ford Explorer and an old Buick. Alex pulled the Blazer up beside them and turned off the engine. Waiting. When no one appeared, he said, "Might as well see if anyone's home."

"You go ahead," Pat said. "I'll wait here, thank you."

Getting out of the car, Alex made his way to the porch, which wrapped around the front of the building, and knocked on the double doors that faced him. There was no response. He looked for a doorbell, but seeing none, knocked again. Harder.

"Lookin' for somebody?" The voice came from behind him and gave him a start. He wheeled around. Approaching him, halfway between the garage and the lodge, was a man Alex judged to be in his fifties, clad in bib overalls and a grimy, sweaty T-shirt. A rifle of some type was slung over his right shoulder.

Alex left the porch to meet him. "My name's Alex Collier, from the Cities," he said. The man wiped his hand on the front of his overalls before returning Alex's handshake. "And that's Pat Hodges, there in the car."

The man turned to look. "How do you like that Blazer?" he asked before saying anything else. "I thought about gettin' one of those before I settled on the Explorer."

"It's okay, I guess," Alex replied. "Never given me any trouble, anyway."

"Uh-huh."

Now that he was next to the man, Alex could see that his skin was well weathered and his teeth uneven and brown, no doubt from too many years of chewing plugs of tobacco like the one bulging in his cheek now.

"You live here?" Alex asked.

The man spat a brown gob into the dirt, causing a puff of dust. "Uh-huh."

"By yourself?"

"Right now, yeah."

"Big place for just one person."

"You got that right."

The man stood studying him, in no apparent hurry to continue the conversation.

"We just happened to be up this way," Alex said, "and I'd heard about this place . . . that it used to be a commune of some type. Am I right?"

"Who'd you say you were again?"

"Alex Collier. I work for a television station in the Twin Cities. Channel Seven."

"We don't get that up here. We just get Duluth TV."

"I know," Alex said.

The man slipped the rifle off his shoulder and leaned it against the railing of the porch, still within easy reach.

"I didn't get your name," Alex said.

"Stanley."

"First or last name?"

"First."

"Do you own this place, Stanley?"

"Nope. I'm just the caretaker." Another gob flew into the dirt, this time a few inches closer to Alex's shoe.

"Can you tell me who does own it?"

"Why would you want to know that?"

This was getting him nowhere fast, Alex decided. Best lie. "Actually, I'm doing some research for a news story on the history of . . . I guess you'd call them fringe groups . . . in the state. I read about the group that used to live up here and thought I'd stop by to get some background."

"Uh-huh."

"Were you here then?"

"That was a long time ago."

"I know. Fifteen years or so."

"Yup."

"Did you know them at all? The people who lived here then?"

"You could say that."

Alex was getting frustrated. "I'd be willing to pay for information about them."

"You would?"

He pulled two crisp one hundred dollar bills out of his wallet. "For starters," he said.

Stanley took the bills out of his hand. "Why don't you and your lady friend come on in," he said, motioning to the lodge.

Alex waved at Pat and then followed the man through the double doors. Pat was not far behind, but not looking all that pleased to be there.

The lodge interior was spacious but dark and musty, like a giant attic that no one had bothered to enter for years. A few pieces of hand-hewn wood furniture were scattered here and there, but not much else. No rugs, no pictures, no deer heads hanging from the wall. All in all, there was an eerie emptiness about the place, as though it had been abandoned in a hurry and never reclaimed.

Stanley opened the shutters on a couple of the windows and turned on some lights. "Grab a couple of chairs," he said. "I got some coffee warmin' in the kitchen."

As he moved away, Alex and Pat exchanged glances. He could read her lips: "Spooky."

Stanley returned a few minutes later with three cups of coffee on a small tray and carefully placed them on the table before taking a seat himself. "So what do you want to know about them people?"

"Everything you can tell me," Alex replied.

"Well, there was about a hundred of them, I guess. Men, women, and kids. Never could figure out who was

married to who, or whatnot. They all kind of lived
together in them cabins you saw drivin' in, or here in
the lodge."

The money had obviously loosened his tongue.

"How long were they here?"

"Three or four years, I guess. Until a few of the
neighbors got to complainin'."

"About what?"

"The noise, mostly. These folks liked to play war
games out there in the woods, and it got pretty wild at
times. That plus their holy roller church services. And
the traffic in and out of here raised a hell of a lot of
dust. But mostly, I think, folks just didn't like the idea
of a bunch of what they figured were hippies livin' this
close by."

"What did they do?" Alex asked. "Aside from playing war games?"

"Never could figure that out, actually. Like I say,
there was a ton of traffic in and out, and there's another
building, back there in the woods, that was off-limits,
even to me. And I was the one keepin' things runnin' for
them."

"So what did you think?" Alex asked.

"To be honest? That they were probably cookin'
some drugs back there. And sellin' 'em in the Cities.
That's why they got so freaked out when the sheriff
started to poke around the place. When they decided to
sell and move on."

"But you never said anything to anyone?"

"Wasn't none of my business. They were payin' me
good wages and I wasn't about to rock the boat."

Alex continued to question him, but learned little
else of value. Stanley claimed not to know who the current owner or owners were . . . that he dealt with a

banker in Virginia who represented them. "It's my job to keep the place up, until somebody decides what to do with it."

"But it's been fifteen years," Alex said.

"I know. Strange, huh?"

Strange indeed, Alex thought. "Tell me about the kids who were here," he said.

"There was a bunch of them. From little ones in diapers to big, strapping kids. They seemed to be everywhere."

"Do you remember any in particular?"

"Not really. There were too many of them."

"How about any of these?" Alex said, showing him a picture of the Hathaway boys that Pat had brought with her from the car.

Stanley studied the picture. "Nope, can't say as I do." Then, after handing the photo back, he said, "But I've got some pictures of my own, if you're interested."

"You do?"

"Yeah. Somebody left 'em behind in one of the cabins. Dropped down behind one of the bunk beds. I found them when I was cleanin' up."

"Where are they?"

"In my room."

"Can we see them?"

Stanley hesitated. "It'll cost you a little more."

Alex pulled two fifty dollar bills from his wallet. "This is all I've got on me," he said.

"That'll do," Stanley said as he took the bills and started walking toward one of the wings of the building. "I'll be back in a minute."

Pat, who had said nothing until now, asked, "Do you always give money away like that?"

"Not hardly. Barclay would kill me. He doesn't like

paying sources. I can't even report it on my expense account."

Stanley was back in a few minutes and spread a group of photos out on the table. Alex and Pat both leaned over, examining them. There were about twenty prints in all, apparently an entire roll of film that somebody had taken and then inadvertently left behind. Most of them were shots of adults, men and women, a few of them in fatigues and camouflage paint—caught in the midst of one of their war games.

Alex picked up each photo, studied it closely, and passed it on to Pat. "Can you give me the names of any these people?" he asked Stanley.

"Sorry. No can do. I never knew any of their real names. They all went by nicknames. Like Tiger. And Shoofly. Amoeba. Things like that. Some of them were pretty crazy."

Alex and Pat continued to pore over the prints, finally coming to four or five that included children. Some of the kids were in swimming suits, apparently taken by the bank of the nearby stream. Others were on the lodge porch.

Alex held each up to the light, squinting. "Look at this," he said, handing the next picture to Pat. "The third boy from the right."

Like Alex, she tried to position it for the best light. Four young boys were in the picture, all about the same age, between four and six, she guessed, holding hands on the porch. "My God," she whispered. "Is it really him?"

Unless they were wrong, the third boy from the right was none other than Andrew, the youngest of the Hathaway brothers.

Stanley stared at them, obviously puzzled. "What do you mean, is it really him?"

"Nothing," Alex said quickly, working to keep the excitement out of his voice. "But I'd like to borrow these prints."

"Borrow them?"

"Yes. I'll return them. If you'd like, I'll even go into the nearest town now and have copies made. It's important."

Stanley appeared undecided. "Have I got your word that I'll get 'em back?"

"Absolutely," Alex said. "And there'll be another hundred in it for you."

That clinched the deal.

"Did they leave anything else behind?" Alex asked. "You know, papers? Journals? Checkbooks? Anything like that?"

"Nope. Nothin' we didn't get rid of during the cleanup. After they'd left. I just kept those pictures for . . . you know . . . historical purposes." He smiled, obviously proud of his vocabulary.

Before they left, Stanley gave them a tour of the entire encampment, including all of the buildings— even the one deep in the woods where he believed the drugs had been cooked. He was right; nothing of value was left.

He also reluctantly provided Alex with the name of the Virginia banker with whom he dealt, the man who apparently represented the new owner or owners of the property. And Alex left Stanley with his business card. "Call me if anything else happens, okay?"

As they left, Alex could see Stanley in the rearview mirror, smiling and waving, Alex's bills still clutched in his hand.

Driving back the way they'd come, toward Virginia, Alex said, "What if we're wrong? Maybe it's just wishful thinking. Maybe it's not really Andrew, and we're getting excited over nothing."

Pat had been comparing the family photo with Stanley's snapshot. "I don't know. A lot of kids that age do tend to look alike. They haven't really had time to form their own distinctive features. But his mother or dad sure as heck ought to know."

"You'd think so, but fifteen years is a long time, even for them."

"If it *is* him," Pat said, "then where are his brothers?"

"They had to be somewhere else when the picture was taken."

"You'd hope so."

Alex glanced at her. "What do you mean?"

"I know this will sound creepy," she said, "but what if these people only wanted the youngest of the brothers? The one who was young enough to eventually forget about his real parents . . . to forget that he'd been taken away from them. What if they had to take all three to get the one? I suspect Andrew was never alone, that he was always with his folks or his brothers."

"Jesus Christ, Pat . . ."

"It's a horrible thought, I know. But can you imagine how difficult it would be to secretly raise three boys, at least one, or maybe two of whom are old enough to know that they'd been kidnapped? Who'd always be trying to get away? Especially a kid like Jed, from what you've told me about him."

"I think you're getting way ahead of yourself, Pat."

"Maybe so, but I wouldn't be so quick to dismiss the idea."

Alex was pretty sure the bank, Virginia Trust, would be closed on a Saturday afternoon, but he decided to try to find the banker anyway. At home or wherever. Getting him to say anything, of course, would be another matter.

He was right. The bank was closed. So while they stopped for a late lunch, Alex looked up the man's name—Herbert Winkman—in the local phone directory. He punched in the number and waited. After three rings, a man answered, apparently on a cell phone, with noisy chatter in the background.

"Mr. Winkman?"

"Yes."

Alex introduced himself, then said, "I happen to be in Virginia now and wondered if I might stop by and chat with you."

There was a momentary pause. "About what, exactly?"

"I'd rather speak to you in person," he said.

"If it's about bank business, then—"

"Not entirely."

"I'm in the midst of a family picnic at the moment . . ."

Alex was persistent. "I wouldn't want to interrupt that, but this won't take more than a few minutes."

After more hesitation, Winkman finally agreed and gave Alex directions to his home. "I'll be there in fifteen minutes," Alex said.

Winkman was not fibbing. As Alex and Pat pulled up to his house on Southern Drive, they could see a backyard full of people, many of the adults gathered around two smoky barbecue grills—drinks in their hands. Alex left Pat and the Blazer in the driveway, and wandered—a bit self-consciously—toward the picnickers. Fortunately, Winkman spotted him before he had gotten too far, and walked over to greet him. "Let's go into the house," he said. "There's too much commotion out here."

Winkman was a short, stout fellow, whose rotund belly was hardly hidden by the "My Favorite Grandpa" barbecue apron that hung from around his neck. His cheeks were flushed, perhaps from the sun, the heat of the grill, or one too many frosty brews, but his gait was steady and he displayed an easy, friendly smile.

"We don't get too many TV fellas from the Cities up here," he said once they were seated inside. "Especially on a Saturday afternoon. So what can I do for you?"

Alex decided it would be best to be direct. No sense in wasting Winkman's time or his own. "I was just up visiting the old commune near Tower-Soudan," he said. "Spent some time with Stanley, the caretaker."

Winkman's smile suddenly faded. "Now, why would you have been up there?" he asked.

Alex thought he might as well tell the same lie, repeating what he had told Stanley about his mythical research project. "But he couldn't tell me that much, actually, and said he didn't know who the current owner of the land is. He said he dealt only with you."

The flushed face seemed to darken. "I'll have to talk to Stanley," he said. "He shouldn't have said anything."

"Why is that?"

"Because it's private property," Winkman said. "And because the previous residents are now history. Distant history."

"I thought the present owner might be able to tell me——"

Winkman got up abruptly. "I think we should end this conversation, Mr. Collier. I have to get back to my guests."

Alex stayed in his chair. "Give me a minute more. Please. If you won't tell me who the owner is, maybe you can give me the names of anyone else who might know more about the people who lived there?"

"I'm sorry, I can't."

"And why the place apparently hasn't been occupied since they left?"

Winkman was by the door, holding it open. "I don't want to be impolite," he said, "but I must ask you to leave. Now, please."

"Okay. I'll just have to get the information from the sheriff and the county tax records," Alex said, although he knew there wouldn't be time for that today. "I thought you might save me the trouble."

Winkman stood aside and watched him walk down the driveway. "Good-bye, Mr. Collier. And have a safe trip home."

As Alex climbed behind the wheel, Pat said, "That was quick."

"No kidding. He wouldn't tell me shit."

Winkman was still watching as Alex backed out onto the street and headed toward the highway.

"But that means something in itself, doesn't it?" Pat said, once he had repeated the essence of his brief conversation with the banker.

"What do you mean?"

"That he's so intent on keeping it secret," she said. "What could he have to hide that's so important?"

"That's one of two big questions," Alex replied. "The other is why the place is still vacant. It's too big and beautiful a piece of property to let stand empty. You'd think somebody would have tried to turn it into a resort . . . or subdivided it. Or something. The taxes alone must be substantial."

Pat turned in her seat, facing him directly. "Maybe

there's something still there," she said. "Something no one wants discovered."

"What are you talking about? Stanley took us around the whole place."

"There's thirty acres of woods, Alex. We saw virtually none of that."

He slowed the car and pulled over to the side of the highway. "You're way ahead of me, Pat," he said, now facing her. "Explain."

"Remember what I said? About taking all three brothers to get the one?"

"Yeah."

"What would they have done with the other two?"

He suddenly saw the light, but didn't like what he saw. "You think they could be in the woods."

She nodded.

"Buried."

She shrugged. "It would explain a lot."

27

Alex wasn't sure if the Hathaways were up north with their daughters or at home for the weekend, but he decided to check their house on the way into town. It was almost nightfall by the time they arrived, and both he and Pat were near exhaustion from their dawn-to-dusk trek.

There were no visible lights on in the house and no sign of activity outside as he pulled into the driveway. "Doesn't look like anybody's here," he said, feeling some relief. Most of all, he wanted to get home, have a drink, take a shower, and head for bed. But as he was ready to leave, Pat said, "You'd better be sure."

He walked to the front door and rang the doorbell, hearing the echo of its chimes inside. He waited, then hit the button again. A minute later, as he was about to step off the porch, a light came on in the inside entry. John Hathaway was at the door, obviously surprised to find him there. "Collier? What the hell?"

"Hello, John. Sorry to bother you, but we need to talk."

He stepped out onto the porch. "Is it Hazel? The girls? Are they okay?"

"I'm sure they are," he said. "It's nothing like that."

Hathaway was wearing a pair of shorts, sandals, and a Grateful Dead T-shirt, wet with sweat. "Hazel's at the lake with the girls," he said. "But I had to work overtime at the warehouse and," with a glance down at his soggy shirt, "was just down in the basement, trying to build a workbench."

"May we come inside?" Alex asked. "We have something to show you."

Hathaway looked toward the Blazer. "That's my friend, Pat Hodges," Alex explained. "She's been with me all day."

"Sure, if it's important, I guess. C'mon in. But you'll have to excuse the mess. I don't keep a very neat house when Hazel's away."

While Alex went back to the car to get Pat, Hathaway quickly changed into a dry polo shirt and turned on the lights around the house. And after he and Pat were formally introduced, they all took seats at the dining room table.

Alex quickly explained how they had spent the day, and why they had gone to the commune in the first place. "There was a newspaper article shortly after your boys disappeared, talking about a militant group that was causing some problems up near Virginia."

"What does that have to do with the boys?" John asked, cutting in.

"We didn't know. But the article mentioned that a lot of children were spotted there," he continued. "And shortly after the newspaper story appeared, the group sold the place and split. Almost fifteen years ago."

"So?"

"So it kept nagging at me," Alex said, "especially when the rest of our investigation seemed to be drying up. We decided to go up and take a look for ourselves."

He went on to describe the encounter with Stanley the caretaker, and how they had come to possess the pictures that Pat was now spreading out on the table in front of Hathaway. "We'd like you to look at them all," Alex said, "but we're especially interested in the one that Pat still has in her hand."

Hathaway took the picture from her and held it about six inches from his face.

"Look at the boy who's third from the right," Alex said.

Hathaway stood up and walked into the kitchen, where the light was better. Alex and Pat followed him, standing in the doorway, watching. "I have a magnifying glass in the den," John said. "I'll be right back."

He didn't return for several minutes, but when he did, there were tears in his eyes, a few trickling down his cheeks. "I can't believe it, but I think it's him. I think it's Andy." He sat down at the kitchen table and buried his face in his hands. "My God, can it really be him?"

Alex and Pat said nothing, standing back, waiting for him to recover. It took several minutes, but finally Alex said, "We thought it was, too. But we wanted you and Hazel to confirm it."

"Can I have the picture?" Hathaway asked. "I'll get in the car and head for Bemidji tonight. Right now. I can be there by midnight. Hazel has to see this."

"That's fine," Alex replied. "But we'd like you to look at the rest of the pictures first. To see if you possibly recognize anyone else."

They returned to the dining room, and Hathaway sorted through the remaining photos, examining each one closely. Then, as if it just occurred to him, he said, "If it is Andy, where are Matt and Jed?"

"We don't know," Alex replied, with a sideways

glance at Pat. "Maybe somewhere else in the compound."

Hathaway went back to the pictures, and when he
was finished, he said, "A couple of these people seem
vaguely familiar, but I can't be sure."

"Which ones?" Alex asked.

He pointed to one of the pictures with several of the
adults in combat fatigues. "I don't know," he said, "it's
like I've seen this couple in the middle before. But with
their uniforms and hats, it's hard to tell."

Alex decided to take a leap. "It's not the Whelans, is
it? The couple that used to live down the street from you
in the old neighborhood?"

Hathaway looked at him curiously. "Maybe. But
God, I don't know. It's been so long. Hazel might remember."

"I'll ask her when you both get back from Bemidji,"
Alex said. "But I need to keep that and the rest of the
pictures for now."

As they prepared to leave, Hathaway stopped them
at the door. "I don't know what's going to come of all
this," he said, "but I owe you a deep apology. I don't
know anyone else who would have done what you've
done, and I'm sorry I've been such a bastard."

"No need to apologize," Alex said. "Not after what
you and your wife have been through for all of these
years."

"Even if we never find them," he said, his eyes
welling again, "knowing that at least one of them didn't
drown . . . and may still be alive somewhere . . . will
make life easier. And give me, at least, a measure of new
hope."

"Good," Alex said, squeezing his arm. "Now just
keep the faith."

*   *   *

Alex dropped Pat off at her town house, then headed for home—trying to shake off his fatigue long enough to stay not only awake, but alert. And in case anyone had been watching Pat's place, he made himself take a few simple precautions to eliminate the chance of being followed.

Malay was at the house when he got there, waiting expectantly. But Alex put him off until he'd taken his shower and fixed himself a cool drink. Then they sat down in the living room as Alex recounted the day's events, as completely yet concisely as he could.

"Holy shit!" Malay exclaimed.

"I know. It's been a hell of a day."

"When will you hear from Mrs. Hathaway?"

"In the morning, I hope," Alex said. "John said he'd have her call."

"So what's next?" Malay asked.

Alex leaned back in his chair, steepling his fingers beneath his chin. "Good question. We have to pin down the ownership of that commune property. Don't ask me how, but that's a priority. I also want to show the pictures to Sean Spangler, to see if he recognizes anybody there."

"You think he might?"

"I don't know. But John Hathaway thought one couple might be the Whelans."

Malay got up and stretched. "I finally found that lock-and-dam guy," he said. "He's retired now, but has agreed to see me tomorrow."

"Good."

"And I also got a message from that state police guy in Missouri. He finally located the skull, and it should be here Monday or Tuesday."

Alex's brain was as tired as the rest of him. "Tell me again. Where did they find the skull?"

"In McLaren County. It borders the Mississippi, across from Illinois. Why?"

"Nothing," Alex said. "I just didn't remember."

By now his eyelids had begun to close, despite his efforts to keep them open. "I've got to get to bed," he said finally.

"Go ahead," Malay said. "I'll get the lights and lock things up down here."

Alex spent a fitful night. Tossing, turning, waking up, drifting back to sleep. In and out of dreams that seemed as real as the daylight, yet as elusive as the darkness. One or two brought him awake, sweating, but later he would recall only one: a hazy vision of Tommy Akers, walking down the sidewalk, newspaper bag slung over his shoulder, retreating into the distance, laughing, oblivious to Alex's calls to come back.

A sharp rap on his bedroom door brought him fully awake. Sunlight was pouring into the room, the window curtains blown high and wide by a stiff but cool breeze. He sat up in the bed. "Yeah?"

Malay opened the door and stuck his head in. "Hazel Hathaway's on the phone," he said. "I knew you'd want to take it."

"Right," Alex said, reaching for the telephone cord that he had disconnected the night before. He plugged it in and picked up the receiver.

"It's him, Alex! I know it is." Her voice was shrill with excitement. "I couldn't believe it when John showed me the picture. You've done it! You've found him."

"Take it easy, Hazel. Please."

"I can't, Alex. How can I?"

Malay was sitting on the edge of the bed, smiling, listening to his side of the conversation. "I'm glad you feel it's Andy," Alex said. "But the picture was taken fifteen years ago. It may prove he was alive then, but it doesn't help us a whole lot now."

"It proves he didn't drown," she exclaimed. "That's enough for me. Now, if we could only find something about the other two."

At her urging, he repeated much of what he had already told her husband the night before, but which she insisted on hearing for herself. "I can't believe you went up there," she said, "knowing only what you did."

"It was more of a hunch than anything," he replied. "Or a lucky guess. But I'm happy it turned out the way it did."

Hazel went on to tell him that Angie and Andrea were having the time of their lives, and that her brother and sister-in-law were in no hurry to see them leave. "But I hear you want me back to look at some other pictures," she said.

"When you get home," Alex said. "There's no great hurry."

"I'll be back Monday," she said, and then, for the second time since he'd known her, she added, "God bless you, Alex."

Later that day Malay had no trouble finding Elmer Jonkowski's home in northeast Minneapolis, a tiny white two-bedroom house on Benjamin Street, just off Lowry Avenue. Like most of the other homes on the street, it was immaculately maintained, with a well-trimmed lawn, carefully pruned bushes, and small flower gardens in front and back.

Jonkowski was sitting on the front stoop, trying to

read the Sunday newspaper, despite the stiff breeze that wanted to tear it out of his hands. He was a man even older than himself, Malay guessed, completely bald but with a ruddy, healthy complexion and a body that, while thin, was not gaunt. He seemed to be wearing his age nicely.

"Mr. Jonkowski?" Malay said as he made his way up the sidewalk.

"You got it," Jonkowski replied, putting aside the wind-whipped paper, anchoring it to the stoop with a small flowerpot. "But people call me Elmer, like in Fudd." Then he laughed.

Malay grinned and started to introduce himself, but Elmer cut him off. "I remember you from your days in the police department," he said. "Your picture was in the paper a lot back then."

Malay sat down next to him. "That was quite a long time ago," he said. "I'm surprised that you do remember."

Jonkowski, Malay would learn, had spent thirty years as a lock man, working the four-to-midnight shift, tending the upper St. Anthony lock and dam near downtown Minneapolis. "It was kind of boring at times," he said, "but I've always been fascinated by the river. It's never the same, you know, changes with the seasons and the kind of weather that Mother Nature decides to throw at us."

It didn't take Malay long to realize that Elmer was a lonely man who loved to talk, and who probably didn't have many people willing to listen to him. So he let him go on, telling story after story about his career and life on the river. The floods and the boats and the barges.

Finally, though, Malay knew he would have to get to the point of his visit. "Do you remember the three

Hathaway brothers? The ones they think drowned in the river back in '83?"

"Of course. It was July sixteenth. I was on duty that day. And the next. I'll never forget it. We tried to lower the river level to help them find the bodies. But they never did, you know."

"I know," Malay said. "That's why I'm here."

"You workin' with that TV guy?"

"Yeah. Alex Collier."

"Right. That's him."

Malay shifted his position on the step to face Elmer more directly. "I'm not so much interested in the search for the boys as I am in what happened at the lock in the five or six hours before you were notified about their disappearance. Like from four or five o'clock that afternoon . . ."

"What are you talking about?"

"Any boats that may have gone through the locks at about that time."

Elmer gave him a shocked look. "You actually expect me to remember that?"

"I was hoping you could," Malay replied.

The old man let out a cackle. "Then you came to the right place," he said, slapping his knee in apparent glee. "Fooled ya, huh?"

Malay couldn't help but laugh with him. "What are you talking about?"

"I kept a log every day I worked on the river. For thirty damn years. Outside temperature, water temperature, wind speed, flow of the water, general weather conditions. And," he said, "every boat that passed through the locks. Names. Port. Registration numbers."

"You've got to be kidding."

"No, it's true. Helped me pass some of the slow time."

"Can you find the log for the sixteenth?" Malay asked.

"Sure, but I don't have it."

"You don't?"

"No, I donated all of the logs to the state historical society when I retired. They tell a lot about the history of the river."

"How can I get it?" Malay asked.

"Just go ask for it," Jonkowski replied. "They'll dig it out for you. But you'll have to wait until tomorrow, when the offices open."

Malay got to his feet. "You've been a big help, Elmer. I appreciate it."

"No problem. Drop by again sometime. I've got some stories that'll crack you up."

"I will," Malay promised.

"And tell that Collier that his sidekick, Maggie whatever, is a hell of a lot prettier than he is." Then he let out another cackle.

Back home, Alex was on the phone, trying to reach Sean Spangler. After several tries over a couple of hours, he finally succeeded. But he immediately noticed a difference in the young man's voice, a hesitation, a reticence. "Are you okay, Sean?" he finally asked.

There was another lengthy pause. "Barney said I'm not supposed to be talking to you."

Alex shouldn't have been surprised, but was. McSwain protecting his ass. "Why is that?" he asked.

"Barney says you may be trying to ruin my mother's reputation. That you think she had something to do with those boys' disappearance."

"And you believe that?"

"I argued with him. Told him you didn't come off

that way to me. But he was pretty insistent . . . said I didn't know the full story."

Alex sat back in his chair. "That's not true, Sean. You'll have to take my word. I'm simply trying to find the truth, and so far I have no reason to believe your mother had anything directly to do with the abduction of those boys."

"But she knew about it . . ."

"That's right. But probably not at the time."

There was silence at the other end of the line.

Alex pressed ahead. "Sean, do you honestly think she would have been willing to give us information about it if she had been involved herself? Does that make sense to you?"

"Not really, I guess."

"Nor to me. I think that's why she called me. Not so much for the reward money as to get what she knew off her chest. Off her conscience."

"God, I wish I knew what to do," he said.

"I want you to look at some pictures," Alex said. "That's all. You don't have to say anything more to me."

"What pictures?"

"I'll tell you when I see you. But it's important."

After more give-and-take, Sean finally, reluctantly, agreed to meet Alex—the next morning, at the same Perkins restaurant as before.

28

Sean was in the same booth when Alex and Malay walked out of a heavy rain and into the restaurant. The skies had opened up with a vengeance in the early morning hours, the rumbling thunder and bolts of lightning awakening Alex from a night of deep sleep. The showers were continuing now, hours later, although the worst of the storm had passed on to the east, into Wisconsin.

Sean looked more physically fit now than the last time they had seen him, although the hesitation Alex had heard on the phone the day before was evident now in his subdued greeting. "I appreciate your seeing us," Alex said as they sat across from him. "I mean that. I know you've still got your doubts."

"Barney doesn't know I'm meeting you," he said, "and I'd like to keep it that way. Things are complicated enough."

"That's not a problem," Alex replied. "I haven't seen him since the funeral."

After they all ordered coffee, Sean told them that he was now back at work and getting along well. "My girlfriend's been a big help," he said. "It's too bad my mom didn't know her better. She's really gotten me through all of this."

He volunteered that McSwain was handling his mother's estate, although there wasn't much there. "She lived pretty much from paycheck to paycheck," he said. "Never did own a house, not since my father left, and spent most of what she earned raising me, I guess."

Alex and Malay listened sympathetically, but— holding to Alex's promise—refrained from asking him any questions. Finally Sean said, "So where are the pictures that you wanted me to see?"

Alex took out the packet of photos. "It's not important where I got these, and I'll warn you, they're old, but I'd like to know if you recognize anyone."

He spread them out in rows on the tabletop, and watched as Sean picked up each and studied it. He took his time, holding the pictures close. When he reached the thirteenth picture, he stopped, glancing up at them, his expression one of surprise. "That's Larry and Emily," he said, "there in the middle."

He handed the picture to Alex. It was the same one John Hathaway had singled out.

"You're sure it's the Whelans?" Alex said, holding his breath.

"Of course. Although they look a little weird in those outfits. But that's them, I'm positive."

Alex put the picture aside. "Keep going, please," he said.

Sean studied the remaining photos as carefully as the first batch, but could identify no one else. "So what's all this about?" he asked when he finished.

"It's better that you not know right now," Alex replied. "But I promise I'll fill you in when we see how everything fits together."

At that point, Sean pulled an envelope of his own out of his pocket. "Back when we met the first time, at

Mom's apartment, you asked if I had any pictures of my father. I hadn't thought about it again until you called yesterday."

Alex had all but forgotten it himself.

"Well, I managed to dig these out," Sean said, opening the envelope. "I hadn't looked at them myself for years."

Alex took the pictures and spread them out between Malay and himself. There were six in all, color snapshots that Sean said dated back to the late '70s and early '80s, before his dad abandoned them in 1983. Two of the photos were of Marvin Spangler and his then-wife, Marie, sitting on the front steps of a house.

"That's when we lived out in Coon Rapids," Sean said.

While the pictures had been shot from a distance, the image of Marvin Spangler was clear. He was thin—skinny, really—with dark hair and beard, wearing a pair of granny glasses that gave him, in total, something of the look of a beatnik professor. Three other pictures included Sean, two of them alone with his dad, the third including his mother. All appeared to have been taken in a park. In each case, Spangler wore a tank top that hung from his slender shoulders, and a pair of baggy pants. Genetically he was a far cry from his well-muscled son.

The sixth and last photo brought a small gasp to Alex's lips. He quickly passed the photo to Malay, who had virtually the same reaction.

"What's wrong?" Sean asked, watching them.

The picture was of Spangler standing alone . . . next to a dark green Chevy van.

"This van," Alex said, holding the picture up. "Did your dad own it?"

"Sure. He got it a year or so before he took off."

"Like sometime in 1982 or '83?"

"Yeah, I guess so. Why?"

"That's another piece of the puzzle that I'll try to explain someday. It may mean nothing, but it also could be important."

Sean sat back in the booth, obviously frustrated and confused.

Alex debated revealing the next piece of information, but finally decided he should. "Sean, did you know that your dad was in trouble with the law a couple of times . . . that he spent some time in prison?"

Sean straightened up. "No, when?"

"He was busted twice on drug charges. Once in 1984, and again in '86. The last time, he spent two years in Stillwater."

Sean shook his head. "I'm not really surprised. I told you my mother thought he might be dealing. So it's no wonder we never heard from him. He was a goddamned con."

"I take it you still haven't heard anything from him," Alex said. "Since your mother's death, I mean."

"No, nothing."

"Would you do us one more favor? Will you let us know if you *do* hear from him? Or about him?"

"Sure, I guess so. I don't figure I owe him shit."

It was still raining, although not quite as hard, as Alex and Malay left the restaurant. They hurried to the Blazer, and once inside, looked at each other. "It's making more and more sense, isn't it?" Malay said. "These can't all be coincidences."

Alex leaned against the steering wheel, watching the raindrops splatter on the windshield and hood. "Tell me again," he said, testing himself, "what kind of vehicle ran down Peter Osborne."

"I'd have to check to be sure, but I think it was an '82 or '83 Chevy van."

"And when did Spangler get out of prison?"

"If he was convicted in late 1986 and spent two-plus years prison, it would probably have been sometime in '89, I'd guess."

"And when was Osborne killed?"

"In the fall of '89. Early October, I think."

"Talk about coincidences," Alex said. "Let's double-check all of the dates, okay? Make sure we're not letting our imaginations get the best of us."

By late afternoon, Alex had met with Hazel Hathaway, who also believed that it was the Whelans who were pictured at the commune. But like Sean and her husband, she could not identify anyone else in the photos.

Alex also returned briefly to the old Hathaway neighborhood, and once again found the grouchy old man, Albers, at home. Alex showed him Sean's picture of his father and the green van . . . and asked if that vehicle was similar to the one Albers had seen parked near the park entrance fifteen years before. Albers grudgingly admitted that it was, but then told Alex to get the hell away and stay away.

Still later, Malay returned from the state historical society with Elmer Jonkowski's logs from the upper St. Anthony lock and dam. "He was a meticulous guy," Malay said, running his finger down all of the data. As Elmer had promised, the logs included detailed descriptions of both the atmospheric and water conditions on July sixteenth . . . as well as the passing river traffic.

They focused on the traffic, especially in the hours after four o'clock in the afternoon, about the time the Hathaway boys disappeared. They found that six vessels had passed downriver through the locks between then and nine o'clock that night, including a tugboat, two barges loaded with cement and gravel, two small run-abouts, and two cabin cruisers. "Forget the runabouts," Malay said, "there's no way you could hide three kids on one of those."

That left the two cruisers. One was named the *Mary Lee*, registered to the port of Duluth, which went through the locks at 7 P.M. The other, *The Patriot*, claimed Bayport as its home port, and had entered the locks an hour earlier. Elmer had also copied the registration numbers painted or stenciled on the bows of both boats.

"What do you think?" Alex asked.

"Let's see when those cruisers went the other way, up the river," Malay said.

Although Elmer did not work mornings, he apparently had persuaded other lockmen to maintain his logs during those earlier hours. And as Alex and Malay flipped through the pages, they discovered that only the *Mary Lee* had made the trip up the river earlier that same day. At about two in the afternoon. There was no indication when *The Patriot* had traveled up the river.

"Don't ask," Malay said. "I'm way ahead of you." He spread out Elmer's logs for the five days preceding the sixteenth, and quickly scanned the pages. "There it is," he said, pointing. *The Patriot* had passed upriver through the locks three days earlier, on the thirteenth.

"So what have we got?" Alex asked. "One boat that's up and down the river in an afternoon. Another that spent a full three days somewhere beyond the locks. Doing what?"

"Waiting, maybe," Malay said.

"For what?"

"The right moment."

Alex watched him, waiting.

"If those kids *were* taken from the river," Malay said, "how would anyone know exactly when they might show up? They wouldn't. They'd have to wait around and hope. I'd put my money on *The Patriot*."

"That sounds reasonable," Alex said, "but since both were upriver at the right time and either could have picked up the kids, let's check them both out."

"You got it," Malay said. "I'll ask Maggie to get on the computer."

Barclay came by Alex's desk after the early news. "I know you've hardly had time to breathe," he said, "but could you spare me a half hour or so?"

"Sure, I guess so," Alex said, having made no other plans for the time between the early and late news. "What's up?"

"I want you to look at some audition tapes," Barclay said as he led Alex across the newsroom to his office and closed the door behind them. "These are the leading candidates for the late news," he added, pointing to four tapes on his desk.

Alex feigned outrage. "You want me to look at my goddamned successors, George? Give me a break!"

"I want your opinion," Barclay said. "Which shows how much respect I have for you."

"Sure."

Barclay put the first of the tapes into the playback machine. "Don't say anything until you've seen them all," he said. "Then I'd like your ranking and comments."

"What am I going to see here?" Alex asked.

"Each of their auditions with Maggie. They're only ten minutes or so each."

Alex settled back in his chair as the tapes played. First up, the tall Norwegian, Hawke's golden boy; then the Hispanic followed by the Denzel Washington looka-like; and finally, by someone Alex had not seen before, a young white guy with a bad complexion and hair not unlike Lyle Lovett's. And whose performance was unbe-lievably bad, from start to finish. He could barely say his own name without stumbling.

"Who in the hell was that?" Alex asked, astonished that the young man could be considered among the finalists.

"Hawke's nephew. He's been working down in Iowa somewhere. Thinks he's ready for a major market."

"It has to be a joke," Alex said gleefully.

"I know, but Hawke insisted we give him an audition, and count him among the finalists. He's just trying to pull my chain, I'm sure, to get me to see things his way."

"You ought to hire the guy," Alex said. "Then leave. Let Hawke sit in his own shit for once."

"Let's forget the nephew," Barclay said. "That's not the real question."

From Alex's point of view, there was no question: The black candidate, whose name was Ted Bryant, was clearly the best of the bunch. Not only did he have Hol-lywood good looks, but unlike the others, he came across as serious and creditable, someone who could connect and communicate with the audience. In short, he appeared to be a real person, not some cloned anchor-man. "I'd need to see more of him," Alex told Barclay now, "but from that short piece, I think he's clearly the pick of the litter."

"I thought you'd say that," Barclay replied. "And I agree. What's more, he's done some real reporting . . . some damn fine work out in the field."

"Then what's the problem?" Alex asked.

"Guess. Hawke says this market's not ready for a major black anchor. That there's not a big enough minority population. That he and Maggie would look like salt and pepper shakers on the set."

What a prick, Alex thought, although he shouldn't have been surprised. Hawke was no different than any of his buddies who ran the competing stations. At the moment, there was but one person of color anchoring the news among the major stations in the Twin Cities. And not a single meteorologist or even a sportscaster who was anything but white as the winter snow.

Hawke and his friends all had their public excuses or rationalizations down pat, but in Alex's view, it came down to the fact that—like Hawke—they all believed a minority face on the news might alienate the majority . . . which could mean lost viewers and fewer advertising dollars. It was as simple, yet frightening, as that.

"So what are you going to do?" he asked.

Barclay slumped in his chair. "I'd fight the good fight, if I thought I could win. But I don't. It's going to take a change in ownership or something before these people finally decide to do the right thing. And even that might not do it."

Alex sat quietly, unable to argue the point.

"And you know," Barclay went on, "the pity of it is that somebody like this Bryant fellow could turn things around. Given the chance. I don't think we've got an audience full of bigots or dullards. They just want somebody who's personable, knowledgeable, and who can read the goddamned news."

"And who's young," Alex added wryly.

"Okay, and young," Barclay admitted.

They spent several more minutes talking, but could

come up with no easy answers. "Hawke is pushing me to make a decision," Barclay said. "And he's made it abundantly clear who he wants."

"The Norwegian."

"Yeah. The kid claims he has a couple of other offers pending, but is waiting to see what we decide."

"Are you going to hold your ground?" Alex asked.

Barclay didn't answer directly. "I've told Hawke I needed a couple of more weeks. I want to see if there's anyone else out there."

Two more weeks, Alex thought. Time was getting tight for him, as well.

Maggie caught up with Alex a few minutes after he'd left Barclay's office. "I got the information on those two cabin cruisers," she said.

"Good. Was it a problem?"

"Not really, but it took some time. The information isn't on-line yet, but the fellow at the DNR was able to retrieve everything from his in-house system and fax it over."

Both took a chair by Alex's desk. "One interesting thing," Maggie said. "A boat like that can be registered in the name of someone who may not be the actual owner, but must also carry a title with the name of the real owner."

"So?"

"So in the case of the *Mary Lee,* the name on the registration and the title were one in the same. A Preston Pranzig of Duluth, who's owned the boat since 1981. But in the case of *The Patriot*, it wasn't so simple."

"Why is that?"

"Because it's changed ownership three times since 1983. The DNR guy had to go back into the files to find out who owned it in '83. And then it turned out the registration was in one name, the title in another."

Alex waited expectantly.

"In 1983, the boat was registered to one John Johnson, which struck me as sounding phony, but was owned by . . . guess?"

"C'mon, Maggie."

She grinned. "You're no fun, at all."

"C'mon."

"The Mullen-McCaron law firm. Barney McSwain's old firm."

Alex's mouth fell open. "No shit?"

"No shit," she said, mimicking him.

Alex's mind was abuzz. What the hell could *that* mean? He was thoroughly confused, and didn't mind admitting it. "You know something?" he finally said. "I think we'd better find out more about the folks at Mullen-McCaron."

29

The Missouri skull arrived the next day, packed tightly and carefully in a box, delivered by UPS. "Hell, from the looks of the box, it could be a toaster or a mixer," Alex said when Malay brought it to his desk.

"This didn't come from any catalogue," Malay replied as he carefully unwrapped and opened the package, using his body to shield it from the rest of the newsroom.

Alex stepped back when the protective wrapping was off and the top of the skull became visible. "I'm not sure we ought to be touching it or taking it out," he said.

"You're probably right," Malay replied. "But I'm damned curious." With that, he picked up the box and walked to a private screening room, with Alex trailing reluctantly behind him, complaining, "You've seen these kinds of things before, but I haven't."

Malay closed the door behind them. "Maybe it's time you did."

He gingerly lifted the skull out of the box and placed it on a shelf, facing them, staring at them through empty eye sockets. "Jesus," Alex whispered.

The skull was small and very white, shiny and

smooth from its years in the river, he guessed. Where there should have been a nose, there was another gaping hole. Below it, in the mouth, several teeth were still intact . . . which Malay said was somewhat unusual since they often would fall out when the gums holding them disintegrated.

He ran his fingers lightly along the bone, feeling for any cracks or indentations. "They told me there was no sign of head trauma," he said. Then, "And I think they're right, that whoever this was, was quite young."

Alex stood back and stared at the skull, trying to picture the human being whose living brain was once housed in it. Whose eyes once saw through those now empty sockets. Could it have been one of the Hathaways? He felt a small wave of nausea as he thought about it. "I think I'd better get out of here," he said.

Malay glanced at him. "You do look a little peaked."

"You'll get this and dental records over to the ME?"

"Yup. I'm on my way."

Once Malay was gone, Alex put in a call to Max Douglas's office. His secretary answered, but quickly brought Douglas to the phone when she learned who was calling. "Hey, Alex," Max said. "I've been tempted to call you several times, but I figured if you needed me, you'd find me."

Indeed, much had happened in the weeks since Alex had last seen Douglas, and he felt embarrassed now that he had not kept in closer touch. "Yeah, I owe you an apology, but things have been happening fast lately."

"Then you're making some progress?"

"I think so, contrary to what you read in the newspaper."

"Good. That's what I was hoping."

Alex knew that Douglas had spent his last couple of

years at the station covering the courts, and probably still had more sources in the legal community than damn near anybody in town. "I'll fill you in on everything the first chance I get," he said, "but right now, I need your help again."

"Shoot."

"Hypothetically, if I wanted to find out everything I could about one of the larger law firms in town . . . and by everything, I mean personal portraits of the top people . . . who would I go to?"

Douglas didn't hesitate. "Tim LaSalle."

"Who's he?"

"He's a lawyer himself and publishes the *Minnesota Barrister Review,* which is the best of the local law magazines. He's got the inside dope on everything and everybody that moves in the legal community. All the gossip, the politics, the skeletons in the closets. Who's getting paid what, who's screwing who. He's a better reporter than lawyer, if you want to know the truth."

Alex knew of the magazine, but did not know LaSalle personally. "Can you trust him?"

"He was always square with me," Max replied. "Back then, he fed me more good stories than I could count."

Alex thought for a moment. "Could you set up a meeting with him?"

"Sure, I think so. But he'll probably want to know what it's about."

"Just tell him that if we can work things out, it could be a hell of a story for his magazine."

"Really?"

"Really."

"I'll call him right now," Max said, "and be back to you as quick as I can."

LaSalle, it turned out, was more than eager to meet—and they got together that evening in a conference room at the station. Max Douglas was also there, as were Malay and Maggie. Alex had considered inviting Pat, since she was also trying to learn more about the Mullen-McCaron law firm, albeit from a different angle. But in the end, he decided against it.

LaSalle was a man in his mid-forties, Alex guessed, tall, with a trim, athletic build and dressed to the nines: a dark blue suit with a carnation boutonniere, a heavily starched pin-collar shirt, gold cuff links, and shoes so well shined they seemed to sparkle as he walked. Like his body, his face was thin and angular, handsome but for the scars left over from what must have been a bad case of acne or chicken pox as a child.

But his smile and presence were so engaging that you soon forgot about the scars.

Once they'd made all the introductions, Alex said, "I appreciate your coming, Tim, but before we begin, we need your assurance that everything we tell you will be considered confidential."

"That's fine with me," LaSalle said with a glance around the table. "You've got my word."

"Good," Alex replied, and then launched into a recitation of their investigation, from the beginning to the present. "It's curious, but things seem to keep coming back to the Mullen-McCaron law firm. There's the Barney McSwain connection, which we still don't fully understand, and then the matter of the mystery cruiser. My guess, although it's only a guess, is that we'll also find some connection between the firm and that commune property up north. We're still trying to check the tax records."

LaSalle listened attentively, only occasionally taking

a sip from the can of Coke in front of him. He made no notes, but Alex had the sense that everything he said was being recorded and stored away mentally.

"Sounds like a hell of a story," LaSalle said. "You're to be congratulated. But what do you want from me? And what does my magazine get out of it?"

Alex took a deep breath. "We'd like to know everything you can tell us about the top people at Mullen-McCaron. Their backgrounds, their politics, their families, their fetishes and foibles. Everything you can think of or can learn that might establish a lead or a link to the missing boys. In return, if our suspicions prove correct, you'll have the print exclusive to the story."

"But my magazine's a monthly," LaSalle said.

"Then we'll try to time our story so that it fits your schedule."

"What about the newspapers?"

"They may have the story," Alex said, "but they won't know the inside of the investigation like you will."

LaSalle took another sip of his Coke. "Okay," he said finally. "But I'll need time to do some digging and get things together."

"Fine, but what can you tell us now?"

"About the firm?"

"Right."

LaSalle leaned back and cleared his throat. "There are only two top people, the namesakes of the firm. The main guy, and the founder of the firm, is Clint Mullen. He's probably in his sixties now, and rich, a tough old bird, a hard-as-a-rock conservative—some would say reactionary—who has built the firm by representing a lot of companies whose CEOs share his particular philosophy. There's a group of them, maybe ten or twelve, who meet regularly at the Minneapolis Club, where they smoke stogies, sip brandy, and talk about free enterprise, the dangers of big government, and how to rid the world of Democrats. Behind their backs, they're referred to as the 'Dirty Dozen.'"

There were smiles around the table.

"Mullen tries to stay out of the public eye, leaving that to his partner, Ralph McCaron. He's a former state legislator and one-time commerce commissioner, a power broker and wheeler-dealer in the old sense of the word. Does lobbying for Republican and conservative causes at the legislature and in Washington. Knows what strings to pull and which skeletons to rattle."

Alex and the others had been listening attentively. "From what you know of these guys," he asked, "can you see either of them involved in something like I described?"

"Not really, but I do know they're a couple of tough dudes who take no prisoners. Mullen, especially. And I speak from experience. A couple of years ago, my magazine did an unflattering portrait of McCaron, focusing on his questionable lobbying tactics and backroom deals. Well, Mullen came after us with a vengeance . . . made some not-so-veiled threats, pulled their advertising from the magazine, and tried to persuade other firms to do the same. Called us a 'yellow liberal rag,' among other nasty things."

"What kind of threats?" Alex asked.

"For one thing, he tried to get me kicked out of the Minneapolis Club . . . which is no big deal, but because I'm still a lawyer, he also tried to get the Bar Association to revoke my membership for 'unethical behavior.' Of course, he had no success, but it wasn't for lack of trying. There were also some anonymous phone calls."

"What kind of calls?"

"To my office. To my home. Warning me to watch my back. To keep an eye on my family. That kind of thing. I can't prove they were ordered by Mullen, but the timing was suspicious. They finally stopped after a while."

"What about their families?" Maggie asked.

LaSalle shrugged. "Don't know much about that, but I can find out. I know Mullen lives out on Lake Minnetonka, and McCaron in Edina, I think."

The mention of Edina made Alex suddenly sit up straight, with a quick glance at Malay. "Do you know a lawyer by the name of Cornelius?" he asked LaSalle. "He lives in Edina, too. Married to a cop's widow, Lorna."

"If you're talking about Richard Cornelius, sure. He works for Mullen-McCaron. One of their senior partners."

Alex fell back in his chair. The coincidences just won't quit, he thought.

"I'm way ahead of you again," Malay said, once LaSalle had left. "I'll check to make sure it's the same Cornelius."

"Good," Alex replied, "and if it is, didn't you tell me once that he was a friend of Lorna's late husband before he was killed?"

"That's what I was told," Malay replied.

"Then it's possible that Pete Osborne may have shared his obsession about the missing boys with him, huh?"

"I suppose so."

"And maybe told him that he was keeping the files at home?"

"That too," Malay said.

Alex could only shake his head in wonder.

For the next hour, Alex fought a nagging feeling that he was forgetting something. Something recent. He reviewed his notes and went back over the conversation with LaSalle, but still couldn't come up with it. Then, a half hour later, it suddenly occurred to him: While they had concentrated on the one cruiser, *The Patriot*, because of its ownership, they had all but forgotten about the second one, the *Mary Lee*, which had been on the river at the same time.

He quickly retrieved Elmer Jonkowksi's logs, found the name, and brought up the national telephone listings on his computer: Preston Pranzig, the owner of the *Mary Lee*, was at home in Duluth and answered Alex's call almost immediately. After identifying himself, Alex asked, "Do you still own the *Mary Lee*?

"My boat? Sure, but what's this about?"

"I can't really explain," Alex said, "but I was wondering if you recall being on the Mississippi in the Twin Cities fifteen years ago, on the day when those three young brothers disappeared?"

"Who could forget that?" he said. "I didn't know anything about it until I went through the lower lock and dam that evening. They asked if I'd help search for the kids downriver, but we never did find them, of course."

"Do you remember another cruiser being upriver at about the same time you were?"

There was a pause at the other end of the line. "It was a long time ago," Pranzig said, "and my memory's not what it used to be, but yeah, now that you mention it, I guess there was another boat."

"Can you tell me about it?"

"I think it was a forty-foot Hatteras. A real big boat, a third again bigger than mine. And white, if I recall."

Alex pushed ahead. "Can you remember when and where you saw it? And what it was doing?"

"Gosh, that's tough. Let me ask my wife. She was there, too." He put the phone down and Alex could hear a garbled conversation in the background. Then Pranzig was back on the line. "We think it was somewhere between the Lowry and Camden bridges. But that's a guess. What we both do remember, though, is that it was anchored along the west shoreline. Like they were fishing or maybe swimming. It was there when we went up the river, but gone by the time we came back down."

"And that would have been about . . . what?" Alex asked. "Six o'clock or so?"

"Somewhere in there. Late afternoon, anyway."

"You didn't see any kids swimming or anything, did you?"

"No, nothing like that." Then a pause. "Say, do you think that other boat may have had—"

"We don't know," Alex said. "We're just trying to check things out."

After he'd hung up, Alex took out his Minneapolis/ St. Paul map, confirming what he'd thought: A stretch of the river between the Lowry and Camden bridges bordered Fairlawn Park.

When Alex and Malay arrived home after the late news, Pat was there to welcome them . . . as she had been virtually every night since the unannounced engagement. And as they all sat down with a frosty glass of ice tea, Alex quickly described the day's events—including their conversation with Tim LaSalle. "I would have asked you to be there," he said, "but I thought it might pose a conflict for you."

"Why's that?" she asked.

"I didn't think LaSalle should know that you're also poking around Mullen-McCaron while working for another law firm. It didn't seem quite proper to me."

She shrugged. "I suppose so."

When Alex repeated LaSalle's description of Mullen and McCaron, she nodded. "I've heard of some of those same things myself," she said. "That they can be bears to work for, and that they tend to hire buttoned-up young Republican-type lawyers. But it's a big and very successful law firm, Alex, and it's hard for me to picture them getting involved in something dirty like this."

"That could be why they're working so hard to protect their reputation," Alex offered. "They could lose the whole thing if it was proved they were part of something—"

"But murder, Alex? Ambushing you?"

"To quote our friend George Barclay, 'Desperate people are capable of doing desperate things.'"

Later, as they lay in bed, Alex told Pat, "You know, it's starting to feel like we're already married."

"It is?"

"Yeah, with you here almost every night and every morning. And I like the feeling."

"So do I," she replied."

"You know something else?"

"What?"

"I don't really care anymore if they bump me off the late news."

She sat up. "You don't?"

"No. We've got a lot of time to make up. Like thirty years' worth, right? And we can't do that if I'm working every night. When the hell would we have fun?"

She chuckled and lay back down. "I think we'd make the time."

"I'm serious," he said.

She snuggled into the crook of his arm. "Let's wait and see, okay?"

30

The report from the medical examiner on the Missouri skull was in their hands by noon the next day. To their relief, the verdict was that the skull was not that of a Hathaway brother. Although the pathologist confirmed that the skull did belong to a boy about the age of Jed, the oldest brother, neither his dental records nor those of the other boys matched the remaining teeth in the skull.

As for the skull itself, the ME—after conferring with a forensic anthropologist at one of the local universities—said he believed it could be older than fifteen years. While there was no way to be absolutely certain, he said the condition of the skull bone—the fact that it was smooth and shiny, and not pitted or stained by algae—indicated to him that it may have been buried in the muck of the river, perhaps for decades.

"What do you want to do now?" Malay asked after both he and Alex had read the report.

"Send the skull back, I guess," Alex said. "And let Hazel Hathaway know that it wasn't one of her kids."

"You want to call her?" Malay asked.

"Sure. She'll be relieved as hell."

Malay also reported that Richard Cornelius was, indeed, the husband of Pete's widow, Lorna. And that yes, Cornelius and Pete Osborne had been friends for years before Pete died. Which was how Cornelius and Lorna happened to know each other.

"So what do you think?" Alex asked.

"Shit, I don't know. It certainly is strange, but it could be the only true coincidence in all of this."

Alex raised his eyebrows. "If it isn't," he said, "and if Cornelius is one of the bad guys, he knew early on what we were up to. Lorna certainly would have told him about our visit, which was long before we went public with the story."

"I don't know," Malay said with a frown. "I just can't see Lorna marrying a guy capable of something like that. Or Pete befriending him, for that matter."

"Maybe Cornelius thought he could kill three birds with one stone," Alex said, playing devil's advocate. "Get rid of Pete, get the Hathaway case files, and get Lorna, all at one time."

"I think you're reaching," Malay replied, although he had to admit that it was not entirely impossible.

It was after Alex's call to Hazel Hathaway, relieving her of worry about the skull, that Maggie came up with the idea. Alex had to give her credit; it had not occurred to him, and probably never would have.

But after she'd been told that the skull was not one of the Hathaway boys, she went—without explanation—to the newsroom library to retrieve a U.S. atlas. Then she spread it out on Alex's desk, opened to the map of Illinois. "Now, where exactly did they find the skull?" she asked.

He remembered what Malay had told him. "In McLaren County, Missouri, across the river from Illinois. Why?"

She ignored his question. "And didn't the medical examiner say he thought the skull could have been in the river for longer than fifteen years?"

"Yeah, but he said it was an educated guess, at best."

"And didn't you tell me weeks ago that your boyhood friend, the paper boy—"

"Tommy Akers."

"—disappeared like forty years ago? And never was found?"

Alex finally saw the light. "Wait a minute," he said. "I know where you're going—"

"And didn't you say you lived southwest of Springfield?"

"In Maxwell, yes."

"Show it to me," she said, pointing to the map.

He found the tiny dot, and put a pencil tip to it.

"And how far is that from the Mississippi River? From McLaren County?"

He tried to gauge the distance by sight. "A hundred miles at least, I'd say."

"Not that far, when you think about it. To dump a boy's body."

Alex sat back in his chair and gazed at her. "You're amazing, you know that? To even think of the possibility."

"I'm surprised you didn't."

"But Malay told me that the Missouri cops alerted the counties across the river in Illinois when they found the skull."

"Maybe not that far east," Maggie said, checking the map. "And hell, the kid had disappeared more than thirty years earlier. Maybe they'd forgotten about him. It's worth a check, I'd say."

"I'll get back on the phone," he said.

But first he had to find Malay and stop him from shipping the skull back to Missouri. Then he asked the chief to dig through his notes to find the name of the deputy in McLaren County who had first alerted the state police about the skull.

Deputy Jim Gibbons was on patrol when Alex called, but the sheriff's dispatcher patched the call through to his squad car and Alex hurriedly explained who he was and why he had called.

"So the skull wasn't one of those you were lookin' for?" Gibbons said.

"No, I'm happy to say. But I need to ask you if anybody from Maxwell, Illinois ... that's in Enright County ... asked about the skull when you first found it six years ago."

"Jeez, not that I remember," the deputy said. "Far as I know, we had no inquiries from any county in Illinois. We put out the word, but nobody hereabouts seemed to be missing a young kid like that. Why are you asking?"

Alex explained the story of Tommy Akers. "It's been almost forty years, but I've been told just recently that neither his body nor any of his remains has ever been found. And Maxwell isn't all that far from you guys."

"I'd better talk to the sheriff," Gibbons said. "This is gettin' out of my area."

Taking Alex's name and number, Gibbons promised to have the sheriff call as soon as possible.

The next call was to Earl Specter, the newspaper editor in Maxwell that Alex had spoken to weeks before. "Have you got a few minutes?" he asked.

"Sure," Specter said. "I'm relaxing. We got the paper out yesterday."

"This is going to sound a little crazy," Alex said, "but if you have the patience, I want to tell you a story."

At that, he launched into an abbreviated account of how they had come to possess the skull. "While it doesn't belong to one of our kids, it is the age of a boy like Tommy Akers. And the cops in Missouri say they can't remember anyone from Illinois inquiring about it."

"Interesting," Specter said.

"Do you know if Tommy's medical and dental records are still around?"

"I'm sure they are. The case is still open. The sheriff must have them."

"Well, the skull still has some teeth in it . . . and we still have the skull. I'd be happy to send it to you for a comparison to Tommy's dental records. If you're willing. It could make a nice story for you."

"Of course I'm willing."

"I know the odds are probably ninety-nine to one against it being Tommy, but what the hell? One chance is better than none."

"I'll alert the sheriff and the county medical examiner," Specter said.

"Good. The skull will be on its way today."

Phil Tinsley stopped by later that afternoon to compare notes. While Alex had kept in touch with him over the past several days, relaying information about all of the new developments, those conversations had been by phone; this was their first chance to visit in person.

"You know, Alex, I hate to admit this, but you would have made one helluva cop."

"Thanks, but it doesn't pay enough."

"You're telling me?"

Malay was also sitting in on the conversation. "He's right, Alex. I've been amazed, and feeling more than a little guilty."

"What are you talking about?"

"About what you've been able to turn up in just a matter of weeks . . ."

"Not me, *we*," Alex said.

"No, you. If we'd done our jobs fifteen years ago, like you're doing now, we wouldn't be sitting here today. We didn't think to check the boats on the river, or to really interrogate any of the neighbors. If we had, if we'd really done a thorough investigation, those boys might have been back with their family for all of these years.

"You were right, you know, the first time we met, back at the cabin. Once we found the caps in the river, we pretty much dismissed any idea of foul play. Never did think that somebody could have put the caps there to confuse us, to lead us to do exactly what we did."

"That's water over the dam, if you'll pardon the pun," Alex said.

"To you, maybe. But not to me," Malay said.

Tinsley got up and walked to the conference room window, overlooking the street. "Let's forget the past," he said. "Where are we now?"

"You tell us," Alex said.

"From our point of view, there's not much we can do. Officially. Not yet. While we know that at least one of the boys may yet be alive, we have no concrete idea of where to look. And while we may think the Whelans and this Spangler character are involved, we certainly don't have enough on them to issue arrest warrants or to notify the FBI." He sat back down and cleared his throat. "And finally, I don't see what we can do about that law firm. They're big shooters in this town, with a lot of political power, and we damned well better have our act together before we start throwing darts in their direction."

"In other words, we're nowhere," Alex said.

"Officially anyway, yeah."

"Have you talked to Barney McSwain about the Stockworth murder?" Alex asked.

Tinsley appeared puzzled. "Our guys did at the apartment that morning, but not since."

"You might ask him where he was the night before," Alex suggested.

"As a possible suspect, you mean?"

Alex shrugged. "To shake him up a bit, if nothing else. But seriously, he is one person Marie would have let into the apartment without question."

"He's also an old man," Tinsley replied. "He wouldn't have had the strength to put a choke hold on her like that."

"But he could have let someone else in who did. While she was in the bathroom or something."

Tinsley grinned. "Okay, Dick Tracy. We'll talk to him. See if we can make him a little nervous for you."

"That's all I'm asking."

It wasn't until the next day that Maggie was finally able to get the information on the ownership of the old northern Minnesota commune property. "But I'm not sure it's going to do us much good," she said. "The owner listed on the county tax records is Z&T Enterprises, with an address in St. Paul. But it turns out the address is simply a mail drop. There's no office there."

"Have you checked on them with the state?" Alex asked.

"Of course. Like any business, it has to register with the state, and include the names of the owners and the officers, along with their Social Security numbers and some other tax information. But not a whole lot else."

She laid a list of names in front of him. "I haven't had a chance to check them individually, but at first glance, I didn't recognize any of these people."

Alex scanned the list, and he didn't either. "First off," he said, "you should cross-check the names against the list of Mullen-McCaron lawyers that LaSalle is sending over. And if that doesn't ring any bells, then . . . I don't know, just try to run them down one by one, I guess."

"You got it," she said, and hurried off.

When he picked up the phone an hour later, Alex immediately recognized the angry voice of Barney McSwain. "You sicced the cops on me, didn't you?" he said.

Alex feigned innocence. "What are you talking about, Barney?"

"You know damn well what I'm talking about. They're asking me all kinds of questions about where I was the night Marie was killed."

"Why would I have anything to do with that?" he asked sweetly.

"I've got friends in the department, Collier. I know that you're thick with this homicide guy, Tinsley."

Alex leaned back in his chair, enjoying the conversation. "I know him, sure, but I suspect he's just doing his job. And why would it bother you anyway? You were home, right?"

"That's none of your damn business, but I sure as hell wasn't in her apartment."

"Then you must be able to prove where you were . . . so you've got nothing to worry about."

"Then why don't you get out of my face?"

"Why don't you stop lying to me?"

"What?"

"About knowing Marvin Spangler. About the reason you left Mullen-McCaron."

There was a long pause. "What do you know about Mullen-McCaron?"

"More than you might think," Alex replied. "Including the fact that you departed under somewhat mysterious circumstances."

"You're an asshole, you know that?"

"So I've been told. But I don't lie. At least, not often."

"You'd best be careful, Collier."

After he'd hung up, it was clear to Alex that Tinsley had accomplished his mission: He had made Barney McSwain very nervous.

31

Tim LaSalle was back the next evening, meeting with Alex and the others in the same conference room at the station. Only Max Douglas was absent. "I'm impressed," Alex told him, "that you were able to get things together so quickly. We appreciate it."

"Don't get too excited," LaSalle said. "I've got more digging to do, but I thought you'd want to know what I've learned so far."

Before he began, Alex told him what Phil Tinsley had said: that Mullen-McCaron carried more than a little political weight at City Hall and the county courthouse, and that the cops would be hesitant to poke around too much on an official basis.

"He's right," LaSalle said. "The firm throws a lot of money into the local elections. They know they've got political muscle, and they're not shy about flexing it now and then."

"So go ahead," Alex urged. "We're here to listen."

LaSalle shrugged off his suit coat and wandered around the room, hands in his pockets. "First of all, you're right about the cruiser. The firm owned it from 1979 to '83, using it mostly to entertain clients on the

Mississippi and St. Croix rivers in the summer, taking it to Florida and the Caribbean in the winter. But they sold it, abruptly and inexplicably I'm told, in August of '83, and never did replace it. To the disappointment of many of the younger lawyers in the firm."

"That fits," Alex said. "Was there a crew?"

LaSalle leaned against the wall. "Funny you should ask. Yes, a full-time crew of three, the captain and two others, who manned and maintained the boat. But all of them were foreigners of some kind, no one is sure what, maybe Bahamians or Cubans. None of them spoke more than broken English, and conveniently, none of them has been seen since the boat was sold."

"So that sounds like a dead end," Alex said.

"Probably," LaSalle admitted.

"What else?" he asked.

LaSalle went back to his chair. "You wanted to know about their families. McCaron is younger than Mullen, and still has one kid—a daughter—in high school. Two other children are grown and living away from home, a daughter in Seattle and a son in Cleveland, I think. Despite his controversial and high-visibility public persona, McCaron is very protective of his family's privacy, keeping his wife and kids out of the public eye as much as possible. You know, private schools, summers in Europe, and all of that."

Alex was taking notes, but so far had heard little of interest.

"Mullen, on the other hand, has been divorced for many years, twenty or so, and has one daughter and grandson—to whom he is totally devoted, I'm told. His ex-wife remarried years ago and is still living comfortably in San Francisco with her new husband and her multimillion-dollar divorce settlement. From what I hear, she's estranged from the daughter and rarely—if ever—returns to Minnesota."

"What about his politics?" Maggie asked. "You said he was a right-winger?"

"To put it mildly. Even keeps a picture of Strom Thurmond in his office, I'm told. But he's no raving zealot. Privately, and quietly, he supports all sorts of far-out conservative causes. With both money and legal services. Like those crazy tax protesters out in Montana. But he's strictly a behind-the-scenes power. As I told you, he hates publicity."

"Would he back a group like The Nation United?" she asked.

"Possibly. At least from what you've told me about them. But I haven't been able to make any direct connection yet."

Alex again had an unsettled feeling, as if he'd missed something. "Hold on a second," he said. "Let's go back to Mullen's family."

"Okay," LaSalle said.

"Tell me more about the daughter and grandson."

"She and her husband and the boy apparently live with Mullen at his mansion on Lake Minnetonka . . . which, by the way, is more like a goddamned fortress. Complete with high stone fences, a steel gate, surveillance cameras, and guard dogs. He justifies all the security on the basis of a couple of high-profile kidnappings in that area years ago."

"Do you know the daughter's name?"

LaSalle reached into his briefcase. "Just a minute," he said, thumbing through some papers. "I've got it here. Yes, it's Jane. Jane Mullen."

Alex felt a stab of disappointment. He'd been hoping for something else.

"She's using her maiden name?" Maggie said. "Isn't that a bit unusual?"

"Maybe," he said, "but not as unusual as her husband. He's taken the Mullen name, too."

Alex sat up straight. "Why would he do that?"

"To preserve the family name, I guess. The old man has no sons."

"He'd change his name to please his father-in-law?"

"If you had a father-in-law as rich as Mullen is," LaSalle said, "you'd probably do the same thing."

"Can we find out what he changed it from?" he asked.

Malay spoke up for the first time. "That shouldn't be a problem, if he did it locally. It's a public record."

"Can you check it?"

"Sure," Malay said, "but not before the county offices open tomorrow."

Alex, his stomach churning, turned back to LaSalle. "What about the grandson?"

"I can't tell you much," he said, again flipping through the notes in front of him. "His name's Ryan, and he's in his late teens."

Alex couldn't resist. "Do they say he's adopted?"

LaSalle gave him a surprised look. "As a matter of fact, yes."

"Bingo!" Alex shouted. "That's got to be it."

LaSalle was obviously confused, but Maggie was grinning from ear to ear. "I know what you're thinking. It's Andrew, isn't it? And the Mullens are the Whelans, aren't they? No wonder we couldn't find them."

Alex quickly left the conference room to retrieve a phone number from his desk. When he returned, he punched in Sean Spangler's number on the conference room phone. "Sean? Alex Collier here. I have one very quick question. What was your Aunt Emily's middle name, if you know?" There was a pause, then, "Thanks. I'll be in touch."

He turned to the others with a triumphant smile. "It's Jane. Emily Jane Whelan."

"Goddamn," Malay said.

They all sat without speaking for a time, absorbing the information and its implications. LaSalle was the last to fully understand what was happening. "You mean to tell me that you think Clint Mullen somehow orchestrated the abduction of these three boys? On behalf of his daughter? And that he now claims one of the boys, the youngest, as his adopted grandson?"

"That's the way it looks," Alex said. "Of course, proving it will be something else again."

"With all due respect," LaSalle said, "that seems preposterous. Even for a man like Clint Mullen."

"There may be another explanation," Alex replied. "But it would have to explain away an awful lot. The cabin cruiser, the Whelans, Barney McSwain. Everything seems to lead back to Mullen and the law firm."

"And don't forget what that old minister told me," Maggie said. "That the Whelans were a really troubled couple, who apparently wanted a baby badly. Maybe they were so troubled that they couldn't get approval to adopt . . . and old Clint Mullen got tired of waiting for a grandson."

"And I remember Hazel Hathaway telling me that Andrew was kind of the neighborhood sweetheart," Alex said. "That everybody loved him. Maybe that included Emily Whelan."

Malay said, "Let's take one step at a time. The first step, it seems to me, is to prove whether this Ryan Mullen is really Andrew Hathaway. To do that, I think we have to set up some kind of surveillance—to find out where he goes and what he does. And to get some pictures of him. It's really police work."

"I don't want the cops involved," Alex said. "Not yet."

"Then why did you bring Tinsley into this?"

"He's working on the Stockworth murder, not the Hathaway kidnappings. Besides, I don't know what he could really do on the basis of what we know now."

After more discussion, it was decided that Maggie and LaSalle would try to learn more about the grandson, using Maggie's computer and LaSalle's sources, while Alex and Malay worked on a surveillance plan.

"I can tell you right now that you'll never see anything from the front of the house," LaSalle told them. "It's set way back on the lot, out of sight behind the stone fence. The most you'd get is a car zipping through the gate. And they'd easily spot you sitting outside. Your best bet is from the lake. There's a large lawn that sweeps down from the house to the water, and if you're lucky, you might catch the kid on the dock or out in their boat. Maybe on the weekend."

LaSalle promised to loan them one of his magazine's still photographers to go along with whatever station photographer Barclay was willing to free up.

"That's all fine," Maggie said, "but I don't want us to forget about the other two boys."

Neither did Alex, but remembering Pat's speculation, he was almost afraid to think about them.

Things began to break quickly the next day. By noon, Malay had confirmed that Larry Whelan had indeed legally changed his name to Larry Mullen, but not until 1986. Which left Alex to wonder what the Whelans had been doing in the years between '83 and '86.

And LaSalle, pumping his sources, learned that Ryan had just graduated from a pricey prep school out east, High Hills in New Hampshire, and planned to enroll at the prestigious Carleton College, in nearby Northfield, Minnesota, in the fall. In the meantime, he reportedly was spending the summer at the Mullen lake home, taking it easy.

LaSalle also said he was trying to obtain one of Ryan's prep school yearbooks, in hopes of finding a recent picture of the boy.

Then, by early afternoon, Alex was summoned to Barclay's office, where he found Nicholas Hawke waiting . . . snappily dressed as usual but looking unhappy and uncomfortable. "Grab a chair, Alex," Barclay said, rolling his eyes behind Hawke's back. "Mr. Hawke here has a couple of questions about your investigation."

Alex had known it would come. As predictable as the sun setting in the west. It was only a question of when . . . of how quickly the word would leak. Must either be McSwain, he thought, or one of LaSalle's supposedly trustworthy sources. Hawke's friends in high places were putting on the pressure.

Hawke straightened up in his chair. "You know I don't like to interfere in any way with what you people in the newsroom do," he said, "but occasionally I have to protect the best interests of the station. I'm sure you understand that."

Alex said nothing, eyes on the ceiling.

"And I'm told," he went on, "that you are . . . what should I say? . . . poking around the Mullen-McCaron law firm."

"Where did you hear that?" Alex said, cutting in, eyes back on Hawke.

"That's not important."

"Yes, it is. I'd like to know the source of your information."

Hawke's face began to redden. "Collier, cut the crap! You're not interviewing me here."

"Relax, Alex," Barclay cautioned.

"I can't imagine what has brought your investigation to Mullen-McCaron, if it has," Hawke said, "but you must know what a prized member of the business and legal community they are . . ."

Alex stood up abruptly. Years of repressed anger and frustration suddenly surfaced. He'd had enough. "Pardon me, Mr. Hawke. And George. I don't mean to be impolite or disrespectful, but we've gone through this once before. With your friend, Judge Steele. And I won't tolerate it again. You will either let this investigation proceed, unhindered by you or anyone else in upper management, or I will walk out that fucking door right now." He paused, catching his breath. "And I won't stop there. I'll be at the newspapers before you can hitch up your britches, and I will tell them exactly how you have attempted to derail important investigations at this station, both now and in the case of Judge Steele. And I will be there when the station's license comes up for renewal. You can fire me or sue me, Mr. Hawke, but don't forget me. Because I will be your worst nightmare."

With that, he turned on his heel and left, not sure whose mouth was open the widest, Hawke's or Barclay's.

His anger was still written all over him when he returned to his cubicle. And Maggie, sitting at her own desk, was quick to notice. "What the heck happened?" she asked anxiously.

He flopped into his chair and smiled. "I just told Hawke to take a flying fuck."

She was aghast. "You what?"

He explained the scene in Barclay's office. "I wasn't going to go through it again, Maggie. Fighting Hawke at the same time I'm trying to get a story on the air. It's not worth it, and I finally decided to take a stand. Screw him. I may be out on the street within the hour, but that's okay, too. I'll just take the story to the papers or to LaSalle's magazine. And I *will* find out what happened to those boys, with or without the station."

Maggie's face had paled. "Jesus, Alex . . ."

"Don't sweat it," he said. "I haven't felt this good in months. It'll be okay either way."

At that moment, across the way, Hawke emerged from Barclay's office and strode out of the newsroom without so much as a glance in Alex's direction. Barclay was right behind him, looking grim, as he made his way toward them. But when he arrived, the scowl turned into a small smile. "You are one stupid son of a bitch, you know that? With more guts than common sense."

Alex grinned. "I'm sorry to have put you in the middle of it, George. But I just wasn't going to sit there and listen to that prick tell me about all of his buddies at Mullen-McCaron."

Barclay pulled a chair up. "Don't apologize to me. I've wanted to do what you did for years, but I've never had the balls."

"So do I still have a job?" Alex asked.

"Yeah, at least through your current contract. But Hawke wants me to try and undo the extension. Based on insubordination or some such thing. He wants you out of here."

"That's fine with me, but is he going to keep his nose out of the investigation?"

"He says he will, but we'll have to wait and see. I think you scared the shit out of him with that bit about showing up at license renewal time."

"Good, because I wasn't kidding."

"I think he knows that," Barclay said.

32

The waters of Lake Minnetonka were at a dead calm, and the sun, unobstructed by any clouds, was hellishly hot. Alex and Maggie were aboard a rented twenty-foot runabout, along with a photographer from the station, Jeff Schmidke, and one of LaSalle's still photographers, Allen Epstein. All were in their swimming suits, but still sweating, as they cruised the shoreline of Wayzata Bay.

"It should be right along here," Alex said, keeping his voice low, knowing how easily sound travels across water, even over the deep rumble of the inboard motor.

They were trying hard to look like four people on a simple summer afternoon outing, lolling about on the deep cushions of the runabout seats, catching the sun's penetrating—almost painful—rays. Out of view, in the well of the boat, were Schmidke's video camera and Epstein's array of still cameras, several of them equipped with telescopic lenses.

"There it is," Maggie said, nodding toward a mansion coming up on their right. Although it was obscured by dozens of shade trees, they could still see a portion of the imposing white stucco home—two stories high with a red tile roof, a wraparound deck and balcony, and giant picture windows overlooking the lake.

At the foot of the meticulously mowed lawn was a T-shaped dock that stuck fifty feet or so out into the water, with a small fishing boat tethered to one side of the dock, and on the other side, a large cruiser raised above the water on a canvas-covered boat lift. The name on the back of the boat: *The Patriot II*.

"Pull a little closer to shore," Alex told Schmidke, who was at the wheel of the runabout. "But not too close."

Schmidke throttled the boat down to its slowest speed and gently moved toward the shoreline.

"Let's not be too obvious," Maggie warned. "We can be looking but not staring at the place."

"Relax," Epstein said. "These rich folks are used to being gawked at by poor folks like us."

On the weekends Lake Minnetonka—one of the largest lakes in the state—was alive with hundreds of boats, jet skis, and water-skiers . . . all skittering to and fro like so many water bugs across the lake. Because of that, Alex would have preferred to wait until then—when they would have been just part of the boating crowd. But, tight on time, he had decided to risk coming on a weekday, knowing there would be fewer boats on the lake to provide cover for themselves.

"I don't see anyone, do you?" he said as they moved slowly past the house. Indeed, the place looked deserted; the windows they could now see were draped shut, with no sign of human activity.

"Isn't that a dog there by the deck?" Maggie said, squinting through her sunglasses.

"Yeah," Alex replied. A German Shepherd, big even for that breed, was sauntering down toward the lake, clearly watching their boat. Then another joined him, as big or even bigger than the first. The guard dogs LaSalle had spoken of. "How would you like to tangle with one of those?"

"After you," Epstein replied.

By now, even at its slow speed, the boat had passed the house and was approaching the next lakeside mansion—if anything, even more impressive than the Mullen's.

"So what do you suggest?" Schmidke asked from behind the wheel.

"Let's keep moving down the shoreline for another ten minutes or so," Alex said, "then head out toward the middle of the lake, opposite the house. We'll have to try to keep an eye on it with binoculars or your cameras."

Once there, they waited for an hour. Then another. With no protection from the sun, now directly overhead, it became unbearably hot. They poured on sunscreen and took turns getting in and out of the water to cool off, two at a time while the other two maintained the watch.

Finally, toasted and ready to give it up for the day, Maggie called out from her perch on the bow. "Someone's coming! Down toward the lake."

Epstein dove for the camera with the longest lens and pulled it up to his eye, focusing fast. "It's a young guy," he said. "Six feet. Blond. A little on the chunky side. Those two dogs are walkin' next to him."

"Can you get a shot?" Alex asked.

"Yeah, but it's not going to tell you a lot. We need to get closer." The camera shutter clicked away anyway, as rapidly as an automatic rifle.

"He's picked up a rod and tackle box on the dock," Maggie said, binoculars tight against her eyes. "He's climbing into the small boat."

Alex tried to think. If he started their boat now and

drove toward the dock, the kid would likely get suspicious. Especially if he'd seen them out there all afternoon. But Alex couldn't just let him motor away. Who knew when they'd get another chance like this? "Let's pull up the motor cover," he said. "Like we're having engine trouble. Now. Quick."

Together they hoisted the backseat and lifted the motor cover. Then, as the boy moved away from the dock and out onto the lake, Alex began to wave a white T-shirt back and forth. "Have you got a camera that doesn't make any noise?" he asked Epstein.

"Yeah."

He continued to wave the shirt. "Okay. If I get him over here, I want you to get as many shots of him as possible without him knowing it. Shoot from the hip or whatever. And hide the other camera gear."

"Gotcha."

By now Ryan had spotted them and had begun to move in their direction.

"Play it cool," Alex said. "If he recognizes us, Maggie, we'll just have to pretend we're out for a day of fun."

She nodded, and loosened the top of her one-piece suit, allowing a little more of her breasts to show below the tan line. "Maybe this will distract him," she said, with a grin.

"How about the rest of us?" Schmidke muttered.

Ryan was now within about ten yards of their boat and reached to shut his motor off so that he could be heard. "You guys must be having trouble," he said as his boat drifted closer.

"Yeah," Alex said. "You know anything about these inboards?"

"Not really," he replied. "I'm not much of a motor head."

Alex studied him. A handsome enough kid, although Epstein was right, a shade overweight. But fine-featured, with close-cropped blond hair, and skin browned by the sun. His teeth were even and white, and if it was any clue, he had Hazel's striking green eyes. It was strange though, Alex thought, seeing him as an adult. He'd always thought of him as a four-year-old boy.

"You know where we could get some help?" Alex asked, trying to keep the young man engaged while Epstein pretended to fiddle with his camera off to one side.

"There's a marina a couple of miles down the lake," Ryan said. "I could tool over there and see if they could come out and give you a hand."

"I'd hate to have you do that," he said. "Maybe it's just flooded, and if I give it some time, it'll take off again."

"You're sure? I was just going to do a little fishing."

"No, that's fine."

The young man was now beside them, holding on to their boat. "Say," he said, shading his eyes against the sun, "aren't you Alex Collier? I've seen you on the news."

"That's right," he said. "We were just trying to catch a few rays, but got more than we bargained for. What's your name?"

"Ryan. Ryan Mullen. I live just over there," he said, pointing.

"A pleasure meeting you, Ryan. If we're still here when you're done fishing, maybe we'll take you up on your offer."

"Okay. I won't be that far away." With that, Ryan restarted his engine and moved off, with a friendly wave back at them.

"How did you do?" Alex asked Epstein.

"Okay, I think. I shot a whole roll. They won't be great, but something should turn out."

Maggie was holding a copy of the computer-aged photo of the Hathaway boys that they had used in Alex's story. "Look," she said. "If he isn't Andrew, I'll eat my swimsuit." Alex and the others looked . . . and she was right. If you could believe the photo, he was a dead ringer.

They waited another twenty minutes, put the motor cover down, and took off—watching as Ryan's fishing boat bobbed in the distance.

Barely making it back to the station in time for the early news, both Alex and Maggie quickly changed clothes, slapped on some makeup, and dashed into the studio with only minutes to spare. "We were wondering if you were going to make it," the floor director said. "It would have been a first for us . . . an anchorless newscast."

"Never fear," Alex said, clipping on his microphone, "your Channel Seven news team is here."

As they quickly read over their scripts, Maggie asked, "Are you going to show the pictures of Ryan to the Hathaways?"

"I don't know," he said. "Let's wait and see how they turn out."

"But if they do?"

He had been debating the question since they'd left the lake. Who better than the Hathaways to tell them if Ryan is really Andrew? *But how could even they be certain?* So much time had passed. Alex knew as well as anyone how much children change as they pass through adolescence and into adulthood. He could certainly see the changes the years had made in his own kids. Would he recognize them today if he had not seen them in a decade or more? He thought so, but wouldn't guarantee it.

"I just don't know," he finally said. "I'll sleep on it."

"I think you should," she said. "They deserve to see them."

The floor director's voice boomed in the studio. "Ten seconds to air! Stand by, everybody."

Alex watched for the director's hand cue, but his mind was back on the lake.

The still photographer, Epstein, delivered the prints to Alex the next afternoon. A few, as expected, were foggy or out of focus, but the bulk of them were sharp and clear. Alex again compared them to the computer-aging of the childhood photos . . . a process that anticipated normal growth and development, and included a blending of the most prominent facial features of both parents.

There was no question: The resemblance was amazing.

Alex had spent a restless night, trying to decide what to do with the photos once he had them. But by morning he'd decided that Maggie was right: The Hathaways deserved to see for themselves what could very well be their youngest son.

That evening, after the early news, he asked Malay and Maggie to go with him to the Hathaway home. He had called in advance and was assured by Hazel that both she and John would be there, but he had put off her questions about the purpose of the visit.

"I debated coming here," he told them when everyone was gathered around the dining room table, "until we were absolutely certain that what we suspect is true. But Maggie convinced me that you deserve to be told now."

He then explained how they had traced the ownership of *The Patriot* to the Mullen law firm, and how they had discovered that Larry and Jane Mullen were really Larry and Emily Whelan. And that their adopted son, Ryan, could be the long-lost Andrew. "He's the right age, and looks like the computer says he should look by now."

"My God," Hazel whispered, eyes heavenward.

Her husband put his hand on hers. "Take it easy, Hazel. Let's see what they have to show us."

Maggie spread the pictures from the lake on the table. "These were taken yesterday," she said. "And this is Ryan."

Hazel took no more than a glance at the first picture and shrieked. "It's him, it's him! John, it's our Andrew!" She buried her head in her hands. "My Jesus," she cried. "Thank you, sweet Jesus."

John took her by the shoulders and held her. "Easy, Hazel. Easy." But then his eyes welled, as he looked at picture after picture. "I think she's right," he finally said, almost sobbing. "I think it is Andrew."

"We need to be sure," Alex said softly.

Hazel straightened up, her eyes afire. "I am sure. A mother always knows." She turned to Maggie. "Doesn't she?"

Maggie nodded. "I think I would."

"There! You see. And I want him back. Now! Not tomorrow, now."

Alex stood up. "I'm sorry, Hazel, but that's not possible. We need proof. Evidence. And that may take some time."

"You have the boys' dental records," she said. "Use them."

"It's not quite that simple," Malay said. "We'll have to convince the police, or a judge, that the likelihood is strong enough to get Ryan's records for comparison. And we're not quite sure how to do that yet."

"Andy did go to the dentist back then, didn't he?" Alex asked.

Hazel quickly regained her composure. "Oh, sure," she said. "In fact, he chipped one of his front teeth badly the spring before he . . . disappeared. The dentist bonded it or something, I know that. Temporarily, of course, because he still had his baby teeth."

"And they took X rays?"

"Yes. They were in the record folder I gave you."

"Good," he said.

Hazel took his hand. "I'm sorry I got so upset. I know you're doing your best." Then, as if she'd just thought about it, "What do you know about him? Where he's been, what he's been doing?"

"We don't know that much," Alex admitted, but went on tell her what LaSalle had been able to learn. "We think he was somewhere else with the Whelans between 1983 and '86, but we're not sure where."

"You mean he may have been here, in Minnesota, since then?"

"He could have been, yes."

"My God," she said. "Then we could have seen him sometime."

"Not likely," Alex said. "I suspect they kept him out of sight as much as possible."

"Have they been good to him?"

"From what we can tell, yes. He certainly looks healthy enough."

John leaned forward. "And the other boys?"

Alex shrugged. "We don't know anything. We hope Ryan . . . or Andrew . . . can help us with that at some point, but we just don't know."

They talked for another half hour, and would have gone on longer, except that Alex and Maggie had to get back to the station for the late news.

As they left, John and Hazel were standing in the doorway, hugging each other. It was the first time Alex had seen them do that.

When they were back to the station and preparing to go on the air, a newsroom assistant told Alex he had a phone call. "Who is it?" he asked.

"He wouldn't give his name, but insists on talking to you."

Alex picked up the phone.

"Mr. Collier?"

"Yes."

"This is Clint Mullen."

Alex sank into his chair and took a deep breath. "Yes, sir. What can I do for you?"

"I understand that you met my grandson on the lake yesterday."

Alex let a few seconds pass. "You mean the young fellow who tried to help us out?"

"I don't believe it was an accidental meeting."

"Really? What makes you say that?"

"I don't like to play these kinds of games, Mr. Collier. As you must know, I am a man of substantial influence in this town. With many resources at my disposal. And I want you to stay away from my grandson. Is that understood?"

"Perfectly." And then, almost as an afterthought. "If he truly is your grandson."

Mullen's voice turned even harder. "You've been warned, Mr. Collier."

"Funny, but I've heard that before, Mr. Mullen."

33

Alex woke with a start in the middle of the night, sitting straight up in bed, sweating. Pat stirred next to him, but then rolled over with a soft moan and was once again asleep. He looked at the luminous bedside clock: 3:15 A.M. Slipping from under the sheets, he made his way downstairs, tiptoeing, but unable to avoid the squeaks in the stair treads.

"Who's there?" Malay's voice in the deep shadows at the foot of the stairs.

"Me," Alex whispered. "Where the hell are you?"

"Here," the chief said, stepping into somewhat better light. He was in boxer shorts, his pistol in his hand.

"Jesus Christ," Alex said, "what are you doing? Put that damn thing away."

"How was I to know it was you, sneakin' around like that?"

"Sneaking around? It's my goddamned house. And don't you ever sleep?"

"Not when I hear strange noises."

They walked together into the kitchen, pulled the blinds, and flipped on the lights. Malay put the gun on the kitchen table and went to the refrigerator for a glass of orange juice. "So what gets you up at this hour?" he asked.

"I'm going to call Tinsley."

Malay stopped, the glass of juice halfway to his mouth. "At three in the morning? Why?"

"It just woke me up."

"What?"

"I told you about Mullen's call. I suddenly realized that there is nothing to stop that asshole, or the Whelans, from taking Ryan out of town . . . to who knows where? He'll be gone again. Tinsley has to get a court order keeping him here . . . and another one to get his dental records."

Malay laughed and shook his head. "Wake up, Alex. You're still dreaming. Not only do we have damn little evidence that Ryan really is Andrew—"

"We've got the parents' word," Alex said. "And the pictures."

"But Mullen is probably bosom buddies with every damn judge in town. Hell, he probably got half of them elected. He's not going to stand quietly by."

"Then what do we do?" Alex asked.

Malay thought a moment. "Watch them. Around the clock. Try to make sure they don't leave with Ryan. At least until we can come up with some real proof."

"And how do we do that? Watch them, I mean?"

"I know about a dozen old farts like myself. Retired cops who'd probably love to do a little extracurricular stakeout work. Especially if I ask them."

"You'd do that?"

Malay looked at the kitchen clock. "Give me an hour. I'll have somebody outside the gates of that mansion by five A.M."

Alex knew he'd never be able to get back to sleep, so

he waited for two hours, drinking coffee and pacing, mostly, and then made his call to Tinsley. Even though it was a more respectable hour, it was still clear that he had pulled Tinsley out of bed. "What the hell, Alex?"

"Sorry, Phil. But we need to meet, like right now."

His voice was groggy. "It's five-thirty in the morning, Alex."

"I know. Time's a wastin'. I wouldn't ask you if it wasn't important."

There was an audible yawn at the other end of the line. "Okay. When and where?"

"How about an hour . . . at the Hilton downtown."

"I'll be there. And it better be good."

Tinsley was already at a table, sipping coffee and munching on a Danish, by the time Alex got to the hotel restaurant. Once he had ordered the same, Alex apologized. "I really am sorry to roust you out like this, and I should have talked to you sooner, but we've come to a critical point and need your help."

Tinsley eyed him suspiciously. "What are you talking about?"

Alex glanced around, to be sure nobody was close enough to overhear. "We think we've found the boy, Andrew. And the Whelans."

"What?"

Alex leaned in close, his words rushed. "Emily Whelan is Clint Mullen's daughter, and they call the boy Ryan. She and her husband are living with Mullen on Lake Minnetonka, and have even taken his last name—which explains why we couldn't find them." He then went on to recount every step they'd taken, including the rendezvous with Ryan on the lake, and the Hathaways' identification of him as their youngest son. "But Mullen knows we're on to him, and I'm afraid that he or the Whelans are going to take off with the boy."

Tinsley was listening intently, taking notes on a small pad.

Alex went on, "Malay's recruited some of his old police buddies to keep an eye on the place for now, but shit, I'm not sure how much good that's going to do or how long they can keep it up."

"So what do you want me to do?" Tinsley asked.

"We've got to get Ryan's dental records," Alex said. "It's the only quick way to prove that he is Andrew."

Tinsley frowned. "The kid's gotta be what? Eighteen or nineteen now, right?"

"That's right."

"Then he's an adult and we'd have to get his consent to get the records. Or I'd have to get a court order, which I don't think is likely on the basis of what you've told me. Unless I could find a very friendly judge. And with Clint Mullen involved, that seems unlikely, too."

Alex took out his cell phone. "Maybe not."

He punched in Tim LaSalle's number. "Tim, this is Alex Collier. I need a quick piece of information."

"Okay," LaSalle said.

"I know Clint Mullen is probably tight with most of the judges in Hennepin County, but there must be one or two who are *not* friends of his. Who may actually dislike the guy."

"Uh-huh. He's tried to unseat a couple of them. You know, by throwing money at their opponents' campaigns and bad-mouthing them around town."

"Who are they?"

"Let's see. One is Nathan Turnbull. The other is Nancy Iverson."

"Which one dislikes him the most?"

"Iverson, without a doubt. Mullen hates women

judges generally, and her in particular. He almost got her beat the last time around."

"Thanks, Tim. I'll be in touch."

Alex gave Tinsley the information. "Now maybe you can find a prosecutor who will take this to Judge Iverson. Emphasize the need for secrecy."

Tinsley took a final sip of his coffee. "Get me an affidavit from the parents, and I'll try to get to the judge by the end of the day."

By midafternoon Tinsley's detectives and Hennepin County sheriff's deputies had completed a telephone canvass of the western suburbs around Lake Minnetonka in search of Ryan Mullen's dentist. It took a couple of hours, but they finally found him in the lakeside community of Mound: Dr. Eugene Scofield, who ran a small two-man practice and who apparently had been Ryan's dentist for years.

By about the same time, the station's attorney had prepared an affidavit for the Hathways to sign—testifying to their belief, on the basis of Ryan's pictures and other evidence, that Ryan Mullen was, in reality, their abducted son, Andrew.

And by late afternoon, Tinsley and an assistant Hennepin County attorney were before Judge Nancy Iverson, in an extraordinary closed session, asking for an order to obtain Ryan's dental records. The judge was provided with the entire background of the case, and because of the perceived possibility that the Mullens could flee with Ryan, was asked to issue the order without the knowledge or consent of Ryan or the Mullen family.

After lengthy deliberation, and admitting she was on tricky legal ground, Judge Iverson did issue the order—justifying it on the basis that if there was no match of the dental records, no harm would be done. However, if there was a match, no one would likely second-guess her decision. The heat on the Mullens would be too intense.

Unspoken, of course, was that she'd been given a rare opportunity to strike back at her nemesis, Clint Mullen.

A deputy sheriff was waiting outside the courtroom, and once the order was signed, he and Tinsley headed for the dentist's office in Mound—with the squad car's siren squealing all the way.

Malay, meantime, had been checking in with Alex throughout the day, reporting on activities in and around the Mullen mansion. "It's been real quiet," he said. "A couple of cars have come in and gone out, but we couldn't spot Ryan in either one of them."

"Have they seen your people?" Alex asked.

"They couldn't miss us. There's no place to hide. But so far, no one's said anything to us."

"How about the lake?" Alex asked.

"I've got that covered, too. One of the guys docks his boat on the lake and is out there, fishing. But he hasn't seen anything move either."

"Okay. If something's going to happen, it'll probably be in the next twelve to twenty-four hours. So stay on your toes."

"You too," Malay said. "Remember, I'm not there watching your ass."

"How can I forget," Alex said.

By evening, a forensic dentist, Dr. Curtis Summers, had compared the two sets of dental records. By a stroke of good fortune, and unknown to them until they'd picked up the records, the Mound dentist had been treating Ryan since 1986, when the boy was seven and the

Whelans had returned from wherever they had been . . . and began living with Mullen.

And at seven, not all of his baby teeth had been replaced by permanent ones, including the chipped and bonded front tooth that had been repaired some three years before. "On the basis of that and the other non-permanent teeth that remain," Dr. Summers told Tinsley and Alex, "I am fairly certain that the two X rays represent the same boy."

"Fairly certain?" Tinsley asked.

"Eighty percent. Maybe eighty-five."

Alex looked at Tinsley. "Is that good enough?"

He shrugged. "Don't ask me. Ask Judge Iverson. She's the one who will have to decide."

"And that can't be until tomorrow, can it?"

"That's right," he replied. "But I'll try first thing in the morning."

By the time Alex got back to the newsroom, Malay was there, waiting. "I may have bad news," he said.

Alex groaned. "What?"

"Three or four people, we're not sure who, took off in the Mullen's cabin cruiser. No way my guy in his fishing boat could keep up with them . . . so he didn't even try. The last he saw of them they were heading off across the lake."

"Maybe they just went out to dinner or something," Alex said, aware there were several fine restaurants on the lake.

"We're checking the eating and watering holes now," Malay replied. "But so far, no luck. We'll try the marinas next. But hell, he could have parked that boat at any friend's house . . . and be long gone by now."

"Shit," Alex muttered.

"I don't know what else we could have done," Malay

said. "I'm going to keep my buddies there overnight, in case they come back. But I wouldn't count on it."

Alex slumped back in his chair. He was out of ideas. Unless and until the judge acted in the morning, there was nothing more he could think of to do.

He was sitting there, exhausted and still stewing, a half hour later when his phone rang. In his lethargy, he debated picking it up, but finally did.

"Mr. Collier?"

"Yes?" He didn't recognize the voice.

"This is Stanley." Then a pause. "You know, from up north."

Alex perked up. "Sure, Stanley."

"You told me to call you, if . . ."

"Go ahead, Stanley."

"I thought you might want to know."

"Know what?"

"They're back."

34

Alex was suddenly alert. But confused. Stanley the care-taker was the last person he had expected to hear from. Especially now, in the middle of all this. "Who's back?"

"Some of them people. The ones who used to be there."

He stood up, the phone pressed so tightly to his ear that it hurt. "Are you sure?"

"They fired me, you know. That Winkman did. After I talked to you."

"No, I didn't know," Alex said. "I'm sorry to hear that, Stanley. I mean it."

"Said I should have kept my mouth shut. Should have kept the gate closed, or chased you off the property. But that's okay. I been there long enough. Fuck 'em."

Alex sat on the edge of the desk. "If you got fired, then how do you know they're back?"

"I been keepin' my eye on the place, you know, just kinda curious like. Nothin' else to do, at the moment. Saw some of them, comin' and goin' today."

"Do you know what they're doing there, Stanley?"

"Not really, no. But there's only a few of them. Eight or ten that I saw."

"And you're sure they're the same people?"

"Damn sure. I remember a couple of them. Shoofly, for one. And Captain Marvel, for another."

"Give me a minute, Stanley," Alex said, thinking. What the hell could this mean? Back after fifteen years. He didn't like the feel of it. "Listen, Stanley. I can't get up there tonight . . . but I'm going to try to tomorrow. Do you think you could get me inside, for a look-see?"

"Hell, yes. I know every inch of that place. But it'll cost ya, you know. Now that I got no job."

"That's not a problem, Stanley. Just give me your phone number and tell me how to get to your place."

Once Alex had the information, he said, "Try to keep an eye out till I get there, okay? And do you have a camera?"

"Yeah, but it's pretty old."

"Well, try to get some pictures of them, if you can. But don't let them know you're watching."

"Don't worry about that. I can be pretty sneaky when I've got a mind to."

Alex quickly went in search of Maggie. "Were you ever able to trace the names of the people who supposedly own that commune up north?"

"Yes. I've been trying to find you to tell you."

"Sorry, but I've been busy."

"Like you suggested, I tried to match the names up with the Mullen-McCaron lawyers, but it was no go. So I called LaSalle, in hopes that he might recognize the names."

"And did he?"

"Remember him telling us about the "Dirty Dozen," that group of CEOs that Mullen meets with at the Minneapolis Club? Well, it turns out that a half dozen of the Dirty Dozen are officers of Z&T Enterprises, which owns the property."

"Surprise, surprise," Alex said, and then went on to describe his phone call from Stanley.

"You're actually thinking about going up there?" she asked.

"Tomorrow, if I can. After I find out what the judge is going to do about Ryan. I don't think it's a coincidence that they've come back to the place now, after all this time. They must have been alerted somehow, and are back looking for something."

"Like what?" she asked.

He hesitated . . . then told her of Pat's fears of bodies in the woods. "I pretty much rejected the idea at the time, but now I don't know. It might answer the question of why there's so much secrecy about the place, and why it's been unoccupied for all of these years. And why some of these people are back now."

Maggie slumped into a chair. "You mean, to move the bodies . . ."

"Maybe. Or to dig something else up. I could be way off, but there has to be some reason to bring them back."

"You won't go alone, will you?"

"Not if I can help it."

The next morning, Alex stood outside Judge Iverson's courtroom, waiting for Tinsley, the assistant county attorney, and the forensic dentist to emerge. They'd already been inside for an hour, behind closed doors, and Alex was growing increasingly impatient.

Malay had not returned to the house the night before, but had called in first thing in the morning. Mullen's cabin cruiser, he said, had not returned during the night . . . and their efforts to locate it on the lake had proved fruitless. "There's a hundred places they could have hidden it," Malay reported. "Like in somebody's boathouse or private marina. And it was damn near impossible to search in the dark. But we're back on the lake this morning, looking."

When the doors to the courtroom finally opened, Tinsley was the first to rush out, his thumbs up. He pulled Alex aside. "We did it. The dental records convinced the judge that there's probable cause to believe that Ryan is actually Andrew. She's ordered that the Whelans, or the Mullens, be detained, and that Ryan submit to blood and DNA testing. She's also ordered that Ryan not leave Hennepin County until the results of those tests are known."

"That's great," Alex said, genuinely pleased. "But it may already be too late."

Tinsley was aware that the Mullens were missing. "We told the judge that, and she's authorized us to issue arrest warrants if we're unable to locate them within a reasonable time."

"What's a 'reasonable' time?" Alex asked.

"That's up to us, I guess."

"So what now?"

"We wait for her to sign the orders, then head for the Mullens'. But a deputy sheriff's going to have to serve the orders, since Lake Minnetonka's out of my jurisdiction."

"Can I come along?" Alex asked. "With a cameraman?"

"I can't stop you from following us, I guess," Tinsley said.

Alex and the station photographer who'd been with them on the lake, Jeff Schmidke, were right behind the sheriff's squad car when it pulled up outside the Mullen mansion. Schmidke jumped out of the Blazer, already taping as the deputy and Tinsley walked up to the gates.

"I don't think you'll find anybody home." The voice came from across the road as an older man, as big and burly as Malay, got out of his car.

"Hey, Ray," Tinsley said as he turned and recognized the man. It was one of Malay's retired cops, Ray Madison, who had been keeping the vigil at the mansion.

"Nobody's come or gone all night or all morning," Madison said. "And I'm told the guys on the lake still haven't spotted the cabin cruiser."

"We've still got to try," Tinsley said as he pressed the button of a small intercom speaker on one of the gateposts. He waited, then hit the button again. Still no response. "Let's check the neighbors," he said to the deputy. "You take the one on the right and I'll go to the left." Then, to Alex and Schmidke, "You better stay put. We wouldn't want to get the neighbors excited, and get you arrested for trespassing."

They waited by the gate for more than twenty minutes, pacing back and forth, ignoring curious stares from the passing cars. One finally stopped. "Is there some kind of problem at the Mullens?" the driver asked.

"No, no problem," Schmidke answered.

"Then why are the sheriff and you TV people here?"

"Just shooting a feature story," Schmidke said with a glance at Alex.

Alex stepped up to the car. "Do you know the Mullens?" he asked.

"No, not well," the driver said. "But I live just up the lake."

"You haven't seen them this morning, have you?"

"No, but you may want to try the Hendersons over on St. Alban's Bay. They're good friends and are over there a lot."

Ray Madison overheard the conversation and immediately used his cell phone to call one of Malay's search boats. "Give St. Alban's Bay a try," he said, repeating the information the driver had just given Alex. Then a pause. "Nope. Don't know which house it is. You'll have to ask."

At the same time, within minutes of each other, Tinsley and the deputy sheriff arrived back at the gate. They reported that neither of the neighbors could say where the Mullens had gone or when they might be back. One, however, had seen the cruiser leave the night before, and confirmed that Clint Mullen, Ryan, and the Whelans had been on board.

"So what are you going to do now?" Alex asked.

"The deputy's going to stay here in case they come back," Tinsley said, "so I'll need to ride back to town with you. I've also got one of my men checking Clint Mullen's office downtown. We'll give ourselves ten or twelve hours and then issue the arrest warrants."

"Ten or twelve hours?" Alex said. "Christ, they could be in Europe by then."

"That's the best I can do, Alex. Unless I get some definite proof that they're on the fly."

"Taking off in a boat and not coming back isn't proof?"

"The judge said reasonable time. I don't want to screw her over, not after what she's done for us."

Alex then took Tinsley aside and told him about the phone call from Stanley the caretaker. "I've got to get up there," he said. "Something's going on and we need to know what it is."

"You're going now?"

"Soon. I don't see what more I can do here. Not until you find Ryan and the others."

Tinsley said he knew the St. Louis County sheriff personally, that they'd been at the FBI academy together several years before. "His name's Louie Stenhouse. He's a good guy. I'll give him a call and tell him you're coming up. And give him some of the background, if that's okay."

"That's fine," Alex said. "We may need him."

As they were about to leave, Madison got a call on his cell phone. He listened, then shouted from across the road, "They found the boat. In St. Alban's Bay." He listened some more. "But there's no sign of any people. Not the Mullens or the Hendersons. The place is locked up tight."

Tinsley looked at Alex. "Maybe you're right. Maybe we should get those arrest warrants out now."

Alex dropped Tinsley off at City Hall and then stopped briefly at his house to pick up some old and dark clothing to take north with him. Plus a toothbrush and other sundries. And a can of mosquito repellent. No telling how long he'd be there, or what else he might need.

By the time he returned to the station, Malay was back from Lake Minnetonka and insisting that he accompany Alex on the trip to the commune. "You don't think I'd let you go up there by yourself, do you?" he said.

"What about the Mullens?" Alex asked.

"I've pulled my guys off," he replied. "It's in the hands of real cops now."

Barclay agreed to replace Alex on the early and late newscasts, and urged him to be extraordinarily cautious. "You don't know what you'll run into up there," he'd said. "Don't play cop or cowboy, please."

"Don't worry," Alex had told him, "I'm not looking to get shot at again."

35

It was somewhere between dusk and darkness as Alex and Malay bounced across the rutted, gravel roads that would lead eventually, they hoped, to the home of Stanley the caretaker. Alex had been trying to follow his directions carefully, but one road seemed no different than the next, and the towering, shadowy forests on either side of them provided no clues.

They would find no street signs in this neck of the woods.

"There should be another road off to the right in a half mile or so," Alex said, trying to read his own writing while also maneuvering the Blazer across the road's lunar-like surface. "And his house should be on the left, after another hundred yards or so."

"I hope we find it before I puke all over you," Malay said, gripping the handhold above him.

Alex knew they were in the general vicinity of the commune, but he also knew he'd probably never find it without Stanley's help. Especially now, with night closing in fast. But he'd called Stanley before they'd left the Cities, and had been assured that he would be at his place, waiting.

And Tinsley, bless him, had been able to get them

two pair of night-vision goggles from one of the department's SWAT teams.

Alex had debated bringing along a station photographer with a night-lens equipped camera, but had finally decided that it would be too cumbersome and too dangerous. They'd go it alone and see what they could find.

They took the right turn and slowed, looking to their left. A yard light shone like a beacon, bringing them to a driveway that led to a small house—more of a shack, really—tucked in behind several huge balsam pines. Stanley's Explorer was there, parked alongside two ancient Artic Cat snowmobiles and a rusted-out and stripped-down Volkswagen Beetle, resting on its wheel rims.

Alex pulled up next to the Explorer, and before he could turn the ignition off, Stanley sauntered out of the side door. "Wondered if you were goin' to make it," he said after shaking hands with Alex and being introduced to Malay.

"Not the easiest place to find," Alex said, looking around him.

Stanley led them to the door. "That's the way I like it. Nobody comes around to bother ya."

If Alex had any doubts before, the interior of the house seemed to prove that Stanley was living life as a bachelor. There was an old woodstove in the tiny kitchen, caked with crusty spills, and a sink filled to overflowing with dirty dishes. The walls and ceiling were grimy from the smoke and tar of the stove, and the floor felt gritty beneath their feet. A spittoon fashioned out of a coffee can sat in one corner, which—judging by the brown spots surrounding it—Stanley missed as often as he hit.

"Sorry for the look of things," he said. "Never can seem to catch up with the housework."

The understatement of the year, Alex thought.

Before they'd taken more than a few steps inside, three scrawny cats had wrapped themselves between and around Alex's legs, and an old, mangy dog—a coonhound, he thought—was sniffing eagerly at his crotch. Another dog, with the look of a basset hound, was leaping at Malay, trying to do the same.

"Get away," Stanley snarled, aiming a kick in the general direction of the animals. "Damn things can be pests, but they do keep me company."

As he led them into a living room not much larger than the kitchen, Alex said, "You know, Stanley. I don't even know your last name."

"Carmichael," he said. "But most people just call me Stanley."

Alex and Malay settled gingerly into a scruffy sofa covered with a virtual blanket of dog and cat hair while Stanley returned to the kitchen for a pot of coffee. "I've got some hooch, too, you know, if you'd rather have that," he said.

They declined, cradling the cups of steaming coffee in their hands as he straddled a chair across from them.

"So what have you got?" Alex asked.

"That depends on what *you've* got."

Alex reached for his wallet and took three one hundred dollar bills out of it. "There are three more just like this," he said, handing Stanley the bills. "Depending on what you can show us."

Stanley stuffed the bills into his pocket. "I've been snoopin' around there all day," he said. "Sneaky as a snake in the grass. They've been out in the woods most of the time, pokin' around. Like they was lookin' for somethin'."

Alex and Malay exchanged glances. "Looking for what?" Alex asked.

He shrugged his shoulders. "Damned if I know. Maybe they buried some of their money there years ago . . . or some of them drugs they was cookin' up. Whatever it is, they don't seem to know where it is. They keep movin' around, pokin' them long steel poles into the ground. Sweatin' and swearin' like crazy."

"You said there are eight or ten of them?" Alex asked.

"About that, yeah. Or maybe a half a dozen. Hard to tell, since they're all wearing that Army stuff. They look a lot alike."

"Did you manage to get any pictures?"

"Nah. Damn camera wouldn't work. Besides, it would have been too noisy."

Malay leaned forward. "They got dogs or anything like that with them?"

"Not that I've seen. But they're all carryin'."

"Carrying what?" Alex asked.

Stanley gave him a disbelieving look. "Guns. Side arms. You know, things that go bang-bang."

"Don't be a smartass, Stanley."

"Sorry."

"Have you been over there at night?" Malay asked.

"Yeah. Last night. But there was nothin' movin'."

"No problems? No guards posted?"

"Not that I seen. Or seen me. They was all inside the lodge, playin' poker or somethin'. And drinkin'."

"Can you take us over there tonight?" Alex asked.

"I can, but don't think I should," he replied. "All you'll get is eaten alive by them goddamned mosquitoes. They're thicker than the hair in a French whore's armpits."

Alex blanched at the image.

"Best wait till early morning. Get there before

they're up and movin' around. If you want, you can sack out there on the couch, or I got a spare bed in the other room."

If there was one thing Alex was *not* going to do, it was sleep in that house. "Thanks, Stanley," he said, "but I think I'll bed down in the back of the Blazer. I brought some blankets and pillows along." Then, with a quick glance at Malay, "But maybe the chief here will take you up on your offer."

Malay gave him a look that could kill. "No thanks. I'll try the Blazer, too."

"Okay, then. I'll get you up just before dawn."

It was still fully dark when Stanley rapped on the car window. Alex sat up, feeling as though he hadn't slept at all, but knowing that he must have. The hours had passed too quickly. He poked Malay, who groaned and rolled over, pulling the pillow over his head. Alex jabbed him again. "C'mon, Chief. Up and at 'em."

"Fuck you," was the muffled reply from under the pillow.

Stanley was waiting as Alex crawled out of the Blazer and stretched, trying to loosen his cramped muscles. He felt as if he'd been sleeping in a bathtub. Malay followed him out a moment later, cussing under his breath.

"There's coffee and toast inside," Stanley said. "Then we better get movin'. The sun will be up in less than an hour."

As they sat sipping the coffee, Stanley darkened each of their faces with a chunk of charcoal, then gave each of them a camouflage jacket. "These will get hot as the day goes on," he said, "but we'll need to keep 'em on."

They decided to take Stanley's Explorer to within a

mile of the commune, then walk from there. They would carry water, binoculars, a cell phone, and the quiet camera with the long lens that Alex had borrowed from Allen Epstein. Malay was also carrying his Smith & Wesson.

"We'll come in from the north," Stanley said. "There's a break in the fence that I never did get around to fixin'. We'll stick together, move quiet, and hope they come to us."

"What are the chances of that?" Alex asked.

"Pretty good, I'd say. Judgin' from where they've been the last couple of days."

"And what are the chances of us getting caught?"

Stanley smiled. "Depends on how quiet you are. The undergrowth is pretty thick in there . . . with lots of fallen logs and all. We should be okay."

To Alex, those sounded like famous last words.

The break in the fence was barely big enough for Malay's husky body to fit through, but with some wiggling and grunting he finally made it. The eastern sky had begun to lighten, although it would probably be midday before they could actually see the sun through the dense foliage that spread over them like some leafy umbrella.

Stanley led the way into the woods, crouching, moving slowly, stopping every few feet to listen. The only sounds were the faraway and haunting cry of a loon and the distant yapping of a dog, maybe one of Stanley's. First Alex, then Malay, followed him along a narrow trail like the ones Alex and Pat had once seen branching off from the road leading to the lodge. Alex tried to place his feet where Stanley's had been, hoping to minimize the noise of the leaves and branches cracking underfoot. And he knew Malay was trying to do the same.

After a few minutes Stanley stopped and turned to them. "Wait here," he whispered. "I'll check things up ahead."

Then he was gone, becoming part of the forest.

Malay tapped Alex on the shoulder. "I hate to say this," his voice low, "but has it occurred to you that your friend could be leading us right to those people?"

Alex shook his head. "No, and it's a little late to worry about that now."

They waited for another ten minutes or so, and Stanley was back. "It's okay," he whispered. "C'mon."

The birds were now fully awake, bringing the woods alive with their darting movements in and among the trees, and with their distinctive songs and cries to one another. It was a chorus the likes of which Alex had never heard before.

By now it was light enough to see and to be seen for some distance, so they crouched even lower, and moved even slower. Finally, after what Alex judged to be about forty-five minutes in the woods, Stanley brought them to a halt. Directly in front of them was a giant Norway pine, apparently uprooted and toppled by some past storm. And as it fell, its roots had been jerked out of the ground, bringing with them a clump of earth the size of a small car. It made a perfect blind.

"We'll stay behind this for a while," Stanley said. "See what happens."

Nothing happened. Not for another hour. They sat quietly behind the fallen pine, occasionally swatting at the mosquitoes that had begun to hover and buzz around them. Except for the birds, there were no other sounds. It was cool and actually quite peaceful, and more than once Alex felt himself dozing off—only to be poked awake by one of Malay's elbows. Getting even.

Stanley was the first to hear them. He sat up straight, head cocked, turned in the direction of the lodge. Then Alex also caught the sound of someone—no, more than one—laughing and talking. Coming closer. Stanley motioned for them to hunker down even lower as he tried to peer through the boughs of the pine. "There's four of 'em," he whispered. "About thirty yards away."

"Let me look," Alex said.

"In a second. When they stop."

Malay had his pistol in his hand, safety on, but ready. By now, Alex judged from the voices, they couldn't be more than twenty yards away. Their words were still not distinguishable, but it was apparent they were making no particular effort to be quiet.

"Okay," Stanley said, his voice low, "take a look."

Alex raised himself slowly, his eyes finding an open space between the boughs. Stanley was right: There were four of them, each carrying a long steel pole, like an ice auger. All were dressed in old Army fatigues, mosquito netting draped from their hats to their shoulders, protecting their faces. They were spread out, maybe ten feet apart, stabbing the soft earth with the poles, pushing down. Maybe two feet, Alex thought. Then moving ahead, repeating the process.

Alex put his mouth close to Stanley's ear. "Where are the others?"

Stanley shrugged and mouthed the words, "I wish I knew."

Malay was now beside them, binoculars trained on the men. "Can't make out their faces with that netting," he said softly. "But they seem to be moving off to the right, away from us."

Alex took the binoculars from him. "Maybe they'll take a break and get those damn hats off."

But the four men kept right on working without a significant pause for another hour, moving farther away. When they were almost out of sight, Stanley signaled to Alex and Malay to follow him as he crawled on hands and knees around the pine and through the underbrush.

This game of cat and mouse went on for two more hours, with Alex and the others always keeping their quarry within view and themselves out of sight from their makeshift hiding places. The men did take one break, but kept their hats on, lifting the mosquito netting to take bites of something—Alex couldn't tell what—and swigs from their canteens. It was impossible to see any of their faces clearly. Then they resumed their search.

The coolness of early morning became the steamy heat of midmorning. Alex could feel the rivers of sweat soaking his body beneath the camouflage jacket, but was helpless to do anything about it. And the mosquitoes and flies, attracted by the sweat, were now attacking with a vengeance—despite liberal doses of repellent on every piece of exposed skin. He wasn't sure how much longer he could stand it . . . and from the looks of Malay, he was no better off. Only Stanley seemed oblivious to the discomfort.

Finally, as the sun was almost directly overhead, one of the men shouted to the others, and they quickly formed a circle around him, looking down. Alex trained his binoculars on them as one, who was taller than the others, brought what appeared to be a walkie-talkie to his mouth and spoke into it. Then listened to the apparent response.

"What's happening?" Malay asked.

Alex gave him the glasses. "Looks like they found something," he replied. "And are reporting in."

"Stay down," Stanley urged.

Not more than ten minutes later, two other men showed up, carrying shovels on their shoulders. Like the others, they wore olive-green fatigues, but unlike the others, no mosquito netting. Alex quickly focused on their faces. Both appeared to be in their forties or fifties and were unshaved, but with the exception of a hawk nose on one of them, there were no other distinguishing features. He was sure he had never seen either one of them before.

Stanley had his own binoculars. "The one with the big nose is Shoofly," he whispered. "I don't know the other one."

Two of them immediately started digging, side by side, carefully piling the dirt as the others stood by and watched, leaning on their steel poles. Alex took out Epstein's silent camera with telephoto lens and began shooting, hoping the exposure and focus settings were right.

The digging went on for about ten minutes, the pile of dirt growing ever higher, until—even at their distance—Alex, Stanley, and Malay could hear the shovels hit something solid. The two men cleared away the dirt from the top of whatever it was they'd struck, then four of them bent down and struggled to lift it out of the ground.

Alex could scarcely breathe. The eyepiece of the camera began to steam up from the perspiration now dripping from his forehead and into his eyes. "Shit, I can't see," he complained quietly, wiping at his eyes. "What is it?"

There was no response for a moment, then Malay said, "I could be wrong, but it sure as hell looks like a casket to me."

Alex brought the camera to his eye again and resumed shooting, ignoring the sweat. Forgetting about the flies and the mosquitoes. Focusing as best he could, snapping shot after shot as the men lifted the wooden box out of the hole and onto the ground several feet away.

"My God," Alex muttered. "Pat was right."

The box was about five or six feet long, and two feet high, made of what looked like rough boards, blackened from the dirt. There was nothing fancy about its construction.

Stanley was kneeling next to them. "I'd say we get the fuck out of here, boys," he said. "You got what you were lookin' for."

"Not yet," Alex said. "I want to see if there's more."

He got his answer a minute later. As four of the men lifted and began to carry the box away, the remaining two once again began poking the poles into the ground. Still searching.

"Okay," Alex said. "Get us out of here, Stanley. Quick as you can."

36

As it turned out, they spent the better part of an hour making their retreat from the woods, moving as carefully and cautiously on the way out as they had on the way in. But they made it without being spotted, and by the time they got back to Stanley's Explorer, Alex and Malay were not only soaked with sweat and exhausted, but covered with dozens of fly and mosquito bites. They itched all over, and Alex, at least, could not remember feeling worse.

Once back at Stanley's shack, Alex quickly put in a call to the St. Louis County sheriff, Louie Stenhouse, Tinsley's friend. Stenhouse answered immediately and told Alex he had talked to Tinsley only a couple of hours before.

"Then you know what this is all about," Alex said.

"More or less," Stenhouse replied.

Alex then described what they had done and seen that morning. "They dug something up," Alex said. "And it looked like a casket to us. I've got pictures."

"So you were trespassing?" the sheriff asked.

"Sure. There wasn't any other way."

There was a pause at the other end. "What would you like me to do?"

"Get up here, for Christ's sake. As soon as you can. With about ten of your guys. I think they're looking for more graves, if that's what they are."

"I'd need a search warrant," Stenhouse said. "I don't know if I could get one, based on this."

"Then get permission," Alex said. "Herbert Winkman, over at Virginia Trust, represents the owners. Tell him you think they're digging up bodies up here. Scare him. I've met him and he's a puss. I doubt that he'd want to be involved with anything like this."

The sheriff agreed to try, but was making no promises. "This sounds pretty weird to me," he said.

"It *is* weird," Alex replied. "But it could be the biggest case you've ever had. I wouldn't fuck it up."

Once he'd hung up, Alex immediately placed another call, this time to Tinsley himself. He quickly repeated what they'd seen and the apparent reluctance of the sheriff to do anything. Tinsley promised to give Stenhouse another call, and also told Alex that there still had been no sighting of the Mullens. "We've even got the FBI involved now," Tinsley said. "So we may know something soon."

"I hope so," Alex said.

Two down and one to go. His next call went to Barclay. Again Alex described what they had found . . . and the possibility that there could be a raid on the place within a matter of hours. "I need to get a couple of photographers up here," he said. "Like now."

"Is there some place for a helicopter to land?" Barclay asked.

Alex repeated the question to Stanley. "There's a small airport outside Tower," he said. "They could put down there."

Once Barclay had the information, he said, "I'll get

somebody in the air as soon as I can." And then, "Are you sure you know what you're doing, Alex?"

"I think so. If not, we could all be in a heap of trouble."

Back at the station, Maggie was surprised to find Tim LaSalle in the lobby when she returned from lunch. "I understand Alex isn't here," he said. "But I need to talk to somebody."

"I'm probably as good as anybody," she said, leading him down the hall, past the newsroom, and into the Green Room, shutting the door behind them. He sank into the sofa. "Alex has to know that all kinds of hell is breaking loose over at Mullen-McCaron," he said. "The word is out that the cops and even the feds are looking for Mullen, and the place is going crazy."

Maggie sat down next to him. "Go on," she said.

"McCaron is locked up in his office and isn't saying anything to anybody, including the cops and the staff, I'm told. No one has seen Mullen, and the place is rife with rumors."

"Like what?"

"Name it. They're all over the place. That he's involved in extortion. Or political payoffs. That the IRS is after him. My phone's been ringing all morning, people wanting to know what I know."

"Has anybody guessed the real reason?"

"Not as far as I know. But the newspapers have gotten wind of the turmoil and are pressing hard for some answers. My deadline is coming up in a few days, and I'm going to need to go with something."

Maggie stood up. "I'll tell Alex. I should be talking to him later on."

"Good. Tell him not to forget our deal."

As they stood at the door, he said, "Oh, yeah. Tell Alex that Richard Cornelius, that lawyer from Edina, is also among the missing. There may or may not be any connection."

Although Alex would never admit it, he was actually beginning to like Stanley's coonhound, whose name was Buster. The dog would not leave him alone, although he had finally stopped trying to lick his crotch. At least he shows me a little affection, Alex thought, unlike that damned cat back home.

They were playing the waiting game, sitting outside of Stanley's shack, but well within earshot of the phone. An hour had passed, and they had yet to hear from anyone. Except for Barclay, who'd called to say Schmidke and another photographer, John Jessup, were airborne in the station chopper and should be setting down in Tower in another hour or so. Stanley had agreed to pick them up.

Malay was leaning against the fender of the old Volkswagen, wearing a puzzled expression. "What I don't understand," he said, "is why they had to poke around to find that casket, if that's what it was. You'd think if they had buried somebody, they'd know where the hell the grave was."

"I know what you're saying," Alex replied. "But remember, it's been fifteen years. The look of the woods changes. And the people who buried them probably forgot exactly where they'd put them, never dreaming they'd have to come back one day and dig them up. Or maybe the ones who buried them aren't around anymore. And these folks were only given general directions to go by."

"That must be it," Malay agreed. "But now that

they've dug 'em up, what are they going to do with them?"

Alex had no response to that.

Another half hour passed before the phone rang again. It was the sheriff, Stenhouse, who said that Winkman—reluctantly and after some persuasion—had finally given permission to search the area. "We'll be there in a couple of hours," he said. "Me and my deputies and a few state patrolmen who have agreed to help."

Alex checked his watch. That would make it five o'clock, still a few hours before dark. "Good," he said. And then, "You don't happen to have a grave-sniffing dog, do you?"

"I'm afraid not," Stenhouse said. "They have one up in Lake County, I guess, but we don't have much call for that."

As Alex looked up, Stanley was signaling him, nodding excitedly and pointing to Buster, who was lying at Alex's feet. "Forget it," Alex said into the phone. "We may have that base covered."

After more discussion, they agreed to meet the sheriff's party at the same place they had parked Stanley's Explorer that morning. Alex couldn't believe it, but he thought the end might actually be in sight.

True to his word, shortly before five, Sheriff Stenhouse and his troops arrived in a string of squad cars. Alex counted seven deputies and six state troopers, all wearing SWAT-type garb and body armor. And all were heavily armed with weapons that Alex had seen before only in the movies.

The station's two photographers, Schmidke and Jessup, were also there, geared up and ready to go. The helicopter pilot had remained with the chopper in Tower, ready to take off and get aerial shots of the commune once the raid was over.

The sheriff took Alex aside. "We're going to look pretty silly if this doesn't play out the way you say."

"I know," Alex replied. "But no one's going to look sillier than me."

Stenhouse took some comfort in the presence of Malay. While they didn't know each other, the sheriff was aware of Malay's reputation in Minnesota law enforcement. And at Alex's urging, Malay spent several minutes with him, providing reassurance and help in developing a plan for the raid.

Stanley, back from a scouting trip, reported that the gate into the compound was closed and locked, but that he saw no sign of guards posted nearby. "I'd guess they're probably gettin' ready for dinner about this time," he said. He also drew a rough map of the commune's acreage. "There's only one road in and out. And from what I seen night before last, they're all stayin' in the lodge. The other buildings should be empty."

It was decided that Stanley and one of the deputies would cut the chain and open the gate, making way for the parade of squad cars that would immediately pass through, lights flashing. "If we surprise them with a show of force," Stenhouse said, "they may be less likely to put up a fight, if that's what they have a notion to do."

After some arguing, Alex finally agreed that he, Malay, and the photographers would remain outside the gate until they were told the area was secure. Then they would be free to come in and tape whatever they could.

"We'd better get going," the sheriff said after conferring with the other officers. "No sense in waiting around."

Stanley and the deputy took off on foot for the gate while Stenhouse organized the squad cars and answered last-minute questions. Then they were gone, with Alex and his crew trailing not far behind.

The raid, Alex was told later, went off exactly as planned. The men inside the commune were—as Stanley predicted—sitting down to dinner when the sheriff and the state patrolmen swept into the clearing and surrounded the lodge. Clearly caught off guard, they offered no resistance—despite the fact that all of them were carrying guns. Ordered outside, they were forced to stand along the porch railing while they were disarmed and searched.

There turned out to be eight in all, none of whom would identify himself beyond his nickname. And a few would not do even that. What's more, none carried any type of identification, not so much as a driver's license, and the two cars and a van parked outside the lodge bore license plates from three different states. Officials would learn later that all of the vehicles and the plates had been stolen in the various states.

Once the area was secured and a preliminary sweep of the compound completed, Alex, Malay, and the photographers were allowed inside. When they got there, the men were still standing by the railing, in handcuffs and ankle shackles, looking confused but not frightened.

Before long the deputies found the box that the four men had carried out of the woods earlier that afternoon. It and another just like it were sitting in the garage across from the lodge. No attempt apparently had been made to hide or disguise them, which led Alex to believe that there had been little or no fear of discovery.

After a few minutes of discussion, the sheriff decided that the boxes should be opened there, on the scene, with cameras and witnesses documenting the event. At his order, two of the deputies, with crowbars in hand, pried open the cover of the first box and flipped it over. Then they stepped back, with pained, stricken expressions on their faces.

Alex and Malay moved forward and peered down into the box.

For the second time in his life, Alex was looking at a skeleton.

It shouldn't have been a shock, but it was. And it took him a moment to recover. It wasn't as if he hadn't suspected it. He obviously had. He'd known somehow, deep down, that that's what they would find. But that didn't lessen the impact of actually seeing the remains. And of knowing they could be one of the Hathaway boys.

He could only think of what he would tell Hazel and John Hathaway. There were no words.

The second box yielded yet another skeleton. This one, it appeared to Alex, was somewhat smaller than the first. But otherwise they looked the same. The boxes and their grim contents were photographed from every angle by the sheriff's photographers. Schmidke and Jessup, however, shot their tape from a distance, knowing images of the actual skeletons would never make the air.

The sheriff walked over to Alex. "I guess I owe you an apology," he said. "For doubting what you were saying."

"I don't blame you," Alex replied. "I'm not sure I would have believed it either."

"We're going to have to spend another couple of hours here, at least," the sheriff said. "And maybe most of tomorrow. Making sure we've got everything."

Alex told him that Stanley and his dog Buster were waiting outside the gate, ready to lead them into the woods in search of more graves. "Stanley claims the dog can find anything, but if I were you, I'd try to get that sniffer from Lake County down here. Just to make sure."

The sheriff agreed, and asked one of his deputies to make the call.

"What about those guys?" Alex asked, with a glance in the direction of the lodge.

"We'll take them into Virginia and hold them until we can find out who they are and what's behind this whole deal. It could take a few days, but believe me, they're not going anywhere soon."

Alex had yet to take a good look at the men. In the flurry of activity after they'd been given entry to the commune, including the discovery of the caskets, his attention had been focused elsewhere. Now he wandered in their direction, staying out of the cops' and the cameras' way, yet approaching near enough to get a close look at the eight of them.

The apparent leader, the man Stanley called Shoofly, was at the far right of the line, and next to him, the other older one Alex had seen carrying the shovel into the woods. Both kept their eyes to the ground, refusing to look up even as he stood in front of them. The other six, four of whom must have been wearing the mosquito netting, were younger—a couple of them quite young. And unlike the first two, their eyes were not averted; they looked squarely and defiantly at Alex as he passed by them. One even spat a gob at him that just barely missed.

All six were well muscled, with features so alike they were almost interchangeable. A couple of them were blond, the other four dark-haired, but aside from that, there was nothing particularly exceptional about any of them. At least at first glance. They would have gone largely unnoticed in a crowd.

All were still wearing their fatigue pants, but had shed the jackets.

Once he had walked past them, Alex stopped abruptly and turned around, returning to the last man in the line, the one who was clearly the youngest. "What's your name?" he asked, knowing that he probably shouldn't be talking to him, and that he'd probably get no answer anyway. He was right.

"Fuck off," was the curt reply.

Alex studied him, and he unblinkingly returned Alex's stare.

Later, much as he tried, Alex could not adequately explain what it was about the young man that made him suddenly realize that he was standing face-to-face with Matthew Hathaway.

37

Maybe it was the computerized photo that he had studied for so long and so often. Or maybe it was having met
Ryan, and seeing in the two of them some indefinable
physical and genetic linkage. Or perhaps it was coming
to know Hazel and John Hathaway so well that he could
somehow recognize their son through them. Whatever
it was, he was convinced that he was right.

But how could that be?

The resemblance to Matt in the "aged" photo was
slight at best, not nearly as strong as Ryan's was to
Andrew. And while both Matthew and Ryan were blond,
there were few common facial features. And unlike Ryan,
he did not have his mother's striking green eyes or any
other outstanding characteristic of either parent.

Still . . . there was something.

But what could he possibly be doing here now?
Exhuming bodies from graves, including one that might
be his very own brother? Alex knew that it made no
sense, that it defied logic and understanding. But he also
believed it was true.

He stepped closer to him now. "Do you know your
real name? Who you really are?"

Shoofly, from the end of the line, suddenly came

alive. His head shot up, and he shouted, "Don't say anything to that asshole. He'll try to fuck with your head!"

Alex ignored him, turning his back, moving even closer to the young man. "Do you know who I think you are? I think you're Matthew Hathaway. Matt. Does that ring any bells? Strike any chords?"

"Don't say nothin', Blue Boy." Shoofly shouting again. Blue Boy?

Without warning, the boy suddenly tucked his head down and lunged forward, head-butting Alex squarely in the chest, knocking him backwards and onto the rough gravel of the parking lot. Alex was so surprised by the suddenness of the attack that he didn't realize for a split second what had happened or where he was. He knew only that he was on his back, seeing the sky, and that he had no breath. He lay there for a moment, gasping. When he tried to move, to sit up, to breathe, the gravel stones dug painfully into his back and neck.

"I told you to fuck off," the kid said from somewhere above him.

Malay, halfway across the parking lot, came running . . . as did two of the deputies. "What the hell's going on?" he shouted, moving faster than his big body should have allowed.

Alex tried to respond, but couldn't suck enough air into his lungs. He was now on his knees, head down, struggling to take small breaths. The deputies, meantime, had grabbed Blue Boy and dragged him back to the line.

Malay knelt next to Alex. "Are you okay? Jesus Christ, I can't leave you alone for a minute."

Alex tried to laugh, but that, too, proved impossible.

Malay got up and walked over to face Alex's attacker.

"You're lucky you got those cuffs on, kid. Or I'd beat you to a pulp."

"Up your ass, old timer!" The young man had lost none of his belligerence.

Alex was finally on his feet, still woozy and hurting. His chest felt like it had been rammed against his spine. But his voice was back. "It's okay, Chief. I'm all right."

Malay turned to him. "You sure?"

"Yeah, but let me tell you, he's got one hell of a hard head."

"So what was it all about?"

Alex approached the young man, keeping a safe distance. "Chief, I'd like you to meet Matt Hathaway. Known to his friends here as Blue Boy."

"What?" Malay said in disbelief.

"It's him, I'm sure of it."

"You're sure of shit!" Blue Boy spat out.

Alex ignored him and spoke to Malay, who was now studying the kid closely. "We'll get a positive ID once they can do some blood work and DNA testing. And once the Hathaways get a look at him."

"I don't see it myself," Malay said.

"Hell, he may not know it himself," Alex replied. "He was only six, for God's sake. Who knows what they've done to his mind and memory in fifteen years?"

Alex and his crew spent another two hours at the commune, until it was nearly dark, taping whatever was within sight—including the renewed search for more graves in the woods by Stanley and his dog. Alex also wrote and recorded several on-camera "stand-ups" that would be used in the story once they were back at the station.

At this point, all Alex could report were details of the raid and the discovery of the bodies. And the possible connection to The Nation United. Without more evidence, he knew he couldn't link this event directly to the missing Hathaway boys. Still, it was one hell of a story. And one they would have exclusively.

To assure that exclusivity, Alex elicited a promise from the sheriff that he would not reveal anything about the raid to any other news organization until Alex had the chance to get the story on the air the next day. "That won't be a problem," Stenhouse said. "We'll keep it as an active crime scene until then, at least. Nobody else will be getting in here, and I'll make sure none of our people talk to anyone else."

With that, and after having found Stanley to give him the additional three hundred dollars, Alex and the two photographers packed up their gear and headed for the Tower airport, where the helicopter was waiting to whisk them home.

Malay, although grumbling, had agreed to drive the Blazer back himself.

At the station, Barclay was clearing the decks for action. Alex had been in touch with him virtually every hour by cell phone—so Barclay knew exactly what he was coming back with. To prepare, he had already assigned two tape editors to work with Alex, all night if necessary, to get the story ready for air the next day. And he had Hawke tell the promotion people to get off their asses and be ready to produce some quick promotional spots.

As the chopper was in the air, Maggie reported to Alex by radio that the Mullens were still on the run, and repeated what LaSalle had told her earlier—that chaos apparently had set in at the Mullen-McCaron law firm. "Good," Alex said, "maybe that will help flush them out."

"One more thing," Maggie said. "I took a message for

you from that newspaper publisher in your old home town. The skull didn't belong to Tommy Akers."

"Damn" was all she heard.

"But he thanked you for trying, and said the skull had rekindled interest in Tommy's disappearance. The new sheriff down there apparently has decided to reopen the case, despite its age."

"Good." And then, "Maggie, do me a favor. See if the Hathaways will come down to the station tonight or tomorrow morning. I have some tape I want them to see."

"What tape?" she asked.

"I'll tell you when I get there, but please make the call."

As it turned out, the Hathaways couldn't make it until the next morning. By then Alex had been working most of the night, scripting and editing his story. Which meant, including his night in the back of the Blazer, that he had been without much meaningful sleep for close to forty-eight hours.

So, as he faced Hazel and John across the conference room table, he first apologized for his near exhaustion. "I'm beat," he told them, "but I needed to see you." He then went on to provide a brief account of the raid on the commune, including a description of the uncovered graves. As he did, he heard a quick gasp from Hazel. "You're sure this is the same place they took the boys, back then?" she asked.

Alex nodded.

She hesitated. "Then . . . whose . . . remains were in the graves?"

"We don't know yet," he replied. "Tests will have to be done. And there may be more than the two. They're still searching today."

Hazel took John's hand in hers and squeezed. Alex could see the fear in both of their faces. "But there may be good news," he said. "Which is why I want to show you this tape."

He got up and put a tape into the playback machine. Before he hit the PLAY button, he said, "I'd like you to study the face of the young man on the tape. I don't know his real name, but they call him Blue Boy, and he was one of those captured in the raid."

"You must think he's one of our boys," Hazel said. "Or you wouldn't have asked us here."

"Just watch," Alex said.

With that, he hit the button and stood back as the first image appeared on the screen. If he had expected immediate recognition, as there had been with Ryan's picture, he was disappointed. They sat erect, still holding hands, watching the screen intently. But with no sign of excitement or hint of recall.

Maybe he was wrong, after all.

After two or three minutes, the tape ended and went to black. Alex shut off the machine and turned to them. "Well?"

They looked at him expectantly, but with obvious confusion.

"He doesn't look familiar?" Alex said.

"Not really," John said, with a glance at Hazel. "Should he?"

Alex took a deep breath. How could he be more certain than the kid's own parents? "I may be way off," he said, "but I think it's your son, Matt."

There was absolute silence for a moment. Then Hazel asked, "How do you know?"

"I don't know, for sure. I thought you might help me."

"Play the tape again," John said.

He recued the tape and let it play once more. The Hathaways leaned forward, across the table, closer to the screen. "Maybe," Hazel said when the tape ended. "But I just don't know."

Her husband was even less sure. "It could be, I suppose, but if it is Matt, what was he doing there now?"

Alex shrugged. "I can't tell you that. But if he's been with this group, whatever they are, for all of these years, who knows what they could have done to his mind? God knows he wouldn't be the first case of brainwashing or mind control."

They were clearly unconvinced, and if he could read their expressions, not necessarily eager *to be* convinced. "I want them to do some tests on him," he said. "But I'll need both of your medical records, and maybe blood samples."

"There may be a simpler way," Hazel said.

"His dental records won't do us any good," Alex said, interrupting her. "It would be comparing mostly baby teeth to permanent teeth."

"I didn't mean that," she said. "Matthew had a birthmark, shaped like a crescent moon, on the inside of his right thigh. It was really quite vivid. We used to laugh about it. Saying that's how he'd have to moon people."

"Good," he said. "I'll try to get the sheriff to check it. But you'd better still get me the medical records."

As they prepared to leave, Hazel asked, "Any news of Andrew?"

"Not yet," he said. "But everybody's looking."

If one could judge by the excitement in the normally unflappable newsroom, and by the flood of calls from viewers, the broadcast that night was a spectacular success. Was it any wonder? After all, it had everything any journalist could hope for: a surprise raid by an army of cops on a mysterious compound in the wilderness of northern Minnesota, and a band of equally mysterious grave robbers, who may or may not belong to a cult-like organization that no one knew anything about. Plus the discovery of two or more unidentified skeletal remains.

And for Channel Seven to have it all by themselves. On tape. Exclusively.

By any measure, it was the biggest story the station had broken all year, the biggest since Maggie's child porn exposé, and it left their competitors—both print and broadcast—scrambling madly to catch up. But because Barclay had held the story until the late news, and because Sheriff Stenhouse had kept his word and had kept quiet, it would be another day at least before any of the other stations could even hope to compete. And even then, they'd be left with only the dregs of the story.

As it was, both the *Star Tribune* and the *Pioneer Press,* facing midnight deadlines, sent reporters to the station to review the broadcast and to interview Alex— with a promise of full credit to the station.

Phil Tinsley was also on the phone, congratulating him. "I told you, you should have been a cop," he said. "Hell of a job, Alex. Now, why don't you solve this Stockworth murder?"

"I already have," Alex said, partly in jest. "It had to be her ex-husband, Spangler. He must have gotten wind—maybe through McSwain—that she was about to tell all. And I think he's also the guy that took the shot at me. Now you just have to find him."

"If it were only that simple," the detective said with a sigh.

Tinsley had no sooner hung up than Alex got the surprise of the night. Nicholas Hawke was on the line, actually offering his personal job-well-done.

Alex tried to take it all in stride, and as pleased as he was with the reaction and attention, he knew full well that an even bigger story was yet to be told.

38

The next morning both newspapers carried front page stories on the raid, including still pictures taken from the Channel Seven videotape and several excerpts from the interview with Alex. Keeping their word, both papers gave full credit to the station, and—in a separate television column in the *Star Tribune*—chided the other stations, and their own newspaper, for having been beaten so badly on the story. The headline on the TV column read:

CHANNEL SEVEN SCORES JOURNALISTIC COUP

Alex read the column and accompanying stories with interest, and with a real sense of self-satisfaction, but he was even more intent on a story in the paper's business section.

MYSTERY SURROUNDS MULLEN-MCCARON LAW FIRM

The story described much of what LaSalle had already told Maggie, and which she had passed on to Alex: that Clint Mullen had been missing for two days, sought by local and federal authorities on unspecified charges, and that the firm he left behind was in a state of disarray. His partner, Ralph McCaron, the story said, disclaimed any knowledge of Mullen's whereabouts or the nature of the charges against him. "I'm as mystified as everyone else," he said. "But I'm sure Clint will be back in contact any day now."

Alex read on, but found no significant new information, and certainly no hint that the paper knew Mullen had fled with his entire family, or the real reason behind his flight. The paper speculated that because of the FBI's involvement, the charges could involve the SEC or the IRS, but made it clear that those were merely rumors.

Barclay had given Alex the day off, to rest and recuperate. He'd assigned another reporter to travel to Virginia for the follow-up to Alex's story, in hopes of keeping one step ahead of the competition. There was no question that Alex needed the time away; his chest still hurt from the head-butt and his breathing had yet to return to normal. And increasingly, he found it was more difficult, and took more time, to recover from the long days and nights of work.

That's what middle age does to you, he thought.

Pat came over in the early afternoon, and they spent much of the rest of the day in or around the pool, absorbing the sun and giving Alex the chance to tell her in detail about the previous day's experience . . . and what remained to be done. "I called the sheriff to see if he'll check Blue Boy for the birthmark, but even if it's there, we may still need some blood and DNA tests for a positive ID."

"And that could take a while," she said.

"I know."

"What about Mullen?"

He shrugged. "Just wait and see, I guess. What does your friend at the firm say?"

Pat laughed. "It's not funny, but she says nobody's getting any work done. Everybody's too busy trading rumors. Or updating their resumes. She says clients are abandoning ship quicker than they can count."

"A pity," Alex said.

"It *is*. For everyone who works there and *isn't* involved."

Alex was back at the station for the late news, but the second-day story out of Virginia did not provide much new information. No additional graves had been found, although the search was continuing, and the suspects were still refusing to cooperate in any way—including giving up their names or anything else about themselves. By now they had all been fingerprinted, and the prints passed along to the FBI for possible identification. At present they were being held without bail, pending formal charges against them.

According to the sheriff, no attempt had yet been made to identify the skeletal remains, but a preliminary examination had determined that both skeletons were those of young males.

Alex had sent the medical and dental records of Jed and Matthew Hathaway with the reporter who had been dispatched to Virginia, and who, in turn, had given them to Sheriff Stenhouse. In a phone call to Alex, Stenhouse said a forensic dentist out of Duluth would check those records against the teeth found in the skulls the next day. He said he had not yet had the time or opportunity to look for the birthmark on Blue Boy.

"I don't want to rush you," Alex said. "But it could be important . . . both to the family, and maybe to your investigation. At least you'd know who one of these dudes is."

The sheriff promised he would have the examination made in the morning, when the prisoners took their showers.

Later, after the news, Alex, Maggie, Malay, and Barclay retired to Tinker's bar for a nightcap . . . and a chance to talk things over. Several other staff members were also there, but Barclay was able to find a secluded booth in the rear of the place—out of earshot, away from the noise and commotion.

After settling in and ordering a pitcher of beer, Malay said, "I still don't get what role Barney McSwain played in all of this."

Alex shook his head. "I don't either. My guess is that he must have somehow discovered what Mullen had done and was trying to put the bite on him. For a lot of money or a share of the firm. Or something. But just the opposite happened and he got his ass fired, along with threats to keep his mouth shut. From what I gather, Mullen's capable of it . . . and the dates do seem to work."

Maggie waited until the waitress had come and gone before asking, "But why would McSwain have been trying to find Marvin Spangler?"

Alex took a moment to think. "If he knew that Spangler was involved with Mullen and the Whelans, he may have been hoping to get some money out of him, too. Who knows?. But maybe that's why he got hooked up with Marie Stockworth . . . in hopes that she could help lead him to Spangler."

Barclay took a sip of his beer. "The fact is, we may never know the whole truth. It's too damned complicated."

"Unless Tinsley gets a break or somebody decides to

talk," Alex said. "And at the moment, neither appears very likely. But," he reminded them, "I only set out to try and find out what happened to the boys. And it looks like we may do that."

"What *about* the Hathaways?" Barclay asked.

"It won't be easy, will it? One of their kids may be dead, another brainwashed, and a third who's alive and well but missing, and who has no memory of them at all. I don't envy them, and you know," he paused, "the more I think about it, maybe John was right all along. Maybe they were better off not knowing."

By ten o'clock the next morning, Alex was proved prophetic. A call from Sheriff Stenhouse confirmed that one of the skeletons was, indeed, that of Jed Hathaway. The forensic dentist said there was no doubt: Jed's dental X rays were an absolute match to the teeth in the smaller of the two skeletons. Which meant, according to the dentist, that Jed must have died soon after his abduction—since there had been virtually no change in the teeth since they had been X-rayed a few months before the kidnapping by the Hathaway's dentist.

The second skeleton, he reported, was not that of Matt Hathaway, and remained unidentified at this time.

"As for the birthmark," Stenhouse said, "I had one of our deputies pose as a prisoner and shower at the same time as Blue Boy. He felt a little strange looking where he had to look, I'll tell you, but he did confirm that the kid had the crescent moon mark where you said it would be."

Before he hung up, the sheriff promised to hold the information in confidence until Alex, or someone else, was able to inform the parents.

Much as he dreaded it, Alex guessed it would have to be him.

39

In the end, it was Clint Mullen's greed that did him in. That, and his unknowing partner, Ralph McCaron.

Alex got the call from Phil Tinsley about two in the afternoon. "Grab yourself a photographer and meet me in front of City Hall in fifteen minutes."

"What's going on?"

"I thought you might want to be there for the arrests of the elusive Mr. Mullen and the others."

Alex was already waving at Schmidke, standing across the newsroom next to the assignment desk. "Are you shitting me?"

Tinsley laughed. "Would I shit you, Alex? Get a move on. I'll tell you about it when you get here."

By then Schmidke was at his desk. As was Malay. "What's up?" the photographer asked.

Alex was slipping into his sport jacket. "Are you free and all geared up?"

"Sure, the cruiser's sitting out front."

"Then let's go," he said, ignoring more of their questions until they were passing Barclay's office. Alex stuck his head in the door. "They're going to bust Mullen."

Barclay was up and out of his chair in a flash. "When?"

"Now."

"Where?"

"I don't know. I'll call you."

Tinsley was standing by his unmarked squad car when Alex and the others arrived outside City Hall. Behind him, three uniformed officers leaned against their marked cars, obviously waiting for something to happen.

Alex jumped out of the cruiser before it could come to a complete stop.

"Hey, relax. We're not in *that* big a rush," Tinsley said with a grin. "We're still waiting for a couple of the feds to get here."

"So where are the Mullens?" Alex asked, catching his breath. "And how did you find them?"

"They're actually not that far away," Tinsley said. "Turns out, they're staying up on the St. Croix River, near Marine On St. Croix. Some friend's place that we knew nothing about."

Alex waited, now joined by Malay and Schmidke.

"McCaron led us to them. Dumb bastard apparently didn't know he was being watched. We—the feds, I should say—collared him as he was leaving the place. He told them that Mullen called him, worried about the firm. He was trying to figure out a way to get his money out of the place before it collapsed. McCaron swears it's the first time he's heard from Mullen or seen him since he disappeared, but they've got him in custody anyway."

"I assume you've got the place under surveillance," Alex said.

Tinsley gave him a look of disgust. "Duh. Golly, gee. Why didn't I think of that?"

"Sorry."

"This is one of those joint jurisdiction deals," Tinsley said. "Between us and the FBI. We're involved because the kids were abducted in Minneapolis, and the feds are here because they believe Ryan, at some point in the last fifteen years, was probably taken across state lines. And because they're trying to learn more about this Nation United bunch. The county attorney and the U.S. attorney are going to have to fight over who gets to prosecute."

At that point a blue Ford sedan pulled up next to them, with two men inside. "Here are our friends from the FBI," Tinsley said, and then, more quietly, "You should know that they're not crazy about you being here, but I told them that if it wasn't for you, none of us would be here."

"Thanks," Alex said.

"Just follow along, and join the fun."

Marine On St. Croix lies some thirty miles northeast of the Twin Cities, one of the small, idyllic settlements that stretch along the St. Croix River—which forms the border between Minnesota and Wisconsin. It's populated largely by the families of well-to-do corporate executives or lawyers, whose lavish homes overlook the river valley, or by less-well-to-do folks who settled there years ago, or who built summer cottages, and have stayed on, refusing to sell out.

The Lester Riley home was one of the former. Set atop a bluff above the river, it was all but invisible from the road, hidden by hedges and trees, and accessible by a long driveway that you could easily miss if you passed by too quickly.

A quarter mile down the road in each direction sat two unmarked cars, with a plainclothes detective in each. Tinsley stopped by one of them for a moment, and apparently was told that no one had come or gone since they'd been on watch.

Tinsley waved the station cruiser ahead until it was alongside his car, and leaned his head out the window. "We're going to go in now and make the arrests," he said. "If you're willing to risk some kind of trespass lawsuit from the people who own this place, you're welcome to follow us."

"Are the owners here?" Alex asked.

"We're not sure, but we don't think so. They may be in Europe and not even aware that the Mullens are wanted."

Alex looked at Schmidke, then at Malay. "Fuck it," he said. "Let 'em sue."

"Okay," Tinsley said. "Just don't get in our way."

By the time Alex and the others got to the house at the end of the driveway, Tinsley and the FBI agents were already out of their cars and pounding on the front door. The uniformed cops had gone around to the back, to block any possible exit that way.

This time it was Schmidke who was out of the car before it fully stopped, camera on his shoulder, tape rolling. But he stayed well back, heeding Tinsley's orders. He needn't have worried. It was all very peaceful.

The front door was opened by a tall, gray-haired, and very distinguished-looking man whom Alex assumed to be Clint Mullen. After a brief exchange of words with Tinsley, he reentered the house, followed by Tinsley and the agents.

"Move in a little closer," Alex urged Schmidke. "I don't think anybody's going to get shot here."

Five minutes passed before Tinsley was at the door again, followed by Mullen, then by a middle-aged couple that Alex knew must be the Whelans, and finally, by

Ryan and the two FBI men. As a favor to Alex, Tinsley made the Mullens stop and stand by the cars for a few moments, allowing Schmidke to approach and get the shots he needed.

Mullen ignored the camera but glared at Alex, who had also moved closer. The Whelans kept their eyes to the ground, but the woman was clinging to Ryan's arm and sobbing. For his part, Ryan appeared utterly confused. Alex stepped even closer. "Ryan, do you know what this is all about?"

"Don't say anything, Ryan!" Mullen snapped. "It's all a mistake."

But Alex pressed on, knowing he was probably out of line, but unable to help himself. The search had gone on too long. His questions came rapid-fire. "Do you know that these people are not your real parents, Ryan? That this man is not your grandfather? That you were kidnapped as small child?"

Mullen appealed to Tinsley. "Shut him up! What's going on here?"

Ryan was looking from one to the other.

Emily Whelan suddenly looked up. "He's *my* son! Don't you dare try to take him away!"

Alex ignored her.

"That's enough, Alex," Tinsley said, moving him aside. "We've got to get going."

Alex followed them to the cars, shouting after them. "You're real name is Andrew, Ryan. And your real parents have been waiting to see you. For fifteen years!"

By then the car door was shut, and Ryan was on his way to an uncertain future.

Alex and Maggie sat beneath the bright studio lights, waiting for the countdown to the early news. Alex was fidgeting in his chair. "Are you sure you're okay?" Maggie asked.

"Yeah," he said. "I'd just like to get this show on the road."

"It's a big night for you," she said. "You should be very proud."

"Relieved, maybe, more than proud."

Alex had been back at the station for only a couple of hours, running between his computer and the editing station, preparing the report on the Mullens' capture and the recovery of Ryan. He had taken only enough time out to call the Hathaways, to tell them what had happened, and to ask if he could visit them after the early news. It was important, he'd told them, and they had been quick to agree.

"Stand by in the studio," the floor director shouted. "Coming out on you, Alex. Five, four, three, two, one . . ."

"Good evening, everyone," Alex said, the camera tight on his face. "Several weeks ago, we reported that we had launched an investigation into the case of the missing Hathaway brothers, three young boys who disappeared and were believed drowned in the Mississippi River fifteen years ago. We told you then that the boys' bodies have never been recovered, and that their parents did not believe they had drowned . . . but instead, that they'd been kidnapped.

"Tonight, we can report exclusively that they were right. One of their boys, Andrew, was found today with the people police believe abducted him and his brothers in 1983. The suspects are prominent attorney Clint Mullen, of the Mullen-McCaron law firm, and his daughter and son-in-law, Emily Jane and Larry Mullen . . . formerly known as Emily and Larry Whelan."

At that point Schmidke's tape of the Mullen's arrest flashed on to the screen, along with Alex's reporting of the details of the arrests and excerpts of his shouted exchanges with the Mullens.

Then the camera was back on him. "Police say the Mullens fled with Andrew, who is now called Ryan, three days ago . . . when they apparently became aware that authorities were closing in on them. Since then, they have been the subjects of a widespread search by both local and federal officials.

"A comparison of dental records has convinced those same authorities that Ryan is, in reality, the Hathaway's son, Andrew, but further blood and DNA testing may be necessary to confirm those findings. In the meantime, Andrew, or Ryan, is being held in protective custody. And charges against the Mullens are pending.

"But what about the other two brothers? Tonight, on our late news, we'll have more on them."

In some ways, it would be the most difficult trip of Alex's life. He knew the Hathaways had to be told about Jed and Matt before he could reveal it publicly on the late news, but he shuddered at the prospect of facing them. He could only hope the right words would some- how come to him, if there were right words.

Because of his fears, he asked Maggie to ride along with him, although she was no more eager to face the Hathaways under these circumstances than he was. But having come this far with him, she knew she couldn't abandon him now.

"I was hoping they might have a minister who could come with us," he said, "but I've never heard them speak of one . . . and I didn't want to ask."

"Minister or not," she replied, "they're eventually

going to have to deal with it themselves. Privately. And with their daughters." She paused for a moment. "I know this sounds callous, but at least they'll know that two of their three boys are alive. Of course they'll mourn Jed, but hopefully, they'll someday be able to celebrate Andy and Matt."

"I hope they'll see it that way," he said.

"They will. But it may take a while."

Hazel and John were sitting outside on the front stoop when Alex and Maggie pulled into the driveway. Smiling, they walked out to meet them, with Hazel giving both Alex and Maggie a hug, and John wrapping his arm around both. Alex's apprehension only deepened.

"I can't tell you how thrilling it was to see Andrew there on the screen," Hazel said as they walked back toward the house. "He looked so . . . I don't know, so healthy and alive. I can hardly wait to see him."

"You understand, Hazel," Alex said, "that he has no idea of who you and John are. It's going to take time . . . maybe a long time . . . for him to get adjusted to the idea. And to accept it. You saw the tape, the confusion he was feeling. His world has to be spinning for him right now."

By then they were inside . . . and once again sitting around the dining room table. Hazel had already cut pieces of chocolate cake for each of them.

"Do you have any idea when we might be able to see him?" John asked.

"A detective, Phil Tinsley, will give you a call. Maybe in the next day or so. He'll set up a meeting. But they have a lot of questions for Ry . . . for Andrew . . . before then. Questions about the last fifteen years."

Hazel said, "I told you once that we've learned to be patient."

"You may not want to allow this," Maggie said, "but

whenever the reunion with Andrew happens, or shortly thereafter, we'd like to have our cameras there."

Hazel and John exchanged looks. "That will be okay with us," John said. "It's the least we can do for you. But it'll have to be okay with Andrew, too."

"That's fine," Maggie said.

There was a moment of quiet, and Alex knew he should wait no longer.

He leaned across the table. "You know that you've become almost like family to me, and I wish I knew an easy way to tell you this, but I don't. So I won't try." He paused, collecting himself. "The people up in Virginia have confirmed that the remains found in one of the caskets are those of Jed."

Hazel's eyes widened and her hands went to her mouth, covering a scream. "No, no, no," she whispered. Her faced paled and the tears came quickly. John slumped back in his chair, his chin dropping to his chest. A small groan escaped his lips.

Alex felt his own eyes well, and he looked across at Maggie, who was trying to comfort Hazel, and making no attempt to disguise her own anguish. He got up and walked into the living room, no longer able to watch silently and helplessly. He needed to be away, to try to get control of his own emotions.

He stayed there, staring out the front window, until he finally heard Maggie call out for him. John was now sitting next to Hazel, holding her, wiping her tears away. "It's time to tell them about Matt," Maggie said.

"Matt's alive," he said, still standing. "He *is* the boy I showed you on the videotape. He has the birthmark you described."

The Hathaways were watching him, but said nothing.

"No one knows what, if anything, he remembers of you or his life before the kidnapping. *He* certainly isn't saying. Whatever he might have remembered has probably been brainwashed away, or he has chosen to forget. But he is your son, and he's going to need your love and support, even if he refuses to accept it for now."

"What will happen to him?" John asked.

Alex could only shrug. "Once it's absolutely proven that he is Matt, the authorities will have to take into account that he's a victim in all of this. He may have been there in the woods in body, but maybe not in mind. I'm going to be around for a while, and I'll do everything I can to help you work things out."

"And so will I," Maggie said.

"But right now," Alex went on, "it seems to me that you have to think about Jed and your girls. To make arrangements. That has to be your priority."

They talked for another hour, Alex and Maggie offering whatever support and suggestions they could. But then it was time for them to leave. Time for the Hathaways to be alone . . . with their grief . . . and their hopes.

For Alex, the broadcast that night was anticlimatic. The thrill that he had imagined he would feel in reporting this story was missing. True, he had found the Hathaway boys—as he had promised himself and his viewers that he would try to do—but he felt little joy. Satisfaction, perhaps, but no particular pleasure.

Jed's death had seen to that.

But again, despite his personal feelings, the story caused a small sensation, within the newsroom and without. Once again, the competing stations and the newspapers had to watch with chagrin, and with no small amount of professional jealousy. The investigation they had once chided, even laughed at, had come full circle . . . to bite them in the ass.

At the end of his report, facing the camera, Alex said, "While two of the three Hathaway brothers have been found alive, emotionally damaged but alive, there are still scores—maybe hundreds—of others just like them, still missing. Children snatched away from their parents and siblings. By strangers. Parents left without the things we value the most in life. Our kids. So until all of them are found and reunited with their real families . . . this story will remain unfinished."

The screen faded to black . . . and a commercial popped up.

In the studio, there was momentary silence, then spontaneous applause. From the technicians, who rarely applauded anything, and from practically the entire news staff, who had gathered there. And from Pat, Malay, and Barclay, and even Hawke, who may have been clapping the loudest.

Maggie leaned over and gave Alex a kiss on the cheek. "You done good, kid. Real good."

Kid? Did she say kid?

40

The first order of business for Alex the next day was to officially and publicly announce to the newsroom—and the world—his engagement to Pat. She was there with him, as she had been the night before, looking pleased and relaxed, with the blush of a soon-to-be new bride. They said they hadn't yet set a wedding date, but would once they had flown to Philadelphia to tell his kids.

The next item on the agenda, once Pat had left, was to meet with Barclay and Hawke—to discuss the station's twenty-five-thousand-dollar reward. "I think we should divvy it up three ways," Alex said. "Among Sean Spangler, Elmer Jonkowski, the lock man, and Stanley the caretaker. We couldn't have solved this thing without the help of each of them."

"How about Tim LaSalle?" Barclay asked.

"He doesn't need the money. Besides, he's getting his story for the magazine."

"And Tony Malay?"

"I made the offer, but he said no. Said he's been on the station's payroll, and wouldn't take it even if he hadn't been. That he was plenty happy to have helped right an old wrong."

Hawke leaned back in his chair, smiling. A regular

Jekyll and Hyde. "I know we've had our differences, Alex, and that I may have been a prick at times, but I hope you'll consider sticking around. We might even discuss your staying on the late news, if you'd like."

Alex smiled. "You have been a prick, Mr. Hawke, no doubt about that. But I'm going to have to think things over. And I'll let George know in a couple of days. You could do me one favor, however."

"What's that?"

"Don't hire that Norwegian. Or Swede. Whatever he is. You'll chase George here right out the door, and let me tell you, you'd miss him a hell of a lot more than you'd miss me."

"I'll think it over," Hawke said, getting out of his chair. "You probably do deserve one favor."

Later that day Phil Tinsley came by the station with an update. All three of the Mullens, he said, had been charged with kidnapping, although it was still not clear whether they'd eventually be tried in state or federal court. Mullen was trying to raise bail to get them all out of jail, but apparently was having trouble because of the worsening financial straits of his law firm. He might even have to take another mortgage out on his Lake Minnetonka mansion.

"So how's Ryan doing?" Alex asked. "I mean, Andrew."

"That's a real problem," he said. "Obviously, we can't charge him with anything, but if we release him, he's got nowhere to go. He's too old for a foster home, and we sure as hell can't let him go back to the Mullens to stay, and he doesn't seem to have any close friends. He needs counseling, that's for sure. But for now, he's across the street at the Hilton with one of our guys watching over him."

"Maybe it's time to introduce him to his real parents," Alex suggested. "They'd certainly love to have him there."

"We've asked, but he's not quite ready for that yet. Maybe once he meets them . . . well, who knows? But he wants to take it slow for now. In the meantime, we've shown him all of the newspaper clippings from back in 1983, and a tape copy of the story you did, with his folks and sisters and all."

Alex told him about the meeting he and Maggie had had with the Hathaways the night before. "They'll probably be okay waiting, too," he said. "At least until they can give Jed a proper burial."

Tinsley also reported that the feds were deeply interested in knowing more about The Nation United, and were hoping that one of the suspects being held in Virginia might break.

As he prepared to leave, Alex asked him about the Stockworth investigation. "No breakthroughs yet," he said. "But we're going to be reinterviewing McSwain, and—as you suggested—are trying even harder to find Marvin Spangler.

"We're also going to be talking to a number of people at the Mullen law firm, to see if anybody else over there might know more about all of this."

"Try talking to Richard Cornelius," Alex said. "If you can find him."

"Who's he?"

Alex gave him the background. "He was a partner with Mullen's firm and knew the late Pete Osborne well. Hell, he married Osborne's widow. He may have known about the Hathaway files, and who knows what else? Maybe Marvin Spangler, too. But I've been told he's taken off."

Tinsley had been taking notes. "Okay," he said. "We'll do that."

Alex was ready to leave for home after the early news when he got a call that he never dreamed he would receive.

"Mr. Collier?"

"Yes."

"This is Ryan Mullen. Or whatever my name is now."

Alex let it sink in for a moment. "Hello, Ryan."

"I wondered if I might talk to you."

"I'd be pleased," Alex said. "When?"

"Could you do it now?"

"Of course. Would you like me to come to the hotel?"

"That would be great. I'm in Room 242."

"I'll be there in ten minutes."

A cop answered Alex's knock at Room 242, but recognizing him, immediately stepped aside and said he'd be down in the lobby, having a cup of coffee. Ryan, or Andrew— Alex couldn't decide which to call him—was standing right behind the policeman, and moved quickly to shake Alex's hand. He had a strong grip, and a slight smile. "My baby-sitter," he said with a nod toward the door.

Alex grinned. "I heard you had one."

"Grab a chair, please. And thanks for coming."

Alex picked one of two chairs in the room, but Andrew sat on the edge of the bed, hands clasped together in his lap. They spent a moment looking over each other before Alex said, "I was glad to get your call. After all this time looking for you, I almost feel like I know you."

"You know I'm not a motor head, right?" His smile broadened. He looked good with a smile.

"I'm sorry about that," Alex said. "But we had to get a picture of you to show to your folks."

"I figured it was something like that. At the time, though, I didn't quite understand why my granddad got so upset when I told him I'd seen you on the lake. I guess I know now."

Alex said nothing, waiting for the young man to go on.

"I'm told I owe you my thanks," he said. "That none of this would have happened without you. But to be truthful, I'm not sure I'm happy it did."

"I can understand that," Alex said, "but I hope you will be someday. I know your real family is."

Andrew moved from the bed to the other chair. "That's why I wanted to talk to you. You probably know them better than anybody."

"I was with them last night. They're wonderful people, Andrew. If I may call you that. They've never given up looking for you. But it was hard last night. They're happy about finding you, of course, but they're crushed about your brother, Jed. And concerned and confused about Matt."

"I have no memory of Jed at all," Andrew said. "Or of Matt. I guess I was too young."

"Do you remember where the Mullens took you before you came back to Minnesota? You would have been about seven, I guess."

"The cops asked me that, too. But I don't, really. Just that it was warm, down south, I think. And there were lots of people around, like a camp, almost."

Alex asked him several more questions about growing up, and was told that the Mullens had been kind and generous and loving to him. "I couldn't have asked for a nicer home," he said. "And I can't just walk away from them now."

"I don't think anybody expects that, Andrew. But

don't ever forget what they did . . . that they did take you and your brothers away from your real parents. That was criminal, Andrew, and caused your real mom and dad more pain and heartache than you or I will ever know. And while you probably won't want to hear this, the Mullens may also have had something to do with one brother's death, and the screwed-up mind of the other. The total truth will come out someday, and you should be prepared for it."

Andrew sat somberly and listened. "What do you think I should do?"

Alex considered the question. "Jed is going to be buried in a few days. I think you should go to the funeral. With me, if you'd like. Meet your mom and dad, and your little sisters. And maybe someday, if things go well, and if it's in you, you'll help them reconnect with Matt."

Andrew got up and held out his hand. The conversation was over. "Thanks," he said. "I'll call you."

The next morning Alex walked directly to Barclay's office and rapped on the doorjamb. Barclay looked up, surprised to find him there. "Alex?"

"May I have a minute?"

"Sure. C'mon in. Shut the door."

"That's okay," Alex said, leaving the door ajar and settling into a chair. "I just wanted you to know that I've made some decisions."

"Really?"

"Yeah. You just tell me what you want me to do and I'll do it. The early news or the late, or both, I don't really care. Just let me know. I'll do whatever you ask, until Pat and I decide what we want to do with the rest of our lives. And if we do decide to pull up stakes and move on, I'll give you plenty of notice."

"You're serious about this?" Barclay said, not quite believing what he was hearing.

"Yes, but there's more."

"All right."

"I plan to be here through Jed Hathaway's funeral, and to spend a day fishing with Malay over in Wisconsin. But then I want to take a few weeks off."

Barclay sat up straight. "A few weeks?"

"Maybe more."

"Into the sweeps?" He was getting flustered.

"If I need to, yes."

"To do what?"

"First of all, Pat and I are going to Philadelphia, to get reacquainted with my kids, and to see if they'll maybe bless our marriage. Then I'm going on to Illinois, by myself."

"Illinois? Why?"

Alex stood up. "If I can, I'm going to help find out what happened to a little kid by the name of Tommy Akers. I owe him that. And it may take a while."

Then he was at the door, smiling. "I'll see you, George."